DATING THE Defensive Back

LISA SUZANNE

DATING THE DEFENSIVE BACK
© LISA SUZANNE 2024

Published in the United States of America by Books by LS, LLC.

ISBN: 978-1-963772-03-6

This book is a work of fiction. Any similarities to real people, living or dead, is purely coincidental. All characters and events in this work are figments of the author's imagination.

Books by Lisa Suzanne

Visit Lisa on Amazon for more titles

Dedication

To the three most important people in my world.

Chapter 1: Grayson Nash

Right On Cue

"Are you sure?" my brother presses.

"Fuck," I murmur in wonder. I've been sure for the last year. I can't believe it's finally happening. "Yes, I'm sure."

"Then we'll have the contract to your agent today, and I'll expect you here in Vegas tomorrow for a press conference. I've got other calls to make."

"Yes, sir," I say, and I practically salute my phone. We've been in talks for the last two days, plus the entire year before that, but we couldn't make anything official until four o'clock today. And now…it'll be official.

Is this the right decision? Time will tell.

It's time for me to pack my shit and get the fuck out of Los Angeles. I've loved playing for the Chargers. I've been here most of my career, in fact, except for my first two seasons when I played for the Bills.

But I'm ready for a new challenge with a new team. I've been contemplating retirement since before last season got underway, and it's still at the forefront of my mind. But this is a one-year contract that comes with a once-in-a-lifetime opportunity to play on the team my older brother coaches and my youngest brother plays for.

I can't pass that up.

I'm a free agent, and if it's my last year...I want to play it on my own terms. And if I retire after the end of this year, I want the chance to join the coaching staff with a team I've played on.

And Vegas sounds pretty fucking attractive, too.

Two of my three brothers are in town. My dad is there, though we're not as close as I am with my mom, who's back in New York at her goat farm. And it's fucking Vegas. The lights, the entertainment, the gambling, the sports...the *women*.

Hell motherfucking yeah, I'm sure.

I unwrap a Tootsie Roll and chew on it, and I debate opening another one while I wait. It takes almost a full two minutes before my phone rings again, and I see my agent's name flash across the screen.

"Right on cue," I answer, tossing my wrapper in the trash.

"I just sent you the document to sign," Isaac says.

I open the email he sent, glance through it, and issue my signature online.

"Congratulations to the newest member of the Vegas Aces," he says when he sees the document come through.

"Thanks, man," I say, a strange sense of emotion washing over me. It's somewhere between excitement and nervousness, I think. "And thanks for everything. You got me a bigger contract with the Chargers than I ever thought I'd have, and you've become more than just an agent to me over the years."

"I think of you as a friend, too. We won't be in the same city anymore, but that doesn't mean I won't come out to Vegas to hit up all the hot spots with you."

"I look forward to it." I cut the call, and I draw in a deep breath as I stare at the figure on the bottom line.

One year in Vegas with an eighteen-million-dollar price tag. The Pro Bowl appearances along with my proven record certainly helped, but my agent and my brother took care of me.

I can't wait to get to Vegas and get started on the next chapter of my career. It might be the final chapter where playing is concerned, or maybe I'll love the new team so much I won't want to hang it up at the end of the season.

There's a lot up in the air right now, and it all hinges on this fresh start.

I should call my current coach and let him know. I should call the front office. I should do about a million things, but instead, I twist the top off a new bottle of Hendricks and take a celebratory swig.

I scroll through my phone, looking for a number to call.

Someone to celebrate with.

My brother already knows, and I'll call the rest of the family later.

Maybe I should call Daphne and let her know, but then I'd have to call her, and we'll get into a whole thing, and I'm not really interested in any of that right now.

So instead, I call the guy who has been my best friend since high school.

He picks up right away. "Grayson Nash. To what do I owe the pleasure of an actual *phone call?*"

"Beckett Maxwell," I say even though nobody calls Beck *Beckett* except for his mother…and me. "I've been a bit remiss in my correspondence. Fucking sue me. I've been a little busy playing football."

He laughs. "Didn't you choke in the playoffs like two months ago?"

I sigh as I think back to the game that ended our season too soon. "I wouldn't call it *choking*, exactly, but I suppose the season has been over somewhere in the neighborhood of two months."

"Two months and this is the first call," he mutters. "You must have big news."

"I'm moving to Vegas," I say.

"You decided to hang it up?" he guesses.

"Nope. I decided to sign with the Aces for a year and see how things play out."

"Well, I'll be damned. Congratulations, man. You mentioned you were leaning that way once Lincoln ended up there. You'll be playing with Asher, too?"

"His suspension will be over by the start of next season, so yeah. A Nash will be on one side or the other when the ball is snapped every play." I take another swig from my bottle.

"Now you just have to get Spencer over to the Aces, and the Nash brothers will be running that city."

"Ah, Spence is soft, Linc's married, and Asher doesn't know what the fuck he's doing. I'll be the one running it." My voice is firm, though I can't argue that it would be fun having all three Nash brothers playing for the team the eldest brother is coaching.

"Do me a favor out there since you'll be the King of Vegas, okay?" he asks.

"Anything for my oldest friend."

He chuckles. "By *oldest*, I know you mean the length of friendship as opposed to my age."

"Well, you are nearly an entire year older than me," I point out. "Now come out with it. What's the favor?"

"My little sister is in Vegas. Keep an eye out for her, would you?"

"Your little sister is in Vegas?" I ask. The last time I saw little Ava Maxwell, she was probably fifteen years old and she wore braces, blue eye shadow, and cat sweaters. "Isn't she like fifteen?"

"She graduated from UNLV three years ago, Gray. She's twenty-five."

"Twenty-five?" I practically spit. I didn't realize she was only seven years younger than us. When I was twenty-two, fifteen felt a hell of a lot further away than twenty-five to thirty-two sounds. "Jesus. When'd we get so goddamn old?"

"Speak for yourself, man."

I laugh, though the truth is I feel older and older every time I step out onto the field. Wednesdays are getting tougher and tougher since they're sort of like Mondays for players. The aches and pains are more intense than they used to be. I'm partaking in more massages and more ice baths than ever.

At first I pretended like it wasn't because of my age. As I look ahead to the next season, I see myself getting more excited about being on a new team, being in Vegas, and playing with my brothers than I am about actually getting into my gear and guarding wide receivers all season.

I shake off the thought. "You got it. I'll check in on her."

"No funny business. You know I'll kick your ass."

I laugh as I think back to braces, blue eye shadow, and cat sweaters—and the threat from a guy with a dad bod versus a guy who plays in the NFL. But he's right. I do know how protective he is of his younger sister, especially since he had to step in and take responsibility for her once they lost their father back when we were sophomores in high school.

"No worries," I finally say, cringing at the mere thought of hooking up with my best friend's baby sister.

Chapter 2: Ava Maxwell

Food Network and Doritos

I toss my phone down on my bed with a frustrated grunt that *might* have come out louder than I intended for it to.

"You okay?"

My head whips to my best friend's voice in my doorway, and I sigh. "Yeah, I'm okay. I'm just tired of fighting with Colin."

Kelly sits on my bed next to me. "What was it about this time?"

"Can I just say I love that you come in here, sit down, and get ready to listen when it's the same old thing time and again?" I ask. She has the patience of a saint as a kindergarten teacher. I do not.

She laughs. "Well, if you'd prefer me to get to the bottom line, then break up with him."

"You think I should?"

"Babe, we're not getting any younger. You have a boyfriend halfway across the country who's been married to his job for three years when he should be planning his wedding to you." She shrugs a little at the end as if it'll soften the blow of her words. It doesn't.

"Don't forget I also have a job I love in my favorite city in the world and the best friend-slash-roommate a girl could ask for. Oh, and that closetful of Radiance Skincare products nobody wants."

She giggles as we both think about the company we somehow were lured into by one of Kelly's old high school friends. It's really not all that funny that we both blew a boatload of cash on the product line, in particular because it set me back a few years on my actual dream of saving enough to open my own bakery, but if we can't laugh about it, we'll just cry.

"Want to watch Food Network and eat Doritos?" she suggests. It's our favorite pastime when we're down in the dumps.

I nod. "Yes please. But add some vodka or something to that."

"You got it. But first, what was tonight's fight about, really?"

"He was supposed to fly out next weekend, and I just had a feeling *this* was going to be the time." I say the word *this* meaningfully since we both know what I'm waiting for. You don't date the same guy for five years without thinking a proposal is coming at *some* point.

But that feeling seems to keep slipping further and further away, especially since it's been an entire three months since I've even been in the same state as him. "But he has some work thing he has to go to, so he canceled."

I don't say it, but it's starting to feel like there's something inherently *leave-able* about me. First my dad, though it wasn't his fault he passed away, then two of my brothers, who scattered to different states for college, and now Colin.

"Do you love him?" she asks me point-blank.

My jaw slackens a little.

"Does he give you butterflies?" she amends. "Does he rev your engine? Make you want to lay back on your bed and kick your feet in the air while you giggle with delight?"

I twist my lips as I bite the inside of my cheek.

I'm not sure I should voice the immediate answer that springs to mind.

"Well?" she asks.

I sigh. "Butterflies, revving, feet kicking…those things are for crushes, not long-term relationships." I think back to the childhood crushes I had on my brothers' friends. With three older brothers, I had *plenty* of nice material to choose from.

There was one in particular who I always crushed the hardest on, but he was seven years older than me and didn't give me the time of day. I haven't seen him since my oldest brother, who was like a father to me, graduated from college. He came by the house to attend the party. I stared at him with hearts in my eyes, and then later I saw him kissing Mindy Ward behind the old shed. I didn't stand a chance. Mindy Ward had big boobs, long hair, and, you know, seven or so years on me.

"What if you could have it for both?" she asks.

"Have you ever had that?"

She presses her lips together and shakes her head. "That's a negative, my friend. But if I ever did, then that's how I'd know. Meet me on the couch. I'll get the vodka, you get the Doritos."

I grin. "Deal."

When I meet her on the couch, she turns on the television, and we settle into a battle of the bakers on a Food Network show.

"That's *so* not how you make ganache," I say.

Kelly rolls her eyes. "If you're such an expert, you should apply to be on this show."

"I should." I pick up my vodka drink from the table in front of me and take a long swig. "It would be my chance to show the world my skills, and I'd win the grand prize and have enough to open my very own dream bakery on the Strip."

"The cash prize is only, like, twenty-five thousand. I feel like you'd need way more than that to start a bakery on the Strip. Maybe somewhere off-Strip. Or downtown."

I set my jaw as I shoot her a glare. "Strip or bust."

She laughs, the vodka clearly already getting to us a little. "You might *have* to strip to make enough for that."

I burst into giggles, and I set my drink down on the table, accidentally bumping into the remote on my way. The channel changes, and suddenly we're watching the sports segment on CBS.

"Rumors from multiple sources say your Vegas Aces have made a big offseason move, trading a second-round draft pick to the Chargers for Coach Lincoln Nash's younger brother, Grayson Nash," the reporter tells us.

Kelly moves to grab the remote, but I snatch it out of the way before she can change the channel back. A video of Grayson in his Chargers uniform is on the screen, and if that isn't the very thing those engine revving, butterfly dreams are made of, I'm not sure what is. He's running along with a wide receiver, and then the footage cuts to another game, and dang...he looks *good* in those tight pants.

Even better than he did a decade ago when I last saw him.

And he's coming to Vegas?

Game. On.

My boobs are bigger now than they were back then. My braces are gone, and my pearly whites are nice and straight. I took up yoga when I was in college, and I've never looked or felt better despite my penchant for sweets. He might not have given me the time of day back then, but I bet he would now.

Except...Colin.

Oh, right.

The guy who just told me his job is more important than his girlfriend.

The guy I've given the last *five* years of my life to.

The guy I thought I was going to marry...the guy I think I'm going to break up with.

The guy I think my heart broke up with as much as a year ago.

I should do it in person...but who knows when that's going to happen? I should just do it. Get it over with. Rip off the bandage. Be done once and for all since I've been done emotionally for months at this point.

"You don't care about football," Kelly says, interrupting my thoughts and reaching for the remote.

"Oh, but I do, my friend. I care very much about football when it's Grayson Nash we're talking about."

"Who the hell is Grayson Nash?" she asks. She's more of a baseball gal herself, and to be honest, I am, too. I gave up trying to understand football years ago, mostly because I always thought of Grayson and how I never stood a chance with him. I buried it in the past with the rest of New York when I moved to Vegas for college.

I'm sure I still don't stand a chance…but if we're going to be in the same town, there's a better chance than there ever has been before.

I nod toward the screen. "Him. The six-foot-four rugged heartthrob on the screen. The football star moving to Las Vegas. And…my oldest brother's best friend."

Her jaw drops. "Your brother is best friends with an NFL player? How have you never told me this?"

"Well, they *were* best friends way back in the day. They went to high school together. I don't really keep up with Beck's friendships these days considering I haven't even seen him since Christmas." I don't go back to New York very often these days, and Beck is in Manhattan.

When our dad died when I was eight, Beck stepped into the role of caretaker since our mom checked out emotionally. And even now that my other two brothers and I are grown adults and have moved away, Beck stays in New York to be closer to Mom.

He's a good guy.

When I first moved to Vegas to attend college, I assumed I'd end up back in New York once I graduated. But then I fell in love.

First with Vegas, and then with Colin.

I could take or leave Colin, who's in Chicago now. I'm not giving up Vegas, though—something I made clear when Colin moved away.

But now that my first crush is moving to town?

Even more of a reason to stay in this city that's become a part of my heart.

Maybe even more of a reason to break up with Colin, too. Stat.

Chapter 3: Ava Maxwell

Everything is Easier When You're Drunk

Everything is easier when you're drunk. Except actually dialing the phone.

I have to be at work in six hours, I've had two too many vodka drinks, and I'm trying to pull up Colin's number. It's not going well.

Kelly is next to me, giggling as she crunches on a Dorito. Cool Ranch, by the way.

I stab at my phone, and then I close one eye and squint with the other in order to focus. I pull up my favorites and click on Colin's name, and then I flash my phone at Kelly.

"Ava?"

Kelly points at the phone. "He answered," she whispers.

"Are you with Kelly?" he grumbles, and oops, I definitely woke him up.

"Of course I'm with Kelly," I say, and I sound exasperated even to myself.

"Why are you calling me so late?"

Honestly because I'm finally drunk enough to admit the truth. But also…time zones. I forgot about time zones. I'm in Vegas, where it's only midnight. He's in Chicago where it's…two hours later than that.

"Because I have to say this while I have the courage," I slur.

"Say what?" he asks, confused.

"That I'm tired of coming in second to your cob," I blurt. Shit.

I meant to say *job*, and I started to say *career*, and somehow they gelled into one word, and this isn't quite the breakup call I meant to make.

"My cob? What are you talking about?"

"I deserve some attention, Colin," I say, plowing forward despite the blunder. "I deserve someone who wants to be with me more than they want to be at the worfice."

"The worfice?"

Dammit. I did it again. Work plus the office...*ugh*.

"The *office*," I say, emphasizing the start of the word.

Kelly starts to giggle, but she's trying to hold it in so Colin doesn't hear, and her whole face is turning bright red as she silently quakes with laughter.

I force myself not to laugh as I turn away from her.

Maybe everything is *not* easier when I'm drunk.

"Do you want to talk in the morning when you're sober?" he suggests.

"No, Colin. I don't want to talk in the morning when I'm sober." I mimic his voice, and this conversation is definitely going off the rails. "I'm breaking up with you."

Silence meets me on the other side as I manage not to fumble any of *those* words.

"Was that clear enough for you?" I ask.

"Let's talk in the morning," he repeats.

"No, Colin. You're in Chicago. I'm in Vegas. We want different things out of life."

"So you're throwing away five amazing years because you drank too much?" he asks. "Let's see if you feel the same way tomorrow."

"I've felt this way a long time. Yesterday, the day before. The month before. Hell, maybe even for an entire year. We were happy when we lived in the same place, and things were good, and they're just…not anymore. So I'm done, and you're free to move on and find a nice lady to settle down with who wants to be in Chicago, but I for one want nothing to do with snowy winters and windy cities even if they turn the river green for St. Patty's Day." I'm rambling, and I need to stop rambling, but it's vodka-fueled rambling so there's a real fat chance it'll stop anytime soon.

He sighs. "You've really felt this way for that long?"

"I really have," I confirm.

Kelly isn't laughing anymore. Instead, she's looking at me with wide eyes as she watches me break up with someone else.

"Drunk or not, Colin, this isn't working for me anymore, and I think it's best if we call it quits." My voice is firm. Resolute, even. I think. It's possible I'm delusional right now, too.

"Okay, then. I guess…I guess I'll talk to you soon."

"I guess so, Colin. Bye." I hang up, not sure what *soon* means or when we'll actually talk again.

And as I end the call and hold my phone in my palm, I feel…free.

For the first time in five years, I feel free.

All the things I've put on hold, all the sacrifices I've made…I can do what I want now.

When I wake up in the morning, I might be sad. I might feel like I just lost my best friend. But the truth is that we were over a long time ago, and he hasn't been a very good friend to me since he moved to Chicago. We moved to a spot of complacency, and I refuse to live there anymore. I deserve better.

"You okay?" Kelly asks me as I stare at my phone.

I set it down beside me, and I glance up at my friend. I nod, my brows crinkling together. "Yeah. Oddly, I feel fine. I feel like I *should* be sad or upset, but I'm not. Instead, I feel like…like…" I slap a hand over my mouth. I can't seem to finish that sentence, but I feel like I'm going to throw up.

I rush to the bathroom. As I expel the vodka from my system, I know the cause is the amount of alcohol I drank, not the breakup.

It's been years since I drank enough to get sick, but here we are. I don't usually drink this much, but tonight, I just wanted to let loose with my best friend. And getting it out now will help me feel better in the morning.

My alarm wakes me bright and early at five so I can get to the bakery by six. I take an extra steamy shower, throw down a few ibuprofen, drink two glasses of water, toss my hair up into a bun, and head to work.

The bakery has been getting a ton of attention lately because it was recently featured on a podcast hosted by the head coach of the Vegas Aces, Lincoln Nash—the same Lincoln Nash who happens to be brothers with the newest acquisition to the team. His wife-slash-podcast co-host talked about our kitchen sink cookies on the podcast in the same episode where he proposed to her, and business shot through the roof.

Those cookies happen to be my very own recipe.

My very own *secret* recipe.

They didn't know there's a small connection from Lincoln to me when they talked about the bakery where I work and my cookies. They don't even know they're *my* cookies. Hell, Lincoln probably doesn't even remember me.

But they're mine. I call them my kitchen sink cookies since I put in everything but the kitchen sink: chocolate chips, of course, and toffee. Pretzels and potato chips for a salty bite, butterscotch and peanut butter, malt balls and caramel sauce. I add in a little sea salt, some pecans, and my super-secret special ingredient.

I've never told anyone my super-secret special ingredient— not even Poppy, the owner of Cravings and my boss.

But it's what makes the cookies melt in your mouth.

How do I get around it so nobody for sure knows my secret? Simple. I prep them at home.

They're our bestselling item, and we're also known for our beautiful cakes and our adorably decorated sugar cookies. And this morning is busy. We have an order for two hundred cookies for a gender reveal party—so a hundred boy and a hundred girl-themed cookies.

Cora, my colleague, and I baked the cookies two days ago, flooded the icing yesterday, and today we need to finish up the decorating by noon so they're dry by the time they're picked up tomorrow morning. This afternoon I need to work on ten dozen kitchen sink cookies ahead of the weekend, and I also have to decorate a birthday cake. This business is no joke, but I'm doing what I love.

Except this morning…I'm moving slower than usual.

"You okay?" Cora asks when I pick up my fifth cookie to decorate, a heavy sigh blowing out of me as Poppy walks by us.

"Yeah. I broke up with Colin last night," I admit over the whirl of the mixer Dom is operating on the other side of the kitchen.

"You what?" Poppy and Cora squawk at the same time.

"Haven't you been together for, like, years?" Cora asks.

I nod. "Five of them."

"Oh, sweetheart," Poppy laments. "Take the rest of the day off."

"Why is she getting the day off?" Dom asks.

"I broke up with Colin, and I'm not taking the day off. We have cookies to decorate, and honestly…I'm not really all that sad about it. It was time," I admit.

"What did he say?" Cora asks.

I press my lips together. "I may have had a few drinks before I made the call in the middle of the night, and he may have thought I was drunk dialing him since I woke him up because of time zones. But then I repeated several times that it's over, so I think he got the message."

Cora laughs. "Only you, Ava. I swear."

21

I shrug and set another finished cookie down. "My slow speed and heavy sighs today are more about the hangover than the breakup."

"Really?" Cora asks. "You're not even sad?"

I shrug. "Not really. I sort of just feel free. And that tells me it's the right thing for me."

"Let's take this girl out tonight!" Dom suggests.

Cora nods enthusiastically. "Yes! I heard the new players who were traded to the Aces are coming into town for a press conference, and a couple friends and I are going to that bar across the street from the practice facility so we can try to snag a baller. Anyone want to go?"

Wait...

What?

Grayson Nash might be in town tonight? And there's a bar where he might go? And I'm single for the first time in five years?

Sign me *all* the way up. I'll be first in line.

I tamper down my enthusiasm—or maybe it's the hangover talking. "I'm in," I say. "And Kelly will come, too."

And then I speed my way through to the end of the day so I can get home and get ready to potentially see the boy I had the biggest crush *ever* on a decade ago.

Chapter 4: Grayson Nash

Nash 24 on Black and Red

"I'm Kyle Broderick with the Vegas Sun. Grayson, tell us your initial reaction to the trade."

I nod at the reporter. "I'm thrilled to be playing for my oldest brother and with my youngest brother. This has been in the works for a while now, and I don't know if it'll be my last season or if I've got more in me, but I knew I couldn't hang it up until I had the chance to play with my brothers."

"What about Spencer?" Kyle asks, following up.

"You'll have to talk to Spencer about that. From what I hear, he's pretty happy in Minnesota."

I field a few more questions, and then the team owner, legendary quarterback Jack Dalton, takes over and fields still more questions about what the team is doing in the offseason. I shoot a look at Lincoln, who's sitting beside me, and he grins at me.

It feels good here. It feels right.

Once the presser is over, Lincoln and Jack take me downstairs to the locker room.

Before the press conference, I was up in Jack's office signing some paperwork. After that, the team doctor gave me a physical to make sure I'm cleared to play. I passed with flying colors, and now I guess I can hit Vegas tonight.

Except…I'm not sure I really have anyone to hit Vegas *with*. Linc's got plans, and who knows what Asher's up to. Off the top of my head, I can't really come up with anybody else, but I'm sure I'll run into someone who wants to celebrate with me.

I head into the locker room and find a few players I recognize gathered there. Wide receivers Travis Woods and Tristan Higgins, running back Jaxon Bryant, cornerback Patrick Harris, and defensive lineman Deon Miller are all here along with a few other players and some of the coaching staff. Lincoln introduces me to everyone, though I've met a lot of these guys before. We've just never played together.

It's a small group of dedicated players, and I get it. It's the offseason. A lot of guys aren't even in town right now because of it. Some don't live here, and they head home to their families in the offseason. But these are the guys who showed up for me today, and that feels good—like I'll have a network of friends here as I make my path in Vegas.

Lincoln shows me my locker, which is next to Patrick's, and I stare at it for a few beats.

Nash 24.

It's the number I've worn my entire life. There's no significance to it other than it was the number assigned to me when the coach threw out T-shirts at my first Peewee League game, and I stuck with that number all through middle school, high school, college, and now in the NFL.

It's nice seeing my number on a black and red jersey. It feels strange after the blue, white, and gold of my former team. All of this feels a little surreal, really.

I'm moving to Vegas.

I need to look for a place to live.

Patrick saunters up beside me. "Nash twenty-four," he says. "It looks good."

"I was just thinking that same thing."

"You want to grab a beer across the street or something?" he asks. "A few of us hit up the Gridiron pretty regularly."

"I'd love to," I say, certainly not wanting to turn down the first invitation from a teammate as I strive to fit in.

Some guys won't like me because I'm the coach's brother.

Some guys will think it's nepotism that got me here—and maybe it is. The rumors are already flying in the media, and I'd likely form more solid friendships somewhere else.

But this feels right for me, and anybody who doesn't like it can fuck off.

We arrive at the bar, and it appears the party is already in full swing. There's a booth in the back corner that Tristan and Travis beeline for, and I follow them as I walk with Patrick. We're stopped in our pursuit of the booth to take photos and greet fans, and I'm given a hearty Vegas welcome by everyone who stops me.

We make it to that corner booth, and we're mostly left alone once we're seated. A server comes by to grab our order, and everyone orders their usual.

I guess it's time to make my own signature splash.

"Hendricks," I say when she gets to me.

She nods and eyes me for a beat as if she's memorizing my drink and my face. I wonder what she's thinking as she associates my choice with me.

Austin Graham approaches our table, and his eyes flick to me before he nods at Tristan across from me, who scoots over to accommodate another person.

"Why weren't you in the locker room?" Tristan asks him.

He glances at me before he looks at Tristan. "I was busy." He's short and to the point.

I get the very strong feeling he doesn't like me.

I'm a people-pleaser. I can get along with anybody. I hate the feeling that someone doesn't like me just because of my last name, but it comes with the territory.

It's something I'll just have to deal with.

Austin Graham is a tight end, and so is my brother, Asher. My brother was chosen as the starter over him before he was suspended, which put Graham here on the bench. And given that my other brother is the head coach in charge of making those types of decisions, Austin isn't hiding the fact that he has something against my entire family.

I'm not going to let him ruin my good time. I've got a few inches and probably thirty pounds on him. I can take him.

Not that it's going to come to that. But if it does…

And a minute later, someone else I recognize comes sauntering across the bar toward our table.

I can't help my wide smile as I push to a stand.

I grab my little brother into a bro-hug complete with back pounding.

"Welcome to Vegas, man," he says, pounding my back as well.

"Thanks. You staying out of trouble?"

He scoffs. "Hardly. Move over."

I slide into the booth closer to Patrick, and Asher sits beside me. I glance across the table at Austin, who looks like he'd rather be just about anywhere but here.

And maybe he will be. My brother was suspended last season after he admitted to gambling on the outcome of games, but he'll be back this upcoming season. Yesterday marked the expiration of last year's contracts, and that means it's a new year. His suspension is over, and the front office has already informed him that he will be expected at voluntary minicamp next month.

He needs to keep his nose clean going forward. But Asher is the Nash brother who's the biggest wild card. He thrives on surprising the fuck out of all of us, and I could see him joining a sex club just as much as I could see him going on an expedition through the Amazon rainforest.

And speaking of sex clubs, I know Vegas has several.

I'm not going to pretend like I'm not interested in learning more, but I can't exactly ask my teammates about them the night I'm meeting them.

There's always next week.

As it turns out, Tristan, Travis, and Jaxon are all married, which means they aren't jumping at the chance to play wingman for the new guy in town. This really is just a group of dudes hanging out and having a drink with their buddies before they head home to their wives and *kids*.

Sounds boring.

I didn't exactly learn about being a good parent or husband from my own father. He was always hard on us, teaching us that football comes first above all else, including personal relationships.

It's probably why he's in his sixties and getting divorced, if I'm being truthful. My mom, on the other hand, is another story entirely. She always had a dream of owning a goat farm, and Linc and I made it happen. Too bad it's in New York—the complete opposite side of the country from what's been home for the last eight years.

I loved California. I never minded the proximity to the beach, the weather, the palm trees, or the nightlife. And to be honest, I didn't mind the proximity away from my family. It gave me the space I needed to spread my wings and prove myself. I'm a Nash, and the dynasty is a huge part of my blood and my reason for playing...but I also needed to prove that I played because I wanted to play, not because I was forced into it.

I love football. I love playing. I love getting on that field and acting like a kid again. I don't know if I'll be ready to give that up at the end of this season, and I had my time alone. I'm excited to be part of something bigger with my biological brothers instead of the teammates who become brothers.

And maybe, just *maybe*...I'm starting to get to that point where I want to figure out my future.

I can't play football forever, and once this season is over, if I decide to call it quits...then what?

I'll go home to an empty house.

Is that *really* what I want?

I just watched Leader Lincoln as he rekindled a romance two decades old, took on a stepson, and knocked up his girl. Serious Spencer, my younger brother, is engaged. Adventurous Asher is not likely to settle down any time soon.

So…I guess that makes Gifted Grayson next.

But as I look around this bar at the fresh meat Vegas is serving this evening, my eyes landing on a gorgeous blonde, I can't help but think that *theoretically* I'm next, but I'm not in a rush to figure out exactly what it is that I want out of life.

At least not tonight, anyway.

Chapter 5: Ava Maxwell

Cookie's Cookies

I spot him the *second* we walk in.

Even from across the room, he's gorgeous. Way hotter than he looked on TV, and also hotter than my memory recalled.

I can't believe my luck.

He's here.

He's actually *here*.

And so is his youngest brother, Asher, who was a year older than me in high school. A whole bunch of football players are smashed into one large booth in the back, but my eyes immediately landed on Grayson.

He hasn't spotted me yet, and I'm trying not to stare as Cora whisper-yells, "Holy shit, we hit the jackpot!"

She's not wrong.

Poppy didn't make the trip to the Gridiron with us *crazy kids*, as she calls us, so it's just Cora, a couple of her friends, Kelly, Dom, and me, and I'm already a little buzzed since we pre-partied before we grabbed an Uber here.

"Aren't most of them married?" Dom asks.

"Does it matter?" Cora asks, and I *think* she's joking, but I'm not sure. "That new guy and his brother are pretty hot."

Kelly opens her mouth, presumably to let them know my brother is actually *friends* with "that new guy," but I don't want them to know that. Not yet, anyway. I shake my head and widen my eyes in that secret *don't say a word* signal that only a best friend could decode.

I'm not saying a thing until I can get a gauge on how all this is going to go down.

But I'm secretly dying inside that he's here.

Those butterflies Kelly mentioned yesterday?

They're flapping wildly all around my stomach as my eyes edge back to Grayson.

God, he's good-looking. Bright blue eyes, dark hair that's sort of lazily pushed back and could use a cut, scruff on his jawline that makes him look both rugged and tough. He tips a glass to his lips. It's a short glass, which tells me it isn't water, but it's a clear liquid. What is Grayson Nash's adult beverage of choice? Is he a vodka guy? Tequila? Something else?

I don't know, but I do know I need a little liquid courage if I'm going to attempt to talk to him. I think I had a total of two conversations with him my entire life, but I'm his friend's little sister. Certainly he'd give me the time of day now that I'm an adult and we have a shared connection in this new space where he finds himself.

I head up to the bar with Kelly, and I order a vodka cranberry while she orders a glass of wine. It's probably a more sophisticated choice than vodka, but I need something that's a little more fast-acting.

The bartender sets my drink in front of me, and I'm about to hand him my credit card when I hear a voice beside me. "You can put it on my tab."

I glance over and see a guy who's probably a football player since I think he was in the same booth as Grayson, but he definitely doesn't have the last name *Nash*.

"Oh, you don't have to do that," I say, trying to be nice as I push my card over to the bartender and shoot him a tight smile.

"I'm happy to. I'm Austin Graham."

"Well, thank you, Austin." I'm suddenly nervous as this football player tries to buy me a drink when he's not the one I want buying me a drink at all.

He's attractive, for sure. But I have my eye on a different player, and I don't know what it's like for these guys. They're teammates, and Grayson is new to the team. I can't imagine he'd want anything to do with me if one of his new teammates is interested.

"And you are?" he presses, not getting the hint that I'm not interested.

"Just getting over a fresh breakup. But my friend Kelly here is definitely interested." I look at Kelly and wiggle my eyebrows, and she looks like she's about to die of mortification.

She doesn't know who he is, either. If it was someone from the Vegas Heat baseball team, like Cooper Noah or Danny Brewer, standing there, she'd know. But this is a football player, and neither of us knows quarterbacks from cornerbacks.

When my brother played in high school, he did something on defense. That's all I know. To be honest, I wasn't really paying attention to the game so much as I was looking at butts. And Grayson Nash's butt? Top notch.

I glance over at him as Austin turns fully around to talk to my best friend who is on the other side of him, and I see his eyes connect with mine.

A wave of anxiety crests through my back as he pushes to a stand, his eyes still on me. He starts his trek across the room in my direction.

Oh. My. God.

He's actually walking toward me.

The anxiety cresting through me stands still for a beat before it snaps fiery rockets along my spine.

My hands tremble as I lift my vodka to my lips and tip it back, hoping it's strong enough to give me the liquid courage I need to face this moment an entire decade in the making.

He stops in front of me, and he tilts his head a little, sending a searing buzz through me that lands squarely between my legs as my eyes meet his.

He's even more gorgeous than teenage Ava remembered. He didn't have that scruff on his jaw the last time I saw him, and he wasn't so…built. Broad. Breathtaking.

He commands the room's attention just by being in it. Maybe he always did, but he's got this energy about him, this positive vibe like you can't help but like him—like he's everybody's best friend. Yet he's standing in front of *me*.

My chest races with anticipation.

"I need a woman's opinion about something," he says, and his voice is deeper than I remember it being. Raspier. Hotter.

I'm nervous, somehow reduced to the squirmy teenager I was the last time I saw him instead of the capable, confident woman I've grown into.

I tilt my head back at him, mirroring his stance. "About what?"

A woman with rather large…*assets* walks over, elbows her way in, and interrupts us before he gets the chance to answer. "Oh my God, it's really you! I'm such a huge fan!"

"Thank you," he says with a polite nod as he looks around her back at me. He seems almost uncomfortable, as if he doesn't want a gorgeous woman walking up to him in a bar.

I wait for her to finish, but she sort of just stares at him. Maybe she's waiting for him to offer to buy her a drink or take her back to his hotel.

"If you'll excuse us," he says to her, trying to give her the hint to get lost, but she doesn't pick up the hint.

"I'd love to buy *The Grayson Nash* a drink," she says, grabbing onto his bicep.

I'm frankly surprised he's *not* choosing her. When I said *assets*, I meant boobs. They're pushed up, and she's shoving them nearly in his face, but he keeps glancing around her at me. I *think* he makes eyes at me to get him out of this, but I've never done this kind of thing before.

The vodka fuels me to try something. I stand and slip my arm around his waist, and he wraps an arm around my shoulder, and *ohmygod* Grayson Nash has his *arm* around me.

He smells good. *So* good.

"Hi, so sorry, but we were sort of in the middle of something," I say.

"Oh!" She looks embarrassed. "Right. I'm sorry." She slinks off after she glares at me.

I rather stupidly slip out from where our bodies are touching, and I sit on my stool and turn back to Grayson. "You needed my opinion about something?"

"If you saw a really gorgeous woman across the room, would you walk up to her and start up a conversation, or is that too direct?" he asks.

I lift a shoulder, a little disappointed that he's asking *me* that question rather than *being* the woman he's talking about. But maybe it's because he recognizes me and feels comfortable asking my opinion. If he wanted that other lady, he should've just taken his chance when he had it.

"I don't think it's too direct," I say, trying to banish all traces of disappointment from my tone. "I guess I'd say to go for it."

He sticks his hand out. "In that case, it's nice to meet you. I'm Grayson Nash."

I blush—hard—as the pickup line works on me.

As I start to say my name, I realize…he doesn't recognize me. Or maybe he does, somewhere in the recesses of his mind, but I'm not the girl I was when I was fifteen.

But if he doesn't know who I am, I don't want to blow my chances at wherever this night might lead with the truth that I'm his high school best friend's little sister all grown up. He wouldn't be looking at me with sex in his eyes the way he is if he knew I was the same girl who used to sit on the living room floor pretending to work out whenever he came over just to impress him with my five-pound dumbbell skills while he totally ignored me.

So I make a snap decision and swap out my name for another. "I'm A—uh, Cookie."

"Cookie? That's your name?"

"Well, no. It's a nickname. I'm a pastry chef."

"A pastry chef, huh? What's your favorite thing to bake?"

"Cookies, of course. But I also love decorating cakes. Someday I'm going to open my own bakery," I say, sharing my dream with Grayson Nash without even thinking twice about it.

"Big dreams," he says.

"Nope." I shake my head. "Sinful."

His brows crinkle together. "Sinful dreams?"

"Oh, I thought you were naming my bakery. I want to open it on the Strip, and it's Sin City, and you know how sweets are a sinful treat...so I was planning to name it Sinful." My other thought was Ava's Haven, but that seems kind of...lame.

"What about Cookie's Cookies?" he suggests, and I giggle.

"Cookie's Cookies? But what if I want to sell cakes, too?"

"Cookie's Cookies and Cakes." He holds his hands out as if that's the solution, and to be honest...it's kind of cute. Or maybe *he* is kind of cute, and I am kind of delusional.

"Considering I'm stuck working for someone else, I guess I have more time to dream about what the name of my future bakery is going to be." I shrug. "What about you? You're new to town, right?" I realize my mistake a moment too late, giving myself away as knowing who he is when I was trying to play it cool.

He narrows his eyes at me. "You know who I am?"

"You're all over the news." I shrug. "And when we walked in here, my friends went bananas that there were football players here. And, you know, Big Boobs over there said your name."

He chuckles at my assessment of the woman trying to hit on him. "Your friends did?" He leans in a little closer. So close. Too close. I can smell him, and...yeah. That clean, woodsy scent does things to me.

Whoa.

34

I feel a little dizzy as I breathe him in and feel his heat so close to me.

I take a sip of my vodka cranberry to force a little cool liquid onto my tongue.

I haven't flirted with anybody in…well, probably close to five years. I'm not sure how to do it anymore, especially not with the man standing in front of me. My ex of five minutes wasn't really the flirty type, so I haven't exercised these muscles in a while.

"Yeah," I say. "My friends. Want to meet them?"

He chuckles. "Eventually, maybe. But right now, I'm most interested in meeting *you*."

"Me?" I squeak as I die inside a little.

"You," he confirms with a nod. His blue eyes search mine, and he runs a hand through the hair that's a little longish on top as he looks away for a beat.

He could have any woman here in this bar. They're all clamoring to talk to him, anyway—as already evidenced by the woman who walked up to us.

But he's talking to me.

"Why me?" The desperate, dumb words are out of my mouth before I can stop them.

He chuckles. "I don't really have an answer for that. At least I don't have one that will make me look like I'm not just a dumb jock who is only out for one thing."

"Are you?" I raise my brows pointedly.

He looks caught off guard by my question, but he shrugs. "I'm a smart jock out for one thing."

I laugh. "And what's that thing?" I have a feeling I know what it is, but I'm…shall we say…*new* at this.

But I've also put a lot of thought into this moment, and by this moment, I mean what I'd do if Colin and I ever broke up.

I'm free as a bird, and I definitely want to exercise that freedom. With Grayson Nash. And by freedom, I mean sex. Tonight.

His lips tip up a little. "I like a woman who's direct, so let me be direct with you. I'm new to town. I don't know anybody here except my two brothers and some acquaintances. It's my first night, I'm staying at a hotel since I don't have a place yet, and I'd love to invite you back to my room where we can talk privately."

"Talk?" I repeat.

He raises a brow. "Where we can get to know each other. Maybe, you know…sample some *cookies*."

Oh. I chug the rest of my vodka.

"Is that how this works? You just…hit a woman with a pickup line in a bar, and she goes back to your hotel room so you can taste her cookie?"

He has the grace to look a little sheepish.

"Because I'm not saying no to that," I add before he can protest or say something that'll make him look like a total jerk.

Maybe it's the courage from the vodka and the buzz. Maybe it's because fifteen-year-old Ava is about to get everything she ever wanted. Maybe it's because he doesn't seem to recognize me, but I know *him*, and that makes me feel a little safer, like doing this with him isn't really that bad of an idea since I've dreamed of the moment he gave me a single second of attention when I first saw him back when I was eight years old and my oldest brother had his friends over to play video games his freshman year of high school.

He looks downright shocked by my words. "You haven't exactly said yes, though, either."

"Okay. Then yes."

"Really? You don't even know me."

"I feel like I do." Because I do. But I'm still not telling him that. "And maybe you could treat me to dinner first so it feels more like a date than just a hookup."

I spot another woman beelining for him. "And, you know…other women. It would be nice to have some privacy without all the competition."

He tilts his head and twists his lips. "Okay. I could eat dinner. I should also mention that I don't know if I'll be able to make a connection beyond tonight. Like I said, I'm new to town, and—"

I hold up a hand, interrupting him. "I never said I want anything more than tonight, either. But don't you want to hang out with your new teammates a little while longer?"

His jaw slackens a little. "Not when your cookies have me so goddamn intrigued."

I laugh. "You're taking cookies over teammates?"

He shakes his head a little as his eyes flick down to my lips. "No. I'm taking *you* over teammates. I have an entire year ahead with them, but I'm not blowing my chance at tonight with you."

I narrow my eyes. "Was that another line?"

He lifts a shoulder. "Maybe a little. But truthfully, there's something about you that caught my attention the second you walked in. And Graham's, clearly. But you pawned him off on your friend. Why are you talking to me?"

"Because you're Grayson Nash. You're a legend, and I'm not blowing my chance at tonight with *you*, either." I set my glass on the bar with a loud clatter, link my arm around his, and escort him toward the door without so much as a backward glance at the woman who was making her way toward him—or at my friends...or his.

Chapter 6: Grayson Nash

I Like Being Your First

I'm trying to think of the last time a woman escorted me to the door so we could go have sex, and I'm coming up blank. I'm usually the one propositioning, and while that was still true this time, she seems somehow…different.

I know, I know. It's the same old cliché about how she's different and blah blah blah. I've known her all of fifteen minutes, so I can't quite commit to her being the one who changes my life just yet.

But there really is something about her. She's familiar, as if we met before in some previous lifetime. She looks at me like she knows me, and while that's not uncommon given my status as a pro football player whose personal life is frequently in the news, I get this sense of something much deeper from her.

She literally linked her arm through mine and walked to the door without even saying goodbye to her friends, which makes me wonder whether this was her plan all along—to come to the Gridiron, which is a known hangout for Aces players, and shoot her shot.

Well, shots have been taken, and it was a fucking swish.

What is it about her? She's a little younger than the women I usually hook up with, and aside from the familiarity I can't quite place, she's got this sweet purity bordering on innocence going for her that makes me want to besmirch and corrupt and…mess her up a little. I want to knock a few hairs out of place. I want to thrust into her and watch her face screw up as she takes pleasure from what I'm giving her.

That's not my usual modus operandi. I play the field. I'm not one of those different women in every city kind of guys, but I'm also not the kind of guy looking for anything more than a fun time. And if I can have a fun time with Cookie again after tonight, great. If tonight is it for us…then that's okay, too.

My last relationship was more of a situationship. A friends with benefits sort of deal but, honestly, minus the *friends* part.

Daphne knew what she was getting into, and she didn't have the sweetness or the purity Cookie has.

She was a fun one, and while she tried to get me to be the kind of boyfriend she wanted, she understood that my career doesn't easily lend itself to allowing time for that unless we're in the offseason. Daphne and I hung out for over a year, but I knew my time was coming to an end in Los Angeles, and I made no secret that I wasn't interested in taking what we had to another city with me.

She got that, and when trade talk turned serious, we had a pretty serious talk, too.

And that was that.

She might've felt the sting, but all I felt was relief.

I thank my father for that shitty attitude.

But now that I see Linc happy, and even Spencer, who just got engaged to some girl none of us have ever met, I'm starting to wonder if that sort of life is in the cards for me, too.

I'm not opposed to it as I stare down the end of my career. It'd be nice to have somebody at home waiting for me, but I have yet to form the sort of connection where I could ever see a woman in my life for more than just a good time.

Maybe it'll happen for me. Maybe it won't. In the meantime, I'm down for a hell of a lot of fun with Cookie.

I can't help but wonder why she gave me her nickname rather than her real name. Maybe it's Courtney or Catherine or Cadence, but none of those fit her. Maybe she'll tell me before our time together is up.

Once we're out front, I call up an Uber to take us back to the Palms, the off-Strip hotel where I'm staying that's both close to the action and has plenty of action.

I was planning to spend the night in the high-stakes poker room, but spending it with Cookie sounds like a hell of a lot more fun. And more thrilling.

Part of me wonders if she makes a habit of heading home with strangers from a bar, but she's the one who said she's not passing up the chance with Grayson Nash, so I'm choosing to think I'm special.

I can't help but ask the question anyway once we've slid into the backseat. She's grasping my arm again, and I kind of love how it makes me feel—strong and protective over her.

"Have you done this before?" I ask quietly so the conversation is just for us and not our driver.

"Taken an Uber? Yeah, lots of times. You?"

I chuckle. "I meant picking up strangers in a bar."

"Oh," she says, and her cheeks turn a little pink like they did when I was hitting her with my best work at the bar. "No. This is a first."

I lean in close and lower my voice to that level that usually makes women drop their panties for me. "I like being your first."

She presses her lips together as she glances out the window, and when her eyes return to mine, they're heated.

I study her for a few beats as her lips become unpressed. They look so soft that I can't help myself.

I have to know what she tastes like. I have to know how she kisses. If I was the romantic type, I might care that this kiss is taking place in the back of an Uber. But I'm not, and we both know what this is.

At least...we both know what my intentions are. Whether it turns out to be more than that remains to be seen.

I lean in and slide my palm around her neck, pulling her toward me as my lips move down to hers.

She lets out a little moan of surprise, spurring me on as her hand comes up to cup my jaw.

I like being this close to her. I like the feel of her lips beneath mine, warm and welcoming as I open my mouth and slide my tongue along hers.

She's tentative and sweet, her mouth like candy under mine, a little tart from the cranberry flavor left behind from her drink. But then she swirls her tongue around mine, and she reaches up to grip the sleeve of my shirt or maybe to grip my bicep, I'm not sure, as if she has to hold on because this kiss is knocking her clean off her feet even though she's already sitting.

Jesus Christ.

It's knocking *me* clean off *my* feet, too.

I feel a weird sensation start to spread through my chest, a warmth where I've only felt a chill.

She's cracking my resolve with just a kiss.

Who the hell is this woman?

She doesn't seem like the kind of girl who goes back to random ballers' hotel rooms, and yet, here she is, heading toward the Palms with the newest player on the Vegas Aces.

I think I could get used to this whole Vegas scene pretty damn fast.

She holds onto me as I deepen the kiss with urgency, and if we weren't in the back of a car, I'd be urging her onto my lap and pulling her as close as I could get her.

Instead, we're making out in the back of an Uber, and it's about to get indecent in here as my incredibly hard cock begs me to take this further than just a kiss. I think about grabbing her hand and placing it there to show her how hard she's making me, but something stops me.

I'm not sure what.

I've never been prompted to stop before—not even in the back of an Uber.

I'm about to slide my palm down from her neck toward her tits when I seem to snap out of it.

She deserves better than a quick grope in the back of someone else's car. I'm not sure I could say that about some of my previous conquests, but there's a refined beauty about this girl I've not seen in the women I've taken back to my hotel rooms in the past.

Instead of pulling away, I slow the kiss. I keep my mouth pressed to hers for a few beats as I put my tongue away, closing my mouth, and I nip a few extra kisses at her lips before I pull back. Her eyes open slowly, and she looks…

Damn.

She looks as horny as I feel.

Her lips are red and a little puffy from our intense kiss, and her eyes are heavy as they land on mine. Her lips curl up a little, and then she whispers, "I can't believe Grayson Nash just kissed me."

One side of my mouth lifts in a lazy smile. "Grayson Nash is going to do a whole hell of a lot more than just kiss you, Cookie."

A whole *hell* of a lot more.

Chapter 7: Ava Maxwell

I Probably Should've Told Him

A text from Kelly interrupts me just as I'm getting out of the back of the Uber. I glance quickly at the screen.

Kelly: You okay? You sure about all this?

I know why she's asking.

I just broke up with Colin last night, and tonight I'm heading to Grayson Nash's hotel room with him under no pretense that we're going up to his room as old friends even though he's taking me to dinner first.

He still doesn't even know who I am, and I'm still thinking I don't want him to.

And he also doesn't know what Kelly knows.

I'm a virgin.

Yep, that's right. I'm twenty-five, I was in a long-term relationship with my ex, and I haven't had sex yet.

To be fair, I wanted to. But Colin wanted to wait until marriage…which is why I thought wedding bells would have been ringing by now.

We met at our college freshman orientation. We were friends first, and it took him two years to ask me out.

He's not particularly religious or anything, and neither am I. We just…*didn't* for the first year of our relationship even though we did *everything* else, and I think it was because we were friends first for so long. Then it became this *big huge thing*, and we agreed without ever really having a big talk about it that we were waiting for our wedding night.

I always had this thought in my head that if Colin and I ever broke up, I'd go out and blow my V-card on the first guy who came along. I didn't want it to be a *big huge thing* anymore.

And somehow the stars aligned and brought me Grayson Nash on a silver platter.

If there's a single man who has starred in my dreams of this moment more than any other man, it's him.

Colin included.

I feel like the monkey face with the hands covering the eyes emoji over that admission.

But I've been dreaming of Grayson Nash for many more years than I even knew Colin, so mathematically…I don't care.

Me: I'm positive.

He walks around to my side of the car and grabs my hand, and it feels so natural as my fingers slide between his.

Those butterflies are flapping. *Wildly.*

I've never had my engine revving quite like this, and I literally want to kick my feet in the air.

Is this it? Or is it just the crush pulsing all these feelings in me?

One thing is definite. I never, ever felt like this with Colin.

Colin was stable. He's a good guy, and he'll make a great husband for somebody. But I was tired of the complacent place where we landed.

I want the butterflies. I want the feet kicking.

And I feel it with Grayson. You know…the guy who just told me he's not sure he can give me anything more than one night.

But I'll take what I can get where Grayson Nash is concerned.

Instead of heading toward the elevators as I'm expecting, he heads to the left. We walk through the casino and stop in front of a café.

I glance over at him with a clear question in my eyes, and his eyes meet mine. His are twinkling a little.

"You requested a date first. I hope this café will do."

My chest tightens as emotion seems to fill me. It's silly, really. So I asked for dinner first.

But he didn't have to remember that I asked, and he certainly didn't have to actually take me out—especially not after the way things heated up between us.

He did it anyway.

It feels more romantic than my entire five years with Colin.

I realize I'm making comparisons, and I don't want to fall into the rebound trap. I really don't think that's what this is, especially since a big part of me knew it was over with Colin a long time ago.

Instead, this feels like every dream I've had since I was a preteen is coming true...except he has no idea who I am.

The host seats us at a round booth in the back of the café, indirectly giving us privacy even though we didn't ask for it.

I'll take it.

We sit, and I peruse the menu as I try to find the exact right thing to order—something light enough that I can do what comes next with enough protein to give me stamina. I don't want to look like a rabbit who pecks at her salad, but I'm also a little nervous, so I don't want anything too greasy.

I glance over at Grayson, and he's perusing the appetizers.

A thrill runs up my spine.

I can't believe I'm actually here about to eat dinner with him. How is this my life?

He must feel my gaze on him because he glances up. "What are you ordering?"

I clear my throat. "Oh, um...I haven't decided yet. You?"

"Want to split some appetizers?"

"Sure."

"What do you like?"

Men named Grayson. I force my eyes to the menu. "The pretzel?"

He nods. "And the nachos."

"Absolutely." And definitely *not* the garlic fries.

"Drink?" he asks.

"Definitely."

He nods, and the server comes by to take our order. He takes over with our food order, and he orders himself a glass of Hendricks. "And a vodka cranberry for my date."

My date.

Grayson Nash just called me his *date*.

I squeal in my mind.

"How'd you know?" I ask.

"I saw your glass back at the bar," he admits, and then he leans in a little closer. "But I also tasted it on your tongue, and I want to taste it again."

I clear my throat as heat climbs up my spine. "You drink straight gin?"

He nods. "It's my usual drink of choice. Low carb, low calorie."

"But the taste…" I trail off and make a face.

"You weren't complaining in the back of the Uber." His reply is cocky and confident.

"Neither were you," I shoot back.

He chuckles. "No, I wasn't. I had to pull myself together if I'm being honest." He clears his throat and shifts his position under the table. "So, Cookie, tell me about yourself."

"What do you want to know?" I ask, riding a line here. Do I tell him who I am?

I don't want to. I like being the mystery woman he just met, not the girl he remembers as his best friend's little sister.

"Did you grow up in Nevada?"

I shake my head. "I went to UNLV and fell in love with Vegas, so I decided to stay. What about you?" I toss the question back to him to try to get the heat off me. The less I have to admit about my background, the better the chance that he won't put two and two together.

"I originated in New York, went to Nebraska, was drafted by Buffalo, where I played for two years, played in Los Angeles for eight years, and here I am, ready to make another move," he says.

"Do you like moving around?"

He lifts a shoulder. "No. Honestly, the whole process of having to pack up and move is...overwhelming. I have to sell my place in LA and find somewhere to live out here."

"Can't you stay with a teammate? Or one of your brothers?" I ask.

"I could, but I don't want to. Linc's married now, and his wife is expecting a baby at the end of the month. And Asher...he's Asher. He's got his own set of shit to deal with, but he's been living with my dad since his suspension started. The idea of backtracking to live with a parent after so many years on my own is..." He makes a face that indicates his distaste over the idea.

"I get that. I love my family, but I wouldn't want to live with any of them anymore." I wrinkle my nose, too. "So will you buy a place out here?"

"I don't know yet. I'm looking at a couple places tomorrow before I head back to LA to talk to my coaches and pack up." He presses his lips together in a way that makes me think he's not looking forward to either of those things.

I almost offer to help him when I realize how out of place that would sound.

"So tell me the truth," I say, leaning in conspiratorially. "Is this going to be your last season?"

He gives me a wry smile. "If I knew the answer to that, I'd tell you. Part of me thought last season was going to be it, but I wasn't ready to hang it up. I'm excited for the chance to play with my brothers."

I tilt my head as I study him. "You sound like you're talking to the press, but I'm not the press."

He eyes me for a long moment before he responds to that. "I don't know you, though. How do I know what I say to you stays between us?"

"You don't," I answer honestly. "But what does your intuition tell you about me? Do you think I'll run out of here and tell everyone your secrets if you confide in me?"

"No," he admits. "You seem…kind. You don't seem like the kind of person who would do that."

"I'm not."

"Then you tell me a secret, and I'll tell you one." His tone is a challenge.

"I broke up with my boyfriend last night."

He looks taken aback by my admission.

Before he can respond to that, I add, "It was over a long time ago. We've been long-distance for a while, and I was waiting to see him in person to do it. When that opportunity didn't come, well…" I shrug.

His jaw slackens a little. "So this, you and me, tonight…this is a rebound bang?"

I laugh. "No. You're Grayson Nash. I would've called him to break up with him the second you approached me at the bar just to be free and clear of him for a shot with you."

He dramatically puts his hand on his chest. "I'm flattered."

My cheeks flush. "Now you go."

His eyes shift over to the aquarium that spans the entire wall of the restaurant behind us. "My father beat into us from a young age that the game comes first above all else, and for a long time, I thought it fucked all four of us up. But Linc's married, Spence is engaged…and I don't know. I don't know what comes next when my playing days are done, and I think it's why I'm back for another season." He glances back at me. "It'll be fun playing with my brothers. That's not a line. But the truth is…I'm tired. I'm only thirty-two, but it's getting harder and harder on my body. On my knees, my back. I feel like an eighty-year-old man who can hardly get out of bed some days, and I don't know how much longer I can put my body through it." He moves his eyes back to the aquarium. "But when I think about really giving up this life, really retiring…I don't know if I can do it. I have nothing waiting for me on the other side. Coaching, probably, which is easier on my body but doesn't change my schedule. Beyond that, I'm not sure." He looks at me again, and I'm surprised at his vulnerability with me.

I reach over and squeeze his hand. "I think it's okay not to be sure, Grayson." My voice is low. "Thirty-two is still young. You can keep playing. You can try coaching. Or maybe there's something else out there for you. It's all about being in the right place at the right time, and what's meant to happen will happen when it's supposed to."

His eyes meet mine. Our fingers are still twined together, electricity flying between us, and I get the feeling that the two of us running into each other tonight is one of those examples of being in the right place at the right time.

Maybe the preteen in me wasn't such a dummy when it came to Grayson Nash. I just had to bide my time and wait for this moment.

He opens his mouth to say something when the server appears at the end of our table with our drinks, snapping the intimacy right out of the moment.

He holds up his gin, and I hold up my vodka drink.

"To the right place at the right time," he says.

I clink his glass with mine, and some sort of unspoken promise passes between us as we each take a sip.

This should feel awkward, right? It's like a first date, but we both know it's going to end in his hotel room, and maybe we'll even have breakfast together. I have to work tomorrow, but that's a minor detail. So I'll be tired in the morning. I was tired and hungover when I got up today, but it's not stopping me right now.

"What's your favorite thing about Vegas?" he asks.

"The weather, except for the super-hot months."

"How long have you been here?" he asks.

"Seven years now."

He twists his lips a little and runs his hand through his hair. "Maybe when I get back you can show me around a little."

My brows shoot up in surprise. I'm about to remind him that he's the one who made the early call that he can't promise anything beyond tonight, but if he's interested in seeing me again, there's no way in hell I'm bringing that up. "I'd love to." I pull my phone out before I lose my nerve and pull up a new contact screen. I slide the phone over to him. "Type in your number."

To my surprise, he does, and he texts *Cookie* to himself. He saves my contact in his phone, too.

Holy shit.

Grayson Nash just gave me his number.

It's all these little things that keep shocking me, but it's also these little things that mean a lot to me.

Our appetizers arrive, and he rips off a chunk of pretzel and hands it to me to go first. I dip it in the cheese sauce and let out a soft moan of delight at the flavors.

He visibly shifts again, and I love that I have this power over him. It makes me feel bold and powerful and *sexy*—something I never felt with my ex.

In fact, just about everything about tonight is different from anything I've felt before.

And I'm not going to be ready to let that go when the sun rises tomorrow.

Chapter 8: Grayson Nash

The Right Place at the Right Time

The longer I sit here with her, the less this feels like a hookup and the more it feels like someone I want to get to know more before I take her upstairs and fuck her until she can't see straight.

I'm not sure when this turned into a date, but it did.

I'm sure I'll get shit from the teammates I ditched to take her back to my hotel, but I'll worry about that tomorrow.

Tonight, all I can focus on is her.

She talks to me like she already knows me, and she makes me feel comfortable in a way that women rarely do. She's obviously more than just some jersey chaser, yet she came back here with me to my hotel.

It doesn't make a whole lot of sense.

And that's why I let it slip that I want her to show me around town. It's why I didn't hesitate when she had me put her number in my phone, and why I immediately texted myself to make sure I had her number, too.

This isn't just going to be some one-night hookup, though I can't define what it will be until I've had the chance to get to know her a little better.

It's all wrong. It's stupid. I can't get caught up in something five minutes after I arrive in town. I have a game to focus on with new teammates. I have to work to find my place in Vegas as I fight against the accusations of nepotism that brought me here.

I have to hold my own against my coach, my troubled youngest brother, and my father...all family members I'll be interacting with more than most grown adults tend to interact with their family members.

I have to move to a new town where I know very few people—including packing up the old place and leaving a life eight years in the making behind me.

And somehow, having this woman next to me as I face all these new challenges feels...

I don't know.

It feels right.

I whisper the word in my own brain because it's ridiculous. I can't come to terms with something this big this soon, but I guess sometimes people have a way of knocking you off balance, and this woman has. Already. In the ninety minutes since I met her.

Is that all it's been?

Because I'm sitting here talking to her as if I've known her my whole life, and that has never happened to me before. Fuck, a woman I've taken back to my hotel has never asked me for a dinner date first, either. I've never shared a soft pretzel and nachos with a hookup before sticking my dick in her.

I haven't had *that* many hookups. Not as many as Asher, anyway, but for the last year, I spent less time hooking up and more time benefiting with my friend. But even Daphne was less of a girlfriend and more of a girl I occasionally screwed—even if she didn't see it that way.

"What was it like growing up with three brothers who all played football?" she asks as we dig into the nachos. She goes for the chips with hardly any toppings while I dive in and get my hands dirty.

"Mostly fun. Linc and Ash are almost a decade apart, so we didn't spend a ton of time playing together when we were kids. We do now when we get together as a family, but that's rare, and we're getting too old for the types of battles we had when we were younger." I chuckle fondly as I think about my grandparents' wedding anniversary almost a year ago. It's always a party when all four of us are together, and we'll be missing Spencer this season as three of the four of us are on the same team for the first time in history.

It *is* a historic moment. It's exciting, and fans are watching us closely.

Which is even more reason why I need to keep my head down and focus on football. I can't come into town hooking up with a different woman every night because eyes will be on me. I need to make a good impression here because every move I make will reflect on my brothers.

"What about you? Do you have any siblings?" I ask. I notice she keeps deflecting anything about herself and tossing questions back at me, and it's just one more thing that's intriguing about her. Most women I've been with love to talk about themselves.

"I'm the only girl among brothers. We all scattered once college hit, and we always get together at the holidays, but that's getting harder to manage now that they're having families of their own," she says. "Which of your brothers are you closest to?"

There she goes again, tossing the conversation back to me. "Probably Lincoln, though we don't talk as often as brothers probably should. I imagine that'll change now that he's my coach. I'm not sure if we *can* be close when he's my coach, and Asher's a teammate now, so I think that'll draw us closer even though he's five years younger than me."

"What about your other brother?" she presses.

I shrug. "Spence just got engaged and he's doing his own thing in Minnesota, so I doubt it. Things will likely change with Ash and Linc as I make the transition to the Aces, but I don't see how it would bring me any closer to Spence. Besides, he's the quietest of the four of us, so I don't really see him reaching out."

"Who's the loudest?" she asks.

I raise my hand.

She giggles. "You? Never."

I offer a wry smile. "I know. Hard to believe, right? I'm also the funniest and the best-looking."

"I'll agree there," she murmurs, and it's almost as if she doesn't realize she said it aloud, but in any event, I like it. A lot. And so does my cock. She clears her throat and shakes her head. "What are some funny things you've done?"

"I don't know. Pranks, jokes, one-liners. That type of thing."

"What pranks have you pulled?" she asks.

"Dumb shit like parking too close to the driver's side so they have to get out the passenger side, or putting googly eyes on all the jars in the fridge. Oh, signing Spence up for a subscription to a dirty magazine that came to the house in his name when we were teenagers. Things like that."

She laughs, and for some reason, hearing her laugh at the expense of my own pranks on my brothers makes me want to pull more dumb shit just to hear her laugh again.

Oh, fuck.

I think that means I might be in a little deeper than I first thought.

We laugh some more, and we get serious, too. She tells me how stressed she is that she got scammed into buying a huge kit of skincare products that she doesn't even use. She was supposed to sell the products, but instead they're sitting in her closet, a total waste of money and space. I tell her how I really feel about getting approached in public like the woman at the bar—I hate it—and I admit to feeling like I need the focus to be on football this season rather than on what conquest the media will pair me with.

As much as I want to take her upstairs, I'm not sure I should. She's too sweet. Too kind. Too…amazing. And I want more.

If I screw her tonight in my hotel room, am I limiting what sort of future I might be able to have with her? Am I putting a stamp on this thing by telling her it's just one night for me?

I said it from the beginning, but I also said I didn't know. The more time I spend with her, the more I want to make the effort for something beyond one night.

And *that* isn't the norm for me. That isn't something I've ever experienced before, to be honest.

I feel like I don't want to ruin tonight with sex.

Our drinks are empty, though, and our plates are cleared.

I order a refill for the road since this is Vegas, and our server delivers them with our check. We're done drinking them by the time we finish paying the bill.

The dinner portion of the evening has come to a close, and now it's time to take her upstairs.

Only…I feel like I want to give her an out. I want to give her the choice.

Of course I want to take her upstairs, haul her into my arms, and strip her naked.

There's nothing I want more, in fact.

Instead, though, I grab her hand and we meander through the casino back toward the front doors. I pause when we get there, and she looks surprised that I'm stopping. I look out front at the line of people waiting for cars to pick them up.

"Well," I begin awkwardly. "I've had a lot of fun with you tonight."

Her brows pinch together as her eyes fly to mine. She looks…disappointed. "I thought we were…"

"Well, we were. But I want to see you again. I don't want this to be—" I fumble for the right words, and I finally find something awkward to finish that sentence. "A one and done."

She stares at me for a few beats, and then she lifts to her tiptoes and reaches around my neck to pull me down toward her. She presses a gentle kiss to my lips, and she breaks the kiss but doesn't let me go. "I'd love to go out with you again. But I also want you to take me up to your room."

I pull back, and my eyes search hers. "Are you sure?"

She sinks back onto her heels, the height difference between us nearly a full foot. She snags her bottom lip demurely between her teeth as she nods. "I'm sure."

I grunt out a soft sound, and then I grab her hand, surprised once more by this unexpected woman. "Then let's go."

Chapter 9: Ava Maxwell

Those Abs Though

I'm not sure if I've ever been so sure and simultaneously so nervous about anything in my entire life before.

Gone from my brain are all thoughts of my ex as I step onto the elevator with Grayson Nash.

This is really happening.

He's taking me up to his hotel room.

He wants to see me again.

At some point, I'll need to fess up to my true identity. I should probably do it before we have sex. But I find that I'm enjoying being Cookie. I'm still one hundred percent me, and it's true that on occasion I've had people call me Cookie because of my kitchen sink cookies. I'm just leaving out the teeny-tiny detail that a decade ago, we were in the same place at the same time—a place which was *not* the *right* place at the right time.

But today is.

We're alone as the elevator doors slide closed, and it feels like the heat amps up a few degrees between us as he pulls on my hand, which he's still holding, and I fall into his chest.

He bends down as his hand comes up to palm my neck like he did in the back of the car, and his lips drop down to mine. I sink into him as I open my mouth to his again, and he backs us up until I'm pressed between his body and the elevator wall.

There's something beautiful about being kissed by Grayson, and it feels as if I'll never get enough of it. I link my arms around his torso as we make out on this elevator. His one palm still cups my neck, and the other slides down until his fingertips find my hip.

The elevator slides to a halt with a ding to let us know we have arrived on our floor, and we reluctantly break away. He moves his arm around my shoulders, and I reach up to grab onto the hand around my shoulder as I look up at him. A tiny smile plays at his lips as he looks down at me, and I smile back at him.

We walk together like that off the elevator and down the hall toward his room, and he slides his phone out of his pocket to unlock his door. He opens the door, and I gasp as I look into the suite.

It's a corner suite, and it's…simply breathtaking. It has wraparound views of the Vegas Strip on one side and the skyline with mountain views out the other window. I'm in awe as I look around the place.

I guess this is what a big-money pro football contract gets you. It's most definitely *not* what a pastry chef at a bakery off-Strip gets you.

A large sectional sofa looks out over the view, and a door leads into another room—presumably the bedroom.

A bar is set up along an interior wall with six stools, and an open bag of Tootsie Rolls sits on the surface beside a bottle of Hendricks. I'm not sure what one man needs all this space for, but I'm really happy he decided to bring me up here.

I head over toward the window and touch the glass, looking out over the view. It's just after nine, and the lights of the Strip twinkle across the highway. "Wow," I breathe. I slip my phone out of my pocket to take a picture if only because I feel like I may never see this view again. I never want to forget the wonder and the pure magic I feel right now.

He chuckles as he watches me in the reflection of the glass, and then he nods toward the bar. "Would you like a drink?"

I turn around to face him, and despite the size of the room, all I can see is him. He's a force, that's for sure.

I shake my head. I don't want another drink. I'm just tipsy enough to think this is still a good idea—just tipsy enough to mask my inhibitions. Just tipsy enough to give myself over to the boy I've had a crush on since I was a kid.

I take a few steps away from the window and back toward him. "I only want one thing right now."

We're mere feet away from each other, and he closes the gap, wrapping an arm around my waist and hauling me to him. "And what might that be?"

"You."

His lips crash down to mine, and this kiss is more aggressive than the previous two. It's faster and more urgent as his mouth opens and his tongue assaults mine in the most heavenly way.

His hand slides from my waist down to my hip and then up my torso, stopping short of my breast. My body seems to automatically move into him, urging his hand up, and he does it. I moan, spurring him on. He moves both hands under my thighs and lifts me, and I wrap my legs around his waist as I move my arms around his neck. He carries us over to the couch, and I unhook my legs from around him as he sits. I rest one leg on either side of him.

He thrusts his hips up toward me, and it's clear he's ready for this. He's hard, and I'm wet, and it's time.

I've been waiting a long time for this moment—not just with Grayson, but with any man. We make out for a bit on the couch, his hands roaming up my back and into my hair as I do the same with him, and then he pulls back.

His eyes are hooded as they land on mine. His lips are swollen from our kiss, and he looks so freaking sexy in this moment that I nearly have a tiny orgasm just looking at him.

He shifts me so I'm lying on my back, and he's so smooth, moving the two of us so easily as he hovers over me, his mouth moving back to mine and his body slamming against me like he's having sex with me only with our clothes on. I wrap my legs around his waist as he drives against me again and again, a desperate plea escaping my lips in the form of a moan.

He lifts off me and reaches his hand between us, cupping my pussy over my jeans. I take the opportunity to slide my hand over his jeans, too, to feel his steel cock through the fabric.

I let out a little moan at the feel of him just as he lifts his hand and slides it down into my jeans. He stays on the outside of my panties, teasing me as my chest lights up with thrills and a rough, needy ache pulses between my legs.

I reach up under his shirt and feel the warm, smooth skin of his back before I allow my hands to trail back around to his stomach. I feel the outline of muscles there even from this angle, and I want to see it all.

I push him back, and he settles onto his knees as I reach for the bottom of his shirt. He's too tall from the angle where I find myself, so he helps, ripping his shirt off over his head, and...

Whoa.

Holy shit.

He's stacked.

He's a pro athlete, and my eyes fall to the muscles in his abdomen. One, two, three...ten. At least ten. I've never seen a ten-pack before. I'm not even sure I've ever seen a six-pack in person before.

If he catches my ogling, he ignores it as he reaches for the bottom of my shirt, too. He pulls it off, and he spots the black bra I wore today. I didn't think I'd actually end up in a man's hotel room tonight, so I didn't put a whole lot of extra effort into my choice. It's just a simple black bra from Target, but his eyes still heat when he reaches around to unhook it. He pulls it off and tosses it to the side, and he ogles me for a few beats.

And honestly?

The way he looks at me makes me feel like I'm the fucking queen of the world.

He clears his throat, and he glances away from me and out the window for a few beats.

"You okay?" I whisper, unable to actually make my voice work.

"Yeah. I just…need a minute."

My brows dip. "For what?" That's definitely my naivete and inexperience talking.

"Well, if I keep looking at you like that looking at me like that, I'm not gonna make it to the big show."

"The big—*ohhh*," I say, cutting myself off.

"Exactly. The big O."

I giggle. He really is pretty funny.

He gets up off the couch and turns toward the window for a beat before looking at me again. "Why does this feel different?"

I shrug and twist my lips a little. "Because it *is* different, Grayson."

He narrows his eyes at me. "I just…don't understand why. I don't even know you."

But you do.

I can't bring myself to say the words. Instead, I stand and walk over toward him, trying not to feel the vulnerability that comes with walking topless through the room. He pulls me in against him when I get close enough. "Sometimes things just don't make sense, I guess."

He lowers his mouth to mine again, and he kisses me slowly. Sensually. With tenderness and abandon at the same time.

He stops the kiss first, and he grabs my hand. He leads me into the bedroom, and he literally sweeps me off my feet and sets me down on the bed. He heads over toward his suitcase perched on a rack to the side, and he grabs a condom out of it as I kick off my shoes.

He kicks his off, too, and then he walks back toward me as he slides the condom into his back pocket as if he's saving that for later—as if he has other plans first.

He flicks the button on my jeans before he lowers them down my legs along with my panties in one fell swoop, and I'm suddenly naked on his bed.

And I feel...

Not nervous.

Not vulnerable.

Not awkward.

I feel free. I feel beautiful, as if the way his eyes are set on me is making me beautiful. I feel like the only woman in his world with the way his attention is focused solely on me. And it makes me feel confident and sexy...two things I don't know if I've ever felt before in the same space, and just because of the way he's looking at me like he wants to devour me.

I wait for him to make a move as I lie there, his gaze moving over the contours of my body as if he's deciding what he wants to do.

A shiver rushes down my spine.

He takes a step toward me, and he circles my ankles with his fingertips. He yanks my body until I'm at the edge of the bed, and then he kneels down on the floor between my legs, pushing my knees open as he rests my ankles on his shoulders.

Oh my God.

He's going to do it.

It's the thing I always wished my ex would do, but the thing he *rarely* did.

Grayson presses soft kisses to my inner thigh, the scruff on his jawline tickling me as he moves closer and closer to my center, and when he sticks his tongue out for the first taste against my clit, my hips jerk off the bed.

He chuckles as he moves his face out of the way by reflex, and then he holds me down with an arm banding across my stomach as he licks into me again.

I grip onto the sheets as he sucks on my clit. I think I'm already seeing stars from the onslaught of pleasure, and he's barely even gotten started.

But I can't help it.

He knows what he's doing with that mouth of his.

He pulls back but doesn't move his eyes from my pussy. "Your cunt tastes so fucking good." His words hum against my body, and he moves back in, flicking my clit with his tongue before he flattens it and moves it down, and then he dips it inside me.

Yep, that's it. That's the thing.

"Oh my God!" I cry out as he moves his tongue in and out of me, and then he flattens it again and moves up toward my clit.

It's a million sensations all at once, but when he brings his other hand up and pushes a finger in while he licks my clit, I'm seconds from falling apart.

He moves the arm banded across my stomach and he grapples with my breast, thumbing my nipple in time as he works my pussy with his mouth and finger. He adds in a second finger, and it's too much.

The climax hits me as if from out of nowhere. I squeeze my legs together around his ears as I moan and scream and swear his name. He fights his way through it, continuing to deliver absolute bliss as my body contracts and pulses with beat after beat of hot pleasure.

Once the pulsing starts to slow to a low throb and I release his head from my knee-lock grip, he rocks back onto his heels, wiping his mouth with the back of his hand before his eyes find mine.

"Jesus, Cookie. That was the hottest thing I've ever seen."

A lazy smile plays at my lips, and I feel like jelly as I lay here on the bed. "That was incredible."

"If you think that was good, you should see how I fuck." His arrogant words take my breath away.

"I'm ready," I pant. "Give it to me."

He lifts to a stand, and he pulls the condom out of his back pocket. He tosses it on the bed beside me, and then he drops his jeans.

He's going commando, and I get the absolute treat of seeing Grayson Nash and all his completely naked glory standing in front of me.

My eyes move from those ridiculously perfect abs down a little lower to the perfect cut of a V leading down to his very hard, very large, very incredible cock.

My jaw drops a little as I take in naked Grayson for the first time. He's reaching for the condom, and I can't help but stare at his cock.

There's no way. There's just no way *that* thing is going to fit into *this* thing.

"Whoa," I breathe.

He chuckles as he rolls it on, and I can't tell if he's a little vulnerable here or if it's cockiness.

"That's, uh…that's quite an um…"

"Is there an end to these sentences?" he teases.

"It's big. You're…big." My dumb, stupid mouth forms even dumber, stupider words.

He twists his lips as he moves to hover over me. "You can take it." He lowers his lips to mine, and I pull back a little nervously.

My eyes meet his. "Go slow, okay?"

He nods, and he grips himself and swipes through my slit, teasing my sensitive clit again with the head of his dick this time.

The thought that he's about to take my virginity pulses through my mind.

I've had fingers in there before. I've even had a vibrator or two in there. Not at the same time or anything, but enough to break through that layer to not give me away as a virgin.

But a cock this size has not yet entered the premises. There's no turning back now, though—not that I want to. I'm ready for this. I'm ready for *him*. He primed me up with that tongue thing he did, and this is it.

His eyes meet mine as he lines himself up, and he pushes just the tip in.

Oh dear Lord.

That's really…that's something else. It feels both good and different at the same time.

"Oh fuck, that's so tight." He inches his way in slowly. "Yes, baby. You can take it." He drops his lips to my neck. "God, that's so good. Does it hurt?"

Tears fill my eyes as he achingly slowly pushes his way in— not because it hurts, but because this is a moment I've dreamed of for so damn long. It's emotional and heavy and at the same time beautiful and light. "No," I squeak. "It feels so good. Give it to me, Grayson."

He pushes in a little more.

"Is it all the way in?" I beg.

"No, baby. Not by a long shot."

"God, just do it," I say, and he takes me at my word.

He thrusts all the way in, and it's a shock to my system as I adjust to his size. I yelp because it hurts, but not unbearably. It's more like a pain lined with pleasure, and I'll take the pain just so I can feel one second of intense pleasure with this man.

"You okay?" he whispers, holding himself steady inside me.

"Oh, God, yes," I moan as my pussy seems to throb all around him.

He inches back with a grunt, and I can tell he's putting everything into moving slowly when he just wants to slam into me.

My body seems to adjust to him, and he pulls back before driving in again. He's controlled and skilled as he moves almost tenderly, like he doesn't want to hurt me even though he wants to find his own release, too.

It's sweet and endearing, and it opens a little piece of my heart that seems to latch onto him in this moment.

I'll always remember my first. I'll always remember this moment.

His mouth finds mine, and I taste my own spicy tang on his tongue as it swirls against mine. I dig my nails into his back as he pushes forward, his drives still slow as he finds a rhythm that works for both of us.

I move beneath him, writhing against him, wanting friction but scared to ask for it, scared it'll hurt, scared I'll fall for him only to be cast aside as a one-night fling.

He pulls back, his eyes finding mine again as he starts to move a little faster still, and I nod, giving him the green light. I still feel a sense of discomfort, but the good outweighs the bad as he picks up the pace. The heat between us is palpable, and his chest glides against my sensitive nipples.

He lifts off me a little and reaches up to grip my nipple between his fingertips, and I whimper beneath him.

He forces himself to slow down again, and I feel like I need him to move faster. I wrap my legs around his waist, and that seems to give me a wider berth for him to move. I dig my heels into his ass to spur him on, and he lets go of my nipple to brace himself before he starts to really pound into me.

God, it hurts so good.

I moan and close my eyes, tilting my head back as my breasts jiggle between us. He grunts and growls with each thrust, and he kicks up the speed a little more as he moves closer to his release.

"Fuck, baby, yes," he growls, and he pushes in and holds himself there as a guttural moan rises up from his chest.

He hammers in a few more short thrusts as he starts to relax into me, and he kisses me for a beat. This kiss is long and deep as he worships my mouth with his, and then he slowly edges his way out.

My pussy hurts as he drops out, and he reaches down between us with his fingers. He rubs slow, lazy circles on my clit as he bends down and drags my nipple into his mouth. He sucks on it as he dips his finger back into me, and the sweet relief of one finger after he filled me with his enormous size is a godsend. He pulls it out and slides my wetness over my clit, and the edges of pleasure start to close in on me as my body bends beneath his touch.

I have some warning this time, but the orgasm plows hard into me as I start to come.

"Fuck yes, baby girl, give me all that come," he murmurs as I drench his fingers. I claw at his shoulder with one hand as I clutch the sheets with my other, and when the pleasure passes through me, I'm left with a warm, soft glow.

And as he moves to settle in beside me and my head finds the perfect nook between his shoulder and his chest, I find myself in a space I'm not ready to move from anytime soon.

Chapter 10: Grayson Nash

I Guess I'm Sweet

I'm at a loss as to how to handle what comes next.

I don't want to move. I think she fell asleep. Her head is nestled on my shoulder, and my arm is around her. I want to pull her closer. I never want to let her go.

What the hell is that?

She fits beside me so perfectly, as if she was somehow made to lay in the place where she is right now.

Right place at the right time, I guess.

I'm not used to feeling anything more than pleasure in the afterglow, but there's something else at play here I can't quite recognize just yet. It's emotions, strange and unfamiliar ones.

I want to fuck her again. I want to rail her.

I certainly will.

But I also know she needs time to get used to my…size.

So I'm well-endowed. It hasn't exactly been a hindrance, but part of the responsibility that comes with having a huge cock is knowing how to use it in a way that won't hurt my partner.

Lube for the win, usually…but she didn't need any. That was a mighty wet pussy, as if she was saving it up for me.

She'll probably be sore for a few days, particularly given how tight she was. But every time she sits, I hope she thinks of me. Every time she feels the sting, I hope she remembers what we just did.

I can't help but think of her ex. Who was he? I'll fucking kill the guy, figuratively, of course. There was something so tentative about the way she was acting, as if she hadn't done this before.

She hasn't said her age, but I'd guess she's somewhere in her mid-twenties based on the conversation we had about how long she's been in Vegas. Surely she's had sex before. Surely I didn't just take her virginity. She would've said something…right?

But *goddamn*, that pussy was *tight* as fuck. Between that and her slight hesitation, I couldn't help but wonder.

Regardless, it was heaven in there, a vice gripping onto me as I moved slowly into her. It was a feeling I won't soon forget. A feeling I'll dream about over and over. A feeling I'll remember as I'm palming my cock over the next few days until I can see her and get up inside that cunt again.

I drag in a heavy breath, and she shifts a little at the sound. I force myself up because I have to get this condom off, and when I return, she's sitting up with a blanket wrapped around her shoulders, and I'm not sure if she's naked beneath it or if she put clothes back on. I don't even know where the blanket came from. The closet, maybe.

She clears her throat a little awkwardly. "I should, uh…I should go."

I pull my jeans back on but leave the shirt off, and I move in beside her, tossing an arm around her shoulder. When I'm sitting next to her, I finally see that she did in fact get dressed in the sixty seconds I took in the bathroom. "You don't have to."

She glances over at me a little awkwardly. My head is angled down as I look at her, and she looks away, fixing her gaze out the window.

"You okay?" I ask.

She nods. "I'm good. A little sore, I think. And I have to work in the morning."

"And I have to look at houses then catch a flight back to LA. Stay the night with me."

She looks surprised, and it's another clue that tells me she's never done this before. A one-night stand, anyway. She's acting like she doesn't know how to act, and if part of my job is to make sure my partner is enjoying herself, then part of my job is also to make sure she feels comfortable afterward.

"Come with me," I say, and I grab her hand and pull her to her feet. I push her toward the bathroom first. "Take a minute in there, and then meet me out on the couch."

She narrows her eyes at me, but she takes the blanket off, tosses it on the bed, and does as she's told.

I pull my shirt back on. I grab the blanket and toss it on the couch before I head over to the bar, where I fiddle around and find a Keurig and some tea pods. I brew a cup of tea, and I sweeten it with a little honey packet.

She emerges from the bedroom a minute later looking freshly fucked and gorgeous, and she sits on the couch, pulling the blanket up over her legs as she looks out the windows at the Strip. I bring her cup of tea over and hand it to her before I sit on the opposite side of the couch, facing the windows overlooking the skyline as I slide my legs under the opposite side of the blanket and twine them with hers.

"Thanks for this," she says, and she takes a sip. "No tea for you?"

I shake my head. "I'm not really a tea drinker."

"How'd you know I needed some?"

"Good guess. You seemed chilly and it's late for coffee. And I wanted you to feel warm and comfortable with me." I say the words almost shyly, which isn't really my MO. I'm more of a confident guy bordering on cocky most of the time.

She tilts her head as a warmth seems to radiate from her, and I get this really strange sensation like I'm looking into the future and we're at home as a couple of kids sleep soundly upstairs and we're about to have the kind of deep conversation that will push me even closer to her.

Where the fuck did that come from?

"That's really sweet," she says softly.

I offer a polite nod as I press my lips together and look out the window over her shoulder. Did I just make it awkward? I feel like I did. I should say something. "People don't usually call me sweet."

She chuckles. "You are to me."

"You're different," I blurt.

She raises her brows. "How?"

"I haven't quite put my finger on it yet."

She ducks her head a little and averts her gaze toward the window, and then she takes a little sip of her tea. "Well, you're different, too."

"How?"

"I've never...um..." She pauses and seems to come to a decision as to what she wants to say. "I've never been with a football player before."

"Good."

"Why is that good?" she asks.

"Because I'd have to kill him if you had been, and I'd hate to start my time with a new team by killing a teammate."

She giggles.

"You mentioned an ex," I say, striding a careful line but also trying to get to the truth of the question I can't seem to bring myself to ask. "Do I need to kill him?"

She makes a face like she's contemplating it, but then she shakes her head. "He's married to his job, and we grew apart long enough ago that he's a nonissue."

She dodges mentioning anything about her sex life, not that I'd really thought she would.

"Have you, uh..." *had sex before?* Come on, Grayson. Just ask her. "You said you haven't had a one-night stand before?"

Her eyes flick to mine, and I spot a question there. "No."

"Good. That record still stands since I'll be back in a few days, and I want to see you again."

"You do?" she asks, and her voice is filled with incredulity.

"Of course I do. You're hot, you're funny, you're kind, you make cookies for a living, and you look at me like I'm a god."

"Have you ever had a one-night stand where you wanted to see the woman again?" she asks.

I shake my head slowly. "Not until you. Maybe that's what it is that makes you different."

Her eyes soften, and she leans forward, so I do the same. We meet in the middle for a sweet kiss, and there's just something about this woman that already makes me feel like I'll never get enough of her.

Chapter 11: Grayson Nash

What's Bought Can Always Be Sold

At some point, we must both fall asleep. We talked late into the night as we watched the lights twinkle on the Strip, and I jolt awake when I hear a phone ringing.

Only it's not a phone ringing at all, it's her alarm clock letting her know she has to get up.

She pulls it out of her pocket and silences it, a groggy look on her face that's downright adorable, and she sits up a little and massages her neck since we both fell asleep as we were, our heads on opposite hotel couch armrests as our pillows.

I crack my neck back and forth as I sit up, too. "Morning," I say softly.

"Good morning." Her voice is hoarse. "This is going to be a rough day."

"Call in sick and spend the day with me, then," I say.

Whoa.

Where did that come from?

Did I really just invite her to crash my day to look at houses in Vegas with me so I could get her seal of approval? It appears I did.

But why?

I don't even know her.

"I wish I could," she says, gently letting me down as she stands. "But it's Saturday, our busiest day. I have to get there early to help set up and make sure all our orders are filled. And probably make another ten dozen cookies. But when you get back and you have some time…I'd love to see you again."

I stand, too, and I pull her into my arms. "I'd love to see you again, too." I drop my lips to hers. "You sure you can't stay for round two?"

She chuckles, and she backs up, pointing toward her pussy. "This kitty needs a rest. She's feeling every inch of that monster you pushed in last night. But when you're back…" She trails off, shrugging at the end to let me know it's an open invitation.

I can't help but laugh and be incredibly turned on at the same time. "Deal." I let out a sigh as she finds her shoes and pulls them on, and she stands by the door.

I don't know how to say goodbye. I don't *want* to say goodbye, and I've never really felt that way before when I've seen a girl out. So I don't say it. "See you soon, Cookie."

She presses her lips together and nods. "See ya, Grayson."

I reach down and take her hand in mine, threading my fingers through hers, and I kiss her once more.

She moans into me, and then she sets a hand on my chest and pushes me back a little. "I need to go."

I nod, and she opens the door and walks out. I think about watching her walk down the hall toward the elevator, but I'm not a psycho, so I let the door latch shut behind her, and then I saunter over toward the bed where I fucked her last night, climb in, and get a few hours of shut-eye as I still smell her on my sheets.

When I wake up, it's four hours later and the sun is streaming in, and I'm jolted awake by the ringing of my phone. Despite the extra rest, I still feel tired, thanks probably in part to the gin. I can't imagine how she's baking cookies at work today after the night we had.

It's probably an age thing. She's a little younger than me, so she can handle it.

I grab my phone to try to silence it, but I miss it just in time as it goes to voicemail. I see it was Beckett calling, and I'll ring him back later, but I can't help wondering why he called.

I take a quick shower, and I listen to his message after I get dressed.

"Hey, man. You're all over the news. Congrats again on the trade. I hope it works out well for you. And I found out my sister is dealing with a breakup, so even more reason to have you check in on her when you can since her big brother isn't there to protect her. I'll text you the name of the place where she works if you don't mind stopping in. I know it's a big ask, but I'm her brother, you know? I just need to make sure she's okay. Anyway, talk to you later."

He hangs up, and I wonder for a beat what it's like to have a younger sister. Sometimes I think that growing up in a family of boys took away certain parts of our personalities that might've developed otherwise.

Our need to protect, for instance.

And yet, somehow I felt it with Cookie.

Cookie.

I still can't believe after the night we shared that she left without giving me her name. We talked about everything in a way that felt like we were each baring our very souls, but the more I think about it, the more I realize we talked about hopes and dreams and the future, but not the past. We didn't get into personal data. And every time I tried to pick at one of those threads, she tossed it right back into my court.

Is she hiding something?

Is that what makes her different? The mystery?

Maybe she didn't break up with her boyfriend at all and I'm just the other man in the equation. Somehow I doubt it, but I can't help the thought as it digs at the back of my brain.

I brew myself a cup of coffee and I stand at the windows, drinking it as I think about pressing her tits up against this very window while I fuck her from behind.

Jesus.

I push that thought out of my brain, not really sure why I can't stop thinking about her.

My buddy John is acting as my realtor, and I get a text from him that he's waiting for me downstairs. That's my cue. I toss the rest of my stuff into my suitcase and head downstairs, ready to look at some places here in Vegas that I can call home.

I'm torn between renting and buying, so he's giving me options for both. But I've barely gotten into his front seat after tossing my suitcase in his trunk when he says, "How are you feeling today? Buying or renting?"

I guess the bottom line is much different for him.

And after the night I had last night, I could see myself in Vegas permanently.

What do I have to lose by buying a place and feeling a little sense of permanence? Nothing. What's bought can always be sold.

"Let's buy, man," I finally say.

He turns out of the Palms entry as he flashes me a grin. "You got it. Let's check out Jack Dalton's newest development," he says. "They've got some spec homes that are move-in ready."

I nod. "Let's do it."

He takes me through three different houses in Jack's neighborhood, and then he takes me through another house a little closer to the stadium.

And through every house, I can't help but see *her* in here. Cookie. I look at the kitchen and imagine her baking, flour dusting her pink cheeks as she tries out new recipes. I look at the bedroom and imagine a bed where I'm on top of her. I look at the view and imagine kissing her under the stars.

This is fucking ridiculous. I don't even know this girl's real name, and I'm reduced to this idiot who can't seem to get his feet under him as I float somewhere high above the clouds.

He tells me he's got another spec in a new community close by, and I nod as I look out the car window.

"You okay, man?" he asks, navigating in the direction of the fifth house of the day.

"Yeah, I'm all right," I mutter.

"I've never seen you twisted up like this. You sure you want to buy?"

I heave out a breath as I look out the window. All four houses he's shown me so far are spectacular. It's not the houses.

"Yeah. I'm sure. You know what? I want the last one you showed me. It's close to the stadium, and it's got a great view."

"And it's in the same neighborhood as Travis Woods."

"Perfect," I murmur.

He nods, and he leaves me to my brooding as I contemplate whether eight hours after leaving each other is enough time before I can text her.

Chapter 12: Ava Maxwell

He's Looking at Me

I haven't had a chance to look at my phone all day. I wasn't kidding when I said Saturday is our busiest day. Sometimes there's a line waiting outside before we open, but not as early as six when I arrived.

Poppy was already there, and I often wonder if she ever leaves. She was likely here late last night, long after we all left, baking and getting things ready for today.

When I first got in, I measured out ten cups of sugar before anyone else got in. I dumped it into our sixty-quart floor mixer, and I got the rest of the ingredients going, too. I was set for a big day at the bakery, and I wasn't wrong. And, really, there's nothing better than warm kitchen sink cookies, so I keep the batches going all day in between my other tasks for those who want them warm.

I should rename them. It was a generic name when I told Poppy about my idea, and I'd told her I'd throw in everything but the kitchen sink. She told me to go for it, and she loved my recipe. It's famous now, and I'm hoping it's enough to help me venture out on my own one day.

You know…once I sell that closetful of Radiance Skincare.

Cora asked me about my night, and I was vague. I didn't tell her I slept with Grayson, but she doesn't know I'm a virgin, either. I learned early on that as much as I like her and as much fun as she is to hang out with, she's also the proverbial office gossip.

But I'm excited to get home and tell Kelly about my night, so after the bakery closes and we clean up and prep for tomorrow, I head home.

Before I go, though, I take a second in the driver's seat, and I pull up the photo I took last night of the view.

I put myself back in the shoes of the girl taking the picture.

I was a virgin when I snapped this photo.

I'm not one anymore.

I don't feel all that different—except for the delicious ache between my legs that I seem to feel each time I sit. Lucky for me, I didn't get to sit much today.

And it's as I look at the photo that I notice a reflection in the glass of the window.

I can see the Strip plain as day, but now that I'm distracted by the lighting, I see something else.

I see Grayson Nash reflected there. And he's not looking at the view.

He's looking at *me*.

My chest ripples with some strange feeling.

It's adorable—seeing him there looking at me as I look with wonder out at the view. He's really something unexpected.

I haven't heard from him yet, not that I expected to.

I should have been honest with him that we have a history, even if we didn't *really* know each other back then, but instead I let him think I was some intriguing stranger. I feel bad about the omission, and maybe I'll work up the nerve to tell him next time I see him.

It's only right. We can't build something from scratch if the foundation is shaky, and this is my chance to build the type of life I've dreamed of since I was a kid.

I think about texting him, but I want him to make the first move. Besides, the things I want to tell him should be handled in person.

When I pull into the driveway of the small, two-bedroom house I rent with Kelly, I spot a car parked in the street. Kelly must have a guest over, which stinks since I was hoping to share every last detail of my first time with her.

And by every last detail, I mean an inch-by-inch replay that would take me all night to chronicle.

I park in the garage and cut the engine as I let out a soft sigh with the memory that washes over me. I get out of the car and close the garage before heading inside, and when I glance toward the couch in our modest family room, I spot a figure sitting on it as Kelly looks wildly at me from the kitchen.

He stands up and turns around, and my breath gets caught in my throat.

"Colin," I murmur. "What are you doing here?"

Guilt racks me as I think back to last night.

Bodies writhing together. Lips meeting. Eyes catching. The intimacy. The heat. The need.

Grayson Nash.

It wasn't this man standing before me—the man who was eighteen when we met, who carried me through a lot of firsts. The man who left for Chicago without looking back, who loves his job more than me.

"I came to save this relationship," he says, and the hope in his tone is overwhelming.

"To save…" I begin to repeat.

Oh, God.

He has no idea how very much I have already moved on.

"I came all this way. Would you at least let me take you to dinner so we could talk?" he asks softly.

I want to shout at him that anything he has to say can be said in front of Kelly, but apparently he'd rather have this conversation in a room full of strangers rather than in front of my best friend, who I'll recount every last word to later anyway.

"I'm not sure I have anything left to say, Colin." I had sex last night. With someone who isn't you.

85

"I have a lot to say, and I came all this way," he says, a pleading tone to his voice.

I stare at him, thinking how fragile and weak he is compared to Grayson. I felt safe and protected in Grayson's arms. In Colin's? I always thought I felt warmth there, but it was nothing like the heat snapping between the defensive back and myself.

But he's right. He came all this way, and a girl's gotta eat.

I blow out a breath. "Let me just get changed." I turn toward Kelly. "Kel, can I talk to you for a second?"

She nods and follows me into my bedroom as I excuse myself from Colin.

"What happened with Grayson?" she whisper-yells.

"We did it," I whisper back, my cheeks filling with color.

"Avelina Marie!" she yells, giving me the pretend full name she can use to scold me with even though my full first name is not Avelina and my middle name is not Marie. Her eyes widen. "You *did it*? As in…sex?"

I nod. "And, oh my God, Kel, it was…everything."

"Are you okay?"

"Oh yeah. Way, way better than okay. I'm great. He was great. He was incredible. So sweet, and caring, and tender. And *huge*." I hold up my hands to express the length, and her eyes widen. "Huge."

"Does your kitty hurt?" she asks.

I laugh. "He, you know, went face-first first, so it was plenty primed and ready for the monster. But yeah, I'm definitely a little sore today."

"Oh my God," she squeals in a whisper, and she grabs my arms, and we dance around in a circle for a beat. "I can't believe you did it with Grayson Nash!"

"I can't, either!" We're both still whispering.

I grab a sweater and a clean pair of jeans from my closet, and I get changed quickly. "We talked, and we got to know one another, and—"

"Did you tell him who you are?" she asks.

I shake my head. "I told him my name was Cookie, and he never pressed for my real name. I feel like I should be honest with him, and I will be next time I see him."

"There's going to be a next time?" she demands.

I shrug. "I hope so. We exchanged numbers. He said he wants to see me again. I just...couldn't bear to give up my shot with him before we had a chance to really connect."

"What are you gonna do about—" She stops short of saying Colin's name as she jerks a thumb in the direction of the family room.

"I'm going to have to let him down gently. What other choice do I have?"

She nods. "Best wishes with that."

I offer her a smile as I run a brush through my hair. "Thanks."

"Are you going to tell him about Grayson?"

I shake my head. "I'm not planning to. It's unrelated, and I feel like it'll only hurt him when it doesn't matter. We were broken up, and I don't want to go back. Especially not now that I've opened up a whole new world."

"Smart move. You got this, bestie." She leans in to give me a hug, and I draw in a deep breath before I head back out to face my ex.

Chapter 13: Ava Maxwell

Welp…This is Gonna Get Awkward.

I slide into the passenger front seat of Colin's rental car.

That's the car parked at the curb.

Colin grew up in Iowa and wanted to go to a school with a renowned business program. The University of Nevada Las Vegas was where his cousin went, and his cousin talked him into it even though Vegas generally doesn't fit with Colin's personality. Maybe it's why I so strongly felt the need to stay here even when he left. Maybe I fell in love with Vegas more than I did with Colin.

Welp…this is gonna get awkward.

I can't exactly tell him that, but he's here to win me back. To…get me to move to Chicago?

It's not going to happen.

If I wanted to go to a big metropolitan area with icy cold winters and humid summers, I'd go back home to New York. But I don't want to go home to New York. I want to stay right where I am. Here I have no snow, hot summers, hotter men, and friendships to last the rest of my life.

And I also have that *feeling* like this is home. This is where I belong.

As I glance over at Colin while he navigates to some restaurant, I realize how very much he is *not* home. That's what someone who is husband material *should* be, and he isn't it…not for me, anyway. I'm sure he'll make someone in Chicago very happy.

"How's work?" I ask awkwardly, trying to fill the silence with his favorite topic, and he flinches.

"Of course that's where you start," he mutters.

"Excuse me?"

He sighs. "I don't want to fight. It's not why I came here."

"Then why *did* you come, Colin?"

He slams on the brakes as the light turns from green to yellow. "Let's just talk at dinner. I need to focus on getting us there safely."

I shouldn't be surprised. He was really never one for multitasking.

He pulls up to an Italian restaurant fifteen minutes away from home. There's a short wait, and he orders a beer once we're seated.

I opt for water.

While alcohol would definitely help the terrible awkwardness of this particular date, I need a night off.

He raises a brow but doesn't say anything, and I'm not sure how to take that. I focus on my menu, suddenly sure I want to gorge myself on Italian food. I spot a pasta trio that sounds perfectly delightful, and while it's normally something I'd avoid since pasta tends to settle right on my hips, I decide to order it anyway.

And I attack the breadsticks the second they're delivered to the table.

I haven't eaten much today, I got quite the workout last night, and I'm surviving on two nights with little sleep. I deserve some damn breadsticks.

"So you skipped out on your work event to show up here?" I ask around a mouthful of bread. "Sorry," I say, pointing to my mouth. "I'm starving."

He looks like he's judging me for talking with my mouth full. Was he always this...straightlaced? Judgmental? Irritating?

Am I the one being judgmental, or did I overlook it because I was in love?

I'm starting to think the latter. I was wearing those old rose-colored glasses, but they've been firmly removed, and now I can see him clearly.

Were we *ever* a good match? Or did I just want a relationship so badly that I sacrificed what I deserved?

His brows dip as if he's nearly offended by my question. "I didn't skip out on anything. I did what I had to do, and then I took a flight out here to see you. I fly back tomorrow morning, so I literally came just to have dinner with you tonight. I wanted you to see that I care about you. I showed up for you."

"Spending an exorbitant amount of money for a plane ride for one dinner seems…" *Unlike Colin.*

He did show up. He's trying.

But all the trying in the world wouldn't be enough to win me back. Not after the night I had last night. Not after I saw a peek of what I could have—of what I deserve.

And I don't just mean the sex.

I mean…the cup of tea.

The blanket.

The talking.

The view.

The man.

Feeling like I matter all the time, not just when our entire relationship is at stake.

I realize it was one night, and it was the night we met. I get it. He might not be the same person on our second date, or our third, or in a year from now. Or ten years from now.

It doesn't matter. It's who he was last night, and it was enough to know I deserve more than what I've had for the last five years with Colin.

My new life mission is going to be landing what I deserve instead of settling for what feels comfortable.

It might've just been one night, but it was enough to tell me it's what I want for my future. People don't change, and getting back together with Colin after one last-ditch effort to win me back just isn't an option. He'll talk a big game. He'll even put in the effort for a week or two, maybe even a month, and then we'll land right back where we were.

It's not the place where I want to be ever again.

I deserve more.

"I know," he says quietly as I never quite finish my sentence. "It's not me. So I hope you can see this is me trying to prove how much you mean to me, Ava."

Too little, too late.

How do I say that nicely?

"I appreciate the effort." I'm about to add that I'm sticking firmly to my decision to end things when he jumps in before I can.

"See? I knew you'd come around."

"No, Colin," I say firmly. "This isn't me *coming around*. I deserve more than you've given me."

"Then I will do what it takes to win you back."

I have no idea what he means by that, but I am sure about two things. For one, history has shown he'll back down. And for two…I'm not a prize to be won. Whatever he thinks he can do, it's not going to work.

Not when I can't stop thinking about Grayson.

Chapter 14: Grayson Nash

Call, Don't Text

We always have exit interviews the day after our season ends, and mine was months ago. But I wasn't sure if this trade was going to go through or not, so I didn't say goodbye to anybody.

When Monday rolls around, I talk to the GM and my coach, and then I clean out my locker. I say goodbye to the place that has been home for the last eight years.

It isn't as hard as I thought it would be, and I think it's because there's so much hope on the horizon.

Not just with Cookie, though she hasn't strayed far from my thoughts. I keep actively *trying* to push her out, but she's ever present, and if someone could keep popping into my thoughts unexpectedly the way she has been over the last twenty-four hours, well, she must've really gotten my attention.

Over the next couple days, I work on packing up my house. I call a moving company once I have the closing date on the new place set, which is nearly a full month from now since they have a few things to finish and the paperwork will take time to go through.

The movers agree to come Thursday morning to pack up my place. I make plans with some teammates for Thursday night to say goodbye, and that's my week. I plan to get a hotel room Thursday night and hit the road toward Vegas Friday morning.

The moving company will store all my shit to deliver to my new house once I close on it, and I'll stay at the Palms until then.

I haven't reached out to her yet. I should...but I don't know what to say.

I don't really have a resource I go to in situations like these. I could call up Beck and talk to him, but we haven't talked about our conquests in years—since he met his wife and they got married—and this girl feels like more than just some conquest.

Lincoln is probably the closest to a person I'd confide this sort of thing in, but now that he's my coach, I don't know where the line is between coach and brother. Will his advice skew one way or the other because he has an agenda for me now? I don't think it would because he's a pretty level-headed guy, but I also don't know for sure.

I settle on Spencer. I dial his number, sure I'm about to make a fool out of myself since we don't really do this, and he picks up right away.

"Gray. Is everything okay?" he answers.

"Bruh. Yeah. It's good."

"What's going on?" he asks.

"I...uh..." I don't know what to say. I blow out a breath. "I met a girl, and I can't stop thinking about her, and I'm not sure what the hell I'm supposed to do next."

He chuckles softly. "That's great news. I'm surprised you called me."

"You're the most logical, and I didn't know where else to turn," I admit. "But she's sort of got me all flipped upside down. I picked her up at a bar, and it was going to just be a hookup, but then...I don't know. I got to know her, and I liked her. A lot."

"Have you spoken to her since that night?" he asks.

"No."

"How long has it been?"

"It was last Friday in Vegas, and I had to get back to Los Angeles to wrap shit up with the Chargers. I've been packing up my place and closing things out here, and I just haven't—"

"Five days?" he interrupts with a loud, frustrated sigh. "You should've gotten in touch with her the next day, man. You might've lost your window."

Jesus. Way to cut to the chase.

"But Amelia says it's never too late to tell someone how you really feel. If you haven't stopped thinking about her, maybe start by telling her that," he suggests.

"Really?" I wrinkle my nose as I think how lame that sounds.

"Really. Be honest. You can't go wrong with honesty. And call, don't text."

"I guess you're right." I pace in front of the fireplace I've never used. "Okay, thanks. You doing good?"

"Never better. Enjoying the offseason."

"Good," I say, and suddenly I'm ready to get off this call so I can send my lame ass text to Cookie. "I'll let you get back to it. Thanks for the advice."

"Anytime. Good luck, man."

"Thanks." I cut the call, and I draft my text despite his advice to call. I'm nervous to call, which sounds absolutely ridiculous. I'm never nervous. Confidence is my whole personality, and maybe that tells me something about my feelings for this girl.

Me: I haven't stopped thinking about you.

I stare at it for a few beats. I recall who the fuck I am, and before I lose my nerve, I click *send*.

Her reply comes quickly.

Cookie: Thank God. I was beginning to think you forgot about me.

I stare down at the text, my chest tightening that she might really ever think that about me, about us, about the night we shared.

Me: Not a chance in hell. When can I see you again?

Cookie: Are you back in Vegas?

Me: No, I'm in LA.

Cookie: Let me know when you're back and we'll make plans.

Me: I'll be back Friday.

Cookie: I get off work at five.

Me: Dinner?

Cookie: I'd love to.

Me: Text me your address and I'll pick you up at eight.

She sends her address right away and follows it up with another text.

Cookie: I can't wait to see you again.

Me: Neither can I.

And now I have to wait forty-eight long hours until that moment arrives.

I shoot Beckett a text next.

Me: Heading back to Vegas Friday if you want me to check in on your little sis.

Beck: That would be great. She's always working, so I'll send you the details for the place where she works.

I text back a thumbs-up, and he sends me the address. I don't bother looking it up. I'll take care of it on Friday as a means to distract me before my date with Cookie.

Time seems to slow down as I sort through my shit and pack the essentials I'll need versus the items that can stay in storage until my new place is ready. I say goodbye to the home I've lived in for eight years, check into my hotel and drop off my suitcase, and head over to my buddy's house for my farewell tour.

I'm seeing Cookie tomorrow night, so I decide not to get hammered even though it's my usual MO when I get together with these guys. An hour into the party, they're all drunkenly laughing about the upcoming season and how I'll be their opponent.

I'm not feeling it. I'm not one of them anymore. I have new teammates to meet, new friendships to create. I'll always cherish the bonds I made here, but there are too many new things on the horizon to feel like I fit in here any longer.

I sip half a drink and stay what feels like a good enough amount of time before I duck out early. I just want to get to Vegas, and with that in mind, I grab my suitcase from the hotel I already paid for, and I hop in my truck and start driving without a single glance over my shoulder as to what I'm leaving behind.

I get there a little after two in the morning, and I head right to the Palms. I check in, and the suite I stayed in last time isn't available, so they just give me a regular room. I booked my usual suite for the next week in advance, though, so I'll move into it tomorrow.

Tonight, all I need a room for is sleep.

I think about calling Cookie as I settle in, but I know she keeps early hours at her bakery. I don't want to wake her up.

I have a Strip view, so I stand by my window for a few beats, staring out at the lights. They're still twinkling even at this ridiculously late hour, and I think of Cookie as she stood at a similar window looking out. I didn't bother looking at the lights. All I could focus on was her.

I blow out a breath. I have got to pull myself together.

I remind myself that I'm moving here because of the team. Because of my brothers. Because of my new job as a defensive back for the Vegas Aces.

I'm not moving here for some girl I've met one time.

I can tell myself that all I want, though. It doesn't change the fact that it's sure as fuck a nice side benefit.

Chapter 15: Grayson Nash

Do You Know Beckett Maxwell's Sister?

I let myself sleep until almost noon after the late night of driving, but I'm still in town and ready to go earlier than I thought I would be.

I have a full eight hours to burn until my date, so I take a shower and decide to check in on Beckett's sister. I click on the address he sent me after reading the text that told me the place where his sister works is called Cravings.

Cravings?

It's Vegas, I guess, and she's in her twenties now, but it sounds like the kind of place that sells lingerie and sex toys. If it is, I can't imagine how awkward it's going to be to walk in and ask for Ava Maxwell.

Either way, it's going to be awkward. But it might be nice for her to feel a little sense of home. I'm doing this as a favor to her brother, and it'll be like she has another big brother nice and close if she needs anything.

I can't imagine Beckett would throw me to the wolves that way. I'm sure it's not a sex toy shop.

But if it is, maybe I can grab something for my date tonight.

The place isn't far from where I'm staying—just down the same street on the other side of the Strip, a ten-or-so minute drive. I head down to the valet, get my Chevy, and slide into the driver's seat.

It's weird driving in Vegas. It takes a vacation place down a few pegs back into reality.

I've only ever been here to play or to party, and I've always had the pleasure of someone else giving me a ride. But today, I'm mid-transition into a resident of this place, and the hope I feel lighting my chest is unexpected.

I cruise down Flamingo Road, the sounds of the country station on the radio blaring in my ears. I listen to all sorts of music, and I guess this is where I landed last night when I pulled up to the hotel.

I make my way toward Cravings, and I spot the sign from the car when I pass by it. There's a small line out front, and I realize it's a bakery and I'm here on the back end of lunch time.

This was stupid.

I should've looked the place up before I drove over here, but I'm invested now. I need to get this over with so my favor to Beck is off the *to-do list*.

There aren't any parking spots on the street, so I opt to pull into a parking lot behind the place, and I pull up alongside a curb that won't block anybody since the parking lot is full, too.

I pull on a baseball hat I keep in my backseat, and I keep my head down as I move over toward the back of the line. The lady in front of me has three kids, and they are not what you'd call patient.

The line doesn't move quickly, and it seems to slow to a crawl as one kid keeps bumping into me. I try taking a step back, but the lady behind me is far too close.

I blow out a breath and do my best to keep my cool.

I sneak a peek at a menu when I get close enough to grab a paper one out of a little holder near the door. It's a relatively small menu for lunch as the focus of this place appears to be on its baked goods, and before I get to the front of the line, I decide on ham and cheese on a fresh baguette with a bag of chips and one of their famous kitchen sink cookies.

Once I step inside, I see there's still a decent line in front of me, but we're moving along as fast as the two cashiers can handle each transaction. It's loud in here, voices echoing in a loud din as patrons enjoy their fresh baked goods and lunches, some people staying to eat while others take their goods to go.

I figure I'll ask the cashier about Ava once I get up front. Or maybe the cashier *is* Ava. She's younger, and she's got blonde hair…but to be honest, I have no idea what Ava Maxwell might look like these days. It's been a good ten years since the last time I saw her, and I didn't pay her much attention back then.

There are still three people ahead of me in line when I see movement in the display case I'm standing next to. I glance up and see someone is restocking some cookies, and when my eyes move up further…

I draw in a sharp breath as I recognize the woman.

"Cookie?" I say, and when she glances up, her eyes meet mine.

"Grayson," she says, surprise clear in her tone as her eyes widen. "What are you doing here?"

"You work here?"

She nods. "These are my cookies," she says proudly, and she grabs one and hands it over the glass display to me. Our fingers brush when our hands touch, and I'm still in shock that she's actually *here*. I found her when I wasn't even looking.

"Then you must know Ava Maxwell. Her older brother is a friend of mine, and he asked me to check in on her since he's back in New York. Is she here?" I ask.

"Ava!" a voice yells from the back, and her eyes widen as she turns toward the voice and then back at me.

She snags her bottom lip between her teeth, her fingers gripping the tray she was holding even more tightly.

She clears her throat, her cheeks turn pink, and that's when I put it together.

"Oh fuck," I murmur as the realization hits me.

The lady in front of me corralling her three kids turns around and glares at me.

"You're little Ava Maxwell?" I ask, my voice hoarse with disbelief.

My Cookie is…Ava?

Reality hits me clean in the face.

The woman I had an instant connection with and immediately wanted more than just one night is my best friend's little sister.

Of course we had an instant connection. We *know* each other. Well, sort of. I knew who she was when she was fifteen, and she knew who I was even though she didn't really know me at all.

Her jaw opens and shuts a few times as she grapples with an explanation.

There isn't one other than the fact that she lied to me.

"Ava!" the same voice yells over the loud din of the bakery. Someone who looks vaguely familiar, as if she was at the bar with Ava last weekend, rushes up to her. "Your dough is ready, and Dom just took out another batch."

She's clearly busy at this bakery, and I'm sort of at a loss as to what to do.

I set the cookie she handed me on the top of the glass display case, give her one last long look of utter disappointment, and I walk out of the bakery, my chest feeling tight as all the hope I walked in this place with is completely shattered.

Chapter 16: Ava Maxwell

The Delusional Phase

"**G**rayson, wait!" I yell after him. I wipe my hands on the apron tied around my waist as I run out to the parking lot.

Poppy will probably yell at me, but I don't care.

This matters.

He stops and turns around to face me. "Your brother told me to check in on you. I don't think this is what he meant." He's hissing at me, clearly disappointed that I didn't fess up to who I was.

"You know what we shared was special, Gray. You know it was. You wouldn't have given me the time of day if I would've told you who I was." While his voice is a hiss, mine is a plea.

"You don't know that. And now I guess we'll never know." He turns to get into his truck.

"Please give me another chance. Please."

"You're Beckett's little sister," he says. He shakes his head. "I can't." He gets into his car and peels out of the parking lot, cutting his way into traffic without so much as another look back at me.

I stand in the parking lot staring after him until he turns at the next block and drives out of sight, and then I close my eyes as a heavy weight seems to push down on my chest, as if it's somehow cracking in half.

It's ridiculous. I can't be heartbroken over one night. I'm just the naïve girl who lost her virginity who's standing in a parking lot up in her feels.

But it felt like more, and I know he felt it, too.

I was so excited for tonight, and now…

I blow out a breath as I force myself to turn around and head back inside.

I shouldn't be out here with my Cravings apron crying in the parking lot, anyway, so I run into the employee bathroom, lock myself inside, and allow the tears to flow down my cheeks.

I hear a knock at the door, which means either someone wants to get in here or someone is checking on me.

"Occupied!" I yell through my tears.

It's Cora's voice that answers back. "I saw you come running in here, babe. You okay?"

I draw in a shaky breath and open the door.

"What happened?" she asks, locking the door behind her.

I never told her my brother knows Grayson. I never told her I slept with Grayson, either.

"It's complicated," I finally say.

"Did he hurt you?" she asks softly.

I shake my head. "This was my fault."

"What was?"

I know better than to blab all this to her when I'm hurting, but that's sort of the whole problem. I'm hurting.

Even so, I'm still not dumb enough to tell her everything. Still, I have to say *something*.

"Grayson and my brother go way back. I had a crush on him when I was younger, and I guess it's just never going to happen." I sigh after I admit a version of the truth.

Somehow the truth hurts far, far worse than breaking up with Colin did. That only tells me that I was more invested in Grayson than I ever was in Colin—even though we only shared one night instead of five years.

How could one night have meant so much to me?

And how can I feel so shattered now that he walked out?

"Oh no, Ava. I'm so sorry. Is there anything I can do?" she asks.

I shake my head a little, not really sure there's anything she can do short of calling up Grayson and getting him back here to give me a second chance.

He was pretty clear that wasn't an option.

"Just...don't say anything to anyone about this, okay?"

She nods, and she pulls me in for a hug. "Now get your ass back to work before Poppy starts asking questions," she warns.

I blink a few times as I realize she's right. I just took nearly a thirty-minute unplanned break on one of our busy days.

I draw in another shaky breath then walk out of the bathroom with her, my head held high. I focus on my tasks so I don't fall apart at work. I bake my famous cookies ahead of our rush tomorrow, but all I can think about as I portion out the dough onto the cookie sheets is how Grayson took a cookie from me that he never ate.

All I can think about is the fact that he called me *Cookie*.

All I can think about is *him*—not the man I broke up with a week ago today.

All I can think about is finishing my task list for the day so I can go home and cry myself to sleep.

But when I get home, I spot a car out front.

I very nearly turn the car around to check into a hotel somewhere just so I don't have to face whoever drove that car here.

Apparently Colin is firmly planted in the *trying to make this work* phase crossed with the *delusional* phase, and that's one combinational phase I'm just not prepared to handle tonight.

I walk in, and it feels like total déjà vu of last weekend. Kelly is making big eyes at me in the kitchen, and Colin stands a few yards away in the family room just waiting for me to get home.

I'm glad he didn't come to the bakery. At least I have the kitchen there as my safe space.

"Colin, I'm not in the mood tonight," I say quietly, giving exactly zero fucks as to putting on any sort of pretense whatsoever.

"I traveled halfway across the country to see you. The least you can do is let me take you to dinner," he complains.

I blow out a heavy breath. "I had a rough day at work, and I just want to slip into a bubble bath, eat some pizza, and call it an early night. I don't have the energy to feed your delusions."

His brows dip together. "Excuse me?"

"You heard me." I pucker my lips at him. "If you got a hotel, you should go to it. You know weekends are the busiest time for the bakery."

Kelly slips quietly out of the room as we argue, and I really could've used her for moral support. And I will. She'll be there when I get him to leave, and I can tell her all about Grayson coming by and shattering my heart when breaking up with the man standing in front of me didn't so much as break a sliver off.

He clears his throat. "But I work all week. When are we ever supposed to see each other to make this work?"

"That's sort of the point of what I'm saying," I say dryly. I turn to walk out of the room to my bedroom, but before I stop, I turn back toward him. "Thank you for coming. Thank you for trying to work on this. I just don't have it in me tonight."

With those words, I head down the hall to my bedroom.

Chapter 17: Grayson Nash

A Bed of Lies

"Hit," I say, looking down at the blackjack table. I bust with a ten on my fourteen, and the dealer pulls in my chips. I set another stack on the little circle where players place their bets as I take a sip of my gin.

I wince a little at the sharp taste, but another glass this full and I won't be tasting much of anything. I won't be *feeling* much of anything, and that's sort of exactly what I'm going for right now.

Because this hurts. It hurts far more than it should given that I shared exactly one night with the girl.

I blow out a breath as the dealer tosses me another four, praying for a seven to go along with it. Praying my luck will somehow change from the absolute shit I've been dealt all night.

Nothing changes. I get a nine. What the fuck am I supposed to do with a fucking thirteen?

I hit.

I get a ten.

I bust.

Vegas is a bust. It's starting to feel that way, anyway.

I haven't told my brothers I'm back in town. I haven't gotten in touch with my dad.

Instead, I'm playing blackjack by myself on a Friday night with an aching chest and a bit of a buzz.

And it's not just my dad and my brothers—I haven't gotten in touch with my new teammates or my new coaches or my buddies in town. I haven't told anybody I'm here. Tonight was supposed to be for Cookie and me, and instead I was dealt the biggest shock of my life when I discovered Cookie is in fact little Ava Maxwell, my best friend's younger sister.

The girl I'm supposed to be looking out for and protecting, not the girl I'm supposed to be railing in a suite at the Palms.

It might not be so bad if Beckett hadn't specifically asked me to check in on her. Instead, I fucked a girl I first met when I was fourteen and she was half my age.

It's not just a huge betrayal of the trust of one of my oldest friends. It's also the fact that she lied to me.

You can't build a foundation based on a bed of lies.

And that's what that bed at the suite upstairs was—a fucking bed of lies.

She knew who I was and didn't have the courtesy to tell me who *she* was. I don't know if that's something I can just get past, and I'm not even sure I want to.

She's dead wrong about one thing, though. She said if I would've known who she was from the beginning, I wouldn't have given her the time of day.

I would've given her the time of day. I might've even found time to reminisce about some shared memories from the past, or we could've compared notes about her brother. But what I wouldn't have done was take advantage of her when she was hurting after her breakup.

Maybe it's my own guilt talking. Maybe I should've known. But I didn't, and I can beat myself up about it, or I can take a fucking night for myself and move on in the morning.

Because that's all this is. It isn't some deep heartbreak. It's disappointment for the things I was looking ahead to with her. She won't be there in the crowd wearing a jersey with my number on it as she cheers me on from the stands...something it's hard to admit I imagined when I thought of Cookie over the last week.

She won't be smiling up at me with that innocence in my bed as I corrupt the hell out of her.

She won't be looking with anxiety at me as she takes in my size or moaning softly as I inch slowly into her.

She won't be deliciously sore, thinking of me every time she sits because of the way I wrecked her sweet, tight pussy.

She won't be impeding on every moment when the sweet scent of fresh-baked cookies wafts to my nostrils.

Oh, wait…

That last one is still true. For now, anyway.

At least until I can find another pastry chef to bang so I can get this girl the fuck out of my mind.

Except I don't want to just bang some other girl.

I still want her. I *only* want her. Is that the gin talking? Because I'm not an *only want her* kind of guy.

I lose my ass at the table, and after a couple more drinks, I head up to my room.

I kick off my shoes and pass out on the couch before I even get myself over to the bed.

Things seem to look a little different when the light of morning dawns and I awake through the haze of a vicious hangover. The sunlight streams in on me, making me squint as a headache wraps around my brain like a vice.

My first thought is of her, and it makes me feel…

Sad.

I don't want to be away from her. I don't want to hold on to anger.

So she lied. Trust is a hard thing to rebuild once it's broken, but maybe we could find a way.

I could talk to Beckett about it. Maybe he wouldn't be so opposed to the idea.

A glance at the clock tells me it's after nine-thirty on the east coast. Is that too early to call a guy with a wife and kids?

I'll admit, that's part of the reason why we haven't kept in close contact in recent years. We do our best to get together at least once a year, and if I'm ever playing the Giants in New York, he makes sure to come see me. We call each other every few months, and we text fairly regularly. But I'm still single, and he's married with two kids. We may be the same age, but our lifestyles are light years apart.

I don't know the proper etiquette here since I don't really know what families do on Saturday mornings, so I send a text instead.

Me: You around?

He doesn't respond right away, which tells me he's busy.

And that's fine…except now I've reached out first, and he might be wondering why, and he might call me back at a time when I'm less than prepared to discuss whatever it is my hungover fingers thought they were doing when I sent that text in the first place.

God dammit.

Why do I keep fucking everything up so royally?

Why did life seem to get harder when I moved to Vegas?

I haven't even officially moved in yet, and I'm already feeling this way. What's going to happen down the line?

A text is waiting for me after I get out of the shower.

Lincoln: Let's meet up when you're back in town. Round of golf?

I'm back in town. I'm not prepared for a meetup. I don't reply.

Fuck it. I grab a few Tootsie Rolls for the road then head down to the casino to blow through some more cash. Good thing these places are open twenty-four seven.

And all I can think as I lose hand after hand of blackjack is whether this is something I can get the hell over.

Am I being stupid? Or would it be even stupider to fall into something with someone who flat-out lied to me and caused me to betray my best friend?

I know how protective Beckett is of his little sister. They were young when they lost their dad. And really, through the same event, they lost their mom, too—in a totally different way. She's still around, but she isn't the same person.

Beckett took over. He protected Ava the way his father did when he was still alive to do it. He made sure she—and her other brothers—were taken care of, had what they needed, and made it to where they needed to be. He sacrificed a lot to do it, too. Instead of going to his dream school across the country, he chose to stay in New York. Even to this day, he lives there so he can be close to their mother, who still carries baggage from losing her husband.

So it's not a small deal that I slept with Ava. It's a huge betrayal, one I'm not ready to admit to my best friend because of his sister's lies.

Did she lie, though?

It's a tiny voice in the back of my mind.

A lie of omission is still a lie.

Is this something I can get past? Maybe. But can I get past the fact that she's Beckett Maxwell's little sister?

I'm not as certain about that, and the more I think about it, the angrier I get.

My phone rings. I can't answer it at the table.

Fuck. What if it's Beckett?

Why did I call him this morning? I can't remember. I'm all fucking twisted up over this, and it's propelling me to *act*. It's propelling me to fucking do something. It's pulsing an anger in me, and I'm not quite sure what to do about it.

"Sir?" the dealer says.

"Hit."

I lose again.

Fuck this.

I cash in my chips and head back up to my room. I stare out the window at the Strip as I wonder if ten in the morning is too early to start drinking.

It is. I know this.

So instead of drinking, instead of calling Lincoln or Asher or Beckett or my dad…I head down to valet, get my truck, and start driving.

Chapter 18: Ava Maxwell

He's Grayman

Another Saturday, another huge line out the door. It's busier than usual, and my guess is because it's spring break around the country, and for some reason people think it's a good idea to bring their families to Vegas for spring break.

Vegas is not for the weak. Or for kids.

I'm glad Poppy's bakery is doing so well, but I have to admit, sometimes I wish I'd saved my kitchen sink cookie recipe for my own place since they're our most ordered bakery item. But at least Beckett talked me into writing up a contract before I baked my first batch for Poppy.

Beckett's a good brother like that—always taking care of me. Always looking out for me. Always protecting me. Even to this damn day when he told Grayson to check up on me.

But he's also a good lawyer, and I suppose I can't get mad that he'd send Grayson to check on me and in the same breath be thankful that he's taking care of me in other ways.

I grit my teeth as I decorate a birthday cake that's scheduled for pickup before we close tonight. It's still early, and I probably need to mix up another batch of cookies, but I want to finish this first.

"Ava, you've got a visitor," Cora says, and she raises her brows pointedly.

My chest tightens. "Is it Grayson?"

She presses her lips together and shakes her head.

Dammit.

Wishful thinking, I guess.

I clear my throat and head out into the bakery, and I see Colin standing on the other side of the counter. I duck under it and storm through the bakery toward the door. I don't want to talk to him in front of our customers, so I pull him out front and around the side of the building.

"What are you doing here?" I spit at him.

"I came to make this work." He stands firm on that.

"Making it work isn't interrupting my busiest day of the week with this nonsense when I've already told you to just. Go. Home." I enunciate each word like it's its own sentence at the end.

He's getting angry, an emotion he's never really directed at me before. In fact, he's maybe *overly* even-keeled most of the time. I rarely see any sort of fight out of him at all, which makes perfect sense in his position as a law firm associate who mostly does research and will likely never see the light of a courtroom.

"My flight isn't until tomorrow, and I don't get why you're being so unreasonable about all this. Why don't you even want to try?"

"I'm not being unreasonable!" I yell at him.

He points at me. "That right there. Unreasonable. You're yelling at me in a parking lot!"

I point back at him. Why's he pointing at me? What the hell even is that? "Well now you're yelling, too!"

Just as I say the words, a silver truck skids to a stop on the street in front of us, blocking the driveway.

And as the man driving the truck jumps down from the driver's side and rushes over toward me, he looks like a damn superhero.

Maybe because he *is* a superhero.

He's not Batman. He's not Superman. He's…Grayman?

I'll come up with something later.

"What's going on here?" Grayson asks, stopping when he's standing beside me, and it feels like I have someone on my side facing off against the ex who can't seem to take a hint.

And then he slips his arm around my shoulders.

He draws me into his side.

Grayson Nash draws me into his side.

The man who's mad at me for lying to him is *here for me*.

I'm not quite sure if this is reality or if I'm so exhausted from the morning rush that I'm hallucinating.

"Holy shit. You're Grayson Nash," Colin murmurs, immediately recognizing him. I *may* have left out the little detail that I knew Grayson in a former life. I wasn't exactly keen on chatting about my former crushes with my current boyfriend, so Grayson never really entered the conversation.

"This is the ex I told you about," I say quietly to Grayson.

"Oh." He tightens his arm around my shoulder as if the very thought that I was with the man standing across from us physically pains him.

He doesn't know that he's the sole owner of my V-card.

And the way he's holding onto me so possessively should be a huge red flag, but it isn't. Instead, it's barbaric and overly macho and really, really sexy.

"Well I'm here now, so you can run along," he says.

I nearly die on the very spot where I stand as the words drop from his lips.

"Excuse me?" Colin asks.

"She's mine," Grayson says, and he puffs his chest out a little. It's a confident move, and Colin is exactly zero match for the athlete currently leaning down to press his lips to my temple.

Colin grabs his phone out of his pocket and snaps a photo of the two of us. I'm not sure what the hell he thinks he's going to do with that photo, but he's got it.

I sort of want a copy, but I stop myself short of asking him to send it to me.

"She's *mine*," Colin says. "She's been mine for five years, and I'm not letting her go without a fight."

"Why don't we go ahead and let *her* decide instead of acting like a couple of fools outside her bakery when she only wants to get back to work?" Grayson suggests.

It's like the man knows *exactly* what to say. He's confident in his suggestion, but Colin is stupid. He's no match for Grayson, yet he's standing here thinking he is when he's literally the one trying to claim me just because we were together for five years. If the length of time we've known each other is a factor, Grayson's actually got him by a long shot, not that he'd ever know that.

"Ava?" Colin says at the same time Grayson says, "Cookie?"

I lean into Grayson a little as my eyes find Colin's. "I'm sorry, but I'm with Grayson now."

Colin's jaw drops clean to the ground—figuratively, of course. He points at me. "You were with him all along, weren't you? Wait a minute. Were you *cheating* on me with him?"

I roll my eyes. "Don't be ridiculous."

Grayson looks down at me, and there's a question there in his eyes, as if he wants to say something but isn't sure he should. I'm not exactly sure what he's asking, but he exudes this warmth that makes me trust him. I gently incline my head a little to tell him to go ahead with whatever it is he wants to say.

"She was faithful to you all along, man." Grayson shakes his head a little. "Not that I didn't want her to give you up years ago."

"Years ago?" Colin repeats, narrowing his eyes at the two of us. "What do you mean by that?"

"Oh, he doesn't know?" he asks, turning to me. He turns back to Colin. "Little Ava Maxwell and I go back many, many years. Her oldest brother is my best friend, and we've known each other since..." He trails off and glances down at me. "Since she was single digits, anyway. And now we've decided to take our relationship to the next level, if you catch my drift. Sorry it wasn't you." He ends with a shrug, and I could freaking kiss him right now.

So I do.

I push up onto my tiptoes and press my lips to his. It may be for Colin's benefit, but I am most definitely the one reaping the rewards.

Grayson slides his arm around my waist to haul me in a little closer. Colin might take another photo—I'm not sure, nor do I care. But he catches the hint that he's out and Grayson's in, and as we kiss in front of my ex, I can't help but wonder what changed Grayson's mind.

Why did he show up here today? Why did his silver truck skid to a stop? Why did he jump out of said truck to rush to be by my side while I fought with my ex in a bakery parking lot?

And...is he telling Colin the truth? Or am I going to be blindsided by this man yet again?

I settle back down onto my heels even if the rest of me hovers somewhere up in the clouds. I'm sure I'll get to the truth eventually, but right now...it's pretty damn sweet up in these clouds.

Chapter 19: Grayson Nash

A Lie of Omission is Still a Lie

S hit.

She just kissed me, and the twerpy ex who is certainly no match for me helped himself to photos, and it's going to be all over social media by lunchtime.

Which means Beckett will catch wind of it all. He'll know that I fucked the little sister he told me to take care of, and he'll smell the betrayal of it all even from where he sits thousands of miles away.

I don't know what came over me, but when I pulled up to the bakery to confront her and saw him yelling at her in a fucking parking lot, I lost my shit.

This primal instinct to protect her kicked in, and...well, maybe Beckett won't kick my ass after all—not that he physically *could*, anyway—if I can make him see that I did what I had to do to protect her from the ex who won't leave her the hell alone.

The ex is still standing across from us, and I still don't know what the fuck his name is, nor do I care. "You can run along now," I say a little more snidely than I probably should. I realize this guy is likely heartbroken, and maybe I should be a little nicer. She broke up with him when she was drunk out of the blue—not out of the blue to *her*, but it probably was to *him*.

It's only been a week, so this is just him trying to win her back. It's not like this has been going on for months or anything, and to be perfectly honest, he *should* be fighting for her. She's worth fighting for. I may not know her very well, but I know her well enough to know that.

He's never going to win against me, so I'm really just helping to push him out of the picture.

"So when you say *next level*," the ex begins. "Do you mean sex?"

"That's none of your business," Ava snaps at him.

"Does he know you're a virgin?" he asks.

All the air deflates out of my chest.

She's…

She's a *virgin*?

"Of course he knows," she snaps.

Hold the fucking phone here, pal.

She's a *what* now?

I put on the performance of my life as I force myself not to give away the fact that I had no idea I took her *virginity*.

I wondered. I suspected.

But to hear it confirmed—and by this idiot ex, no less—is a gut punch.

"Well, to be fair…she's not anymore," I say, my voice low and hoarse.

Ava gasps, the ex looks like he's about to vomit, and I feel like I just got run over by a truck.

"Okay, then," the ex says to me. "I guess you win." He gives Ava a long look, and then he walks away. He gets into a Honda and drives away. Once he's turned the corner, she peers up at me.

"I, uh…I need to get back to work. But thanks."

"Thanks?" I echo. Is she really not going to address the giant elephant in the parking lot with us?

"For scaring him off. Hopefully that's the last I'll hear from him." She clears her throat. "Oh, did you come by for something?"

Yes, I fucking came by for something. But I'm blanking on what it was since all I can think about is the fact that she was a virgin before she met me and now she isn't and I'm the person who took that from her.

Me.

Why me?

Why did she lie?

I blow out a breath. "I did."

"What was it?"

"Are we really not going to talk about the virgin comment?" I hiss.

She draws in a deep breath. "I need to get back to work. We can talk about it later."

"Fine." I clear my throat. "We've got another problem. He took a photo of us."

"So?"

"So…what will he do with it?"

She shrugs. "Who knows. Sell it to the highest bidder? Use it for insurance and leverage? But who cares?"

"I care," I say through a clenched jaw. "I don't want your brother seeing them and getting the wrong idea."

"Is it the wrong idea, though?" she challenges. "We did have sex."

I glance around, completely at a loss as to what the fuck I'm supposed to do or say right now. "Because you lied to me. Apparently about more than one thing."

"I didn't lie about a damn thing," she says sharply. "You never asked whether I'd had sex before, and some people really do call me *Cookie*."

"A lie of omission is still a lie!" I roar.

"Not when it never came up!" she yells, defending herself.

"I'm not talking about the virginity thing!" I yell back, and then I draw in a breath to force myself to calm down. I lower my voice. "You. Your name. Your identity. You kept it from me, and I fucked you, and that made me betray my best friend. Don't you get that?"

"So we don't tell him, then." Her voice is so flippant. "It's not like I send him a weekly list of my conquests. Do you?"

"You don't even have conquests!" I yell with a heavy dose of exasperation as the realization that I fucked my best friend's *virgin* sister still hasn't quite hit me. "Do you just, like, lie by omission to everybody? Because I can't honestly be with someone who does that."

She looks taken aback by my words. "No, I don't. But don't stand here and tell me you always tell the whole truth and nothing but the truth."

"Are you accusing me of lying?"

She purses her lips. "Did you ever tell my brother that you kissed Mindy at his college graduation party?"

I take a step back as if she just issued a physical blow. "How do you know about that?"

"Because I have eyeballs." She rolls them for effect then holds out her hands. "Well?"

"No," I mutter.

I swear to God, only Ava Maxwell could catch me being a hypocrite and get away with calling me out on it—especially in a tense situation like this.

And the only reason she could get away with it is because something flipped in me that night we shared.

It was instant, and it was intense.

But just because I've left words out of the story in the past, too, doesn't make this sit any better with me. "That's different." I realize how weakly constructed my argument sounds the moment the words fall from my lips.

"How?" she demands.

"Because it didn't matter. I didn't tell him because he was over her, and telling him I kissed her when I was drunk at his graduation party would only hurt him."

"So you did it to protect him," she says.

I nod. "Exactly."

Her voice is eerily quiet when she finally replies. "I didn't tell you who I was because I needed to protect myself. Now if you'll excuse me, I need to get back to work."

She spins on her heel and heads back inside, leaving me standing alone in a bakery parking lot with my truck blocking the parking lot entrance.

Chapter 20: Ava Maxwell

It's Not Lying, It's Bending the Truth

"Are you okay?" Cora asks quietly, and yet again I'm wondering how much to tell her.

I love Cora, and it's one thing to ask because you're trying to be there for a friend.

It's another entirely when you're also the bakery gossip.

I don't really need word getting around that I lost my virginity to Grayson a week ago, so I just nod and keep my head down as if I'm too focused on the task at hand to chat.

I know she'll ask again. I know I can't dodge her forever.

But in all honesty, I can't believe Colin had the audacity to bring up the V-card.

I know it just made Grayson angrier with me. I know he's seething about all the lies. I know I've wrecked any chance at a happy ending for the two of us.

But as I'm rolling out dough for sugar cookies, an idea occurs to me.

It's an explanation. A way to throw Beckett off the scent, a way to help solve Grayson's media issues where his love life is concerned, and at the same time, it would give the two of us a shot at getting closer. Maybe even close enough that we could give this obvious attraction between us a real shot.

It's dumb, though. Grayson will never go for it, particularly not when he's clearly such a staunch advocate for complete honesty, and this would be...*bending* the truth.

I'm an advocate for honesty, too—not that my track record proves that. But what's one more little thing that would benefit both of us?

If he's worried about his loyalty to my brother paired with already feeling like he betrayed him, this is one idea that might help. And the other benefit is that maybe it'll be enough to convince Colin to back all the way off.

I can't see any downsides at all other than the fact that it's not the whole truth. But before I can tell him my idea, I have to finish my day at work, and I have to potentially face Colin at home.

And...then what?

I have Grayson's number, but I haven't used it except for that one time when he texted me first.

I know he's still mad. But if Colin sells those photos of the two of us kissing to the media and my brother sees them...this really does feel like the perfect solution.

I cut circles out of the dough and set them on the cookie sheets. I stare at the rows and rows of unbaked cookies. Our sheets have circles on them to make it easier to place the dough, and since the dough was chilled, they won't spread very much once I stick them in the oven.

It's rinse and repeat. Make dough, chill dough, roll dough, portion cookies, bake cookies, flood cookies, decorate cookies.

It's one of those mindless tasks I can do on autopilot, which is perfect since my head is stuck in the clouds.

How do I regain his trust when we never even got off the ground? Maybe it's my inexperience talking, but I thought the night we shared was special. The text he sent me telling me he can't stop thinking about me meant something to me. Maybe it was just words for him—another shot at the virgin.

My cheeks burn even as the thought enters my brain again. I cannot believe Colin had the nerve to bring up my virginity to

Grayson. To be fair, he handled it smoothly in the moment, but clearly he was taken aback by it.

And he wants to talk about it. He brought it up again when Colin left.

What am I supposed to tell him? That I had a crush on him since I was a preteen, and he made my childhood fantasies come true?

Okay, no. Come to think of it, that actually sounds pretty disgusting.

But the sentiment is there. How many people get to say they got to have sex with the guy who they've crushed the hardest on their entire life?

I do.

And I'm not going to pretend I didn't love every second.

But now I'm in a jam, and I'm not sure how to get out of it…unless he agrees to my plan.

If he does, then it'll mean more time together—more time to figure out a way to get him to fall so in love with me that he won't ever want to let me go.

Once I get off work, I slide behind the wheel of my car and stare at my phone. I draft a text, and before I lose my nerve, I hit send.

Me: Can we talk?

His reply is nearly immediate, as if he was sitting on his phone waiting for me. I'm sure he wasn't. Right?

Grayson: I think we need to.

I stare at his words, and then my phone starts to ring, startling the hell out of me. I pick it up when I see it's Grayson.

"Hey," I answer quietly.

"Where are you?"

"I just got off work. I'm in the bakery parking lot."

"I'm at the Palms. Come over."

"*Come over?*" I repeat. Is he seriously commanding me to come over? This guy's got a lot of nerve.

"I'm sorry. I didn't mean to come off rude. It's…it's been a day."

I guess it was a day for me, too, and I'd rather go to the Palms than run into Colin at home. I should text Kelly and ask if she's having to deal with him. God, I hope not.

"Have you seen the picture?" he asks out of the blue.

My brows dip together. "What picture?"

He clears his throat. "Your idiot ex sold the photo he took of us. It's all over the internet, and I'm just standing by waiting for your brother to call me about it."

I sigh. "I'll be right over. I actually, uh…sort of came up with an idea that I'd like to run by you. It might help."

"Valet your car when you get here. I'll meet you down there."

"Okay. Fair warning, I smell like cookies and have flour everywhere."

"Fair warning back, Cookie," he says, his voice raspy. "I like the smell of cookies." He cuts the call, leaving me to wonder what he meant by that and why he's flirting with me after everything that's gone down between us.

I guess I'll find out in a few minutes.

Chapter 21: Grayson Nash

Fake It Til You Make It

A little red Nissan Versa comes pulling into the valet area, and a beautiful blonde hops out of it. She looks around and spots me as the valet attendant walks up to her, and I meet her by the driver's side.

"You can charge this to my room," I say. "She won't be long." I realize how that sounds after I say it. "I mean…I didn't mean she's coming by for an hourly visit or anything. We're just talking."

What the fuck am I doing? The valet doesn't care. It's his business not to care.

I shake it off, not sure why I feel nervous.

Maybe because the last time Ava and I were at the Palms together, I took her virginity.

Looking back, all the signs were there. She was tentative and nervous even though she was enthusiastic and ready. She was tight. God, she was so tight. Perfectly tight.

Maybe that's why I'm nervous. The mere memory of sliding into her cunt is causing me many issues, from an accelerating pulse to heavy breathing to all the blood rushing straight for the cock.

I lead her through the casino toward the elevator, and as it happens, I'm back in our suite. I mean *my* suite. Not ours. We don't have anything together. I certainly haven't been calling the bed *our* bed in my head all day—especially not when I jerked off while I thought of her as she moaned beneath me.

Fuck.

Fuck.

There's no way in hell I'm getting her up to that suite and not getting her naked again.

I blow out a breath. I can do this. I can control myself. We need to talk anyway, and apparently she has some idea that's going to fix all this. I already feel like all eyes are on us as I try to hide my raging boner and she walks a few strides behind me, trying to keep up with my pace.

I'm nearly a foot taller than her. There's no way she can keep up with my pace, and I realize I'm walking fast as it is.

I hit the button to call the elevator, and we head up to the suite, both of us silent in the already awkward silence of the elevator. Both of us remembering the last time we rode an elevator together as sweet anticipation built between us and we made out like we needed each other's tongues to breathe.

This isn't the same sort of visit.

Now she's my best friend's little sister, not some conquest I brought back to slam.

"You okay?" she asks quietly as the elevator finally skids to a stop on my floor.

I nod, and I give her a strange look. "Yeah. I'm fine. Why?"

"You're breathing really loudly. You seem like you're out of breath, so I just wanted to check."

"Sorry." I'm about to say that I was working out before I came down to get her, but that would be a lie. I can't lie to her when that's one reason I'm so angry with her.

I draw in a deep breath and try to calm my racing heart.

It's *her* that's making me breathe harder, but how can I admit that to her? She's the very person I should be staying away from, and instead we're feeding anyone who wanted to snap a photo of us exactly what they want since we just walked through that casino together.

At least we weren't holding hands. At least the anger on my face was apparent. At least I was practically running through the place. Maybe that's why I'm panting.

We walk into the room, and the door clicks shut behind her with a loud echo.

"Same room," she says. It's not a question, merely a comment.

"Yeah."

She wanders over to the window and lightly trails her fingertips down the glass. "I didn't think I'd get to see this view again."

"Didn't you?" I accuse. "Because you sure as fuck knew who I was even though you acted like you didn't. And if you knew who I was, you'd know that I would've likely invited you back knowing you were the little sister of my best friend. Until we fucked, that is."

She winces at my vulgar word for what we did, and she has every right to. It was her first time, and it wasn't fucking. It was something deeper for both of us, and I feel like an asshole for making light of that.

But the truth remains that I'm mad, and she needs to know exactly why.

"I'm sorry," she says. "What can I do to earn your trust back?"

I shake my head a little. "I don't know." And then I flip it back around to her. "You said you have an idea?"

"Right," she says, drawing in a breath. "Cutting right to the chase. Could, uh…could we sit first?"

I nod toward the couch, and we end up sitting exactly as we were when we fell asleep the last time we were here. She's leaning against one armrest, and I'm leaning against the other, and our feet meet somewhere in the middle of the large sectional.

"Can I be honest with you?" she asks.

"Now's a hell of a time to start," I mutter, and maybe I'm being a little immature about the whole thing, but the level of shock I feel at all the secrets that I keep finding out about her is astronomical.

First, who she is, then the virginity thing…it feels like for as much as I got to know her in that one night we shared, I really didn't know a damn thing about her at all.

She bypasses my comment, and she sucks in a nervous breath. She rubs her hands together, and one part of me wants to walk over and put my arms around her and tell her whatever she has to say, it'll be okay. The other part of me wants to sit in my anger forever. I'm not quite sure which side is winning.

"The first time I met you, I was seven. You were just my older brother's best friend. You were fourteen, and I didn't care about boys yet. I cared about flavored lip gloss and my stuffed animals and baking cookies with my dad. But by the time you were a senior, I was eleven. I was starting to notice boys. I cared about more makeup than just lip gloss, and the stuffed animals had been long gone, and I wished my dad was still around to bake with me. And when you came back from college for the summer, I was a preteen. By that time, I'd already built you up as the hero in my love story." Her cheeks burn as she says the words. "Every time you came over after that, I'd do anything I could to get you to notice me. I'd pretend I was working out because you seemed to love athletics so much. You'd just walk by me with a forced hi or a smile, and you made it clear you wouldn't give me the time of day. It didn't matter. I had a huge crush, and it wasn't on Asher or Spencer, boys much closer to my age. It was you. It was always you." She shrugs a little at the end.

I don't know what to say to that. "I…I'm sorry I acted like that when I was younger."

She shakes her head. "I'm not telling you this to make you feel bad. I don't want an apology. You had every right to be civil but ignore me. I was just a kid. But I'm telling you this now to try to get you to understand why I felt like I couldn't give you my real name. I'd just dumped Colin, and I knew you'd take care of me. I knew you were a good guy. I'd always told myself that if Colin and I broke up, I'd finally be free to do whatever—or *whoever*—I wanted. And I knew you'd make my first time

132

memorable. I knew you'd be even better than the girl with a crush dreamed you'd be. And you were, Grayson. You *are*. I just wish you could find it in yourself to forgive me for leaving out the things that would've prevented my dreams from coming true that night."

My jaw slackens a little as I try to figure out what the hell to say to any of that—as I try to figure out how to *feel* about it. My mouth flaps open and closed a few times, and thankfully she steps back in with more words before I say something stupid—before I get a chance to process any of this.

She draws in a breath. "All that aside for the moment, because I know it was a lot, I had a thought that could potentially help us even before you told me about the photos being public."

I nod as if to tell her to go ahead, and it's as if my mouth has ceased working.

"My idea is just a way to throw my brother off our trail and, at the same time, get Colin to back off. It's a win-win that way. And you had mentioned the other night that you want the focus to be on your career rather than on what different woman is on your arm at every event, and this would be a way to, uh…have the *same* woman on your arm at every event."

My brows crash together as I have no idea what the fuck she's talking about. "Okay…" I say, drawing out the word. "Out with it. What are you thinking?"

"A fake relationship," she says, and her tone is a little proud, a little confident, and a little nervous all at the same time.

"A fake what now?" I ask.

"We pretend we're dating. For the media, of course, and we tell Beck it's just for show, a way for you to protect me from my ex since he asked you to protect me." She lifts both shoulders and holds them up for a few beats.

I shake my head as I push to my feet. "No. Absolutely not. I don't want to make this any worse, and I don't want to lie to Beckett."

"We wouldn't be lying to Beckett," she says.

"How is that not a lie?" My tone comes out with a huge dose of exasperation. "We'd explain away the photos by telling him we were faking it?"

"We *were* faking it in front of Colin. How is that a lie?"

He sighs. "It's not the whole truth."

"No, it's not. And do either of us *really* want to give Beckett the *whole* truth that you laid me down on the bed right in the next room, stripped me naked, sucked on my—"

"Okay, okay, I get it," I say, holding up a hand as I interrupt her before she says exactly what I sucked on since hearing those words fall from her mouth will only make me want to do it again. Harder. Faster. More. Now.

I exhale roughly, and then my phone starts to ring. I slide it out of my pocket and glance at the screen, and then I flash it at her. "Great. Just fucking great. I'm sure he saw the photos by now."

"Then ignore the call," she says, shrugging.

I press my lips together as I slide to answer the call. I wander over toward the window and start pacing in front of it. "Beckett Maxwell, how the fuck are you doing, man?"

"Care to explain why your tongue is shoved so far down my sister's throat you're probably tasting what she had for lunch?" He's seething, clearly asking from between a clenched jaw, and I...

I—

I think fast.

"Dude, that's why I called you earlier. To explain before the pictures hit the media." Fuck! Shit! That's a lie. I called him hungover this morning to ask him if I could date his sister, but his reaction to the photo of me kissing her is not a great one, so I'm guessing the idea of me being with her isn't going to fly.

"Okay. Then explain."

"Yeah, okay. So…" I trail off, and my eyes meet hers. And then, before I know what the fuck is happening, the lie falls from my tongue. "Your sister and I are in a fake relationship. Her ex is trying to win her back, and she just wants him to disappear, so I did what I had to do when I said I'd protect her."

Beckett is silent on the other end of the line, and Ava sits up a little straighter from her position on the couch as she watches me carefully.

When Beckett finally speaks, his tone is much more relaxed. "Oh. Uh…I guess—thank you, then. For protecting her."

"Of course, man. It's what friends do."

What they *don't* do is fuck their friends' little sisters and then lie about it.

And yet…here I am, doing exactly that.

Chapter 22: Ava Maxwell

Little Ava Maxwell

I may have to physically pick my jaw up off the ground after the shock of a lifetime there.

I can't believe he just lied to Beck.

But even more than that, I can't believe he told Beck we're in a fake relationship. I'm not exactly sure what this all means. Do I get to be his girlfriend now?

Um…side note: Do I get the benefits that come with being his girlfriend?

And maybe most importantly…can all this fake business turn into something real?

"I promise," Grayson says, clearly trying to wrap up the call with my brother. He doesn't mention that I'm here. Is that a lie of omission?

It's not like every person tells every other person every single detail of their lives. So I left a few things out. Who hasn't?

But what he just told Beck…that wasn't a lie of omission. It was just a straight-up lie, even if I told him it wasn't one. The truth is that I don't want to *fake* date him.

I want to give this a real shot with him.

Only…he doesn't trust me, and I don't know what to do to get back in his good graces. And beyond that, he's not okay with dating his best friend's little sister. I need a plan.

I'll just have to figure out how to become irresistible to him.

"I will. Talk to you soon." He hangs up and stares at his phone for a beat before he pushes it back into his pocket. He turns toward the window and stares out over it.

I give him a few seconds to brood, and then I have to break the silence. "Why'd you tell him it was fake?"

He blows out a breath, and he runs his palm along his jawline before he turns to face me. "He was pissed about those photos. I couldn't come up with an explanation, and what you said before was right. The truth is that we *were* faking for your ex's benefit."

"So you liked my idea of a fake relationship?" I ask.

He shakes his head. "No. I hate it, actually. But something snapped in me when your brother was asking. You need help keeping your ex at bay, and I don't want people to think the only reason I came to Vegas was to play with my brothers. So maybe it'll work. For now."

"Isn't the only reason you came to Vegas to play with your brothers?" I ask a little stupidly.

"Well…yeah. But if I'm in a relationship with someone local, it'll take a little of the heat off the bullshit nepotism rumors flying around that I didn't get the trade on my merits but on my connections." He shakes his head to switch back to the matter at hand. "We have a lot of logistics to figure out first."

"Do we?" I ask, my voice a little higher than I mean for it to be. "Or could we just…you know, like, get to know each other and actually date?"

He blows out a breath and turns back to the window, and I wish I had a window into his thoughts to see what he's really thinking right now.

But I don't. Obviously.

"I don't know, Ava," he says, his voice raspy and low. "I don't know if it's a good idea. I guess after you said all that stuff before, I get why you didn't give me the whole truth. And the omission is a big deal, but not so big I can't get past it."

"Then what's holding you back?" I ask softly.

"You're little Ava Maxwell." He shrugs. "You're my best friend's little sister."

I swear to God, if he calls me *little* one more time, I'm going to lose it.

The word pushes me to my feet. I take a few strides to close the gap between us, but I stop short of actually touching him while he still faces the view out the window instead of me. My eyes are on him, and I see his flick over to me in the reflection.

"First of all, I'm not so little anymore. I was big enough to catch your eye at the bar the night you wanted me for nothing more than sex, and you got it. And if we're telling the truth here since you're so fucking big on honesty, you wanted it again until you found out who I was." I toss in the f-word to emphasize the fact that I'm not that seven-year-old girl anymore. "And second…if Beck doesn't like it, so what? He'll get over it." I realize how flippant I sound, and we both know the truth. He won't just get over it.

He's not just an overprotective brother. When I was eight, he became a father to me. He played football in high school with Grayson, and they bonded on the field. But when practice was over, *he* was the one making sure my homework was done. *He* was the one making peanut butter and jelly sandwiches while our mother couldn't force herself to get out of bed even with the cocktail of pills the doctors had her on.

We both know he's so much more than just an overprotective brother.

"Agree to disagree on your brother. Regardless, you and me? Not a good idea." He's quiet as he shifts his gaze back out the window.

I don't want to keep pushing. I don't want to sound desperate. But I have to know. "Why?"

He finally turns around to face me. "I'm afraid I'll only hurt you in the end." His voice is raw and filled with sincerity.

"The very fact that you don't want to tells me you won't."

He shakes his head. "You don't know that. There are no guarantees other than the fact that I have never had someone I'd call my girlfriend. Hookups, sure. One nights? Lots of 'em. Benefits all over the damn place. But the last woman who even came close to that line was Daphne, and I did everything I could to keep her at arm's length. I'll do that to you, too, before we ever even give this a chance."

"So the fact that you're sure you'll fail is going to keep you from trying?" I ask.

"I think it might. On top of the fact that you just got out of a long-distance relationship and I know you don't want to jump right into another one."

My brows pinch together. "This isn't long-distance. You're moving to Vegas, remember?"

"What about traveling to half our games? What about when we go to training camp in California?" He presses his lips together, and I get the very real sense that he's setting us up for failure without even giving us a chance.

He has lots of excuses why this won't work.

But I have one big one why it will…the fact that *I want it to*. I just have to figure out how to get him on the same page.

He's the loud one? I'll be louder.

He's the funny one? I'll be funnier.

Now that I've got his attention, all I have to do is figure out a way to make him fall in love with me.

Easy, right?

I blow out a breath. Wrong. Especially because I'm not sure I actually *do* have his attention.

Chapter 23: Ava Maxwell

One Kissing Pic a Day is Enough
to Keep the Media at Bay

"**K**el?" I yell as I walk in the door. I'm thankful there's no car at the curb. It means Colin isn't here, though he may still be in town.

Grayson didn't kiss me goodbye. I didn't even get a freaking handshake. I just got a *see ya* once the valet brought my car around. I suppose one kissing picture a day is enough to keep the media at bay.

It's not enough for me, though.

"In my room!" she yells back, and I step into her doorway a short while later. She's sitting on her bed, reading a book. "Where've you been?" she asks a little absently, setting the book down beside her.

"Have you seen the photo?" I ask casually.

"What photo?" she asks, narrowing her eyes at me. "Was I supposed to see photos?"

"Oh, only a picture of Grayson and me kissing outside Cravings earlier today." I brush my fingernails on my shoulder with exactly zero modesty.

"You were kissing? You were kissing! And I'm just finding out about this?"

I plop down on her bed beside her. "Long story short, Colin came to confront me at work, I told him it's over, we were arguing in the parking lot, Grayson showed up, I kissed him to prove to Colin I've moved on, and he took a picture. He must've sold it to the media because it's all over the place."

"I've been grading spelling tests and making lesson plans, so I didn't see it."

"That's what you get for being so dedicated to your job," I tease.

"But wait…why did Grayson show up?"

I twist my lips as I try to think back to a part of the day that feels like it happened forever ago. "You know, I asked, and we never got back around to it. But Colin took a shot and asked him if he knew I was a virgin, and Grayson told him that I'm not anymore."

Kelly's eyes widen to an almost comical level. "Whoa. How'd Colin take it?"

"It was definitely a gut punch, but I *think* he got the idea that I've moved on. Has he been here?"

She shakes her head.

"Okay, good. Hey, you okay?"

She nods. "I was invited to go out with a group of teachers tonight, but I declined."

"Why?"

She shrugs. "I wasn't in the mood for all the politics that go along with what's supposed to be a fun night out." It's not the first time she's said something similar. One of her colleagues turns every conversation into a complaint about the principal, whom Kelly happens to be friends with. She picks up her book. "And I just got to the juicy part, so I wanted to plow through some chapters."

I giggle. "Book boyfriends beat the real thing every time. Speaking of which, I need your help."

"With?"

I pull a face before I get right down to it. "How to make Grayson Nash fall in love with me."

She laughs, but when she sees the dead serious expression on my own face, she grows serious. "Uh...what?"

I run my palms along my jeans-clad thighs. "Long story short, he told my brother we're fake dating so he can protect me from my ex and protect his relationship with Beck. But even if it's starting out as fake, I'm looking for a way to make it...you know, real. All the pieces are there. I just need to figure out how to make myself irresistible to him, get him to trust me again, and *boom*! Before you know it, he'll be head over heels."

"That seems like kind of a tall order, don't you think?" she asks.

I shrug. "What's the worst that can happen?"

She offers a rather unladylike snort. "Do you really want me to answer that?"

I heave out a heavy breath. "I guess not."

"Okay. What do we know about him? What's he like? What *does* he like?"

"He likes football. He's athletic and strong. He likes working out."

"Oh! Get some dumbbells to impress him with your athletic prowess!" she suggests.

I roll my eyes. "I'm not fifteen anymore, Kel."

She giggles. "Did you really do that when you were fifteen?"

My blush gives me away.

"Okay, not dumbbells." She sighs. "What else does he like? Did you dig any deeper when you spent the night with him?"

I shrug. "Kinda. Not really."

She taps her chin thoughtfully. "So you're in the getting to know you phase."

I nod. "Right. Even though we sort of know each other, we don't really *know* each other. He said he used to pull pranks on his brothers, so maybe there's something there."

She wrinkles her nose. "You want to act like one of his brothers?"

"No, but I want to make him laugh. I want to bond with him. I want him to find me funny."

"By pranking him?"

"I don't know," I say, a touch more frustration in my tone than I mean for there to be. "I'm just spit-balling here."

"That's such a gross phrase, spit-balling."

I sigh. "Can we stay focused?"

"Right, pranks. What kind of pranks?"

"I think that's where I need some help. And you're a planner, so, you know…help me plan, or whatever." I'm very clearly *not* the planner in this friendship. I'm more the *bumbling through life hoping for the best* kind of gal.

"We should go back to that bar," she suggests.

"Why?"

"Maybe he'll be there. And maybe Austin Graham will be, too." She raises both brows, and I raise both of mine back.

"Austin Graham?"

"What, you can snag an NFL player, but I'm shit outta luck? I think not, my friend."

"Did we ever talk about how it went when you started talking to him?" I ask.

She shakes her head. "Nope."

"Well?"

"We didn't exchange numbers or anything, but we had a nice chat. And I'd like to see if we can *chat* more again sometime." She throws air quotes around the word *chat*.

"Then let's go."

Maybe Grayson will be there, and maybe I can get started on this big plan to make him fall in love with me.

But first…

I need to figure out how in the hell I'm going to make that happen.

Chapter 24: Grayson Nash

When Your Brother Blows
Your Big Plans

I'm still staring out the window, this time with a glass of gin glued to my palm, when my phone rings.

I glance at the screen and slide it to answer, clicking the speaker button. "Hey, Ash."

"What's up, G? A few of the guys from the team are meeting over at the Gridiron tonight and wanted me to extend the invite to you," my brother informs me.

Fuck.

I feel a little stuck.

I don't *want* to go out tonight, but I know how this works. The more times you tell someone no, the less likely they are to ask the next time.

This isn't my brother extending the invitation. It's our teammates. They want to get to know the new guy, and they're issuing the invitation through Asher.

Which is fine. It's good. It's great. Whatever.

I need to get to know these guys, and I need to get my ass over there. But I'm still reeling over the confessions Ava made on the couch earlier tonight, and I'm not really in the mood to put on the Grayson act where I'm everybody's best friend when I just want to drink some gin, tug on my dick, and call it an early night.

I guess I'm letting my little brother blow my big plans for the evening.

"Yeah, okay. I'll be there." I hang up without thanking him for the invitation. It's rude, but I'm already halfway to drunk and only have a few fucks left to hand out tonight.

I take a shower, which sobers me right back up, and then I order up a car to take me over to the bar. I draw in a few deep breaths before I get there, and I force myself to call up the act.

The one where I'm the boisterous, loud, fun-loving brother, the guy everyone loves to be around, the guy sought after by women, the guy who can make anyone laugh. Tonight, and most nights since last Friday, I'm feeling much more like the introspective guy who just wants to sit in my hotel suite on a couch opposite Ava, our legs tangled together while the lights of the Strip blink outside and her face lights up everything inside as we talk about nothing and everything.

Fuck. Fuck fuck fuck fuck fuck.

I need to shake that shit right out of my head.

That's not who Grayson Nash is, and it's not who I'm here to be tonight. I'm here to get to know my teammates, and I want them to see the fun side of me, not this whiney little sap one night with a virgin has turned me into.

I get out of the car and hold my head high as I head inside, and I beeline for the same table in the back where I sat last time. It must be a standing Aces table because it's already filled with guys I recognize, some who were here last week, and some who weren't.

And the reason I beeline for that damn table? It's so I don't have time to stare at the place where I met Cookie…or, rather, the place where I re-met Ava Maxwell. The woman who had a dream that night, the woman who asked me to forgive her for leaving out details that would've prevented that dream from coming true.

Is she right?

It's not over the top to think that yes, absolutely she was. It's not out of line to think that if I would've known her name, I never would've fucked her. And what's more, if I'd known she was a virgin…

Well, I can't say I wouldn't have fucked her if I knew she was a virgin but *didn't* know she was Ava. But I might have handled things differently. I might've been more careful, or gentler, or maybe I would've talked to her longer or given her more foreplay or stopped before I stuck my dick in her.

We'll never know the answer to that since she didn't trust me enough to give me the whole story. And to be honest, I can't really blame her for that. I can't be mad that she didn't want me to know she was a virgin when she willingly gave it up to me.

And she said I made her dreams come true.

I don't know if that was just lip service or if she meant it, but these are the things I'm quietly processing while I prepare to project the persona I'm really not feeling at all tonight.

"What're you drinking, Nash?" Travis Woods asks me from across the table as the server approaches. His arm is slung around a woman, and I'm not sure if she's his girl or just some conquest for the night.

"I'm a gin guy," I say more to the server than to him.

I slide into the booth beside Patrick, the only other guy on D here besides me, and I spot my brother across the table in the corner. I give him a nod even as I make a face at him when I look at his choice of shirts this evening—a button-down with rather large dinosaur faces.

Does he really get pussy dressing like that?

"Really, man? Gin?" Patrick asks, making a face at me.

"What are you drinking?" I challenge with a laugh.

"Tequila." He holds up an empty glass.

"I'll stick with my Hendricks, thank you very much. Bad memories with tequila. Or, rather…no memory."

He laughs. "Been there, my friend."

We get to talking about our backgrounds and where we've played, and I start to relax a little. It almost feels like, at some point, I might even find my place with this team.

Asher holds my gaze as he nods over toward the bar.

Clearly, he wants to get me alone to tell me something, so I nod, and we head up that way without another word.

"What's going on?" I ask him once we're standing out of earshot of the other players. There are a lot of people around, but between the music and the loud din of the place, we're safe to have a quiet conversation even in this rather large crowd.

"Be careful, man."

My brows pull together. "With what? Getting eaten by one of the dinosaurs on your shirt?"

"Fuck off. I mean, be careful with these guys. Getting too close. They're all great, but they're playing a game, too. They're being careful with us since we're related to the coach. You got me?" he asks.

"Why the fuck did you invite me out tonight if you just wanted to warn me not to get close?" I can't help the rather annoyed face I pull at him.

"I haven't had much chance to hang out with them given my suspension. But I did have a hard time fitting in when I got here, and I think it's because they put up a wall around me thanks to Lincoln." He shrugs. "I guess I just wanted to warn you, but I also wanted to give you a shot at developing your own friendships here since I know they all meet here fairly often."

"Well...okay. Thanks, I guess?" I say it more as a question than out of actual gratitude.

"You're welcome. And by the way, what the hell is up your ass?" he asks.

"Nothing's up my ass. What's up your ass?"

He rolls his eyes. "You think I can't tell when something is going on with you? You've been all stiff and just...not yourself since you walked in here. What's going on?"

"Nothing," I mutter, honestly a little surprised that my little brother not only recognized that I'm all fucked in the head, but he also called me out on it.

I turn to head back to the table, and wouldn't you fucking know it?

Out of the crowd appears none other than the woman throwing me all out of sorts herself: Ava Maxwell.

I blow out a breath.

I can't fucking get away from her.

My big plan to get to know my teammates as I try to push her out of my head appears to have been blown to bits once again.

Chapter 25: Ava Maxwell

Asking for Favors

I t was just a really good guess that he'd be here tonight.
We got lucky.
Or not.

He looks angry as his eyes meet mine, and I'm not sure how to take that.

"Did he call you, too?" he demands.

"Did who call me?"

"Asher!" he yells at me.

My brows draw together as I try to remain calm even though he clearly is not. "Asher? Why would Asher call me? He doesn't even have my number. At least not that I know of." I'm babbling, and he's angry, and I feel like I walked into the middle of a conversation I'm not part of.

"Sorry," he mutters. "I just…don't even know why I bothered coming here tonight."

"Hoping to run into me?" I say brightly, trying to be the sunshine to his grumpy. But he's clearly not feeling it tonight.

"I can't seem to escape you," he says under his breath. At least that's what I *think* he says. I'm not really sure. It's loud in here.

"Ready to pretend?" I ask, leaning in conspiratorially.

He pinches the bridge of his nose then draws in a heavy breath. "Do I have a choice?"

"Nope! But first, I need a drink. And so do you."

"I have a drink over at my table," he says.

"Have you met my friend Kelly?" I sling my arm around her.

"Pleasure," he says gruffly as he glances at her.

"I've heard so much about you," she says with a grin.

My cheeks warm.

"Ava speaks highly of you, too," he says, finally relenting from the storm cloud he seems to be walking under this evening. "Would you two like to join us?"

I lean in toward him. "I told Kelly everything, just so you know."

He nods as he snags his bottom lip between his teeth. "We need to be careful."

"Does this count as a public appearance?" I ask.

He shrugs. "I guess we should have some conversations about that."

"Yeah, probably."

"Just let me lead the way, then." He looks angry, and I think he still *is* angry with me for the omissions that I refuse to call lies. But I follow him over to his table anyway, and Kelly trails on my tail.

I spot Austin Graham at the same time she must because I feel her grab my hand and squeeze it. If anyone deserves a hot night with a football player, it's Kelly Kaplan. She dated the same guy all through college, and he broke her heart just after graduation. She's gone on a few dates here and there, but I haven't seen her genuinely excited about anybody until Austin.

I hope she scores.

I hope I do, too.

I lean forward toward Grayson's ear. "Kelly is interested in Austin Graham if you have any strings you can pull."

He stops short and turns around to face me. "You're seriously asking me for favors when you've now interrupted *both* nights I've been out with my teammates?"

I shrink back, and he looks immediately apologetic.

He sighs. "I'm sorry. I'll see what I can do."

It's the first time I realize the tremendous amount of pressure he must be under. He's new to town, playing for a new team where his brother is the coach and his other brother was suspended for the last year, and he's already dating somebody—all while his life is under a microscope since he's a professional athlete from a family of football royalty.

I didn't realize all I was in for when I propositioned him with a fake relationship.

I'm starting to get it now.

"This is Ava and Kelly," he says, introducing us to the table. "And this is…well, a bunch of Vegas Aces players and their significant others."

We both giggle, and each of the guys and their dates introduce themselves. I try to remember all the names, but there's just no way.

Kelly slides into the booth first since the seat next to Austin is open. I move into the booth next to her and find myself across from Travis Woods, whom I recognize from Instagram, and his wife, who I think said her name was Victoria.

"So, how do you know Grayson?" Victoria asks as Grayson sits next to me.

I glance over at him, waiting for him to field the question, and he does.

"We actually grew up in the same town. Her brother is one of my oldest friends, and we sort of just…found ourselves in the right place at the right time." He glances over at me and winks, really laying it on thick as I think back to the night we ran into each other.

There's something sweet about him quoting those words again. I just wish he was doing it sincerely rather than for the benefit of faking it.

"I had the *hugest* crush on him when I was eleven years old. And now…" I trail off with a big smile and pink cheeks.

"You're together?" Victoria guesses.

"Jeez, Hartley. Give them some space," her husband says.

She rolls her eyes. "Look at the way they look at each other. It's kind of like how you used to look at me."

He laughs. "Back when we first met and we hated each other?"

"No, just after that, when the hate melted into…well, you know." Victoria's cheeks burn, and I giggle.

"Oh, yeah. I definitely know," Travis says, and he wiggles his eyebrows, garnering laughs from all around the table.

Grayson gets to talking with the guy sitting across from him, and I gather from the conversation that they play the same position. Victoria seems really nice, so I start asking her questions about how she and Travis met, and they're all too happy to tell their love story. I finish my first drink and order another, and I find that I already feel like part of this crew.

I hope Grayson does, too—particularly since I've interrupted his time with them now twice. But it's not like it's a team meeting. There are significant others here.

And I hope I get to be a significant other for a little while longer. I hope there are more nights just like this in my future.

It's all part of my plan, really. I'm finding ways to bond with the teammates he's bonding with, too. I'm inserting myself into this group so it'll be harder to extract me in the end. I'm weaving my way into the fabric of his life here in Vegas.

Maybe eleven-year-old me was onto something. Maybe she knew that eventually this is where we'd end up.

He gets up to go to the bathroom, and I see he left his phone unlocked on the table. I pick it up off the table as I think to myself that it was awfully trusting of him to just leave his phone sitting here open for anybody to take a peek through.

Not that I'd do that…but I do have a different plan I want to execute. I spot a text from his mom as I open up his timers.

Mom: Daily check in! How was your day?

I feel a little twinge of something in my chest. I wish I had a mom who checked in daily with me. It's been months since I've communicated with my own mother.

I shake off the thought as I set the timer. At eleven in the morning tomorrow—and every day, on repeat—he'll get a reminder: *Are you thinking about Ava?*

It's not a prank, per se, but more of a way to make sure I don't leave his mind for too long. All part of the grand plan to show him how irresistible I am.

"Are you spying on him?" Victoria asks, leaning across the table with wide eyes.

I shake my head, and I flash her the phone to show her what I just did.

"Oh my God, that's genius. Trav, gimme your phone."

He rolls his eyes but hands it over dutifully. "Like I need the reminder."

They seriously are couples' goals. They just seem to be so in tune with each other, and that's all I want—somebody who looks at me like I hung the moon. Somebody who would do anything to make me happy. Somebody who gives me butterflies.

Somebody like Grayson Nash.

Grayson's phone is long off when he returns, and I hope he texts me tomorrow when the timer goes off with the reminder.

Grayson is chatting away with everybody, and I have yet another early day tomorrow. I think I'm ready to call it a night, but I'm sandwiched into the booth with Grayson carrying on and on about something football-related that goes completely over my head. He's talking to Patrick across the table, and they're both laughing while I'm lost.

"I need to get going," I finally say when there's a break in the conversation.

"Okay." He starts to scoot out of the booth, but then he leans in toward me. "Do you need a ride home?"

I turn to Kelly and whisper, "Are you staying?"

She nods. "If it's okay."

"Of course. Shoot your shot, bitch."

She giggles, bids me goodbye, and turns back to Austin.

"I'm heading home solo, but if you're offering a ride, I'll take it," I say to Grayson, raising my brows.

What I'm really looking for here is a ride back to his place followed by another ride on him, but I'll take what I can get.

Chapter 26: Grayson Nash

Typically My Cock Has the Final Say

I could've just sent her home in her own Uber, and I probably should have. But then I think of what Beckett would want me to do, and ultimately I decide he'd want me to make sure she got home okay.

I need to get him out of my head. It's too conflicting to think what he'd want me to do when what I *really* want to do to her would not top his list of priorities.

Nor would it be protecting her.

So I slide into the backseat with her as the driver heads toward her place, and I recall the last time we rode in the back of a car together.

Fuck. I should've taken the seat up front.

My cock is begging for this girl, but my brain keeps trying to slow me down. It's a big conflict, and typically my cock has the final say. But this is different.

She is different.

She has no idea the power she holds over me—the same power I'm trying to slowly back away from. I don't want to hurt her. I *can't* hurt her. But I'm afraid I already have.

"You okay?" she asks quietly.

I glance over at her as I realize my focus has been carefully placed out the window for the duration of our car ride thus far. "Fine," I grunt.

"You don't seem fine."

"You really want to have this conversation in the back of an Uber?" I throw back at her.

I think we'd both rather be doing what we did the last time we were in the back of an Uber, but I can't.

She sighs, and I go back to staring out the window as I try to figure out why I'm being such an asshole. We pull up in front of a small house a few minutes later.

I thank the driver as Ava storms toward the front door and unlocks it, and I really debate asking the driver to hang tight for a bit. I realize we need to talk, as much as I don't want to. I suck in a fortifying breath as I saunter up behind her, frankly a little surprised she didn't slam it in my face.

Her hands are on her hips, and her eyes are shooting fire at me when I walk in and shut the door behind me.

"Well? We're not in the back of an Uber anymore," she practically spits.

"Right. You asked if I'm okay, and I said I'm fine. I'm not fine, Ava. I'm not even close to fine." My voice is low and nearly threatening, though I don't mean for it to be.

But she needs to be careful here. She's standing there challenging me, and she has no idea what she's asking me for.

She's asking to be hurt in the end because that's the only way this will go.

Even my fucking parents are getting divorced. They were married nearly forty years, and *bam*, out of nowhere…done.

You'd think as a grown ass man, it wouldn't affect me. It does. Deeply.

And maybe that's the root of the issue here.

No woman has ever pulsed these thoughts in me, yet here I am having them at the same time I'm watching dear old Mom and Dad get a divorce.

I've learned from my parents. They've taught me now that happy endings are simply illusions we can strive for, but they're not real. None of us gets out of this life alive, so we're either doomed to fail at relationships or doomed to lose the people we love most if we're not the ones to bow out first.

That's a little deeper than I plan to go tonight with her, but I do want her to feel the confusion pulling at me.

"I can't stop thinking about your words the other night about how you had this crush on me when you were just a kid, and you're not a kid anymore. You proved that the night we were together. But for me, this isn't just about trust and truth versus lies. I can't be with you because doing so is betraying the guy who has been there for me since I met him our freshman year of high school. Don't you get that?"

She rolls her eyes. "This again? Really?"

"Yes, really. Our friendship means something to me, and I'm not going to fuck it up when we don't have any guarantees."

She shifts to fold her arms across her chest, clearly protecting the heart that she laid out for me to take. "That's kind of the whole thing with relationships, Grayson. There aren't any guarantees."

I nod as I press my lips together. "And that's why I don't want one—particularly with someone who I care about and don't want to hurt in the end. Because *that* is a guarantee. I *will* hurt you."

She shifts her gaze to the floor as she nods, and I think she's starting to get it.

Except her next words tell me the opposite. "What if that's a risk I'm willing to take?"

"Then I guess we're at an impasse because it's not one *I* am willing to take." I lean back on the door as I watch her chew on the inside of her cheek for a beat.

She finally nods a little resolutely, and then she drops her arms to move one of her hands to her face, where she swipes away a tear. "Was it bad?"

My brows draw together. "Was *what* bad?"

"The sex. Was it so bad you don't want to go it again?"

Jesus.

Fuck.

"No!" I practically roar at her. I draw in another breath to try to calm the rage I feel that she'd really think that. "No," I say much more calmly. "I can't believe you'd even ask that."

"Well?" she says in the form of a question—as if that must be why I don't want to be with her.

But that's sort of the whole problem. I *do* want to be with her.

Everything south of my dumb brain—including both my heart and my cock—is telling me I should give this a try with her. But my brain keeps stopping me short.

"Were you there? It was fucking incredible, Ava." I lower my voice at my next admission. "And that's what scares me so goddamn much."

"I scare you?" she asks, surprise coloring her tone.

"You terrify me." I give her my most honest answer.

One side of her mouth tips up at that—as if she likes having that power over me.

"Look, I know it was your first time, and I know you don't have the…uh…*experience* I do. But if I'm being honest, you blew all those other experiences right the fuck out of my head. It's not even a comparison. And I don't know if that's what you want me to say or if—" I stop when she rushes toward me, slamming into me with her body so that an *oof* sound escapes me as I'm suddenly sandwiched between her and the door.

I look down at her as her gaze moves to my eyes, and the heat that passes between us is fucking unbelievable.

It's unbearable.

She leans up and presses her mouth to mine, and goddamn, I'd never believe this woman is as inexperienced as she claims because she certainly already has a lock on how to handle me.

I'm momentarily shocked as her mouth molds to mine, and she pulls back as quickly as she rushed at me.

I don't dare move. I simply stare at her as I wait for her next words.

"Sorry," she says a little sheepishly. "I just...couldn't help myself. You were saying such nice things, and—"

I shake my head and cut her off. "It's fine. I should go."

"No, wait," she says. "Come on in. I shouldn't have done that. I'm sorry. We have some things we need to talk about." She freezes for a beat, and then she rushes to add, "Not related to any of that."

"Then what?" I ask a little stupidly.

"The media. How to handle the attention. Our backstory— making sure we're on the same page. That sort of thing."

I nod. "Okay."

"Want a drink?" she asks, leading me into the house. It's on the small side—a foyer, a short hallway into a family room with the kitchen attached, and two other hallways that probably lead to the bedrooms.

"Sure. Got any Hendricks?" I ask hopefully.

"Sorry, no. Vodka is the drink of choice around here, and we might have some beer in the fridge."

"Whatever you're having is fine," I say. On second thought, alcohol is probably a bad idea. It might end with us in bed together again. Honestly, I'm starting to get tired of fighting against it. But I also know if we're really doing this fake relationship thing, then we're going to have to get used to being around each other.

I wander around the family room as I wait for her to get us some drinks. The house doesn't tell me anything about her. There isn't any artwork hanging on the walls, no comfortable recliner to relax in after a long day of baking.

In fact, I realize I don't really know much about her at all, and if we're really going to convince the media and her ex that we're dating, we should probably get to some details.

"Do you own this place?" I ask.

"No," she says from the kitchen as she pulls two glasses out of a cabinet. "Kelly and I split rent. We've been here…oh, nearly three years now. Since we graduated from college."

"What does Kelly do?"

"She's a kindergarten teacher."

I wrinkle my nose at the thought of working with children all day, every day. "She must really like kids."

"She does. And she has the patience of a saint. And then there's me."

I chuckle. "You're not a kid person?"

She wrinkles her nose. "Not teaching a classful of them every day."

"Do you want kids?"

"I'm not sure. I always think maybe if I wasn't the youngest, I'd want kids. Like Beck. He took care of us, stepped into that fatherly role way too young, and now he's the best dad to my nieces." She shrugs, basically leaving out the ending and how she feels about having kids someday. "You?"

I shake my head. "I'm not really a kid person. I always liked the idea of having a couple sometime down the road, but I'm not sure if I still feel that way."

She adds ice to each cup. "Why not?"

"I guess it might have something to do with watching my parents get divorced." The words slip out before I can stop them, and they happen to be words I haven't spoken aloud to another soul. And then somehow, I keep going. "I guess I thought after nearly forty years, they'd just be together forever. But clearly, it can still fuck up adult kids since it's showing me that nothing's meant to last forever, and I don't know that I want to bring someone else into that kind of world."

She stops making our drinks to stare at me, her head tilted a little as she takes all that in.

I feel a little self-conscious as I wait for her reply, and she shakes her head before she pours a healthy dose of vodka into each cup.

"I get that," she finally says. "Totally. But it's your life and your mistakes to make, not your parents'."

It's your life and your mistakes to make.

Why do her words seem to really put it all into perspective?

Why am I letting what somebody else is going through control me?

They're good questions, but an even better one enters my mind unexpectedly.

Why am I so hell-bent on pushing this woman away when she seems to be the only person who knows exactly how to handle me?

Chapter 27: Ava Maxwell

Cookies Are the Way to a Man's Heart

I hand him the drink I just mixed, and he holds up his glass. I clink mine to his.

"Cheers," I say, and then I take a sip.

Okay, so I made them strong.

Maybe I'm trying to get him to loosen up. I just need him to abandon his morals a little so I can break away at his shell, we can have all the sex again, and we can get started on this whole him falling for me thing.

And on that note, I like to keep my hands busy while I talk. "Can you help me with something while we talk through some of this?" I ask.

His brows dip. "What do you need help with? Changing a lightbulb or something?"

I laugh. "No, we're not helpless housewives from the nineteen-twenties. We're pretty good at lightbulbs. I have an idea for some cookies I've been wanting to try, but I haven't had time to execute them at work. Want to be my helper and guinea pig?"

Cookies are the way to a man's heart, right?

It's worth a shot.

He looks a little hesitant, but then he says, "Sure."

"Any food allergies?"

He shakes his head, and I nod over toward the kitchen—the place where I feel most myself.

I grab some ingredients from the pantry and set them out, and he takes a seat on the stool at the counter.

I narrow my eyes at him. "Sitting is not helping."

He immediately stands. "Yes, ma'am."

Why do those words falling from his lips as he follows my directions pulse a needy ache solidly between my legs?

Oh, right. Because I want to have sex with him again, and pretty much *everything* he does is sexy as hell.

I hand him a measuring cup and push a bowl over to him. "I need three cups of flour in this bowl."

I set to work on the wet ingredients, and I start to make conversation as I methodically pick up each ingredient I need and measure it out before dumping it into the bowl.

"So we're sticking with the backstory that we've known each other for years and just ended up in the right place at the right time?"

"Well, the truth is probably the easiest thing to stick to." He clears his throat. "I mean…as closely as we can. It'll come off a lot more genuine if we tell the truth, anyway."

He dumps the first cup of flour into the bowl after carefully measuring it, and he somehow spills a bunch on the counter on his way. I brush it into my hand and throw it in the sink.

I nod. "Right. And how, exactly, do I handle the media?"

"It might be a good idea to have you sit down with a publicist to discuss some of that, but my own training has taught me that less is more, and maintaining privacy is key."

"Right. Less is more. The same is not true for cookies." I sprinkle in some more brown sugar, and he chuckles.

I hand over a teaspoon. "Let's go with one teaspoon of baking soda and a half teaspoon of salt."

He nods and adds in those dry ingredients.

"I get the theory behind maintaining privacy, but people are going to want to know who you're dating, and I'm just a normal pastry chef who likes to bake cookies. We need some sort of story to explain why you'd be with someone like me."

He looks surprised by my question. "You think you're *just a normal pastry chef?*"

I glance over at him after I set my bowl onto the mixing stand. "Well…I am." I pick up the bowl he added the dry ingredients to.

"You're a lot more than that." He reaches over with his thumb to brush away a smudge of flour from my cheek, and his gaze is so tender on me that I think he's going to lean down to kiss me for a beat. "You're beautiful, Ava. You're funny and smart. You're talented and kind. You're sexy as fuck without even knowing it."

He draws in a deep breath before he seems to snap out of whatever thought he's having.

He clears his throat. "You're, uh…you're definitely more than just a pastry chef, but the fact that we share a history is enough of a story to keep the wolves at bay." His voice is a little robotic at the end, as if he's saying something he feels he needs to say even if he's not sure he believes it. Or maybe that's just me reading too much into things.

He grabs his phone out of his pocket and appears to send a text.

"What was that?" I ask.

"I texted Linc to ask about local publicists. From what I remember, he's working with someone he really likes. Got him out of a whole heap of trouble with Jolene when they first got together."

I vaguely recall something of a rivalry between the Nashes and the Baileys, but clearly that's over if his brother is married to Jolene now. I didn't know much about the story since it all went down over twenty years ago when I was barely in kindergarten.

But my mom was friends with Mrs. Nash since their boys were so close, and I recall gossipy discussions between my mom and Mrs. Nash about some bar the Nashes and Baileys had invested in together.

His phone dings with a new text, and he scans it before giving me the summary. "He's working with someone named Ellie Dalton, the wife of former player Luke Dalton. She represents a bunch of players on the team, and he highly recommends her." He shrugs as he looks at me.

"Can't hurt to give her a call," I say. I have no idea who Luke Dalton is, but the name is vaguely familiar. I really should brush up on my football knowledge if I'm supposedly dating a player. "So talk to me like I know nothing about football. You play defense?"

He chuckles. "*Do* you know anything about football?"

I twist my lips and shake my head. "Honestly? No. I've never understood it. My brothers tried to explain it to me, and they'd always draw these things out with Xs and Os and squiggly lines, and I had no idea what any of it meant."

"I'll teach you without drawing anything." He laughs. "The very bare bones basics is that the goal is to score more points than the other team."

"Like in most team sports," I say.

He nods. "A field is a hundred yards, and we take it ten yards at a time. We get four tries, or downs, to move the ball ten yards. Do you know what it's called if a team moves it those ten yards?"

I bite my lip. "A first down?"

"Very good! And if they don't move it those ten yards?"

"Then the other team gets the ball?" I guess.

"That's right! See, you know more than you think." He beams at me a little—or maybe I'm just delusional. He fills me in on more of the basics with no Xs and Os, and I learn that he's a cornerback, which is a type of defensive back. His job is mostly to guard wide receivers, who usually run down the field to catch the ball.

"So I'm dating the defensive back?" I ask.

He flashes me a smirk. "It appears that way."

By the time he's done explaining it to me, our last batch of cookies is almost done baking, and I feel like I understand the basics of a game I've never taken the time to understand.

Just the way he's explaining it shows me how passionate he is about the game, and the best part is that we're talking about it while indulging in *my* passion, too.

"Ready to try one?" I ask, picking up a cookie from the first batch which has been cooling on a rack.

He nods, and I hand it over.

"Are you trying one?" he asks.

"You go first." I'm not sure why I'm suddenly nervous, but this is the first cookie of mine he'll be tasting, and we made them together. It feels like a lot hinges on him actually liking them.

He takes a large bite and chews, his face giving nothing away as he lets the flavors roll over his tongue before he swallows.

"Well?" I ask.

"Jesus Christ," he mutters. "Is there anything you can't do?"

I pump a fist into the air then pick up a cookie for myself.

And he's right. It's pretty damn good. I guess I'm not just a normal pastry chef after all. I'm a damn good one.

We're both finishing our first cookie when the door opens.

"Ava? You home?" Kelly yells from the front door.

"In the kitchen!" I yell back, and she appears there a moment later.

And she's not alone. It looks like my roommate scored herself a baller, and the wide smile stretching across her lips tells me she's happy about it.

"Graham," Grayson says cordially.

"Nash," Austin says back with a nod.

"Anyone want a cookie?" I ask as a way to break up the sudden awkwardness. Grayson and Austin don't really know each other yet, and now they're thrust into an interesting situation.

"I'll try one," Austin says.

"Give me two seconds, okay?" Kelly says to Austin, and she scurries out of the room, presumably to clear the papers she was grading earlier from her bed. And maybe put away her stuffed teddy bear.

I should do that, too. Grayson doesn't need to know I snuggle a stuffed bunny every night while I'm sleeping.

His eyes find mine after I hand Austin the cookie, and it seems like he's trying to tell me something. We're not quite at the level where the two of us can communicate without words just yet.

With any luck, we'll get there someday. But that day is not today because I have no idea what the fuck he's asking me.

"This is great," Austin says as he munches the cookie.

"It was all Grayson," I say modestly, and he laughs.

"Yeah, it totally was all me."

Austin looks like he's not really sure what to do with our banter, and Grayson doesn't seem to be saying anything. I get the sudden inclination that he might not like Austin, but I can't imagine why, and I can't exactly ask him in front of the guy.

"Hey, are you going to the Heat's home opener next Friday?" Austin asks.

"I'm not sure yet," Grayson says. He avoids looking over at me, and thankfully, Kelly steps back into the room before Grayson has to expand on that.

She's a little stilted and awkward, as if she's not quite sure how to handle herself. We all know why Austin's here and what they're about to go do, so there's no sense in beating around the bush.

"Guess we'll see you at breakfast!" I say brightly, clearly only making the awkwardness even worse, and Austin glances at me and nods a little before Kelly grabs his hand and pulls him out of the room.

"Well, that was awkward," I mutter.

"We? *We* will see you at breakfast?" Grayson says.

"It was a blanket *we*. Not a *you-and-me we*."

"It was *totally* a you-and-me *we*. And you just basically told him I'll be spending the night, and now if I don't, he'll know something's up!" He's hissing at me so Austin doesn't overhear, but maybe he's right.

"Oh, I, uh—I didn't mean to…"

He purses his lips, and he's angry again. It felt like we were making a breakthrough tonight, and now this.

I sigh. "I'm sorry. You're free to go whenever. What we do isn't any of his business."

"He's going to make it his business, which is probably why he showed up here tonight."

My brows dip. "What are you talking about? He came here tonight because of Kelly."

"I don't trust that guy, and you shouldn't, either," he warns in a whisper.

My brows dip. "Why not?"

He glances back toward the direction the two of them disappeared. "We'll talk later."

"Fine. What's this Vegas Heat thing?" I ask.

"Lincoln sent me a text last week about it. Jack apparently rented out a huge suite for players to attend the first home game of the season for the Vegas Heat baseball team."

"That sounds fun," I say.

"It does, and he invited families, too." He pauses, and then he adds, "It might be the right time to put in my first public appearance with my new girlfriend." He nods meaningfully at me.

"Are you inviting me?"

"Do you want to go?"

"Hell yeah, I want to go! Will Danny Brewer be there? Oh my God, will Cooper Noah be there?" I'm babbling now, but I can't help it. I'm a baseball girl.

"I assume they'll both be there since they play for the Heat," he says dryly. "But they're also both in relationships, and you'll be there with me, so…" He trails off, and I sort of like the fact that he sounds almost *jealous* that I know who those two players are.

"A girl can dream," I say with a smile, and he rolls his eyes.

And now I'm wondering how I can use this little dose of jealousy to my advantage.

Chapter 28: Grayson Nash

Nightlights and Stuffed Animals

"For the record, I don't want to go with you to the game if you're still mad at me."

I *am* still mad. First for the omissions, and then for what she just blurted to Graham. Now I have to spend the night, and I have no choice but to stay in her room with her, and how the fuck am I going to keep fighting against my feelings for her when we keep getting slammed into each other?

"For the record, I'm still mad," I say.

She purses her lips, and I'm not sure what she wants me to say. I can't just magically get over my anger. She folds her arms over her chest and glares at me.

"But come anyway," I finish.

She stares at me a long time before she relents. "Fine. I have to get up early tomorrow for work. Are you ready for bed?"

Right. Bed. A thing I'm going to have to share with her tonight. I sigh, and then I nod.

We head down the opposite hallway from the one Kelly and Graham went down. It's a split floor plan, and we pass a bathroom before we get to Ava's bedroom.

There's a nightlight plugged in, and there's a stuffed animal on her queen-size bed. Just when I was starting to see her as a woman, it feels like we're reverting backwards.

I blow out a breath. "I can, uh…I can just sleep on the floor."

"Don't be silly. We can share a bed without touching each other, right?"

I don't *want* to share a bed without touching her, but I hold back from admitting that to her as she grabs the stuffed rabbit off the bed and tosses it onto the dresser.

"Right. Sure. Of course," I say instead. It's all lies. I can't sleep next to her with this throbbing erection, particularly not in a bed that's smaller than the one I'm used to sleeping in by myself.

"If you'll excuse me, I'm just going to go wash my face." She grabs her pajamas, too, and I feel like I'm displacing her.

I'd love a shower and a shave plus a toothbrush myself, but I'm sort of stuck. She leaves, and I drop my jeans and pull off my shirt. I slide into her bed wearing just my boxer briefs, and I shimmy under the covers, doing my best to cover the thick monster so she doesn't suspect that I can't seem to get it down when I'm around her. He's begging me for another shot at that tight little cunt, but I will not give in.

I can't.

I scroll my phone as I try to focus on something other than sex, and Ava, and sex with Ava, but it's useless.

I pull up Candy Crush, my classic go-to game every night before I go to sleep. Hey, if she can admit she still sleeps with a stuffed animal, I can admit I play candy games on my phone before bed.

I'm mid-game two when she walks back in.

She's wearing a silky, short nightgown thing that would look much better on the floor. Does she seriously sleep in that? Or did she choose it tonight to purposely tempt me?

I realize I'm staring as she walks in. She doesn't look at me, but her face is scrubbed clean, and her tits look fucking amazing in that thing, and Jesus Christ, I've never wanted anything as much as I want to be inside her right now.

Fuck.

I force my eyes back to my game as I realize the time ran out and my score is awful. I close down the app and toss my phone on the bedside table. "Is this side okay for me?" I ask. My voice comes out all low and grumbly, and I swear to God I'm not going to be able to sleep until I take care of this raging boner.

She looks up at me all shyly, and it's my fucking undoing.

I nearly come in my boxer briefs.

"Yeah, it's fine," she says softly. She flips off the light and clears her throat as she gets ready to climb in.

"Excuse me," I say, and I bolt out of her bed and head for the bathroom.

I lock the door behind me, and then I rub one out.

It doesn't take much.

I'm fisting my own cock as I think about her wearing that little nightie thing, and I come all over my hand.

A sense of relief swells in me, but it's not enough.

I can jerk it all I want. It's no substitute for the real thing, the gorgeous woman who has every fucking ounce of my attention as I try futilely to get her the fuck out of my head.

Maybe it wouldn't be so bad to give it a try.

A little voice whispers to me in the back of my head, but I have to ignore it. I have to.

What would happen if we *did* give it a try and I fucked her over the way I'm terrified I will? Then I could lose my best friend on top of losing the girl I already care so much about. It's hard enough to make real friends when you're a professional football player, and maybe that's just a small part of why my friendship spanning back to my high school years is so damn important to me. He's not friends with me because of what I can do for him— and I can't say the same about the bonds I've formed since I snagged my first contract.

It's not a risk I'm willing to take.

I use the restroom while I'm in here, scrub my hands clean, and head back to the bedroom, feeling a small measure of calmness after what I just did.

But it doesn't last long.

She's scrolling her phone now, the light of the screen illuminating her face, and she doesn't acknowledge me when I come back in.

The moment I slip into bed beside her and get a whiff of that sweet, fresh-baked scent she seems to always have about her, the raging monster is back in action and ready for a go at her.

"Night," I grumble, turning away from her and closing my eyes.

Her nightlight is right in my eyes. I should've chosen the other side of the bed.

I want to ask why she has a nightlight. I don't. It feels rude and oddly personal even though we're getting *very* personal since we're sharing a bed.

The bed rustles a little, and I assume she's shifting down and setting her phone down. Before she says goodnight, though, she asks, "Can you tell me why you don't like Austin now? I'm worried about Kelly."

I flip over to face her, and I can see her clearly in the glow of the nightlight. We're closer than I thought we'd be, but the bed isn't that big, and I'm a rather large dude. "Between us?" I ask.

"Of course." She looks mildly offended that I'd even ask that.

I study her for a beat before I determine that I can trust her. "Linc said he didn't react kindly to the fact that Asher was going to start over him."

"Who's the better player?" she asks.

"Ask anybody else, they'll say Asher. Ask Graham, he'll say himself."

She presses her lips together. "Thanks for telling me."

"I'm a little worried he's using your friend as a way to get close to me, so just tell her to be careful," I warn.

"I'll let her know—without saying anything about what you just told me. Thanks for saying something," she says softly.

I nod a little, and our eyes lock.

I have this sudden feeling like I should kiss her. I *want* to kiss her.

Don't do it, my brain screams, but my dick is louder. My fucking *heart* is louder. I'm about to lean in toward her to do it when she shifts.

"Well, goodnight." She turns to face away from me.

I'm tempted to be the big spoon and hold onto her, to shift my cock so it settles near her ass.

I don't.

"Night," I mutter, and I reluctantly turn away from her, too.

I try not to toss and turn since it's a small bed that's rather bouncy on the shifting, but she seems to be sleeping soundly.

I draw in a deep breath as I move slowly to my back, and I stare up at the ceiling as I try to process these unfamiliar feelings. Not only am I spending the night in a woman's bed without having fucked her properly before we fell asleep, but I'm also going to be *dating* this woman—publicly, at least.

How the hell am I going to hold back from falling for her when every second I spend with her pushes me further and further in that direction?

The answer is less and less clear every time I ask myself that question.

And the boner? Harder and harder every time I ask that question.

Maybe I should just get up and rub out another one.

I glance at the clock. It's a little after two, which means I've been lying here for nearly two hours trying to fall asleep.

I should go back to my hotel, but I can't. I need to be here to put in face time with Austin Fucking Graham—and to take the pulse of what he's doing with Ava's best friend.

I shift again, and that's when I hear it.

A yelp followed by a gasp from beside me. She sits up as she pants wildly, and then she starts to cry.

"Ava?" I ask, sitting up beside her.

"Oh my God, I'm so sorry," she wails, clearly embarrassed.

"What's wrong?" I reach over to put an arm around her quaking shoulders, and I pull her in a little closer.

She sniffles, and I reach my other arm around her front so I'm holding her in a side hug.

"It's okay," I say softly, soothingly. "Whatever it is, I'm right here."

"I'm so sorry," she says again.

"Don't be. Talk to me, Ava."

She draws in a shaky breath and sniffles again. "I, um…I sometimes have bad dreams. They started when my dad died." She sniffles again, and I reach over to the box of tissues I saw on the nightstand when I first came in. I hand her one, and she blows her nose and sets the tissue on her nightstand. "I'm so embarrassed."

"Don't be," I say, my voice quiet and soothing. "I'm right here. Do you want to talk about it?"

She clears her throat. "It usually only happens if I have a drink right before bed, and even then it's rare. It's been a long time since I've had one."

"How long?"

"Months. Maybe a year." She reaches over to her nightstand, slipping out of my hold, and grabs a bottle of water. She gulps some down.

"Do you want to talk about what was in the dream?" I ask once she sets her water down. I keep my voice low and quiet, not really sure how to help her but wanting to do *something*.

"It's the same one every time. I'm eight, and all my brothers are with their friends. You're there, upstairs somewhere with Beck, I guess. And I'm in the kitchen with my mom. The phone rings, and she screams before she breaks down sobbing, and I know something's wrong. She hangs up and ignores me and calls for Beck, and she tells him that Dad was in an accident at work and he died on the scene, and then Beck tells Alex and Oliver, and nobody tells me. Nobody talks to me. It's just a rush of people in and out, walking by me, and nobody seems to care that

I just lost the most important person in my world." She draws in a shaky breath, her voice cracking at the end like she's going to start crying again.

I reach around her and pull her into my chest, and she silently quakes as I wrap my arms around her. I get the very real sense that it's not a nightmare so much as it's reliving her reality. It's a flashback to that day.

I remember that day, too. I *was* over at their house. Beckett and I were playing some video game that seemed to be the most important thing in the world, and we both heard his mom scream. He went down to check things out, and I stayed upstairs. I kept playing the game.

I didn't know his dad was dead. I didn't know the entire family would need the support of their friends in the coming days. I was just a teenager. There was a whole lot I didn't know about life at all.

Hell, I'm thirty-two now, and there's *still* a hell of a lot I don't know about life.

"It's okay," I say, trying to keep my voice low and soothing as I hold her close and rub her back slowly. "That sounds terrifying." I'm about to say *it was just a dream*, but the truth is…it wasn't. It's her memory tossing one of the worst moments of her life into play by way of her dreams, and that's a shitty thing for her own memory to do to her.

God, it's not like we can stop these things. I can't believe I'm getting defensive about *her own memory* to *her*. Have I really fallen in that deep after a single night with her?

It's not possible. It's merely my need to protect her—even if it means protecting her from, well…herself.

"It's why I have the nightlight and the bunny," she says quietly. "Usually I wake up alone, and those things help."

I feel like a royal asshole for judging any of that before I knew the truth.

"We all have bad dreams," I finally say, trying to come up with something to soothe her. "There's nothing we can do to help that, but I'm right here next to you, okay?"

"Thank you, Gray," she mumbles into my chest.

I get up for just a beat, grab her bunny off the dresser, and hand it to her. I pull her back into my arms and shift down, pulling us both under the covers but not letting her go. She settles onto my chest with the bunny held between her arm and my chest, and I link my arms around her.

"Tell me a story," she mumbles.

"About what?" I ask, feeling suddenly insecure. I can't just whip up a story on the spot, though my friends would say I'm quite the storyteller.

"I don't care. Just talk so I can fall asleep listening to your voice."

"Okay. Um…" I glance around the room as I wait for inspiration to strike. I start talking about the first thing that pops into my head, which is the last time I was with my entire family. It was back when my parents were still married instead of going through a divorce, and none of us had any idea where we'd end up a year later.

"About a year ago, we celebrated my grandparents' sixty-fifth wedding anniversary, and the entire Nash family went to our parents' goat farm in New York. It was the last time the six of us were together as a family," I muse, wanting to keep the story light and fun but realizing I'm taking it in a different direction already. I switch tracks. "I pulled up a minute after Lincoln and he hadn't gotten out of the car yet, so I parked about an inch from his door so he couldn't open it to get out." I laugh at the memory.

I go on to talk about how much fun it was spending the weekend with my brothers. As I'm talking, I can't help but put myself back in the place I was in a year ago.

I was thinking about retiring. Lincoln and I had a long talk well after midnight over beer as we each perched on a counter in the kitchen while everyone else slept.

I still am. I'm fucking tired, and my body is beat to hell. The offseason is no longer a long enough break from it all.

I was starting to see how important family is.

I still am. It's what brought me to Vegas, after all.

I was starting to think I wanted to settle down. Lincoln was talking about Jolene again, and Spence mentioned he met a girl.

I'm right in between the two of them by age, yet I'm still living life most like Asher. I don't want to be like Asher.

I don't want to get in trouble for stupid shit and get suspended for an entire year.

I don't want to be living with Dad again.

I don't want to be the spontaneous guy that nobody trusts. That's never really been me anyway.

But what *do* I want?

As the woman in my arms lets out a soft sigh and her breathing starts to even out as I talk, an icy fear grips onto my heart.

I think I have my answer.

Chapter 29: Ava Maxwell

Overanalyzing the Ass Grab

I'm exhausted when my alarm wakes me, but the second half of the night was some of the best sleep I've had in a while.

When I was with Colin, I didn't want to cuddle. We rarely shared a bed, anyway, especially since he moved to Chicago.

But somehow, having Grayson's arms around me made me feel safer than I've ever felt in my life, and hearing his voice hum from his chest as he told me about the last time he was with his family lulled me into a deep sleep filled with much happier dreams.

I'm careful to slip out of his grasp so I can go shower, and he groans his displeasure when I get up—but he doesn't move from my bed.

I take a beat to stop and stare. I could really get used to seeing Grayson Nash asleep in my bed. What a lovely sight to behold…and even lovelier that he didn't want me to get up out of his arms.

Maybe last night was a breakthrough. If everything happens for a reason, perhaps my nightmare was to push us closer together. He was so sweet in the moment, making sure I felt cared for and safe, and as embarrassing as it was, he even got up to bring me my bunny.

It's those little details that make me feel like this could be the start of something really, really special—if I could just get him to trust me again. Oh, and, you know—that other hurdle called *my brother*.

I get ready quickly and figure I'll just let Grayson sleep in my bed. I head over to let him know I'm leaving, and I stare at him sleeping for a beat.

God, how I wish this was real.

I don't have the heart to wake him, so instead I lean down to press my lips to his forehead. As I straighten to leave, he reaches up and pulls me back down.

"Where do you think you're going?"

I giggle. "I have to get to work."

"Are you okay after last night?" he asks softly.

"Yeah. I'm okay."

"Let me walk you out," he says, finally relenting as he lets go.

I don't want him to let me go. Ever. But I straighten and turn to leave. "Don't be silly. You stay and sleep."

"I should get back to the hotel anyway since I'm paying to stay there."

"Then stop paying and just stay with me until your place is ready." The words are out before I can stop them, and I nearly slap a hand over my mouth at the random outburst.

Instead, I wait to see what he's going to say. I can't really see his face to get a good gauge on his reaction since the sun is just starting to rise and it's still dark in here, but he freezes for a beat.

Is he contemplating it?

"That's a nice offer," he says.

That's a nice offer.

He doesn't say yes…but he also doesn't say no.

I head to the kitchen to fill my water bottle, and he follows me out there.

"What are your plans for the day?" I ask.

"Checking in with my agent, giving that publicist a call. Maybe finally calling my dad to let him know I'm in town."

"Why don't you stay with him?" I suggest, and I could kick myself for suggesting it.

"Yeah, that's a no."

I chuckle. "Is he really so bad?"

"For one thing, I'm a thirty-two-year-old man who really doesn't want to revert back to living with my father. And for another thing...Asher is living with him."

"Is that a bad thing? Are you not close with Asher?" I ask.

"No, we're close. It's just...we'll be playing on the same team, so a little separation won't hurt anybody, you know?" He shrugs.

I really don't know, but just the thought of living with a colleague—say Cora, for example—is fairly taxing.

I screw the lid back onto my bottle and turn to face him. "Thanks again for last night. You were—"

He cuts me off as he shakes his head. "No need for all that." He takes a step toward me and pulls me into his arms, and I settle there on his chest for a beat.

We both hear the door on the other side of the house open, followed by footsteps.

He leans down and presses his lips to mine.

It's a warm, sweet kiss, and I want to bask in it, but I really do need to head to work. I pull back first—reluctantly, but I have to.

"Have a great day, baby," he murmurs, and he hugs me once more just as Austin clears his throat behind him.

"Morning," he says.

I recall Grayson's words from last night about Austin, and I can't help but wonder if he's up to no good with my best friend. I'll have to warn her, but I'll have to be careful about how I go about it, since from the look on her face last night when she walked in with him, she is one smitten kitten.

"Morning," I say brightly, moving out of Grayson's arms. "Gotta run to work. Have a great day!"

Grayson reaches down to squeeze my ass, and between the kiss, the *baby*, and the ass-grab, I'll definitely use the rest of my day to overanalyze whether all that was sincere or just for Austin's benefit.

My heart is trying to convince me he was being sincere—that something changed last night when I woke him crying in the middle of the night after my recurring dream.

But my brain is fairly convinced it was just for show.

I ponder it on my drive to work, and it doesn't get pushed to the back of my mind the way it should when I'm at work. Part of me wants to talk about it, but the person I'd talk to about it is Kelly—not Cora. Kelly's not here, though. Cora is.

I keep my trap shut. It's the wisest move considering we don't want it getting out that we're not *really* in a relationship even if I *really* want to be in one.

But how exactly does one level up with a pro football player? How does one move from the little sister of the friend zone up to banging against the windows overlooking the Strip?

With any luck, time will tell, and eventually I'll have an answer to that question.

Chapter 30: Grayson Nash

Fake Relationships Are My Specialty

At eleven o'clock, a reminder dings on my phone.

Are you thinking about Ava?

I can't help a smile as I look down at the phone.

Of course I'm thinking about her. I haven't stopped.

I don't mention it, but I do text her after I get the confirmation appointment a few hours later.

Me: Are you available to meet a publicist with me around four o'clock today?

It's a Monday, and I think she went into work at six, so I assume she'll be off by four. My meeting actually starts at three thirty, and I figure it'll give me the chance to make sure I like this publicist before I give her the back story and ask for her help in training Ava to handle the media.

I call my agent next. Isaac informs me that he has several interviews lined up for me along with some new sponsorship opportunities, three of them local to Vegas. I tell him to send them over, and I take a look through them. I sign off on the three Vegas ones, figuring I may as well get started on making a name for myself in the community.

I stare out the window for a while as I think about this whole situation with Ava before I finally decide to call my dad.

"I was wondering when you'd finally break," he answers.

Yeah, that's dear old Dad. Never a hello or friendly greeting, that's for damn sure.

"Consider me broken."

"Asher said you've been in town a while now."

"I have," I admit. "Been busy getting my shit together."

"Getting your shit together? Or finding the first girl who catches your eye?" he presses.

"I take it you've seen the pictures. You recognize her?"

"No. The name's familiar, but with four boys and a life of my own, it's hard to keep up."

"She's Beckett Maxwell's little sister," I say. I'm about to tell him we're just faking it for the media when I realize…why the fuck would I tell my dad that? So he could lord it over me? Thanks, but no thanks.

"Okay," he says, as if he doesn't even know the name of the man who has been my best friend since I was fourteen.

I feel like my mother would have a completely different reaction to my news.

And I might even tell *her* the truth.

"Well…should we do dinner or something?" I ask.

"Sure. You, me, and Asher? Tonight?" he suggests, and why do I get the sudden inclination I'm going to get stuck with the bill?

"Fine," I say with a sigh. "I'll pick you two up around seven."

Ava texts me back around lunchtime.

Cookie: Yes, I can make it. I'll come straight from work, so just send me the address.

I text it over to her, and then I resume my brooding as I stare out the window.

Eventually it's time to head over and meet this publicist, and I get the feeling that if she's married to Luke Dalton, she knows what she's doing. He's a legend with the Vegas Aces, and I've never met anybody who didn't respect the hell out of him. I remember playing against the Aces when I was in Los Angeles, and twice I spent the whole goddamn game trying to keep up with the guy only to have him duck away and pull moves I never saw coming.

Plus, his brother owns the team I play on now, so there's that.

Ellie works from her home office, so I ring the doorbell promptly at three thirty. It's not a woman who answers the door, though—it's Luke.

"Grayson Nash," he says, reaching his hand out to shake mine. "Good to have you on our team for a change. I always had the hardest time outrunning you."

I chuckle as I shake his hand then slap his back. "I was just thinking the same goddamn thing about you."

He laughs and invites me in.

"Are you still working with the Aces?" I ask.

"I am. I've been a consultant to the wide receiver coach for the last few years. It's the best of all worlds. I can keep my foot in the game without the grueling schedule." He leads me through the house toward a hallway as we talk, and then we appear in a white office with purple décor. "This is my wife, Ellie. She's the best in the business, and she'll take good care of you."

She blushes a little at her husband's compliment, and she stands and walks around the desk to shake my hand. "Nice to meet you, Grayson."

"And you," I say with a polite nod.

"I'll leave you to it," Luke says, and he ducks out as Ellie nods toward a chair on the opposite side of her desk while she slips back into her chair.

"So, Mr. Nash, what can I do for you?" she asks.

I contemplate where to start, and ultimately I decide to dive right in. "Well, I have a publicist I worked with back in Los Angeles, but I think I'd like to work with someone local. And, uh…I'm in a relationship with someone who could use some media training."

"A relationship?" she asks, resting her hand on her chin as she leans forward conspiratorially. "Tell me more."

I twist my lips for a beat. "This doesn't leave this room, right?"

She picks up a folder and tosses it across the desk. "If you sign that NDA at the end of the contract to hire me, it doesn't."

I scowl, but I glance through the details, and it all seems pretty standard. I sign on the dotted line and push the folder back toward her. "My first night in town, I met a girl. Took her back to my hotel room. Things were great. Found out a week later she's my best friend's little sister."

"You don't know who your best friend's little sister is?" she asks.

"Not when I'm originally from New York and somehow met up with her in Vegas, and I haven't seen her in a decade." I shrug.

"I'm kind of teasing. The truth is I didn't know who my brother's best friend was, and then I married him."

My brows dip. "Luke? Who's your brother?"

"Josh Nolan."

"Ah," I say with a nod. "Yeah. Nolan's a beast." He's another now-retired receiver I had a hard time blocking back in the day.

"He's just my brother," she says with a laugh. "Actually, he and his wife live across the street, and we see them all the time. Anyway, back to the matter at hand. So now you're in a relationship with her?"

"Kind of. The truth is that I was pretty angry with her for lying to me, and then her ex got involved, and photos were posted...long story short, I told her brother that we're in a fake relationship."

"Fake?" she asks, her eyes lighting up. "Fake relationships are my specialty!"

Oh Jesus. What the hell have I gotten into with this woman?

"But I do have just one very important question I have to ask you, and since you signed the paperwork, this really does stay between the two of us."

My brows dip. "What is it?"

"Is it fake for both of you?"

"What do you mean?"

190

"Exactly what I said," she says, as if this isn't the most confusing conversation I've had today. "Is it as fake for her as it is for you?"

I think about holding her last night in my arms after a nightmare woke her up. I think about climbing out of her bed this morning and kissing her the way I've wanted to for days. I think about the anger I'm still holding onto. I think about her brother. I think about our night together at the Palms.

"Well?" she prompts me.

I guess I was thinking about all of that shit longer than I realized.

I blow out a breath. "To be honest, I'm not really sure."

"That it's fake for her? Or fake for yourself?"

"Both. Either. Neither. Fuck, I don't know," I say, running a palm along my jaw.

"Do you have real feelings for her?" she asks.

"Yes. But I promised her brother I'd look out for her, and a real relationship with me wouldn't be protecting her the way she needs me to."

She stares at me a long time as she processes that, and then she finally says, "Don't you think it would be worth the risk?"

I avert my gaze out the window. "Not for her."

"How do you know that?"

"Because of my track record. I fuck up everything that's good." Whoa. Where did that come from?

And…do I?

I don't even feel like it's a conscious thought I've had before, but there it is, as if Ellie has this magical ability to expose my soul right here in her office.

Maybe she should've gone into psychology instead of publicity.

"What have you fucked up?" she presses.

"My friendship with Beckett if I bang his little sister again," I admit.

"Okay, but what if it doesn't fuck it up? What if he's okay with it?"

"You didn't hear him when he saw the photos her ex posted of us. He was *pissed*, Ellie. He would not be okay with me dating his little sister, and to be honest, I don't blame him." A vague memory comes back to me from when I was fourteen and I was with Beckett just after his dad's funeral. He told me his dad had gone out of town for work one time and he promised his dad he'd be the man of the house any time his dad was gone. He promised to take care of his mom and his siblings.

He took that promise to heart. His dad wasn't just gone for a few days on a business trip. He was gone for good.

And then he reached out and asked me to help him keep that promise.

I didn't. I failed. I fucked up because she lied.

Of course I'm holding onto anger because of that.

But I'm also holding onto something else because of that— something much, much stronger than anger.

I just haven't quite identified what that is yet.

"Sometimes people surprise you," she says softly. "What else have you fucked up?"

"I just left an old team for a new one, and everyone thinks it's because of nepotism."

"Nobody thinks that," she says.

I raise my brows pointedly.

"Okay, fine, some uninformed idiots might think that. But the truth is that you're a kick-ass defensive back, and before I met Luke, I didn't even know what a defensive back was." She shrugs.

"Neither did Ava."

"Ava? That's our girl's name?" she asks.

"Yeah. And I hope it's okay, but I invited her to come here at four for her first lesson with you."

She narrows her eyes at me. "How'd you know you were going to sign with me?"

I laugh. "You're married to Luke Dalton. I saw your client list. I think that speaks for itself."

She grins. "Welcome to Prince Charming Public Relations. I think we're gonna have a really good time working together."

I smirk at her. "Now I'm scared."

"Yeah, you probably should be." She winks at me, and then she gets down to business.

We talk through my current list of sponsorships, and she takes notes as she has some ideas for redirecting my image. Instead of focusing on my relationship with my brothers, she wants me to build my own image in Vegas, which means working with charities or even starting a foundation of my own. She wants to use the *relationship* I'm in to showcase my dependability and my commitment to the Vegas community since that's where she lives. She also thinks it's a good idea to make it seem like I made the move to Vegas for *her* instead of allowing the focus to be on my brothers.

And the next thing she suggests knocks the wind out of me.

"She needs to move in with you to make it look serious. If you're going to fake it, then you have to fake all the way around."

Just after she says those words and before I even get the chance to react to them, there's a knock at the office door. Ellie gets up to answer it, and I stand from my chair.

There she is.

My chest tightens as Ava walks into the room a little timidly. She has flour on her sleeve, but none on her face today. She's somehow this combination of sexy and cute all at once, and I've honestly never met anyone like her.

She's modest and sweet, yet that night we shared was the complete opposite of all of that.

And I think…I *think*…holding her in my arms last night when she was scared did something to me.

Something irreversible.

Something terrifying.

Something that makes me want to break that record I just shared with Ellie of fucking up everything that's good.

I don't want to fuck up Ava. I want to be better with her. I want to be better *because of* her.

I want to do right by her.

I don't think I want to fake this, either. But for now…it's the right thing. It's the only way to keep Beckett in the dark while I explore whatever this is with her.

"Hey," Ava says quietly to me.

"I'm Ellie, Grayson's new publicist," she says, sticking her hand out to shake hers. "I hear you two are in a fake relationship?"

Ava's eyes go wide. "You told her?"

"I signed an NDA, so anything we say in here stays in here," I say.

Ellie takes her seat behind the desk, and Ava sits beside me.

"I was just telling Grayson how fake relationships are my specialty," Ellie begins.

Ava's eyes widen as they meet mine, and I'm not sure why, but I get the feeling that this is going to be a whole hell of a lot of fun.

Chapter 31: Grayson Nash

Civil Wars Are Not Laughing Matters

"What the fuck are you wearing?" I ask my brother when he opens the door to the house my parents bought when two of their boys landed in the same place.

As I glance around, I see my mom's touches are everywhere. She decorated this place, but it's my dad who's living here. It hits me once again how strange it is that they're getting divorced.

I always figured *kids* were the ones affected by their parents' divorce. I didn't realize how much it could fuck up adults, too.

Asher is my dad's favorite of his four boys, and he's never made a secret of that. I'm certain it's why he agreed to allow Asher to stay with him when he got into trouble last year, but I think Asher might be good for my dad, too—at least as he's going through the divorce, he's not alone.

My mom, though…she's all alone in upstate New York, two hours from civilization on her goat farm in the middle of nowhere. There's a little downtown area with a diner, a market, and a gas station, but otherwise there's not much around unless you're interested in a solid thirty-minute drive.

I worry about her, but she insists she's happy with her goats.

She comes out to visit, and now that three of her boys are on the same team, certainly she'll spend most of the season either out here or traveling to our games.

She always loved watching us play, and I know it's been hard on her having us all in different cities. She'd make it to at least one home game and one away game for each of us during the season, but it's a lot to manage with four boys in the league.

Asher looks down at his outfit—a bright ass purple velvet tracksuit. "What's wrong with it?"

"You're wearing velvet. To dinner."

"It's velour," he says, as if that's a solid defense.

"That doesn't make it better."

"Well, you like Tootsie Rolls," he says.

"Yeah, because they're a fucking delicious, low-calorie treat, and that's got nothing to do with your ridiculous *velour* tracksuit." I pull one out of my pocket, and he laughs.

"Okay, then. Bet. I pick up more pussy wearing this than you do wearing that." He nods pointedly to the black T-shirt and jeans I've had on all day.

"I'm not taking that bet," I say. I'm not taking it because I'm supposed to be in a relationship with Ava, but he takes it to mean something else entirely.

"Because you know I'll win."

"Yeah, exactly that." I roll my eyes. "Where the fuck is Dad so we can get this over with?"

"I'm right here," he says, walking into the foyer. At least he's dressed normally, though black slacks and a short-sleeve, button-down plaid shirt are very much a *dad* move. "And why are you so eager to *get this over with*? Got somewhere to be?"

"Always."

"Never anywhere more important than with family," he says, pursing his lips.

Do I really have to sit through this dinner with him? I'm starting to remember why I didn't rush to call him when I arrived in town.

He's always been about family loyalty, family ties, family this, family that. Yet he's the one who fucked everything up so badly that my mom filed for divorce. Where's the family loyalty in that?

Pushing away the woman who supported him for the last forty years doesn't seem so devoted, but I guess I don't know what the fuck went on in their marriage. All I know is he's cried family loyalty my entire life, only second to football coming first.

I unwrap the Tootsie Roll I found in my pocket and pop it into my mouth. It's a little stale, but when they're hard, it just means I can make the deliciousness last a little longer.

Asher rolls his eyes.

"You two ready?" I ask.

They follow me out to my truck, and Asher slips into the back while Dad rides shotgun.

"Where are we headed?" I ask from the driver's seat.

"There's an excellent steakhouse at the Venetian," Dad says.

Of course he'd pick a steakhouse on the Strip. I force myself not to roll my eyes, but in all honesty, I should start eating less red meat and sugar and start preparing for the upcoming season.

And so should Asher—but that's on him to decide. I can't help but wonder if he's been working out over the last year or if he's taken it off to play video games.

I should know these things about him, and maybe I will now that we're in the same town. But even though he's only five years younger than me, it feels like we come from different eras.

Which is strange considering the woman who currently has my attention is *seven* years younger than me, and it *doesn't* feel like that's too far removed.

Maybe women are just more mature than men.

And I suppose we prove that once we're seated at our table.

"Good evening, gentlemen," our server says. "Are we celebrating anything tonight?"

I nod at Asher to give him the signal.

You know…that signal between brothers where we silently agree that we're going to annoy our father at this meal and where it becomes our sole mission to get the other one to crack first.

"Well, it's April first, which is National Trombone Players Day, so we figured a steakhouse was an appropriate place to celebrate," I say.

Asher smirks at me. "It also marks the ending of the Spanish Civil War, and if that's not a reason to celebrate, I'm not sure what is."

I keep my face smooth at his words, but in all honesty, that was a pretty good one.

Our server just looks at us like we're a couple of weirdos, which we are. It's fine. "Oh, I get it. April fools!" she says.

"No, these two jackasses are just playing a game to see who can get the other one to laugh first," Dad says. He rolls his eyes.

"That's not what we're doing," I say solemnly.

"Yeah, Dad. Civil wars are not laughing matters," Asher says just as solemnly as me.

I guess I've got my work cut out for me.

We each order our signature drinks—Hendricks for me, a beer for Asher, and whiskey for Dad—and I peruse the menu as I try to come up with something to make my brother laugh.

To that end, I get up, head to the host stand, and let her know we're actually here tonight celebrating our dad's birthday, and if she could be so kind as to find a way to *really* embarrass him, I'd be forever in her debt.

Usually I flirt my way to getting what I want, but tonight...I don't. Instead, I simply ask a favor, and I hope she'll do it. If she doesn't, that's cool. If she does, great. But I'm not in the mood to flirt when I can't get Ava Fucking Maxwell out of my goddamn mind.

Speaking of which, the second I sit back down, Asher glances at me. "So, Ava Maxwell, huh?"

"Fuck off," I mutter.

His brows shoot up. "Ooh, seems like a touchy subject. Think I'll press on that nerve just a little more. Are you really doing your best friend's little sister?"

"Not that it's any of your business, yes, I'm seeing Ava."

"I remember little Ava Maxwell," he murmurs. "She wasn't so little by the time I went home between my sophomore and junior years of college."

"Yeah? You saw her back then?" I ask.

"I banged one of her friends. Ava was more the innocent type who didn't have a clue what was going on in the Taco Bell parking lot on Friday nights." He shrugs. "Not that I wouldn't have taken a shot at her, if you know what I mean."

"Yeah, well, she wouldn't have taken one with you."

He holds up both hands. "My-oh-my, we're getting awfully defensive over the new girlfriend."

"She had a thing for me back then," I admit. "She wouldn't have blown her chances on the likes of you."

"The *likes of you*? Who the fuck talks like that?" he asks.

Dad just watches us like we're in some sort of tennis match. I can't tell if he's impressed or embarrassed.

"The brother of the guy wearing velour to a steakhouse," I say dryly. That gets a laugh out of Dad.

The server delivers our drinks along with a basket of bread, and I snatch the first piece of bread after we order. The three of us make small talk about the voluntary minicamp that's just three weeks away. It's *voluntary*, but since Asher was out for a year and I'm new to the team, we'll both be there.

I continue my quest to make Asher laugh first after our food is delivered. I pick up the bottle of ketchup sitting on the table, make a space between my steak and my vegetables, and start squeezing the bottle.

"What do you need ketchup for?" Dad asks.

"My veggies." I keep squeezing, and I catch Asher watching me as a pool of ketchup forms on my plate.

He keeps watching as the pool spills over the side of my plate and onto the tablecloth.

He glances up, sees me watching him with intensity as I keep squeezing the bottle, and he bursts into laughter. "Fine, you win, you win," he says, and I start to laugh, too.

Damn, it feels good to laugh with my brother.

It's been a long time.

Dad just looks at us like we're both idiots, and maybe we are. But at least we're two laughing idiots who are about to play on the same team for the first time in our entire lives.

And I, for one, cannot wait.

Chapter 32: Ava Maxwell

I Thought D Meant Dick

I take a final look at myself in the mirror, and I hope my skinny jeans and Vegas Heat tee are good enough for me to appear on the arm of Grayson Nash. I curled my hair, put on a little extra makeup, and went over Ellie's advice a hundred times in my head.

I'm ready for this.

Our first official date.

We'll be with his teammates, including at least one of his brothers, and I think we're set to have a really good time.

If I can get my nerves in check, anyway.

I only have about fifteen minutes before he's going to pick me up, so I head to the kitchen to find the vodka. I could use a shot to calm my nerves.

I hear the garage open, which means Kelly's home from work. As far as I know, Austin didn't invite her to the game. They've only been together the one time, and we haven't had a chance to talk about his intentions with her yet—or about how their night together went.

I know I need to warn her, but I'm also a little afraid to have that talk. We've only seen each other in passing since she had late nights with parent-teacher conferences this week and I had early mornings at the bakery—on top of late evenings so I could leave early today and go in late tomorrow morning. I've been working seven days a week lately because I could use the paycheck, and frankly, while I love it, it's also exhausting.

I guess it's now or never, though.

She walks in with a bright smile. "There you are!"

I smile nervously, glad I took that shot. "Here I am. How was work?"

Her smile fades a little. "What's wrong?"

Leave it to your best friend to correctly read the situation. "I don't know how to say this, so I'm just going to say it. Grayson doesn't trust Austin and is worried he's using you to get to him. I just want you to be careful."

The smile that faded drops completely off her face. She's silent for a few beats, but then she asks, "Why would he think that?"

I sigh. "You know Grayson and Asher's brother is the coach of the Aces, right?"

She nods.

"Well, Asher and Austin play the same position, and Lincoln was going to start Asher over him until he got suspended. So Grayson thinks Austin might have a grudge against the Nash family."

Her brows dip. "I didn't really get that vibe from him, but I'll be careful."

"I'm sorry I had to be the one to tell you."

She walks over and hugs me. "Don't be. I appreciate you looking out for me, really."

I squeeze her. "Love you."

"Love you, too. And have fun at the game. Tell Austin hi for me." She winks at me, and then she shrugs. "Hey, if he's using me, then I can use him right back. That night we shared..."

"You never really gave me all the details," I press.

She grabs the bottle of vodka and helps herself to an after school on a Friday afternoon kind of swig. "It was good."

"Good?"

"*Good.*" She nods meaningfully as she holds her hands out to indicate his rather generous size, and I giggle.

"Nice. Just be careful."

"I know the reputation a lot of these guys have, so I'm going in with eyes wide open, don't you worry. What about you? What's been going on with you and your man on D?"

"Man on D?" I repeat.

"Yeah. You know, D. *Defense?*" she says, as if she knows a damn thing about the game.

I laugh. "I thought D meant *Dick.*"

"It does, depending on context. Just like my man on O definitely was on the O the other night." She looks up at the ceiling dreamily. "Multiple times." She wiggles her brows.

The doorbell rings before I can respond to that, though before we got on the subject of orgasms, I was going to tell her about my nightmare the other night and how sweet Grayson was as he held me through it.

"Well, thanks for all those details," I say dryly. "Looks like my date is here."

"You look gorgeous, and you're going to smash your way into his heart. Guaranteed."

"You're the best." I head toward the door to answer it, and there stands Grayson Nash, here to pick me up for our date.

He's wearing jeans, a white Nike T-shirt, and a hat...*backwards.*

What is it about a guy with a backwards hat on his head? He has great hair, but tossing on a hat and turning it around turns him into this sort of bad boy. A bad boy who I want to rock my entire body like he did that night at the Palms.

Sometimes I think I'm in some alternate reality. This man who is talented, hilarious, absolutely gorgeous, and...*endowed*...is here to pick me up for *our date.*

But then the truth clobbers me right smack dab in the middle of the nose. We may be going on a *date,* but we're not really together.

And it sort of pops the balloon that I was starting to float up toward the clouds upon...until I remember my promise to myself.

I'm going to get him to fall in love with me.

"Hey," he says, and his blue eyes seem extra bright for a beat. Maybe it's the sunshine behind him, or the white shirt, or the backwards hat.

And then his eyes flick down my figure before landing on mine again, and they're just a little darker than they were before.

"You look…" He trails off, and he clears his throat. "Wow. You look great."

One side of my mouth lifts in a smile. "I was just thinking the same about you."

We sort of just stand there staring at each other for a few beats, taking each other in.

And then he seems to gather his wits about himself again. "You ready to go?"

I nod. "Come on in. Let me just grab my purse."

He follows me in and spots Kelly in the kitchen. They exchange pleasantries, and then we head out after I tell Kelly not to wait up.

I'm not sure why I say it other than the fact that I'm hoping this date ends up in his hotel room.

I'm certain I won't get that lucky tonight, though.

We hop into his truck and cruise down the highway toward the stadium. It's the first time he's actually driven us somewhere, and I can't help but notice a few things. First, his car is spotless. Second, his car smells like him. And third, the second we got in the car, he shut off the radio so we could talk.

There's something really sweet about that last one. And it gets even sweeter when he says, "What did you do to my phone?"

I can't help a giggle as I shrug as if I have no idea what he's talking about. "When's your house supposed to be ready?" I ask instead.

"Around the first of May. Less than a month now, and it'll have everything I want when I move in, but it's kind of a pain in the ass to live out of a hotel for the next few weeks," he says.

"I offered for you to stay with me," I point out. I don't dare look over at him. I'm not sure my heart could take hearing the rejection or seeing the look on his face that tells me he's not interested.

He clears his throat. "Uh, yeah. About that."

My brows dip as I glance over at him. "About that?" I prompt.

He sighs. "Ellie thinks we should be living together if we want this to look genuine."

Oh. So Ellie thinks that. He didn't say what *he* thinks, but if this is my chance to spend more time with him, I'm going to grab the hell on with both hands.

"Then let's do it. I can stay with you at your hotel, or you can move in with Kel and me for now."

"I can't impose on you and your life like that, Av."

Av.

He's never called me Av before. Kelly sometimes calls me Avelina, and my brothers call me Avabear, which my dad used to call me. But Av...it's really just my name turned into one syllable, the second syllable dropped, and it used to be my least favorite nickname if I'm being honest, so I told people not to call me that.

In any event, because *he* is the one who said it, somehow it's hot as hell. I want to hear him rasp it when I'm naked beneath him and he's driving into me.

Whoa.

All that from just simply abbreviating my name? I'm in deep here.

"It's not imposing when I'm inviting you to, *Gray*," I say, abbreviating his name, too.

He chuckles a little. "You sure?"

How the hell else am I supposed to execute my little plan here if we hardly ever see each other?

"I'm sure."

"What about sleeping arrangements?" he asks.

"You can stay with me. We're two grown adults. We can handle it, don't you think?"

He glances over at me, and I swear there's a little smirk there, but he looks away so quickly back to the road I think maybe I imagined it.

But the truth is…maybe he doesn't think we can handle it. And if he thinks that, maybe I'm closer to reaching my goal than I first thought.

Chapter 33: Grayson Nash

The Tootsie Roll Connection

She's full of surprises.

She thinks we can share a bed because we're two grown adults who can handle themselves?

Maybe she hasn't looked in a mirror today, but fuck.

What is it about jeans and a T-shirt on a woman that's just... *hot?*

She's casual, and something about that is even sexier than seeing her all dressed up for some other event. I'm more of a casual dude myself, unlike my eldest brother, who enjoys suits, and my youngest brother, whose preference leans toward velour and stupid shirts.

Her ass looks mighty grabbable in those tight as fuck jeans, and I'm impressed she thinks I can keep my hands to myself sharing a *bed* with her when I'm not even sure I'll be able to keep my hands to myself sharing a suite at a baseball stadium.

Which is fine. I shouldn't keep my hands to myself if we're faking it the right way.

Except it's starting to feel less and less fake and more and more real.

We arrive at the stadium and head toward the suite, and the party is already in full swing in there by the time we walk in. Buffet tables are filled with food, the bar is open, and my teammates are already having a good time.

I don't walk in as tentatively as I should, given the fact that I'm the new guy.

I have this uncanny ability to make friends, and even though my brother is the coach of this team, I still think I can have friends here.

Luke and Ellie are standing near the door, and it feels good to see familiar faces immediately. Ellie hugs Ava, and she whispers something to her. Ava's cheeks turn pink, and I can't help but wonder what words were exchanged there.

"Heard your niece is coming any second," Luke says.

"Yeah, Jolene was due a few days ago. I haven't talked to Lincoln in a few days, but I imagine he won't be here today," I say.

"We'll all kick his ass out of here if he shows up," Luke says with a laugh, glancing at his wife. "If his own wife doesn't take care of that herself."

I chuckle. Jolene is definitely the perfect match for my rather stubborn brother.

I glance around the suite and spot Patrick—someone I've already bonded with because we play the same position and we've hung out at a bar a few times. Tristan and his wife are here, too, and so are Travis and his wife. I see Ben Olson and Jack Dalton along with their wives, and Austin is here, too—solo, talking with Declan, the punter. Our quarterback, Miles Hudson, is here, fresh off the IR, and our backup QB, Brandon Fletcher, is here, too, along with a few other guys I haven't met yet, some older who appear to be coaches and others who might be players.

We head toward the bar first, and my hand grabs her small one—for the act, of course. Hers is chilly, and she flexes her fingers as they fold around mine. I tighten my grip around hers, and she glances up at me.

"What did Ellie say?" I ask.

She just smiles, lifts a shoulder, and orders herself a vodka cranberry. I order a Hendricks, naturally, and we head toward the box seats to enjoy our drinks and keep our eyes on the field as the home opener gets underway. I try to push away the unfamiliar feelings pulsing through my chest as I have the sudden need to hold her hand again.

What the fuck is that?

I've never cared about holding a woman's hand, and somehow it's all I can think about right now.

I finish my drink and grab a Tootsie Roll from my pocket just to keep my hands busy.

I open the wrapper, and I hear her mutter something as I pop the candy into my mouth.

"Huh?" I ask.

"You still eat those," she says quietly. Her eyes are shining a little.

"Still?" I've been eating them my whole life, and I have no idea what she's talking about, but she seems emotional about whatever link we share over the chewy chocolate candy.

She glances away from me and down to the field. She clears her throat. "My dad's funeral. You were there, and you had a pocketful of them. You gave me one, and I came back around and you gave me another one. My brothers always made fun of you for eating them, and I'm sure Beck gave you hell for giving his baby sister candy. But I always loved them."

"So have I," I say quietly, not realizing we shared that connection.

To be honest, I rarely share my Tootsie Rolls with anyone. But I guess that day I saw a little kid who was hurting, and it was my way of making the day a little more bearable.

"And maybe because of you, they've always been my favorite candy," she says softly.

I slip another one out of my pocket and hand it to her. I let my hand linger in hers when I press it to her palm, and she glances up. When our eyes meet, I see a little pain there, but I also see a little hope in them.

It might be the same sort of hope reflected back at her.

It's a heavy moment, and I do the only thing I can think of.

I lean over and lower my lips to hers.

She sighs softly into me, and I pull back before I take it to another level—a level that wouldn't be appropriate here in this suite with my teammates, my coaches, and my team owner.

Though I'm definitely not opposed to it, and the more time I spend with her on this *date*, the more I want...*more*.

Our eyes meet, and hers look confused.

She's clearly wondering whether I just did that for show or if there was more to it.

And there was *definitely* more to it, but I'm not sure this is the time or place to admit that.

This is all so confusing. I want to be with her, but I can't. I like her—a lot—but I promised her brother I'd take care of her.

How is kissing her at a Heat game taking care of her? How is it protecting her?

Every time we start to get close, I feel myself pumping the brakes.

But isn't that always what I do? How do I make things different with her when she deserves so much more than what I can give her?

"Nice, you two," a voice whispers from behind us, interrupting the rather intimate moment. I glance back and see Ellie, who clearly just saw me kiss her and obviously believes it's all part of the act.

It wasn't. And I'm torn between telling Ava the truth about that or not.

Maybe it's better not to. I should play it safe. Protect her like I promised I would.

Ava unwraps the Tootsie Roll and pops it into her mouth, and she closes her eyes for a beat as she chews.

I shift in my seat as my cock throbs.

This is ridiculous.

I sigh, turn my attention to the field, and focus on the proverbial baseball as a way to get my raging boner to calm the fuck down.

But when I'm sitting next to Ava Maxwell and she's moaning her delight over a fucking Tootsie Roll, there's little chance that's ever going to happen.

Note to self: buy more Tootsie Rolls. Stat.

Chapter 34: Ava Maxwell

So Smart and So Goddamn Clueless
at the Same Time

The Heat win on opening day at home, and we have the best time together. It feels like we're in a real relationship—we don't stick only with each other the entire time. I sit with Ellie for a bit, who introduces me to her sister-in-law, Jack Dalton's wife, Kate. I chat with Victoria and Tessa for a while, too. Grayson chats up his teammates, and I watch him from across the room.

I never feel that awkward sense of loneliness even though we're not side by side for the entire event. He's free to do his thing, to get to know his teammates, to have some fun, and the girls chat me up as they try to figure out my secret ingredient in my cookies, but I won't tell a soul.

Especially not now—after the intimate moment I just shared with Grayson.

He's such a force, even in this suite with a whole bunch of other forces, too. He still somehow stands above the crowd even though he's not the tallest man here, or the biggest, or the loudest. He's magnanimous, and it's this charismatic energy that he carries that turns him into the center of attention.

The guys on his team all seem to like him already, and I love that for him. I think he was initially worried about fitting in, but I can't see why he'd have any problem with that at all.

I hang around with Grayson toward the end since he's the kind of guy who's the last one standing as he talks to everyone and makes the rounds. As they leave, I hug the girls who feel like friends goodbye. Eventually, it's just Jack and Kate remaining, and we say our goodbyes before Grayson drives me home.

He's quiet on the car ride home, and I can't help but wonder what he's thinking. At times it feels like I know him so well I can read his mind, and other times it feels like I hardly know a damn thing about him. Maybe we've known each other for seventeen years, but knowing who somebody is and actually knowing them are two different things.

If Beck's held onto a friendship with him for this long, though, I think that means I can trust him, too.

"You're quiet," I muse.

"So are you," he counters.

Neither of us asks what the other is thinking. We're probably both too scared to ask.

What I wouldn't give for a window into his thoughts right now.

Was that kiss back there genuine? It happened during a moment of emotion, and it didn't *feel* like it was just for show. It felt like a sweet moment between us when he just couldn't help himself.

But sometimes the things he says and the things he does seem to conflict with each other, and all it does is leave me in total confusion.

The thought grates on my nerves the closer and closer we get to my house. Part of me hoped he'd take me back to his hotel room. Part of me wonders if he'll stay. Part of me thinks a confrontation is the right move here. Part of me doesn't.

And when I'm confused and conflicted…well, it's not pretty to be on the receiving end of that.

We get back to my place, and it's a little before nine. Still early by all accounts, and I don't have to be at work tomorrow until noon. The house is dark, which makes me think Kelly must've gone out—maybe with her teacher friends, whom she's been avoiding lately.

It should be the right opportunity to invite him in.

"Would you like to come in?" I ask once he has pulled into the driveway and put the truck in park.

He sighs and leans his head back on the headrest. He doesn't answer. He doesn't look at me. He also doesn't cut the engine. "I don't know if it's a good idea."

"Can I ask you a question?"

He turns his head to look at me, which seems to be the signal to plow ahead.

I clear my throat. "Was the kiss back there…was it just for show like Ellie assumed it was?"

He turns his head back so he's looking out the windshield rather than at me. He's quiet a few beats before he finally says, "No."

My chest tightens and my heart races.

"What was it?" I ask.

"I don't know." He shakes his head a little. "It just felt like the right thing to do. It felt like we were on a date, and you admitted something personal, and…" He trails off, leaving me to wonder what the *and* might have been leading to.

"I think we should talk," I say softly.

"I think talking might be a bad idea."

"Fine." I toss open my door, slam it shut behind me, and head up to the front door without so much as a goodbye or a backward glance.

I fumble around in my purse to try to locate my house key, but I can't seem to find it through the hands shaking with anger nor the eyes blurring with tears.

I shouldn't be this affected. This upset.

But I am.

Because this feels big, and I realize for the first time how right he is. He has the power to shatter me completely. He shouldn't. We've really only known each other as adults for the last three weeks. This is still new—really new. We haven't defined what we are. Not quite friends, not quite something more than that.

But maybe that's what I wanted to talk about. Why would he kiss me in a personal, emotional moment?

My hands are trembling once I finally locate my key. I try to shove the key into the keyhole in the darkness of my front porch, but between the blurry eyes and the shaking hands, I'm struggling.

That's when I hear footsteps behind me, and then the light from a phone illuminating the door to help me fight my way in.

He comes in after me, and he shuts the door quietly as I storm through the house to the kitchen. I slam my purse down onto the counter, and I set my hands on my hips to face off when he appears a few beats later.

"What the fuck is your problem, Grayson?" I yell at him.

He looks surprised by my outburst, but he doesn't answer my question. He just stares at me while my anger boils over.

"One minute you're kissing me as we talk about my dad's funeral, and the next minute you're holding me at arm's length. You're leaning into me then pulling back, and I can't tell if you like me or if you're disgusted by me, and I just want some goddamn answers, but when I try to talk, you tell me it's a bad idea. So what is it, Grayson?" I practically spit his name at the end.

His eyes flash at me, and then it's like something snaps. He takes a few steps toward me until I'm backed up against our pantry door. He pins me there with his hips against mine, and it would be impossible not to feel his rock-hard cock as it settles between us.

He's...*turned on* right now?

His eyes fall to mine, and he just stares at me for a hot beat while I try to figure out what he's thinking.

"I like you, Ava. A lot. Too much, I think." His voice is a low snarl, and he pushes his hips against me to prove what he means by *too much*. "The idea that you might think I'm disgusted by you fucking kills me. I've never met a woman who's so smart and so goddamn clueless at the same time. But I'm still not sure I can trust you. And it's not just that. I made a promise to your brother, and I find myself crossing lines. Getting too close. That's why I keep pulling back. You're drawing me in. You're making me want shit I have no business wanting." His lips drop to my neck, and he lets out a strangled groan as he tastes my skin. "Fuck it."

My spine lights with the thrills that zip up it at his words, and then his lips slam to mine.

He's aggressive as his mouth opens and his tongue assaults mine. He drives his hips toward me like he wants to fuck me, and God, I want it, too. I want *him*. I've always wanted him, and now that I've had a single taste, I can't go back.

Maybe it's the naiveté talking, the inexperience of never having had sex with another man. Or maybe we made magic that night, and he's the one I'm supposed to be with.

We won't know if we never even give this a try.

I kiss him back like my life depends on it—and maybe in a strange way, it does. My future hinges on him accepting who I am. Because I know we can have a beautiful future together if he could just find it in himself to trust me.

We're good together. This kiss tells me that much.

We're fire. We're hot. We're smoldering.

I link my legs around his waist, and he holds me up with a hand under my ass. I hold his jaw between my hands, and I slide one back to run it through his hair.

My chest quakes with anticipation for where this might be leading.

We make out there for ten seconds or an hour—I'm not sure because I lose track of time as his mouth explores mine. I lose all sense of *everything* except for this man and the way he makes me feel.

Just as all good things must come to an end, so does this kiss.

He pulls back, and he gently sets me to the floor.

He looks confused, and then he looks…guilty.

"I should go," he says softly. His lips are red from kissing me, and disappointment lances through me.

"Okay," I say, the sting of rejection fresh and cold on top of that disappointment.

I want to ask him if he's going to move in with me. I want to ask him to stay. I want to ask him to kiss me more. I want to ask him to sleep over.

I don't do any of that.

Instead, I stay right where I am, my back against the pantry door, until I hear him close the front door behind him.

Chapter 35: Grayson Nash

A Recipe for Disaster

What the actual fuck was I thinking?

I'm not sure if I was dumber for leaving or dumber for kissing her.

Either way, seems like I'm dumb.

I was seconds from jamming my hand into her jeans so I could reach down and feel how hot and wet she is for me on the inside.

If she were anyone else, I would've.

But she's not anyone else. She's my best friend's little sister, and I'm falling in love with her.

I'm angry with myself for letting this happen, for allowing my feelings to go there when it hasn't even been a month since the night we spent together.

I knew she was different the very second she asked me for a date before we hooked up. My reputation precedes me, and typically the jersey chasers I hook up with just want to get to the main event.

She didn't. She wanted to get to know *me*, and even though she kept some things from me in the process, she also wanted to share some of herself. I get why now since it was her first time. She put a whole hell of a lot of trust in me to hand that over to me.

She didn't know *me*, exactly…but maybe she did.

Maybe Beckett shared stories with her about me so she felt like she did. She remembered the Tootsie Roll thing, and that left some sort of impression on her even though it was just an innocent sharing of candy for a kid who looked so damn sad all I wanted to do was make her feel some measure of happiness.

I was just a dumb teenager after one thing back then, and she was too young to fall into any sort of category that would allow me to remember anything else about our interactions together.

But *she* remembered.

And who knows what that means? Who knows what that moment did to shape who she is as a person today? Who knows what *any* singular moment might do to change who someone is at their very core?

All I know is that I'm changing. She got into my core in the short time we've shared, and that's one hell of a heavy and terrifying admission to make—even if it's just to myself. Even if I can't share that with her, or my best friend, or my brothers, or anybody else in the world.

Because I can't.

It doesn't matter how I feel. I made a promise to the guy who has been my best friend for eighteen years, and I can't go back on that now.

These feelings will pass, won't they? It's just the shiny newness of it. It's just wanting what I can't have.

And I'll keep telling myself that until these feelings fade. Because if I don't, it's her heart on the line.

I'm not willing to risk that.

I pull into the valet lane and take the ticket from the attendant before I walk through the casino to head upstairs.

A woman's voice stops me midway in my pursuit. "Grayson?"

I whip around and come face-to-face with Daphne...my *situationship* from Los Angeles.

My chest tightens as I suddenly feel a little lightheaded. What the fuck is she doing here?

"Daphne. What're you doing here?" I can't quite hide the surprise in my tone.

"I came to see you," she says.

Why? It's what I say in my head, but not what I say aloud. She has no clue that I just came from a house where I kissed a different woman and didn't give Daphne a second thought. She has no clue I haven't given her a second thought since I left LA...maybe even since I officially pulled the plug on our *situationship*.

A term she coined, by the way, not me.

I wouldn't have called it anything more than friends with benefits, but she insisted we were in some sort of relationship.

I guess when you bang somebody more than a couple nights in a row, it comes with the territory.

"I...uh..." I'm not sure what to say. "It's good to see you." It's not. I don't know why I say it.

I lean in for a polite hug. She doesn't take it that way. She clings on for a few extra beats.

It feels like she's showing up out of the blue simply to throw a wrench into everything else.

"Can we go somewhere to talk?" she asks quietly in my ear.

It's her way of inviting herself up to my suite, but I have no intention of taking her up there. I don't really want to take her to the café where I had a date that meant something to me with another woman, either. So instead, I lead her over toward the casino bar.

It's probably not the privacy she was hoping for, but I can't give her that. That was always part of our problem. She wanted more of me than I was ever willing to give her.

That thought unlocks something new in my brain. I think I might be willing to give those things to Ava.

But I can't.

It's a lose-lose-lose situation. I have feelings for her, and if I acknowledge them or act on them, it could fuck up my friendship with Beckett. If it doesn't do that, it'll fuck me up. And because I fuck everything up, it'll fuck her up too. We all lose, and why risk an eighteen-year-long friendship with somebody over something that I've already determined is doomed to fail?

What if it's not?

It's the first time that particular thought has snuck its way into my consciousness, and it takes me by surprise.

It's as I'm staring at Daphne, a meaningless woman from my past, that I get the first inkling of what I want in my future.

And the woman sitting in front of me ain't it. That's when I realize I can use this whole fake relationship business to my advantage.

"I have to tell you something, Daph. I started seeing someone a couple weeks ago, and it's actually already pretty serious."

"You started seeing someone?" she repeats. It's clear from her tone that she doesn't believe me.

"It's complicated, but I've known her since I was a teenager. We just found ourselves in the right place at the right time." I try to keep my tone apologetic even if I don't really feel that way about it.

Her face falls, as if the hope she carried in with her just slid right away. "I don't even know what to say to that. You always told me you wanted nothing to do with relationships."

"I know, and I didn't. It wasn't a lie, and it wasn't just some line I used on you. But I guess things change when you find someone you can't be without."

She looks like I just issued a physical blow, and I feel a little sick to my stomach.

Not because of the look on her face.

It's because I'm not sure whether what I just said is true or if it's lip service to get the fuck out of this situation with Daphne. And if it's true…then I'm fucked.

I sit with her until she finishes the drink I bought her.

"I have some things I need to take care of," I say, trying to sound apologetic again as I push to a stand.

"I knew it was risky coming to town not knowing your schedule. I guess I was lucky I ran into you."

I wonder for a beat how long she was waiting to run into me. I was gone all afternoon at the game.

I give her another hug—one that she doesn't cling to as much as the first one—and bid her goodbye before I head upstairs. And I feel restless once I arrive back in my suite. I fill a glass with gin then take it over by the window. I stand there thinking about what just happened.

It affected me far more than it should have…and by *it*, I certainly don't mean my run-in with Daphne. I mean my date with Ava, followed by that kiss.

That fucking kiss.

Dammit.

My cock aches as I think about her.

I chug down the gin in my glass and slam it on the counter, and then I sit on the couch we've shared more than one time, pull out the beast, and get to work.

I'm not slow and steady with myself. Instead, I yank like I need this release to survive, and I think I do.

Sweat beads on my forehead as I stroke up and down, back and forth, desperation running through me as I move steadily toward the finish line. The animalistic need to come pulses everywhere in me.

I think of her sweet, tight cunt as I slid into it, inch by hard inch, and she laid back and took it all. I think of her tits bouncing, of her mouth, and what I want to do to it.

But it's when I think of her in her jeans and T-shirt at today's game, the easy way her little hand fit in my big one as we played the part that's becoming less and less of an act and more and more real, that my balls tighten up as fire tears through me.

I grunt out her name as I start to come, and it's only after the release grabs hold of me and my throbbing cock pulses out jet after jet of hot come that I realize it wasn't the sexual thoughts of her that pushed me into my release.

It was the relationship part. The hand holding. The little gazes across the room. The Tootsie Roll moment.

I slump back, relaxing on the couch cushions for a few beats as I let myself feel the warm afterglow of ejaculation. I draw in a few deep, calming breaths in those moments.

It doesn't last long. I want to see her again. I want to kiss her again.

I want to fuck her again.

I finally tuck my cock back into my jeans then head over to the bathroom to wash all the come off my hands.

I grab more gin, bypassing the glass this time and going right for the bottle.

And then I find myself haphazardly throwing all my shit into my suitcase as I wonder what the fuck I'm doing.

I can't go there tonight. Not like this. Not when I'm angry and confused and halfway to drunk.

Ellie said we should be living together.

It would only make sense for me to stay at her house until my house is ready.

Can I really do that, though? I already find myself falling for her. Spending more time with her, sleeping in the same bed as her…it's a recipe for disaster.

And she's the chef.

Chapter 36: Ava Maxwell

Am I Still Your Fake Girlfriend

"I'm so sorry, Ava," Kelly says quietly. "But I had to show you as soon as I saw."

I close my eyes and suck in a breath. This could go one of two ways here.

Either A, I could get pissed off and fall into the whole miscommunication trap, or B, I could give him a chance to explain since there might be an explanation…not that he owes me one.

Because we're not *really* dating, right?

Except I'm totally there, and I've been in love with him since I was a teenager, and I think he's feeling it too, but I'm probably wrong. Either way…I'm not missing my chance.

I opt for B. I'm not a real confrontational person, but he's the one who agreed to the fake relationship thing, and getting photographed hugging another woman definitely contradicts our whole story.

And Tito's. Three shots of Tito's plus some Tito's and Sprite, and here we are—with enough liquid courage to make the call.

Interestingly, however, I retreat to my bedroom for privacy for this call. It's not like when I broke up with Colin while Kelly was sitting beside me. For some reason, I want to call Grayson alone.

"Hey," he answers, and I can't quite read how he sounds from his tone. I was half-expecting some joke about how I must not be able to get enough of him if I'm calling already, which is also true, but he sounds…subdued?

"Hey. Kelly saw some pics of you hugging some woman in the Palms casino an hour ago, and there was a whole caption about how you spent the day with your girlfriend at the Vegas Heat game. So, I guess I just called to ask…am I still your fake girlfriend or what?"

He's silent on the other end.

"Well?" I push.

"Yeah. A friend from LA came to see me, and I told her I'm in a relationship. Okay?" Now he doesn't sound as subdued. He sounds…angry. At me?

"Okay," I say, definitely more meekly than my first question was asked.

He blows out a loud, harsh breath. "I shouldn't have hugged her. She kind of clung to me, and I had to let her down gently that it wasn't going to happen."

"Did you want to?" I ask. No way in *hell* would I be asking that question if I wasn't slightly drunk.

He's quiet a long time again before he answers. "Not with her."

"With who?" I whisper.

"I can't talk about this with you over the phone."

"Then come over," I suggest.

"I don't think that's a good idea."

"You keep saying that, but…" I trail off as I hope he fills in the blank there that *hell yes* it's a good idea.

"But what, Ava?" he demands. Before I can answer, he jumps in. "But you're Beckett's little sister."

"Stop saying that!" I yell into the phone. "I'm a goddamn adult, and I'm so tired of you acting like I'm not. Why can't you just admit that you want me too?"

"Fine!" he yells back at me. "Fine. Yes. I want you. Okay? I want you so fucking bad that I just rubbed one out thinking about you, not her, and when I came all over my own hand, I yelled out *your name.* I'm staying in the same damn suite where I fucked you, and I see you everywhere. I can't think, I can't sleep, I can't eat. I know how this is going to turn out, Ava, and I refuse to hurt you."

I'm shocked into silence for a beat by his words. His passion. His admissions.

But one thing remains the same.

"You keep saying that, but you're hurting me more by refusing to give this a chance."

I hang up on him after I say those words.

I hope they're enough to convince him to move to action. We can handle Beckett later. Just because we give this a real try doesn't mean it has to ruin anything between the two of them. It's not like Beck and I see each other every day and it's going to drive some big wedge between us if things go south with Grayson.

I head back out to the family room, where Kelly is sitting on the couch.

I debate how much to tell her as I collapse down next to her, my head on the top of the cushion as I stare up at the ceiling.

I don't like fighting with Grayson. That whole exchange should have me feeling giddy and excited. He just admitted he has feelings for me.

Instead, all I feel is sad.

Kelly and I tell each other everything. She's my best friend.

But saying that he *rubbed one out* while he was thinking about me feels too personal to reveal to my best friend.

"How'd it go?" she asks.

"Instead of being accusatory, I told him you saw the pictures, and I asked if I'm still his fake girlfriend. He said she's a friend from LA, and he told her he's seeing someone."

"Why would he need to tell her he's seeing someone if she's just a friend?" she asks, and part of me wonders if she's reading more into him than she should because of the warning he issued where Austin is concerned.

I shrug. "We didn't really get into that part. We started fighting instead, and I told him to come over, and he said it's not a good idea because he'll only hurt me, and then I told him he's hurting me more by not giving this a chance, and I hung up on him."

"You hung up on him?" she repeats.

I twist my lips and nod.

"Well, maybe he'll come over then," she suggests.

I shake my head. "I doubt it. I'm worried I've pushed him further away than ever, and I'm not sure where we go from here."

"Then wait it out. If you're still dating, fake or not, he'll be in touch soon."

"I hope. What's been going on with you and Austin?" I ask, changing the subject to her.

"Nothing. He went to Florida where his mom lives. We've texted a few times. We had that one night, and it was incredible, and then…" She trails off and shrugs as she twists her lips. "I've been busy. He's been busy. I guess if it's meant to happen again, it will."

"And you're okay with that?"

"I don't want to be the desperate girl chasing him down."

I study her, and she really does seem to be okay with whatever arrangement they have. We shift topics to work, we eat our pizza, and we drink our vodka.

As it turns out, the *soon* Kelly was referring to in Grayson getting in touch with me comes the next morning after a rather fitful night's sleep.

I don't have to go into work until noon today since I wasn't sure how late I'd be at the game yesterday, though I debated going in earlier since I'm not waking up in Grayson's arms.

I'm awake since I wake up early every morning, and I'm scrolling my phone at six thirty when a text comes through from Grayson.

Grayson: Are you up?

My chest tightens with anticipation as I wonder if this is it. Is he going to admit he was awake all night thinking about me?

Me: Yes.

My phone rings a beat after I send the reply, and I answer with a groggy, "Hey."

"Hey." His voice is low and raspy. "Did I wake you?"

"No. How'd you sleep?"

"Like shit, but that's not why I'm calling. My sister-in-law went into labor late last night, and my first niece is here. I'm going to the hospital in a bit to meet her, and I was wondering if you'd come with me." He pauses, and then he adds, "So, you know…so we're seen together."

Right.

It's for show.

We're showing the world, which apparently includes his family, that we're together. And it makes sense. All eyes will be on who is entering and exiting the hospital to visit Vegas's hottest football coach's new baby.

"Oh, sure," I say, my voice flat to try to hide the hurt I feel that he's still just doing this for show despite his admission last night. "I have to be at work at noon, but I can meet you at the hospital and head in from there."

"Can you, uh…" He pauses as if he's trying to choose the right words. "Can you call in sick and spend the day with me?"

"Oh," I say, surprised by his question. *Why?* I want to ask, but I'm terrified to know the answer. "Let me check in with my boss, okay?"

"Of course."

"What time are you planning to go?"

"I'm just going to take a quick shower, and then I'll be ready. Asher and my dad are heading in after breakfast, my mom flew in yesterday, and Spence is on his way today. I figured we'd all spend the day together."

"That's…that's lovely," I say softly, and suddenly I want more than anything to spend the day with Grayson and the Nash family. "Let me call my boss. I'll call you right back."

"Okay."

We hang up, and Poppy gives me the go-ahead to take the day off. "You haven't taken a day off…ever, my girl. Take two days if you need it. We'll survive."

Not with my recipe, but she's right. They'll survive.

I call Grayson back.

"Hey," he answers, and why is just a simple *hey* from him enough to send my pulse into overdrive?

"She told me to take two days," I say with a light laugh.

He chuckles softly. "Great. I'll be by to get you in a half hour."

I take a quick shower and do my best to look presentable, and he shows up right on time, knocking quietly on the front door so as not to wake my roommate.

I open it, and he stands there looking absolutely freaking delicious in jeans and a red Aces T-shirt. He's wearing a backwards hat again, and my *God*, he's hot.

"Did you eat?" I ask after I pick up my jaw off the ground.

"I figured I'd just grab something at the hospital, but I wouldn't say no to a cup of coffee."

"Come on in," I say, opening the door a little wider to allow him in. I offer him a bagel while his Keurig brews, and he takes me up on it. We're in the car ten minutes later on our way toward the hospital.

"So this is your first niece, huh?" I ask.

"By blood, yeah, but Beck's kids are like nieces to me, too. What's it like having one?" he asks.

It strikes me that the kids he considers nieces already are my actual nieces. "It's pretty cool getting to know kids who are made from one of your siblings. Everleigh is eight now, and she's so calm and cool like Beck, and then Isla is almost five, and she's a firecracker like her mama."

He chuckles. "Yeah, *firecracker* is one way to describe Rachel."

My sister-in-law fell for my brother when they were in college. She chased him for three years while he was busy focusing on his studies, but eventually he put it together that she wanted him. He always knew he wanted to be a lawyer, and she was in school to become a teacher. She decided she didn't want to do that anymore, so she jumped to being a journalism major. She hated her professor, so she switched tracks to biology, and it took a semester for her to realize she hated science.

She ended up graduating with a degree in business, and she's been working as Beck's assistant for the last nine years.

"She's the best, though," I say softly. And she is. She'd tell me to just go for it with Grayson. She doesn't care what anybody else thinks, and that's one of the things I admire most about her. It's also one of the things Beck fell hardest for when he finally saw what was right in front of him.

An awkward beat of quiet passes between us, and then I ask, "Did you get anything for the baby?"

"Get anything?" he repeats. "She's a newborn. What am I supposed to get?"

I laugh. "You're such a man. Maybe flowers for your sister-in-law, or a balloon, or…*something* so you're not walking in empty-handed?"

"No. I didn't get anything. I honestly thought stopping by to visit and spending the day there was going to be my big grand gesture." He pulls into the parking lot of the hospital and starts the search for a space. It's not too crowded yet this early.

"They'll have a gift shop. We can stop and grab something," I suggest. "And diapers are always a good idea. Or a cute stuffed animal that can sit on a shelf until she's old enough to play with it. Wouldn't that be sweet? She could snuggle her favorite stuffy from Uncle Gray."

"Yeah. Sweet," he mutters.

"Have you asked to make sure they even *want* visitors?" I ask.

"My brother texted me at three in the morning to let me know he's a dad, and he told me to come by to see her. I think it's safe to say he wants to show off the baby," he says.

He pulls into a space, and we walk toward the hospital entrance.

We detour to the gift shop first, and he finds a little balloon proclaiming that *It's a Girl!* We swing by the stuffed animals, and he picks a stuffed bunny up off the shelf.

"Perfect," he mutters more to himself than to me, and my heart lifts up a few pegs.

He wants this. I want this.

Now the challenge is getting him to see that maybe we could make it work after all.

Chapter 37: Grayson Nash

Gray Brought a Date

A stuffed fucking bunny.

Nothing felt more right when this should all feel so wrong. I got it for *her*, but I'm giving it to my niece, which is probably extra stupid on my part since every goddamn time I look at the dumb thing, I'll be reminded of Ava and how I royally fuck up all that's good since I'm never going to be able to actually make the move I want to make.

I'm trying to remember why I thought it was a good idea to invite her along with me today.

The conclusion I keep drawing is that I'm an idiot.

I did it to be *seen* with her, and we were seen as we walked in together. Someone somewhere snapped a photo of us, and it'll be posted online soon. It'll erase the rumors about who the woman last night was, and I won't ever need to address it.

I shouldn't have to.

It's my fucking life, and just because I play a sport people tune into every Sunday, they think they deserve the inside track to what I do in my spare time.

They don't.

Nobody does.

I pay for the bunny and the balloon, and we head toward the elevator. We're buzzed into a waiting room, and my brother comes down to collect us.

"Congratulations, bro," I say to Lincoln when he walks in the room.

He looks...*exhausted*. Like he hasn't slept in a week. And maybe he hasn't, though I don't comment on that. I grab him in a hug and slap him on the back.

"You remember Ava Maxwell, don't you?" I nod toward the woman beside me.

"Beckett Maxwell's sister, right?" Lincoln says, eyeing her.

She nods and steps in to give him a hug. "That's right. Congratulations."

"Thank you," he says with a smile. "I'm so glad you're both here. I can't wait for you to meet them, but Jolene and the baby are both sleeping. Do you mind waiting here until they wake up and she has a chance to try feeding her again?"

"Not at all," I say, sliding onto a chair. Ava takes the seat beside me, and Lincoln sits across from us. "So...how is she?"

His smile widens. "Jolene? Great. And the baby? Amazing. Six pounds, seven ounces of literal perfection."

"What name did you decide on?" I ask.

"I'll let Jo tell you that." He yawns.

"Go get some rest," I suggest. "We'll be fine here."

"Seriously, this kid wakes up every hour, so you can come meet her soon." Lincoln pushes to a stand, and the door to the waiting room opens.

"Two of my boys in the same room? How'd a mom get so lucky?" Mom says as she rushes to hug Lincoln first, and she says something into his ear. She squeezes me next, and she's beaming when her eyes land on the woman beside me. "And Gray brought a date?"

"You remember Ava Maxwell, don't you, Mom?" I ask.

"Oh, of course! How's your mom doing, sweetheart?" she asks as she pulls Ava into a warm hug.

"She's okay," Ava says, and for the first time, I wonder how she's *really* doing. It's not something Beckett and I talk about, and

I don't think Ava is very close with her. In fact, she rarely mentions her family at all.

I wonder about how long it's been since the last time Ava and Beckett spoke. Or Ava and her brother Alexander, or Ava and her brother Oliver.

I touch base with all my brothers fairly frequently. My mom texts me once a day at a minimum. I can't imagine not feeling that connection with them, and I can't imagine how the beautiful woman standing beside me hugging my mother feels about not having a mother figure in her own life. I wonder if she chose Vegas on purpose to escape her family and create her own life somewhere far away from them.

It pulses more feelings in me about how I don't know her as well as I want to.

And as if the thought comes out of absolutely nowhere, I wonder if I could give her the type of family she deserves.

"When can I meet my first grandbaby?" Mom asks Linc.

"Let me go see if Jo and the baby are awake," Lincoln says, and he heads down the hallway, leaving the three of us in the empty waiting room.

She glances between Ava and me, and I get the feeling she wants to ask what's going on between us. Thankfully, she doesn't—but I get the feeling she *will* when she corners me later.

"So what is Ava Maxwell up to these days?" she asks Ava.

"I'm a pastry chef at a bakery just off the Strip with aspirations of owning my own place someday." She has this glow about her as she answers the question.

"Oh, I love the ambition," Mom says. "Isn't running your own bakery a lot of work and long hours?"

Ava nods. "It is, but when you're doing what you love…"

"It doesn't feel like work," Mom finishes for her.

"That's right," Ava says.

"Tell her about your cookies," I say, nudging her.

Her cheeks turn a little pink as she says, "Our bakery is known for the kitchen sink cookie recipe I created. I have the recipe copyrighted, so if I leave, I can take it with me. Still, I tend to do some of the prep work at home so nobody learns what my secret ingredient is."

"That's so neat! When can I try one?" Mom asks, and I realize I haven't tried one yet, either. I held one in my hand and handed it back over the counter, but the sweet delight her bakery is known for hasn't crossed my tongue yet.

Her cunt has, but her cookie hasn't.

Wrong time to be thinking about that, and an even worse time to pop a boner.

Fuck.

"Maybe we can swing by later and grab some for everyone to try," I suggest.

We talk more about what it takes to run a bakery, and it sounds like the startup for it requires a lot of cash that Ava doesn't have right now.

Lincoln shows back up a short while later, interrupting the easy conversation with, "My girls are ready for you."

"My girls," Mom says, holding a hand to her heart. "I'm just so happy for you, Linc."

He grins and tosses his arm around her shoulders. "Thanks, Mom." He kisses her on top of the head, and then the four of us head down toward his room.

"Grandma's here," he says softly, and he leads Mom in first. Ava and I walk a few paces behind her, and I'm a whole head taller than my mom, so I spot Jolene holding the baby with a soft smile playing at her lips as she gazes down at the little bundle wrapped in pink.

She doesn't look like she just put in the hard work of labor even though she did, and the little baby she's cradling to her chest is just like Lincoln described. Perfection.

I'm not a baby guy, but damn, she's adorable.

I'm not sure why, but I can't help a quick glance over at Ava.

Her eyes are a little misty as they fall onto the new mom and baby. I think she might be feeling the same strange pulse of emotion I am.

It's not what I was expecting to feel today.

I thought I'd put in my time with my family, show off my new "girlfriend," and we'd call it a day.

Instead, I can't help but wonder about a future with said "girlfriend" and maybe one or two of these little perfect creatures born from the intimate connection we share.

Is it a possibility for my future?

I have no idea.

But I think it's more of a possibility now than it ever was before, and that alone is really fucking terrifying.

Chapter 38: Ava Maxwell

It's Worth the Risk

"Meet Josephine Lorraine Nash," Jolene says, handing her over to Mrs. Nash.

The first-time grandma coos over the sweet baby as Grayson makes the introductions between Jolene and me. I know who she is since we all grew up in the same town, but she's nearly ten years older than me, and we never attended school together.

He hands her the balloon and the stuffed bunny, and she thanks him, and I can't help but stare at the tiny bundle Mrs. Nash is holding. It's not the first time I've held one so little. Both of Beck's girls were born by scheduled C-section, and I was a senior in high school when they had Everleigh. I was in college with Isla, and he flew me out so I could meet her the day she was born.

I couldn't have afforded to go otherwise, but he's a high-powered attorney who makes bank in Manhattan.

My other brothers could've afforded it—Alexander, an anesthesiologist in Philadelphia, and Oliver, a software developer in Chicago, both make plenty of cash. It's a reminder how my siblings are all much, much more successful than me, and I have to admit, it's not a small part of the reason why I enjoy being out west, far, far away from the rest of them.

But Alex and Oliver had to work, so they didn't bother flying in to meet their nieces. They finally met each girl when the next holiday came up that forced us all to get together again.

And the Christmas after Isla was born—five years ago this year—was the last time we were all together in the same place at the same time.

It was awkward and stilted. We were forced together for two whole days, and my brothers—all three of them—spent most of their time on their laptops working. I played with my nieces, chatted with Rachel, and did my best to ignore my mother, who drank too much wine and pointed out everyone's flaws the whole time we were together.

I don't fit in with my family.

I'm the baby. I'm the only girl. I'm still chasing my dreams while my brothers have already achieved them.

It's not like that in the Nash family. It's four boys, all successful professional athletes. They seem to be very close, and I've never felt that way with family.

I think it's why I made my own family when I came to Vegas. Kelly's been like a sister to me since we met, and for a long time, she was all I needed.

Yet as I sit here with half the Nash family, I can't help but feel like I wish I had something like this, too. I wish I was a part of a family where it didn't feel like an obligation to reach out. It's not that way with Beck, but he's so busy with his job and his family that oftentimes I feel like I'm bothering him if I'm so moved as to send him a text.

And so I usually don't. It's him who keeps tabs on me instead.

I get the sense it's not like that with this family. I don't know the ins and outs, and I know Mrs. Nash and Mr. Nash are going through a divorce, so it's not all perfect. They're all coming together to be with their oldest brother to meet his baby, and there's something really special about that. It's the first grandbaby, and Lincoln is the first one to get married and start a family.

Spencer appears to be next since he proposed to his girlfriend not too long ago. As far as I know, Asher is enjoying the single life, and that leaves Grayson.

He's still a huge, unsolved mystery.

My eyes shift over to him, and he's staring down at his new niece while his mom holds her. He's clearly already in love with her with the way he's looking down at her, and my chest tightens as this fantasy plays out in my head that it's us here, and everyone is gathering to meet our baby, and we're married, and it's the happily ever after I've dreamed of since I had my first crush all those years ago.

As if he can tell exactly what I'm daydreaming of, his eyes flick up to mine.

His are warm, and my cheeks redden as he catches me staring at him.

"Want to hold her?" Mrs. Nash asks the room in general, catching me off guard by interrupting the lock his eyes have on mine.

Grayson looks back at her, but I don't miss the terror before he shifts his gaze. I stifle a giggle.

"May I?" I ask.

"Of course," she says.

I head to the sink first, scrub my hands, and then walk back to Mrs. Nash. She hands the baby over, and I stare down at her as I gently sway.

She's all bundled up in her swaddle, and she wears a pink hat on top of her head to keep warm. She's sleeping with her little button nose and her pink cheeks.

And I get the strangest feeling that I didn't have back when I held my nieces.

Maybe it's age. I was in high school and college with them, but now I'm an adult on my own in the world, and I'm starting to get this feeling that I want one of these in my own future.

It hits me out of left field.

I don't know a ton about kids, but I know how busy Beck's two keep him and Rachel. I know when they're first born, it's all sweet bliss and sleepless nights, but then they grow into actual people with opinions and voices and backtalk.

What would it be like to raise one of them? Would I be any good at it? Is *anybody* any good at it, or are they all just winging it?

Beck and Rachel seem to have it down pat. When I have kids someday, I want to parent the way they do.

But that also means I need a partner who also wants to have them someday. Is that Grayson? Or am I just chasing down a dream that doesn't have any possibility of coming to fruition?

Tears fill my eyes as emotion seems to get the better of me.

"She's so beautiful," I say to Jolene, who smiles at me. I glance over at Grayson, and he's watching me intently, with something akin to curiosity in his eyes. "Would you like to hold her, Uncle Grayson?"

"Oh, uh," he says, and he shifts a little on his feet. "I, uh—"

"Dude, it's fine," Lincoln says, slapping his brother on the back. He gently takes the baby from me. "Wash your hands, then sit, and I'll hand her to you."

Grayson follows his brother's instructions, and I can't help but feel a twinge of something in my belly as Lincoln hands the baby to his brother.

I feel myself falling deeper and deeper, and that's terrifying.

Sure, he admitted he has feelings for me. He even went so far as to tell me he masturbated last night while thinking about me.

But he's also dead set against anything ever really happening between the two of us, and I'm terrified he's stubborn enough to stick to that forever. I'm only setting myself up for heartbreak.

On the other hand...what if it works?

What if my persistence pays off and I end up with everything I ever dreamed of?

I have to believe it's worth the risk.

The door opens, and a nurse walks in. "Time to check the baby's blood sugar," she says cheerfully.

Grayson hands Josephine back to Lincoln, and they prepare to do their little test while Grayson and I head back to the waiting room with his mom. A man and a woman who look vaguely familiar are standing there with a little boy, and Mrs. Nash runs over to them.

"Joanna!" she exclaims as she grabs the woman into a hug.

"Have you met her?" Joanna asks, and I assume this is Jolene's parents.

"She's precious. So perfect!" Mrs. Nash says, hugging Jolene's dad next. "The nurse came in, so we gave them some time. I'm sure Lincoln will be down to take you in soon."

Mrs. Nash makes the introductions between us all, and I learn the boy, Jonah, is Jolene's son and Lincoln's stepson. We all chat for a few minutes when, sure enough, Lincoln comes back.

"I'm going to run down to the cafeteria for some water," I say to Grayson. "Need anything?"

"A cup of coffee would be great. Just black."

"You got it," I say.

"I'll come with you," Mrs. Nash says to me.

Grayson glances at me to make sure that's okay, and I nod and smile. He heads down the hall with Lincoln, Jonah, and Jolene's parents, and Mrs. Nash and I turn in the opposite direction.

"It's so good to see you, sweetheart," Mrs. Nash says to me. She squeezes my arm.

"You, too, Mrs. Nash," I say, leaning into her a little.

"Stop that Mrs. Nash silliness. Call me Missy. And it's just us girls now. Tell me what's going on with you and my boy." She hits the button to call the elevator.

I giggle, not sure how much to tell her. So I dodge it instead. "That's probably a better question to ask him."

She raises a brow. "Do I need to have a talk with him?"

Oh, God. I have no idea what to say to that, so I just laugh. The elevator arrives empty, and we step on it together.

She fills the silence of the car. "For some reason, I always saw you ending up with my Spencer. Even way back when. There was always something about you even when you were much younger that told me you had a good head on your shoulders."

"Thank you for saying that. The truth is that I always had eyes for Grayson. He was my first crush." And my first bang, but I refrain from telling her that.

"How adorable is that? And now you two…" She trails off. "Well, I don't know what it is, but I saw him looking at you when you were holding the baby, and…" She doesn't end that sentence, either, and I'm dying to know what the ending is.

"And?" I prompt. I can't help myself.

"I'll be honest with you. He's never brought a girl around before. But when I saw him looking at you, I had the strangest feeling that he'd be next. Not Spence, who just got engaged. Definitely not Ash. But Gray." She shrugs a little. "There's just something about the way he looks at you. He's never looked at anyone like that before." Her eyes get a little misty, and I think mine do, too.

I want to tell her the truth about how I'm falling for him and he will never see me as anything other than his best friend's little sister, but I can't make myself form the words.

The elevator opens to the floor with the cafeteria, leaving the conversation behind us as we focus on the reason why we came down here.

But her words echo in my head. He's never looked at anyone like that before.

Maybe there's a chance for that happy ending for us after all.

Chapter 39: Grayson Nash

Risks Versus Regrets

I
t feels like an ambush…like she's been waiting all day to get me alone.

As if it wasn't bad enough that she decided to accompany Ava down to the cafeteria.

"What are you doing with that sweet girl?" my mother asks me when it's just the two of us.

I excused myself to the restroom shortly after Asher and my father arrived, and my mom said she had to go, too.

And now here we are, standing in an empty hallway near the restrooms, and I really do have to go take a piss, but now I have to answer to my mom. She raised four boys who all ended up playing football professionally. If you think this woman can't take every single one of us on, you'd be wrong.

"We're just having fun," I say, my tone more defensive than it should be.

"The way you were looking at her when she was holding Josephine was more than fun." She raises her brows pointedly.

"I don't really want to talk about this with you, Mother, and I have to use the restroom."

"She's young, honey. And she looks at you like you're her everything." Her voice is quiet as she ignores my words.

"It's complicated." I lower my voice and sigh. "We're faking it for the press for multiple reasons. She's Beckett's little sister, and

I know she has feelings for me, but I also know my track record, and I don't want to hurt her."

She closes her eyes and shakes her head as she purses her lips. "God, we really messed all four of you up." She draws in a long breath. "Your track record is meaningless, okay? If you like her—or more, whatever it is you might be feeling—you're doing more harm than good to both of you by pretending you don't."

"She said something similar," I admit.

"Then take the chance, Grayson. It's better to live with risks than regrets, don't you think?"

"Do you regret marrying Dad?" I ask. My voice sounds like a little kid's as I ask the question.

"Oh, honey," she says softly. She squeezes my bicep. "No. Not for a second. We were very happy for a long time despite the things I swept under the rug, and we wouldn't have the four most important people in my life if I hadn't spent all those years with him."

I nod as I consider all that. "Okay."

"I guess what I really want you to hear is that whatever happens, it'll turn out okay."

"You didn't hear Beckett, Mom. He asked me to check in on her. To protect her." I shake my head. "Not to take advantage of her and make her fall for me only to hurt her in the end."

"You don't know you will," she points out.

"Everything ends," I say, trying to mimic the pointed tone she used earlier as I hold out a hand to indicate her situation with my dad.

"You look in that room with that newborn baby, and you look at Linc and Jo's second chance twenty years after they first met. You still want to tell me everything is meant to end?" she asks.

It's something to consider, I guess. They battled their way back to each other, and it's working for them.

That doesn't mean it's meant to work for everybody else that way, but why can't I have that, too?

"Okay, now go pee," she says. "I just had to tell you that."

I chuckle and disappear into the bathroom, but her words play on my mind for the rest of the day.

It's a little after six when we're saying goodbye to the new parents for the night, and we're all gathered in the elevator when Asher says, "You all want to grab some dinner?"

I glance at Ava, who nods. "Count us in."

My parents and Spencer are in, too, and we make plans to meet in an hour at a Mexican restaurant at the Aria that Asher can't stop talking about.

We swing by Ava's place so she can change clothes, and the house is quiet as I wait for her in the kitchen. She's in a black dress when she emerges from her bedroom, and we've sort of avoided each other today as we each chatted with different members of my family. Or maybe we were avoiding each other on purpose because we weren't ready to face the reality of what's going on between us.

So I bring it up first…only, I'm not exactly sure *how* to bring it up. "You hung up on me last night."

"Yeah. You made me mad." She lifts a shoulder.

"Do you really believe what you said?"

"Which part?" Her tone is a little guarded.

I clear my throat. "The part about it hurting you more by not giving this a chance."

"Yeah. I do. You admitted you had feelings for me, but I think you're so convinced that you're doomed to fail at relationships that you're throwing in the towel without ever giving it a try. But what if it *doesn't* fail? What if it's everything we ever wanted?" she asks.

I shift my gaze to the counter. "I never wanted any of this." I lift my gaze to hers, and she looks like I struck her with a physical blow. "I know that sounded harsh, and I didn't mean it that way," I hurry to say. "I just meant that I never dreamed of this life with a wife and kids and a white picket fence."

"It doesn't have to be white," she says, a little teasing in her tone.

I chuckle. "I know. This is just all new to me, and it started with a lie, and that scares me, Ava. You kept a secret from me, and if there's one thing I've learned in my life, it's that secrets kill relationships. My dad kept secrets from my mom, and now they're getting divorced after forty fucking years. I can't just let it go, and being together with my whole family today even though my parents are apart..." I trail off, but the truth is that it's triggering me.

I'm just not sure what it's triggering me to do.

Ultimately, the way my dad treated Lincoln was what led to the divorce. Even when the kids are grown and gone, they can still fuck relationships up. Sure, my mom pointed out how happy Lincoln and Jolene are today, but will they always be that happy?

I have no idea.

And I don't know what the future holds for me, but despite the fears pulsing through me, after watching my brother and his wife and their baby today...

They were so happy.

Deliriously so.

I want to feel what it's like to be in love, and I think I could have that with Ava if I could just step over those fears and give this a real shot.

"I wish I knew how to earn your trust back." She takes a step toward me, and she touches my shoulder as I can't help but think to myself that she has it. She's proven that I can trust her over the last few weeks despite that first night together. It makes sense why she felt like she had to keep things from me, and I can't continue to hold that against her.

She's so close that I could just reach out and grab her.

I could pull her into me and never let her go.

"You know what scares me?" she asks quietly.

I lift my eyes to hers. "What?" I ask, my voice raspy and low.

"Everyone always leaves me. My dad, my mom, my brothers. Colin. I'm scared there's just something about me that makes people run, and I'm terrified you'll give this a shot with me only to eventually leave me, too."

"What if I do?" I ask softly.

"You won't." She says it so resolutely that I very nearly believe her.

"I wish I could make that promise to you. But I can't."

She tilts her head a little. "I know you can't, and that's okay. Whatever this is, if we decide to explore it and really give it a try, then we work through these things together. And if you leave, well…then I guess I pick myself up and figure it out."

I stare at her for a long time as I wrestle with myself, and eventually I lean in a little closer to her. My eyes flick to her lips.

I want to kiss her.

I've never wrestled with whether or not to kiss a woman before…and I guess that's part of what makes her different.

"Promise me you'll be okay," I whisper. "Promise me this won't change my friendship with your brother."

"You know I can't promise any of that, just like you can't promise me you won't leave," she says softly. "But try this with me anyway."

My eyes lock on hers, and as the feelings I've developed for her race through me, I know I can't deny this any longer.

My eyes flick to her lips again, and then I reach for her, loop an arm around her waist, and haul her into me.

I drop my mouth to hers, and she relaxes into me as she links her arms around my neck.

I hold her to me as tightly as I can, as if I'm trying to get inside her body even though we're both fully clothed.

Fuck that.

I need her naked.

Now.

I need to be inside her.

Now.

I hold myself back, though.

She's not like the other women who can take on this monster so easily—and I'm not sure if I'm talking about my cock or myself.

She deserves every piece of me, and for the first time in my life, I actually *want* to hand it all over.

I open my mouth to hers, and her tongue meets mine. They tango together as I run my hands down her body toward her ass. I reach under her dress and give myself the utter pleasure of squeezing her ass, and she moans into me.

Fuck.

That little sound out of her pulses every primal need inside me to hear it again.

I lift her up by her ass and set her on the counter, and she widens her legs to allow me to stand between them. I run my hands along her thighs and under the bottom of her dress as my mouth continues its assault on hers.

I reach for the side of her panties, and I yank before I slide one finger through her.

I groan as I feel how wet she is.

"Oh, God," she moans into my mouth, and *yes*, that's exactly what I needed to hear to spur me to action.

I push my finger into her wet heat, and she gasps into my mouth as I keep kissing her. She's still holding on around my neck, and she widens her legs a little more to give me more space to work with.

I thrust my finger in and out of her, and she shifts as she holds onto me, fisting my T-shirt before digging her nails into my shoulders. She moans with every slow, languid thrust in, and when I pull my finger out to coat her clit with her own wetness, I'm rewarded with a sweet gasp followed by a cry of need. I growl as the need to chase my own release starts to pull at me.

I slide my finger back in and add a second one this time, and she's so fucking wet. She's primed and ready for me, and I want with everything inside me to slide into that tight, sweet cunt.

I didn't bring any condoms with me, though.

Or lube, not that she needs it.

I nibble on her neck for a few beats before I suck her earlobe into my mouth, and then I ask softly, "Where are the condoms?"

She freezes for a beat, and I pull back to catch her eyes with mine even though my fingers don't stop driving into her.

Hers are hazy and heated as she says, "I, uh…I don't have any. Kelly might."

I nod. "Where?"

She shrugs, and it's probably weird to have a conversation about her roommate while I'm fingering her, so I drop my lips back to hers as I drive into her a few more times, picking up the pace a bit to a steady rhythm before I pull my fingers out, leaving her teetering on a needy edge.

"Don't stop, Grayson. Please don't stop," she begs.

Jesus.

Why is hearing her beg me so fucking hot?

I stare down at her for a few beats, feeling like the most powerful man in the world as I hold her pleasure in my literal hands. I drop my lips to hers again for a short kiss, and then I kneel down. The counter is about at the perfect height for me to treat myself to a delicious meal of pussy.

I push her knees open wider, and I slide my tongue through her folds that are slick with need. The tang of her flavor is fucking addicting, and as I push my tongue inside her, she leans back, her palms on the counter behind her as she thrusts her pussy against my face.

I slide my fingers back into her, and I take her clit between my lips. As I suck on it, her hips buck toward me as she becomes greedy for pleasure.

Her thighs start to quiver, and I know she's right at the edge. I suck a little harder and thrust my fingers a little faster.

"Oh, God, yes, yes, yes!" she moans as her pussy tightens around my fingertips and a fierce orgasm rips through her. She clings onto me, her fingernails clawing at my neck as the pulses of pleasure surround her.

I keep driving my fingers into her and sucking on her clit as she crests through her release. I kiss her thigh as she lies fully back on the counter, and I murmur against her skin. "Fuck, baby. That gorgeous cunt feels so tight and perfect." My voice is low as I think about how much I want her wrapped around my cock.

I'm not sure how we went from *you hung up on me last night* to *this*, but I'll take this over fighting every damn day of the week.

All I can do is hope that I can figure out a way to break my historical pattern of fucking everything up. Because right now, in this moment, there's nothing I want more than to be able to make those promises to her as I do everything I can to hold onto her.

Chapter 40: Ava Maxwell

He Wants to Have Sex. Again. With Me.

He pulls his fingers out of me, and a long, deep, satisfied sigh escapes me as he slips my panties back into place. Once the waves of pleasure have waned, I finally sit up and open my eyes to find his. His normally bright blue eyes are black as night with lust, and I'm not sure I've ever seen a hotter sight in my twenty-five years on this Earth.

It's Grayson Nash. It's still absolutely surreal to me that he's any part of my life at all, and now he's admitted he has feelings for me that he can no longer deny.

It's like in the recesses of my mind, of course this was going to happen. It makes perfect sense. We were always destined to end up right here.

But I still can't believe it's actually happening.

It's a literal dream come true. *He* is a literal dream come true, and whatever that crush was has definitely found its way to something deeper, something *real*, something terrifying. Something mutual. Something perfect.

He lifts to a stand, and I tip my chin up. His lips find mine, and he kisses me again in that way he has—it's slow and tender and beautiful, and at the same time it's deep and urgent and needy.

I want to…*return the favor*, but I also am not fully sure I can move right now since my entire body feels like very satisfied Jell-O.

Oh, and condoms.

He said he wants condoms.

He wants to have sex. Again. With me.

My brain might be malfunctioning a little at the thought of it.

I force myself to pull back. "Do, uh…do you want me to…?"

Pull it together, Ava. Stop being so awkward.

"To?" he prompts, not sure what I'm trying to ask.

"To make you come?" My cheeks burn as I say it, but if he catches onto my awkwardness, he doesn't acknowledge it.

His eyes burn into mine. "I want your mouth on my cock possibly more than anything I've ever wanted. But we need to get to dinner, and I'd rather save it for tonight when I get you back to my hotel suite."

I draw in a breath as I realize we're about to head to dinner with his entire family, and his breath is going to smell like my pussy.

My cheeks burn at the thought.

"Are you sure?" I ask.

He shakes his head with a wry smile. "No. But we're already late."

"Do you, uh, want some gum or something?"

He shakes his head. "Fuck no. I don't want anything taking away the aftertaste of your hot cunt."

That word used to make my skin crawl, but somehow hearing it out of his mouth after he just had said mouth on said body part…I'm nearly ready to combust all over again.

"Okay. So, we're just going to sit across the table from your mom with your mouth glistening with my wetness. Cool, cool."

He laughs. "Maybe a quick stop in your bathroom to wash my hands."

"Be my guest," I say, sweeping an arm in that direction. He heads that way, and I slowly get down from the counter, my legs still a little shaky after all that. I use the bathroom next, passing by him in the hallway, and then we head toward the restaurant.

"Will it be weird being with your whole family minus Lincoln?" I ask when we're on our way.

He shrugs. "Maybe a little. Would it be weird with your family if one brother was missing from dinner?"

I shake my head. "Nah. I talk to Beck the most, and even that is fairly limited. He's busy with the kids and work. And Oliver's in Chicago, Alex is in Philly. Everyone's busy being successful at young ages, and I'm the black sheep in Vegas working at a bakery after blowing my life savings on a dumb skincare line."

He reaches over to set his hand on my thigh. "I'd hardly call you a black sheep, Ava."

I lift a shoulder. "Feels that way sometimes. I mean, Oliver's the youngest senior software developer at his firm. Alex just finished his schooling, and he's the youngest anesthesiologist on his staff. Beck's the youngest senior partner at his firm. Everyone is doing these amazing things, and I'm stuck in neutral."

"Didn't you invent that special recipe that's the bestseller at your bakery?" he asks.

"Yeah. Fat lot of good it's doing me."

"Stop," he says, taking my hand in his and threading his fingers through mine. "It's incredible. You're working toward your dreams, and owning a bakery is a huge and expensive dream, but I have every faith in you that you'll make it happen, and it'll be the best bakery Vegas has ever seen."

"Thanks, Gray. That's really sweet of you to say."

Financially, I'm fine. I can afford rent and living expenses with what I make at the bakery, and I still have enough to tuck a bit into savings each month. Eventually I'll reach my goal. I know I will.

But I also know Grayson has a lot of money, and I never, ever want him to think that's something I'm after.

Still, it's like he senses it, and he addresses it without making it weird. "Hey, what would you think about maybe baking some shit for my teammates when we're in season, and I could pay you for it?"

"I'd do it for free," I say.

"I know you would. But I also know you're saving for a dream, and maybe I could contract you on the side for cookies or granola bars or something. It's a win-win. I get to bring something for my teammates, you get to make a little side cash."

It takes me all of two seconds to think it over. "On one condition."

He glances over at me with narrowed eyes.

"You have to be my taste tester. I refuse to send in something to your team without knowing it's up to par."

He chuckles, and he lets go of my hand to stick his out toward me to shake. "It's a deal."

We arrive at the restaurant, and Asher, Spencer, Missy, and Eddie Nash are all waiting for us at a large round table.

Grayson takes the seat beside Asher, and I slip in beside Missy.

"What was the hold-up?" Asher asks loudly, and Grayson gives him a *shut-the-fuck-up* kind of look as he reaches for the chips and salsa. "Ohhh," Asher says knowingly.

My cheeks burn.

So that's how this meal is going to go.

I order a margarita, which Missy is drinking, and Grayson gets a Dos Equis, which all three men sitting at the table are also drinking.

I peruse the menu, and so far, the company isn't all bad despite the earlier teasing. Eddie is sitting on Asher's other side, so Grayson's parents are separated with Spencer in between them—which is a good thing since they really don't seem too keen on interacting with each other. It's not to the point where it's awkward—at least not to me, an outsider—but it's still noticeable.

"When are we going to get to meet Amelia?" Missy asks Spencer. "I thought for sure you'd bring her this weekend."

"I wanted this weekend to be about Lincoln and Jolene, and I knew it'd be a circus to bring her," he says. He's definitely the quietest out of the Nash brothers. He seems the most serious of the four boys, though I don't know any of them that well apart from spending the day with them today.

"Have you two picked a date yet?" his mom asks.

"You'll be the first to know when we do. I'm not really in any rush," he says, and he picks up his Dos Equis.

"Turning thirty and not in a rush," Missy says. She glances at Grayson as if to note that he's over thirty, and then there's the baby, Asher—at twenty-seven. "At least I have one grandbaby."

"Leave 'em alone, Miss," Eddie scolds from across the table.

She just purses her lips then lifts her margarita, and we start up a side conversation about the bakery while the men talk football.

All in all, it's a fun meal with the Nash family, and I feel more and more like I fit in with them.

I like that feeling, but the anticipation of what's coming next is absolutely killing me. I know he already got me off once tonight, but knowing his plan is to take me back to his hotel and bang me is making me want to rush through the meal so we can get to the dessert course.

Eventually it does come to an end, and we say our goodbyes.

"Will we see you tomorrow?" Missy asks me, and I glance at Grayson.

"If she wants to come," he says.

I smile. "My boss told me to take two days off, so I'd love to be there."

She gives me a hug. "I've loved spending time with you today, sweetheart."

"You, too, Missy," I say, and I squeeze her.

When I glance up at Grayson, I can't quite read what's on his face. But something tells me he likes seeing me with his mom.

I like it, too.

When we pull in front of the Palms, Grayson grabs my hand and leans down toward my ear. "You want me to take you on a date first like last time, or are you ready for me to take you upstairs so I can fuck you?"

My cheeks turn bright red. "Upstairs," I say stupidly, and he laughs then pulls my hand as we practically run through the casino toward the elevators.

There's another couple on the elevator this time, so we force ourselves not to make out. When the doors open on our floor, we head down the hallway toward his suite, and the second the door closes behind us, he grabs me into his arms as his lips slam down to mine.

Yes. This. This right here. It's exactly what I've been waiting for all night.

We kiss near the doorway, and he backs us up until I bump into a wall. I'm a little tipsy from the two margaritas I had, but he only had the one beer.

His hands move up and down my torso as I slip my fingers into his hair, and then he wraps his arms around me and buries his face in my neck as he draws in a deep breath.

It's sweet and romantic, as if he's breathing me in for sustenance, and I pull back a little as he does, too. His eyes meet mine.

"You were...God. Tonight was perfect, Av. I loved seeing you with my family. I loved knowing this moment would come, that I'd get you back to my hotel room so I could fuck you until neither of us could see straight. I loved the anticipation of wanting to kiss you, wanting to hold you, wanting to sleep next to you. What the fuck are you doing to me?"

I don't know how to answer that, so I just press my lips to his. The words come as I back up in a haze of lust. "The same thing you're doing to me."

His mouth crashes back down to mine, and we kiss there against the wall near the entry for a while. Eventually, he pulls back and lifts my dress over my head, depositing it on the floor beside us. I pull his shirt over his head, too, and drop it on top of my dress, and then I go for his belt buckle.

"Hang on. I'll be right back." He disappears for a beat, and when he returns, he's standing in his boxer briefs and holding a condom and a bottle of what looks like lube. He takes my hand and leads me over toward the couch, and he sets the condom and the bottle down on the cushion while I kick off my shoes. He slides my panties down my legs and unhooks my bra. He pulls his boxer briefs off, too, and we're both standing naked in the living room of his suite.

He pulls me into his arms, and I feel his cock as it nestles between us. I tip my head back, and our eyes meet, exchanging a heated and intimate moment before he lowers his mouth to mine.

Thrills light up my chest as anticipation for this moment climbs through my spine. I've been waiting for another chance at this since we parted ways the last time, and I can't believe it's really happening.

He opens his mouth to mine, and he kisses me slowly, that magical tongue of his moving skillfully against mine as I kiss back with everything I have, pushing every longing feeling I've had for him for a decade into this kiss.

His scruff is rough against my mouth, and I'm reminded of the way it tickled my thighs earlier. A pulsing ache rockets through my core as he shifts his hips, and then he pulls back, licks his two fingers with his eyes on mine, and he moves his hand down to push those two wet fingers right into me.

I grip onto his shoulders as I close my eyes at the feel, and he grunts as he feels how wet I already am.

"Open your eyes," he orders, and my eyes fly open as they land on his. "That's better. I want you looking at me while I finger fuck you. I want you to know who's doing this to you. I want you thinking only of me."

"I *do* only think of you," I protest, my voice breathless and needy.

"That's right, you do," he says, and he shoves his fingers in a little harder. "And this pussy? It's mine."

"Yes, Grayson," I groan as I fight the urge to close my eyes and give into the pressure building.

His eyes flash at me. "I'm the only man who's ever fucked it."

"Oh, God," I moan as he shoves those fingers in and curls them up.

"Tell me it's mine," he demands.

"It's yours. Only yours. Forever yours." Oh my God. What did I just say? Did I just say *forever* as if we might have an actual future together?

I expect him to freeze, or freak out, or…something. But that's not at all what I get.

His eyes grow even more heated as he holds his fingers inside me for a few beats, curling them upward in this way that makes me want to come, but then it all stops.

"Only mine," he repeats. "Now bend over the couch so I can show you how I take care of what's mine."

I scramble over to the armrest and bend over it, and I hear the rip of the condom wrapper. I turn around and watch him over my shoulder as he slides it on, and he strokes himself a few times, letting out a low grunt as he does it.

The whole view is like something I dreamed of in a sexy fantasy, but this is my reality.

He grabs the bottle of lube from the couch, and I hear him squeeze the bottle.

And then I feel his heat as he moves in behind me. He slides his finger through me again then grabs onto my hip with one hand while he aligns himself with my slit. He glides through me and lands on my clit, and he teases me there for a few beats before he slides his giant cock up to push himself all the way into me.

We both moan once he's all the way in, and he holds himself steady as my body gets used to his size. It's not painful at all this time, but he's stretching me to fit all the way in, and all that lube is just making him feel like heaven.

He pulls back and slowly eases forward again, going deep into me, and I have the sudden need for friction.

"Can you go faster?" I ask, my voice a little low, a little tentative.

"It's okay to tell me what you want, baby," he grunts. He picks up the pace a little, and it feels so good. So damn good.

But it's still not enough. I want him to push me to the edge.

"Faster," I say with a little more confidence this time.

He moves a little faster, and God, yes, it's so good.

"Tell me what you want," he demands.

I feel weird saying it, but I do it anyway. "Touch my nipples."

My breasts swing beneath me, and he reaches around to grasp one of them in his palm. He takes my nipple between his thumb and the side of his forefinger and rolls it, and yes, that's exactly what I needed.

"Oh God, yes!" I scream.

He's bucking into me more wildly now with shorter strokes, and I can tell he's getting close.

He's still gripping my hip with his other hand, his fingers digging in as he tries to hold himself off so we can come together.

He leans over me so I can feel his heat along my spine, and his lips find my neck as he continues to pound into me and roll my nipple. He lets go of the one to grapple for the other, and his hot, growly moans as he pounds into me are going to be my undoing.

"Fuck, Ava, your pussy is so goddamn tight. Tell me again how this is my cunt," he grunts.

"It's yours, Grayson. Only yours." My own voice sounds like a whiny cry to me, but it spurs him on as he lets go of my hip to reach for my other breast.

"These tits are mine, too," he declares.

"You own me," I cry. "All of me."

"You're goddamn right, I do," he says, and he rolls both my nipples as he drives into me a little harder, a little faster.

I cry out as my body starts to tighten, and then he reaches down with one of his hands to caress my clit as he slows the shorter thrusts to long, deep strokes—as if he knows exactly what my body needs before I need to ask him.

It's my undoing.

I scream out incoherently, some mix of his name and the fact that I'm coming and a bunch of curse words, as my body tightens and contracts beneath him. He moans as he feels my come drenching his cock, and he glides easily in and out of me as he waits through my release. It's long and it hits me hard, and once it starts to slow, my body trembles.

He moves his hands back to my hips as he keeps plunging into me with those deep, wonderfully slower thrusts. I want to make him come, too, so I reach down between us and make a V with my first and second fingers around his cock as it slides in and out of me. I twist my hand and reach a little lower with my other fingers to grasp lightly onto his balls.

"Holy fuck," he says, and I feel his balls tighten in my gasp. A loud roar fills the room as he starts to come, and I keep doing exactly what I'm doing as he rides out his orgasm. As soon as he's done, he pulls out of me and helps me up, spinning me around before grabbing me up into his arms—literally. He's carrying me like I weigh nothing, and his cloudy, hazy eyes fall to mine. He presses his lips to mine gently before pulling back. "Jesus Christ, Ava. That was…" He trails off as his eyes glaze over.

"Amazing," I say softly.

He nods, and he carries me around the couch, through the bedroom, and to the bathroom. He sets me on the ledge of the tub then turns on the water and runs a washcloth under it. He returns to me, and I expect him to just hand me the washcloth, but he doesn't. He pushes my knees open then uses the washcloth to wipe me clean before he takes care of the condom.

He's quiet during the process, and I wish I knew what he was thinking.

I wish I could tell him what I'm thinking, and maybe I will. Or maybe it'll scare us both for me to admit that I'm head over freaking heels in love with this guy.

"I'll give you a minute," he says softly, and he leaves the bathroom, closing the door behind him.

My body is warm and tingly after that. It was only my second time, but it was in a completely different league from the first.

This time, mutual feelings were involved, and it was absolutely magical.

I only hope he's feeling the same things I am and that I'm not just setting myself up for an epic heartbreak.

Chapter 41: Grayson Nash

I'll Never Know If You Don't Tell Me

I pull a pair of shorts on and stand by the window, looking out over the Strip as I wait for her. I'm holding a glass of straight gin in my palm, and I made her a vodka cranberry that's perched on the table beside me.

Jesus.

That was…

I still can't quite come up with the word for it.

It wasn't just the sex. It was the entire day. Seeing her with my family—with my mom. Feeling like she has a place with us. Holding her own against my father, not that they interacted all that much. Feeling like I had a safe space if I needed one, which sometimes happens in this family full of incredibly hard-headed men.

Amazing, incredible, fantastic—none of them quite encapsulate everything that I was feeling when she told me I am the sole owner of her pussy *forever*.

Terrifying, alarming, shocking—those aren't quite it, either, though they're definitely a part of it.

One word keeps pulsing around my brain, and I'm scared to even acknowledge it.

My brain does the work for me.

Love, Grayson. It's fucking love. You're in love with her.

I am.

I realized it the very second I slid into her. It felt like home.

It's been a long time since I've felt at home anywhere. With this line of work, nothing is guaranteed, so as much as we call a place home and try to make the best of it while we're lucky enough to be there, it's fleeting.

Ava, though? She feels like forever.

No admission I've ever made has been more terrifying.

And to teach her to ask for her pleasure, to demand what she wants, to be the one making sure she's happy, making sure she's getting what she deserves—it's the honor of a lifetime.

I see her emerge from the direction of the bedroom as I spot movement in the reflection of the glass.

"There you are," she says softly. She moves closer to me, and I don't turn around until she's right behind me.

"I made you a drink," I say, and I grab it off the table and hand it over. She's wearing one of my T-shirts. It's huge on her, and somehow it's hot as fuck.

"That was sweet of you." She clinks her glass to mine, and I'm not sure what we're toasting. She's standing right next to me, but it feels too far away. We're quiet for a beat as we each sip our drink. "What are you thinking about?"

That I'm in love with you.

I clear my throat. "How incredible you are."

"The sex?" she asks.

"Well, yeah. But not just the sex. It's everything about you. You weren't sure how to tell me you wanted it faster, but when you asked for it, it was so goddamn hot."

"Oh," she says, and she ducks her head a little.

"Don't be embarrassed, Ava. I'll never know if you don't tell me."

"Okay. Well, then, on that note…I liked it when you were being all demanding and making me tell you that you own me. It was so, like, aggressive and cocky and erotic and hot at the same time."

"You liked that?" I ask.

She nods slowly and hides behind taking another sip, and I'm not sure what it is about her—maybe the easily corruptible innocence—but Christ, I'm already in deep.

"You tell me when it's too much, okay?" I request, and she nods.

I have no doubt that she will. She says what's on her mind, and that's one of the very things I've fallen for. And the more we're together like this, the more we experience together, the more we'll find what works for us. The more we'll fall into an easy pattern together.

The more we'll fall.

I chug what's left in my glass for liquid courage, and then I set it down on the table. I take hers and set it down, too, and then I pull her into my arms.

She leans her head on my chest as we look out the window together at the magic of the lights illuminating the Strip.

I draw in a deep breath. The words are on the tip of my tongue.

"This is nice," she says with a soft sigh.

It *is* nice. It's incredible, if I'm being honest, and it's what I want going forward. I want to close on my new house, and I want her to be there when I get home. I want to stand near our patio doors overlooking the Strip much further away in the distance as I hold her in my arms. I want her in the stands wearing number twenty-four as she cheers our team to victory.

I want a life with her, and it's confusing as fuck because I've never felt like this before.

But just like I told her... *I'll never know if you don't tell me.* It works in reverse, too. She'll never know if I don't tell her.

And so, before I lose my nerve, I shift us so I'm looking down at her and she's looking up at me.

"You okay?" she asks, her brows pushing together with concern.

"I think I'm in love with you." I blurt the words before I can stop them.

A soft gasp of surprise escapes her, and she stares at me, her eyes searching mine. She doesn't say anything, and now I feel stupid for telling her, for scaring her, for…whatever this is.

But then she touches my jaw with her fingertips, and she rises up to her tiptoes. She presses her lips to mine. She breaks apart from me and lands back on her heels, and then she says, "I think I've been in love with you for half my life."

My eyes soften as I stare down at her, and then my lips fall to hers. We kiss there in front of the window, two souls who were maybe meant to run into each other that night at the Gridiron here in Vegas despite having first met in New York all those years ago.

I'm lost in the moment, lost in her, lost in everything about this day. It's the first time since we ran into each other that she took an entire day off to spend it with me, and it feels like somehow saying those words is the perfect endcap to this day.

Eventually, I take her hand and lead her to the bedroom, where we fall into bed. We're kissing again—or making out, really, with me hovering over the top of her—and I have the sudden need to make love to her. I have this primal, carnal urge to be inside her with nothing between us.

The monster down below is locked and loaded.

I pull back and murmur my question. "Are you on birth control?"

She shakes her head. "No. I, uh…never really had any need to be."

I nod as the words from earlier hit me over the head again. I own that pussy. It's mine.

And I'm going to claim it again.

"Right," I mutter. "We should fix that."

"I'll call my doctor tomorrow."

"I need to be inside you again." I trail my hand down to her thigh, and I reach around to grip her ass as I push my hips to hers.

"Now?" she asks.

"Yes."

"Yes," she agrees, drawing out the word on a moan.

I was smart enough to leave the box of condoms on the nightstand, so I reach over and grab one. I yank my shorts down and roll it on, and she's still wearing just my shirt. I put my knees on either side of her body, and I reach under the shirt she's wearing to feel her breasts. I lift the shirt up a little and kiss the valley between her breasts as I shape them around my cheeks, and then I lift up and suck one of her nipples into my mouth.

Her hips rise off the bed at the feel of it, and I take the moment to reach down and feel if she's ready for me.

She is. She always is.

I line myself up and push my cock into her. I hold myself up with one arm, and I start with those long, deep strokes—the ones that allow me to feel her tight pussy as it clenches over me. I want to make it last longer, but I know she likes the shorter, faster strokes—the ones that will push me to the finish line way, way too fast.

But it's okay. Even if this moves too quickly, we have tomorrow.

That's something I've never counted on before, but it's something I'm actually looking forward to with her.

She moans as I keep the pace slow, and I know she's enjoying it. We don't need the quick release we were both craving earlier. We can take our time and enjoy the feel of each other. I'm too tall to get a tit in my mouth while I'm fucking her, so I reach up just to feel her tight nipple between my fingers as I press my mouth to hers again. Her tongue fights its way into my mouth, and she moans as her tongue batters mine. It's hot and primal, and I can't help but pick up the pace. She wraps her legs around me, urging me into her deeper with her feet pushing against my ass, and the old, familiar fire tears through me.

But it's different this time. As I let her know I'm coming, an unfamiliar warmth fills my chest. My eyes meet hers as her pussy takes every last drop out of me, and she rolls right into her own orgasm. Her fingernails dig into my back as her body takes over, filling her with pleasure as her pussy clenches onto me and holds me in place. I'm powerless to move as I watch her give in, her face twisting and her body quaking in the most beautiful way.

When it's all over, we each take our turn in the bathroom, and I pull her shirt off so we can both sleep naked in each other's arms.

It's warm and comfortable, and I play big spoon as I wrap her into my arms.

I love you. I want to say the words. If I don't tell her, she won't know.

But saying *I think I'm in love with you* and saying *I love you* are worlds apart, and I'm not quite ready for the heavy admission.

Someday, I will be. Someday, we'll get there. But right now, I'm basking in the place we're at.

I'm almost asleep when she asks, "Do you think we should tell Beck it's not fake anymore?"

I'm not sure how to answer that. On the one hand...yes. Absolutely. On the other, this is still so new, and I'm dreading that conversation. I decide to throw it to fate as I answer sleepily. "What do you think?"

She traces a little circle on my chest. "I think we should wait. Explore, get to know one another, fall harder. He's across the country. What he doesn't know won't hurt him."

"Works for me. Oh, and if I haven't mentioned this yet, I loved spending the day with you today. You should quit your job since we'll have events to attend on weekends coming up."

"I can't," she says, and there's a hint of apology in her tone. "You know I need to save up for my own bakery."

I think fast. "Then cut your hours, and I'll pay you to bake for me." I already offered this deal once, and I'll keep offering it until she takes me up on it.

She sighs softly. "Maybe."

I shift to hover over her again, and I drop my lips to her neck in the darkness of night in our hotel room. She arches back a little to give me more space.

"Say yes," I murmur against her skin.

"Oh my God," she moans. "Okay, fine, yes."

I laugh as I roll off her and settle in beside her.

"You play dirty."

"Maybe. But I also get my way." I lean over to kiss her again.

"Good thing we're on the same page."

She's not wrong, and it pulses yet another new fear in me. What if one day, we're *not* on the same page?

Who's going to win?

Chapter 42: Ava Maxwell

I Want You There When I Get Home

I spend Sunday with Grayson and his family.

We're all in Jolene's private suite at the hospital cooing over the baby when I hear Lincoln ask Asher and Grayson, "Are you two dickheads ready for minicamp?"

"I thought it was voluntary," Grayson says. I can tell from his light tone that he's teasing his brother.

"Well, you're being voluntold that your ass better be there," he says.

Grayson and I haven't talked about minicamp or when it is or what that means.

I think there's a *lot* we haven't talked about.

We haven't had a chance, though. This is all still really new and fresh, just sealed into perfection twice last night (and once this morning), and we're feeling things out.

But does minicamp mean we'll be away from each other? And for how long?

And what's the season going to be like? Is he different in season than he is out of it?

Maybe he's right. If our time together will be limited once the season gets underway and our routine shifts, maybe it makes sense for me to quit my job. You know, in the future. When and if things get serious so we can maximize the time we have together.

Are things serious *now* for us?

I'm not sure.

It *feels* pretty damn serious after the admissions we made last night, and I did tell him I'd cut back hours at the bakery to make myself more available for events with him. But I still need a paycheck if I ever want to reach my dreams. I can't be a woman who gives up on my own dreams for my man...even if my man was technically my dream before the bakery was.

It's on our way back to my place in the evening that I finally ask the questions on my mind. "What's minicamp?"

"It's basically non-contact practice for a few days toward the end of April. Individual drills, routines, position practice, things like that. Since I'm new to the team, it would be good to put in face time with the coaches and my teammates."

"So you'll be gone?"

He shakes his head. "It's held at the practice facility across from the Gridiron, so I'll be in town but gone all day."

"When's your new place going to be ready?" I ask.

"I just got word that it's closing on the first of May. So just a few more weeks."

"Do, uh..." I feel awkward asking. "Have you thought any more about moving in with me while you wait rather than wasting all that money on a suite at the Palms?"

I suppose money's not an object to him, but my guess is that what he's paying for that suite over the next few weeks would be enough capital for my bakery.

I don't mention that, obviously. I'm not with him for his money.

"I mean...Ellie said it would look good if we did. It would make things easier for the press." He clears his throat, and then he glances over at me.

I feel a twinge of disappointment spear me in the stomach at his words.

"I don't care about the press, though, Av." He reaches over and grabs my hand in his. "I want to spend as much time with

274

you as I can before the season starts and everything gets thrown into chaos."

My chest warms at his words. "Really?"

He nods. "Really. And I want you to think about moving in with me when my place is ready."

"What?" I gasp.

"It just makes sense," he says, rushing his words. "It's closer to the Strip, it has a bigger kitchen so you can bake for the team…"

He's not wrong, but I was hoping there was more of a personal reason why he asked.

And then he assures me there is.

"And I want you there when I get home."

Tears pinch behind my eyes at the sweet sentiment. He could've said any number of things—he wants to have more sex, or it's easier for the press to catch us together…but he didn't say those things.

He said he wants *me* there.

And that means more than I thought it would.

I don't answer because I'm not sure I'm ready to move out of the house I've shared with Kelly since we graduated from college, though, to be honest, I haven't spent much time with her lately.

If she's not working, I am—or I'm out with Grayson. It isn't until a few days later that we're finally home at the same time.

"Pizza and Doritos?" I propose.

"And vodka, obviously," she says with a grin, and I nod as I call up our favorite pizza place to place our usual order.

She meets me on the couch with vodka drinks, and she starts in first. "So what's going on with you and Grayson?"

I think my smile must give me away because she squeals.

I giggle. "It's kind of crazy. I yelled at him that night when you saw the photo, he called me the next morning to go with him to meet his niece, and something changed when I spent the day with him and his family."

"He saw you in it," she says, nodding meaningfully.

"I don't know. Maybe. And I need to tell you something."

"You banged him again?"

"Well, yeah. A few times, actually. But that's not it."

She giggles, but I stay serious. "What is it, Avelina?"

"Is it okay if Grayson stays here with us for a while until his place is ready?"

"Of course! I didn't realize you two were already *there*. That's amazing!" She throws her arms around me, and a little of her drink sloshes over the side and onto the couch. "Oh shit," she says, and she jumps up to grab a towel to dab it up.

"And, uh, there's more…" I say as she scrubs at the couch.

"What's more?" she asks a little absently.

"He asked me to move in with him once his place is ready."

"He…he…" She freezes and drops the towel as her eyes meet mine. "Are you serious?"

I nod slowly as I await her reaction.

"Oh my God, Ava! That's amazing!" She throws her arms around me. "I'm so happy for you!"

"But what about rent? What will we do?"

She shrugs. "We'll figure it out. I can move to a one-bedroom somewhere, or I'll see if there's someone at school looking for a roommate, or whatever. I'm not going to be the one to hold you back from everything you've dreamed of."

I squeeze her. "You're the best friend in the world, do you know that?"

"Yeah, I do." She grins at me, and I have this feeling things are going to work out for both of us.

The next couple weeks pass in a bit of a blur.

Between him leaving the Palms to stay at my place, attending events on his arm so we're photographed for the press, trying our hardest to make sure Beck still believes we're faking it, having lots of sex where we're *not* faking it, visiting Grayson's niece, and slipping in hours at work in between everything, suddenly it's the Monday morning that minicamp begins, and Grayson is up and at 'em bright and early.

I head into the bakery to fill the hours while he's gone, but I'm still home before four. He isn't.

I don't hear from him all day, which feels…odd. I know he's busy. He's bonding with his teammates. He's getting to know a whole new routine with a brand-new team. He's spent so much of his time with me over the last month and a half since he first arrived in Vegas that he hasn't gotten much bonding time with anyone else.

I have to admit, I kind of liked not having to share him.

Since he moved in with Kelly and me two weeks ago, I have been the one leaving to go to work. I cut back from close to sixty hours a week at the bakery to thirty, and most of the time I spend there is baking my cookies.

I miss decorating cakes and cookies, but the tradeoff is charity events and concerts and nightclubs with Grayson.

He has invitations to different events nearly every night, but he picks and chooses the ones he wants to go to. He's in high demand, especially since he's new to town, and there's something really damn special about being the woman he wants on his arm at all these events.

Beckett has checked in with me a few times to make sure I'm okay with this arrangement, and I've assured him I am. We haven't told him I'm moving in with him just yet.

We get through those three days of minicamp, and we find ourselves spending yet another weekend together as we prepare for the closing on Grayson's new house in the morning.

It's as we're lying together in my small bed in the afterglow of another exhausting release after an appearance at a nightclub tonight that Grayson says, "I need a snack after that round."

I giggle, and we both put on clothes and head out to the kitchen, where we happen to run into Kelly.

And she's not alone.

"Graham," Grayson says with a nod.

They're on different sides of the ball, so I'm not sure if they had much interaction at their minicamp. I do recall Grayson mentioning that Austin plays the same position as Asher, though, so I wonder how important these minicamps are for the coaching staff to determine who will start.

I'm happy for Kelly, but I'm also worried for her.

"Nash," Austin says back. He eyes Grayson a little warily, and there's something in his eyes that I can't quite identify.

An awkward beat passes between the four of us. "Anybody hungry?" I ask.

"We were just heading to bed," Kelly says, setting her glass down on the counter. She gives me one of those looks that tells me she's ecstatic he's here, so I give her an encouraging nod before they head out of the room.

I dig through the pantry for something to eat, and Grayson searches the shelves beside me.

"Damn shame," he mutters.

"What is?" I ask. I half expect him to make some comment about Austin, but he doesn't.

"No Tootsie Rolls in here." He purses his lips and shakes his head disapprovingly, and all I can do is laugh.

He grabs a loaf of bread and takes it over to the stove. "Grilled cheese?"

"You're cooking?" I ask.

He nods. "As long as you have cheese and butter, this is my specialty."

I open the fridge and grab what he needs, and I set it on the counter. "I am all in."

I perch on the counter next to where he's cooking, and while we wait in between steps, he slips in between my legs and leans in for soft kisses.

I feel giddy. Butterflies are flapping wildly, and my engine is revving, and I feel like I want to kick my feet in the air with happiness.

All I can do is live in the moment and pray there isn't some rocket on its way to collide with this feeling.

But that look Austin gave Grayson is still in the back of my mind, and I'm worried he, or Colin, or some woman from Gray's past, is just waiting for the moment to blow this all up.

Chapter 43: Grayson Nash

You Know How Much I Love to Eat Your Cookie

Ava heads to the bakery the next morning, and I head to the title company to sign off on my new place. I get the keys, and I meet the moving company along with the internet guy at my new house.

I have the basics, and they make quick work of unpacking my stuff—including unpacking boxes and putting items away. I'll find what I need when I need it.

Ava hasn't packed yet to move in with me, but to be fair, we've been busy.

I found out the lease on her house expires in June. They moved in when they graduated three years ago, and we haven't really talked about what she wants to do about that.

Having her move in with me is fast, and I want her to still have that out if she needs it. I want her to be able to get together with her friend and have girl time whenever she wants. I don't want her sitting alone at this big ass house while I'm traveling during the season if she doesn't *want* to be in this big ass house all alone.

So I make a decision. I just haven't shared it with her quite yet, and knowing how stubborn she can be, I'm not sure she's going to like it.

I'm doing it anyway.

The doorbell rings a little after lunchtime, just after the internet company finishes their installation. I head over to open it, and I find Travis Woods standing there.

He's a wide receiver for the Aces, and in the back of my mind I remember my realtor telling me that he lives in this neighborhood.

"Hey, neighbor," he says. "You know that's my house, right?" He points to the one two doors down from me. "My wife made me bring this over." He hands the basket he's holding in his hands over to me.

I chuckle as I glance at the contents of the basket—a bottle of Hendricks, a couple tumblers, and a spread of cheese, sausage, and crackers. "That was nice of your wife. Be sure to thank her for me." I pull the bottle of gin out. "Want to come in?"

He makes a face. "Not for gin, but for the company? Sure."

I open the door wider, and he steps in. He glances around as I lead him toward the kitchen, and we both look out the back at my pool.

"Nice place," he says.

"Thanks. I didn't have anything to do with the design, really, but I'm happy with it."

We're making small talk, and I'm debating where to take this conversation next. I can't really comment on the coaching staff since I'm not sure how careful I need to be given that my brother is the head coach, and I don't know my teammates very well since I've been a little busy with Ava. I've only had those three days of minicamp with my teammates so far, apart from a few nights at the Gridiron.

I tend not to be an awkward guy, so I start with something we have in common. "Do you like this neighborhood?" I ask. It's a question I probably *should have* asked before I moved into it. Little late now if he says he hates it.

"Yeah, I do. It's quiet. The gate at the front helps ward off the paparazzi, and it's close to the Complex and my daughter's school."

"You have a daughter?" I ask.

He nods. "And a son, actually. My daughter is eleven, and my son is eight months."

"Oh, wow. Busy house. Congratulations."

He smiles. "Thanks. My wife runs that ship, and she's pretty damn incredible. To be honest, I don't know the first thing about kids, but I'm learning."

I chuckle. "As you know, my brother just had his first. She was the first baby I've ever held."

"That was me with my son."

"Not your daughter?" I ask, realizing the words might be insensitive a bit too late considering I don't know his situation.

He shakes his head. "No. I just met her a little over a year ago. Long story, but the moment I met her, she owned me. Kids will do that to you." He chuckles a bit, and it's weird how I never even really thought twice about kids, and now this is yet another newish dad convincing me that having kids is this whole magical thing.

I'm sure it's magical when they're new. Is it still magical when they develop attitudes and sassiness and opinions? Doubtful, but what the fuck do I know?

Still…I'm starting to think about it more. That life. I'm starting to wonder if it's something I want. I've never felt that urge before, but I've also never been in love before. Now that I'm with somebody who I've fallen for, I can't help but wonder if kids are coming in the semi-near future, too.

"How was minicamp for you?" he asks, changing the subject to something I'm more comfortable with.

"It was good," I say. "Nice to get to know more of the defensive guys." I pull the box of crackers out of the basket and open them, leaving them on the counter for us each to pick at.

Travis takes one after I do. "I've gotten tight with Evan Wilkinson on the D-line. His daughter and Harper are the same age."

"Harper? That's your daughter?"

283

He nods. "And my boy is Henry. We had a hell of a time deciding on a name for him, but I call my wife by her maiden name, Hartley, and with Harper...we liked another H name. It felt right."

"It's great," I say, not really sure how we got back on the topic of kids. Do all parents do this?

We switch gears back to football for a bit, and then the movers interrupt us to let us know they're all done. They take the boxes with them, and this is really first-class service. I don't have to do anything but sit back with my sausage and gin and enjoy the view. And, you know...search for all the shit they organized into cabinets for me.

"I should head back home, but I'm glad to have a neighbor I can carpool with to practice," Travis says, and I laugh.

It feels good to make a friend on the team even if we're on opposite sides of the ball, and as I recall, Ava and Travis's wife seemed to hit it off at the Gridiron.

"Let's make dinner plans soon," I suggest. We exchange numbers, and he walks down to the house on the other side of the one that sits between us.

I've just settled onto the couch that definitely isn't big enough for this room when I get a text from Ava.

Cookie: Just leaving the bakery.

I decide to call her rather than text back in case she's driving.

"Hey," she answers.

"Hey. How was work?"

"Screw work, how's the new house?"

I chuckle. "It's incredible. Come see it."

"You're there now?" she asks.

"Yeah. And I have something I want to talk to you about."

"Well, that sounds scary. Text me the address, and I'll be there soon."

I send her the details, and fifteen minutes later, I hear the doorbell.

When I open it, she's standing in front of me looking nothing less than gorgeous. She smells like cookies, and she's holding a box that says *Cravings* on it.

I narrow my eyes as I grab her arm lightly and pull her into my chest. "What's in the box?"

"Housewarming cookies." She tips her head up, and as I stare down into her eyes, I can't help but think how this is our future.

I'm excited for it. I'm *ready* for it.

"That was nice. And you know how much I love to eat your cookie."

"Why do I feel like you don't mean these?" she asks, shaking the box.

I reach for her hips and pull her against my already hard cock. "You know exactly what I mean."

Her cheeks flame red, and I love surprising her in the best way like that.

She clears her throat. "Before you make a meal of me, you said you have something you want to talk to me about?"

"I do. Maybe over cookies." I press a soft kiss to the corner of her mouth before I finally let her go. I sweep my arm out gallantly. "Welcome home."

She tilts her head as her eyes get a little misty. "Aw, Gray. That's adorable."

"As are you." I nip a kiss to the tip of her nose, and she giggles.

I lead her toward the kitchen, and she glances around in awe of the place. It's just after four o'clock, and the sun is shining through the windows, making it look even brighter with all the natural light. The design is very modern, mostly black, white, and gray, which isn't something I necessarily would've chosen, but it works in here.

It already feels like home, and having Ava in here makes it feel warm and comfortable.

She sets the box of cookies on the counter as she inspects the place, twirling in the middle of the kitchen as she runs her fingertips along the huge island. "This is incredible, Gray," she murmurs.

She runs to the windows as if she just noticed the backyard, and she looks out over the luxurious pool and the resort-style setup.

I take her through the rest of the house—all seven thousand square feet of it. We walk through the huge living room and kitchen on the first floor, plus the office and the guest suite. We look through the ensuite bedrooms and rec room on the second floor—including the huge primary suite with separate his and hers walk-in closets.

She's in awe of the place, and I'm in awe that she's here.

We step out onto the balcony outside of the primary suite, and she takes in the view. I can see the Strip perfectly across the distance from the Stratosphere on the north end to Mandalay Bay on the south end.

"Wow," she breathes. It's a different view from here than the one out the window of the Palms, where we could only see from the Wynn to the Bellagio—much closer, but still only a snippet compared to the grandeur of the whole thing.

We have mountain views out the other side of the house, and I can see this becoming our sex palace. Or, you know…a home.

"I can't believe I'm really going to live here," she breathes.

"Believe it, baby," I say softly. I move in behind her and rest my palms on the railing in front of us, pressing my front against her back. I drop my lips to her neck, and she squirms a little as she spins in my arms.

"Before you start all that, because then you know I'll be incoherent for the rest of the night, what did you want to talk about?" she asks.

It's just like her to cut right to the chase. I suck in a quick breath. "I did a little research and got in touch with your landlord. I, uh…I paid the rent for the next couple months and set up an autopay from my account so you and Kelly have a little breathing room and she doesn't have to move out just because you are.

And, you know, in case you want to head back there and have a sleepover while I'm out of town, or if—"

She cuts me off as she moves to her tiptoes and presses her lips to mine. She pulls back. "Shut up. You did not do that."

I can't help but laugh as I tighten my arms around her. "I did."

"I just…how? How did I get so lucky?"

I think about throwing out some cheesy line about how I'm the lucky one, but instead I settle on, "No clue, but good for you."

She giggles. "Well, this place is amazing, and you are amazing, and, God, I just love you so much." Her smile fades as her words seem to register. Her eyes widen, and her face blanches. She reaches up and covers her eyes with her hand. "Oh, Jesus. What did I just say?"

I gently tug on her hand so I can look into those gorgeous blue eyes of hers. "You just said you love me so much," I say, and her cheeks go from pale to red in a heartbeat. I say the words before I lose my nerve. "And to be honest with you, Ava, I love you so much, too."

Her eyes soften as she stares up into mine, and I've never felt so sure about anything in my life.

I lower my mouth to hers, and what starts as a sweet kiss on the balcony turns heated nearly immediately. It's urgent and needy from both sides as we both rush to prove our words valid—to show each other with our actions how much we mean the words we just said.

She takes charge this time, and seeing her get more and more confident in the bedroom has been nothing short of incredible. She backs us up until my knees hit the back of my bed, and she pushes me down. She climbs on top of me and takes my jaw between her hands as her mouth drops to mine. She shifts over me, rotating her hips as the anticipation builds between us, and I thrust up to let her know how ready I am for her. How ready I *always* am for her.

Her lips part as she releases a small moan into my mouth, and she pulls back, her eyes sparkling as she pulls her shirt over her head then reaches behind her to unclasp her bra. She tosses it on the floor and tugs at the bottom of my shirt, and together we pull it up over my head. She runs her hands along the plane of my chest to my shoulders, and then she pulls me into her as she hugs me tightly, her tits smashed against me.

I shove my hips up toward her again, and she groans. She moves off me and pulls her jeans down, kicking them off along with her panties, and then she helps me out of my pants, too.

She moves back over me, her hair swinging around her shoulders, and her eyes find mine. "I have a surprise for you, too."

"Oh?" I ask, my cock pulsing with need between us.

She grips me in her fist and strokes me a few times, aligning her cunt with my cock as she pumps me against her clit. "I finally got on that birth control we talked about." With those words, she pushes my cock inside her.

Holy. Fuck.

Her eyes are hot on mine as there's nothing between us for the first time, and our breathing becomes ragged and the sound of our panting and grunting fills the air.

She moves slowly at first, tentatively, and not because she's intimidated or shy anymore, but because of my size. I know it takes a little time for her body to get used to me, and the last thing I want to do is hurt her.

But I need to move like I need to breathe.

It's velvet in here, or maybe velour, soft and warm and luxurious. The feeling is like no other I've ever experienced before because I *haven't* experienced this before. I've never gone bareback with a woman. I've never wanted to take that risk.

But with her, it's not a risk. It feels like every time we've been together has been leading up to this moment, and there's literally no better time for this to have happened than after we just said the words we said on the balcony in our new house.

She shifts up, rolling her hips over me, and I give her an encouraging, "Yes, baby, yes."

We move slowly as the need starts to build, her tits brushing gently against my chest with every passing thrust, and she lowers her mouth to mine again. I reach around to hold her under her ass as our mouths move as languidly as our bodies.

She holds me close, too, as she reaches around me to hug me to her. Her nails dig into my shoulders again, and when she does that, it sets me on fucking fire. It tells me she's getting close, that I'm giving her everything she needs, that she's taking pleasure from my body, and there's somehow no greater compliment than that.

I have to hold myself off. I have to make this last. If I knew how to make it last forever, I would.

She pulls back, and her lips are against my neck as I start to stroke more deeply into her. She shifts to move a little faster over the top of me, digging those nails into me, and I know she's getting close.

Her voice is low and silky when she moans, "Oh, God, Grayson. I'm going to come."

"Fuck, Av. So am I," I groan. I move my lips toward her ear. "Come for me. Now."

Her body seems to burst at my words, and she clings onto me as she takes me for a fucking ride. Her body writhes over me as the intensity reaches its peak, stoking the hot fire of my own release as I shove up harder into her and hold onto her through her orgasm. As her sweet cunt constricts over my cock, my entire body tenses as the tidal wave crashes into me.

A loud growl rips up from my chest as I start to come, and I bury my face in her chest as my release hits me hard. Her pussy milks my cock, stealing all my come greedily, and I give it to her willingly.

It's inside her now. Nothing between us.

She fucking owns me.

As much as I called her mine…I'm hers, too.

Whatever happens from here, we'll both know at least that much is true.

Chapter 44: Ava Maxwell

This Is About to Get Complicated

We're doing an appearance at a nightclub the next night with some of the other defensive players on the Aces, including Patrick Harris, Dave Redmayne, along with his wife Leah, and Evan Wilkinson and his wife Trudy, when a text from my brother comes through.

Beckett: Hey, just wanted to let you know I'm bringing the family out to Vegas next month for a summer vacation. Hope we can get together.

A summer vacation?

Beckett *never* takes vacations.

And having him here will mean Grayson and I might have to tone it down a little.

It's been easy *faking it* for the media since we're really not faking it at all. But when Beck comes out here…I can't help but wonder if it's the right time to tell him the truth.

Sure, he might be mad at first. But once he sees how *good* we are together, he'll get it. He has to.

I sort of don't want to bring it up with Grayson. Everything is going so well, and I'm worried it's a wrench. But it's a wrench we'll have to deal with at some point, especially if we continue on the track we're on.

I don't let it dampen my good time tonight. Grayson and I can talk about it tomorrow. Instead, we've spent the night dancing, and he even took me to a dark corner booth where we made out a little. He reached under my dress and fingered me right there under the table with nobody around us any the wiser before we returned to the dance floor. Or maybe I'm drunk and delusional, but I'm at a point where I'm not sure I care.

I just want to be with him.

All the time.

Butterflies race through me every time our eyes meet, and I feel safe and protected when I'm in his arms.

It's pure magic, and if my brother can't see that, then maybe I don't care.

Grayson will, though. He's closer with my brother than I am, and the last thing he wants to do is upset him—or worse.

Grayson flashes his phone at me, and I see a text from my brother to him, too.

Beckett: I'm heading to Vegas with the family for summer vacation next month. Will you be able to show me the sights?

Interesting how he wants Grayson to show him the sights, and he just wants to see me.

It's a clear signal that he still sees me as a little kid. He doesn't see me as someone old enough or versed enough to show him the sights of Vegas.

And that's fine. His best friend can show him.

But I'll be there, too…probably telling Grayson where to take him since I've lived here seven years and Grayson's barely lived here seven weeks.

"I got a similar text," I yell in Grayson's ear.

He drafts a text back and shows it to me.

Grayson: Of course. You're all welcome to stay at my place. I have a pool, and we can kick back with beer like the good old days.

I widen my eyes at him. "You do realize this means that unless you're ready to tell him the truth, I won't be sleeping in your bed."

He twists his lips as if he hadn't really considered that.

Beckett: I'm more of a whiskey guy these days.

Grayson: Truth be told, I'm a gin guy.

Beckett: That sounds good, though. I'd rather have the girls at a house than a hotel anyway. We'll be there June 13-17 on our way to Hawaii.

Grayson: Looking forward to seeing you.

"Do you want to tell him?" I ask before I lose my nerve. It's definitely the vodka talking.

He shrugs, but he doesn't answer, and then Patrick grabs him and pulls him up on stage with the deejay, and the moment is lost as he puts on his party hat and sets this crowd on fire.

That's my man up there.

My man that my brother doesn't think is my man.

Whew boy. This is about to get complicated.

We have more events lined up. We make more appearances. We have more sex. A *lot* more sex.

It's almost daily now, sometimes multiple times a day, and somehow it gets better every time. He doesn't have to go as slow as he used to since my body has made room for him, and he really knows how to work me until I'm wrung out and completely sated.

He invites me to the charity ball the Aces hold in mid-June each year, and I'm excited to attend a team event with him.

He also lets me know that my brother has secured tickets to the event since he'll be in town, and he's looking for a babysitter to watch the girls so he can take his wife to the ball.

Since I cut back my hours at the bakery and Grayson asked me to bake for his teammates, I make some fruit and nut bars before his organized team activities, or OTAs, at the end of the month. He pays me handsomely for them, and I have to admit, I'm building up my savings rather quickly without rent to pay.

I still have a lot of stuff at the house with Kelly, and I stop by often to check in with her. She has continued talking to Austin, but she's taking things slow, and I'm not sure how serious either one of them is. For now, they seem to be having fun, and if she's happy, I'm happy.

He's gone three days a week the last week of May and the first week of June with OTAs, and the second week of June finds him at mandatory minicamp for three days. I make something for him to bring for his teammates each day, from cookies to protein muffins to banana bread.

Either he's a great liar, or they love everything I'm sending in. He comes home with empty trays and begs me to send in more. He said it's helping him bond with his teammates, and they're looking forward to what he's going to bring in next every day.

And I know he's not lying when I get a call from his brother Lincoln one afternoon.

"Hello?" I say when I see the unknown Nevada number on my screen.

"Ava, hello, it's Lincoln Nash."

I'm not sure why hearing him call me sends a pulse of fear through me. He's at OTAs with Grayson, and suddenly I'm nervous he got hurt or sick or…something.

Fear climbs up my spine as I say, "Hey, Lincoln. Everything okay?"

"Everything's great. I'm calling because I just put together that the delicious treats my brother has been bringing to OTAs are from the same woman who made those fantastic kitchen sink cookies we featured on our podcast not terribly long ago. I was wondering if I could contract you to make some pastries for our annual charity event coming up."

"Of course. I can put you in touch with Poppy, the bakery owner," I say.

"No, Ava. I don't want the bakery. I want *you*. Grayson told me those were *your* cookies. You have a real talent, and I want Ava Maxwell's pastries. Not Cravings'."

"Oh," I gasp, a little shocked. I glance around the kitchen where I'm standing. A million ideas plow through my mind. Petit fours, mini souffles, truffles, and tortes. Oh! Mini cheesecakes!

It's the opportunity of a lifetime. This could really get my name out there in the community. *My* name. Not Poppy's. Not some other bakery. Me.

I could handle it here, but it would be easier to do it at the bakery where we already have the equipment I'd need.

I shake my head as I realize I haven't actually answered his question, and silence is spanning between us and I need to say something.

"I'd love to, Lincoln," I say, forcing myself to stay calm. "Thank you so much for thinking of me."

"Great. I'll have our charitable contributions director get in touch with you with quantities and that sort of thing, but I think this is going to be a really great fit."

"So do I." We hang up, and I twirl around Grayson's kitchen. Holy shit!

Things are really starting to fall into place, and I could not be more excited.

Everything's coming up Ava. I refuse to believe that I can't have it all.

Chapter 45: Grayson Nash

I Like Her

I hated watching her pack her shit and move out of my house, but her brother arrives in town today, and we're trying to play it cool in front of him.

She asked me the one time if I'm ready to tell him, and I shrugged. I played it off.

The truth is that I probably *should* tell him, but I'm just not ready to. It's easy to ignore the reality of the situation when he's all the way on the other side of the country. It's a little harder when he's staying with me.

And so I'll tell him when I'm ready to put a ring on her finger, and likely not a moment sooner.

She's back at her place, which sucks. She makes this house feel like a home, and for the next four days, I'm going to have to sleep without her in my arms.

Unless I can sneak her in. Maybe I can sneak her in…

I have one last day of mandatory minicamp, and our position coaches put us through the fucking ringer yesterday, so I'm having a hard time mustering up the right words to tell her how much I miss her already.

She doesn't know Grayson in season, and sometimes the pain gets to me. It's a harsh reality that she might not be expecting, but as the season gets underway, it's not like it gets *easier* for me to get out on that field every week.

So why do I continue to play if that's how I feel?

Because I fucking love the game. It's the best game in the world, and it's been my life's honor to be a competitor in it. Maybe this will be my last year, and I'm giving it my all just in case it is. I'm leaving every last bit of myself out on that field, practice or not.

And it's not just that.

I'm not ready to give it up because I don't have a plan. I don't know what comes next.

We have a max of twenty-four practice hours for the week, so today will be lighter than the first two days were. But I'm sore as fuck after those first two days as I prove I'm the cornerback the Aces need.

It's going to be a long season, and so far, Ava has been nothing short of incredible as she caresses me with her light touch, feathers kisses along my skin, and works the knots out of my back and shoulders.

It's like she knows exactly what to do, and having her here when I get home after a hard day of practice is somehow the exact medicine I need.

I haven't told her that yet. I should, but time seems to have slipped away from me before I could form the words, and now I'm on my way to the Complex and she's on her way to the bakery, and her brother gets here in a few hours.

I gave him the code to get into my house. I didn't know what else to do. Having Ava there felt too personal, like he'd be able to read into it and see what's going on.

I'm not sure how I'm supposed to take her to the charity ball this weekend and act like I haven't fallen head over ass for her.

The day drags, especially when it comes to the position meetings toward the end, and I'm itching to get home to see my guests—and my guest's sister. I'm not sure if she headed over there after work to see her family or not, but I'm interested to see her interact with her brother after all this time. And, of course, after I've gotten to know her the way I have.

I think after all these years, I might actually be closer to Ava than I am to Beckett.

He's still my best friend. We have a history together. But he's also the kind of friend who will be there in a month or a year. We don't have to talk every day to know our friendship remains strong and healthy.

Ava, on the other hand…I don't want to miss a day with her. I don't want to wait a month or a year to talk to her. Hell, I don't even want to wait an hour to talk to her.

I know that's not feasible, but I like her. I like spending time with her. I like laughing with her. I like fucking her.

I like my life with her in it.

It's a strong realization to have as I head home to meet her brother and his family as we continue this sham that's purely for his benefit.

Her little red Versa isn't there in my garage where it has nestled in its own space for the last month. Instead, a rental luxury sedan sits in my driveway.

That means her brother is here, and she is not.

I text her when I pull into the garage before I head into the house.

Me: Home from practice. Your brother is here. Are you coming over?

I don't wait for a reply. Instead, I head inside to greet my guests.

Beckett looks the same as the last time I saw him. He's clean-shaven, and he's neat as a pin, with not a hair out of place in his polo shirt and slacks. He greets me with a hug.

Rachel looks sophisticated even in her dark pants and white sweater, and she hugs me next as I realize how quiet the house is.

Beckett nods upstairs. "We put the girls to bed a little while ago. I hope that's okay. It's past their bedtime on the east coast."

I nod. "Of course." I head toward the kitchen. "What can I get you two?"

"Got any scotch?" Beckett asks.

"I do," I say, and I fumble around on the top shelf of my pantry for the bottle. "Rach?"

"I'm fine with my water," she says.

Water. Water? Rachel *always* has a glass of wine. It's practically glued to her hand. I step back from the pantry and glance over at my guests, and Rachel gives Beckett a *look*.

One of *those* looks. Even *I* notice it, which means it must be glaringly obvious.

"Water?" I repeat, staring at the two of them. Eventually, Beckett's eyes shift to me.

"Water," he says quietly.

"Okay," I say, and I pour two fingers of the scotch and grab a bottle of water from the fridge. I hand the drinks to my guests and grab my gin before I sit in the recliner across from where they sit on the couch. "So, what's new?"

"Just tell him," Rachel mutters.

Beckett's face lights up. "We're having another baby."

"Holy shit, man," I say, rising to my feet to shake his hand. Rachel stands, and I hug her. "Congratulations. You feeling good, Rach?"

"No. I feel like shit. I'm always nauseous and cranky, and I very nearly canceled this trip because I didn't want to travel, but Beck insisted we come. And it's early, early days, so please don't say anything to anyone yet. We're only eight weeks in."

Don't say anything to anyone. So…they want me to keep this a secret from Ava, Beckett's sister. And we're keeping our own secret from Beckett, and I get a really, really bad feeling about all the secrets bouncing around this house.

"You finally getting your boy?" I ask Beckett.

He chuckles. "Praying for healthy, and we'll take whatever we get." It's the standard answer parents must be trained to give when they're pregnant, but I also know that Rachel has had two miscarriages, and I'm sure that's a lot of where his answer stems from.

They tell me the girls don't even know yet, so I promise to be careful about not spilling the secret.

And it pulses something else in me. I don't want to overshadow their news with our news. I don't want to admit to what we're doing when Beckett is already worried about his wife and the baby she's growing. I don't want him worrying about his sister, or me, or our friendship on top of what he's already dealing with.

The doorbell rings a short while later, and when I open it, I find Ava standing there.

A huge bag is slung over her shoulder, and it takes everything inside me not to grab her into my arms. But I'm determined to be the friend Beckett needs me to be, and the time just isn't right for a confession.

I take the bag from her as her eyes meet mine, and I think there might be a question there. But then Beckett walks up behind me to greet his sister, and the moment is gone.

I see in her eyes how much she hates keeping this secret, and now that Beckett has asked me to keep one from her, I'm a little nervous about how the next few days are going to play out.

Chapter 46: Ava Maxwell

God Bless Gray Sweatpants
and Their Inventor

After I greet my brother and sister-in-law with hugs, I send Grayson out to my car for the huge box I packed to bring over.

"Grayson's brother asked me to bake for the charity ball, and Grayson said I could use his kitchen since it's so much bigger than mine. And now that you're here, I'm definitely putting you to work."

Beckett laughs. "As fun as it sounds to be put to work while we're on vacation, we're taking the girls to the children's museum tomorrow, and then we have tickets to the Heat game."

"If we're not too tired when we get home, we'd love to help," Rachel says.

They'll be too tired, but it's fine. What they just told me is that Grayson will be home alone tomorrow, which means *he* can help me.

You know, in between sex and stolen kisses. Oh, and he can help me with my orgasms.

"How was practice?" I ask Grayson.

"Day three was tough, but I've got this."

"Yeah, you do," I say, and I hold my hand up for an awkward high five.

He chuckles and slaps my hand, and I nearly grab his in the process before I remember that as far as anyone here is concerned, we're just *faking*. We're nothing more than friends.

This is going to be a tough four days.

"How was Coach Turner today?" I ask. While he really likes the defensive coordinator, Andy Glen, he mentioned that his position coach, Jordy Turner, hasn't given him the warm fuzzies just yet.

"Tougher on me than on Pat again," he admits, and Beckett looks between us with a crinkled brow.

"You two talk about that stuff?" he asks.

"You know this guy," I say, rolling my eyes as I jerk my thumb in his direction as I try to cover for my blunder. "Once he gets started, he never stops talking."

"Yeah, she's attended some events with me where she caught us talking about Turner. He's not been overly welcoming to me so far, but I'll win him over," Grayson says, ignoring my jab.

The boys chat about Grayson's new team while Rachel helps me unpack my box and my bag filled with supplies and ingredients for the desserts I'll be making.

I'm keeping it simple and delicious with mini fruit tarts, cake pops, truffles, and petit fours. I've spent the last week working on prep. I've already made the shortbread crusts for the fruit tarts along with the truffles, which are currently stored in the refrigerator in Grayson's garage.

I still need to make the cake pops, the filling for my tarts, and the petit fours. Erin, the woman who runs the Aces charities, told me the final count for the ball is just under twelve hundred people. With an estimate of three desserts per person, well…it's a lot of desserts for little old me to undertake, which is why I have tomorrow and Saturday off from the bakery. I'll spend all day tomorrow baking and dipping, and I'll put the final touches on my desserts Saturday before I deliver them to the banquet facility.

And then I'll have to get ready for my date since I'm attending this who's who of Vegas event on the arm of the newest, hottest teammate of the Aces.

I stay and chat with my brother and sister-in-law, and they call it a night pretty early since they traveled halfway across the country today. I do a little more prep work in the kitchen, and Grayson asks if he can help.

I tell him to sit since I know he's suffering after minicamp the last three days, and he watches me work while I ask him questions about camp as I prep so I'm ready to go tomorrow.

It's as I'm wrapping things up and getting ready to leave that he stands and walks over toward me. I turn to face him, and he backs me up until my ass hits the counter. He leans forward, placing his palms on the counter behind me, and my breath hitches when he's so close to me.

He drops his lips to my neck. "I miss you," he groans.

"I miss you, too," I whisper.

His lips move to mine, and it's a short kiss that's far too brief.

"I think we should tell him," I say softly when he leans his forehead down to mine.

"We can't."

"Why not?"

He sighs and pulls back. "He's got his own shit going on, and the time isn't right."

I narrow my eyes. "His own shit?"

He presses his lips together and takes a step back, and I don't like that he's putting physical distance between us when we already *have* physical distance between us.

I grip his biceps and pull him back into my orbit. "What's going on?"

"I promised I wouldn't say anything."

I nod. "Okay. Okay, don't say anything."

"Rachel's pregnant," he blurts.

I gasp.

He rushes to add, "She's not very far along. They didn't want to tell anyone, but she asked for water instead of wine…so I had a feeling."

"Oh, God. After the two miscarriages, I don't blame them for not wanting to say anything. I promise I won't say a word that you told me. And you're right. We can't tell them right now."

"We will. When the time is right, we will. I promise," he says softly.

I nuzzle into him for a beat, and then I pull back. "Thanks for telling me."

He nips my lips with his for another kiss that's far too short, and then he backs up out of my reach.

I take it as my cue, and he walks me out.

When I arrive back at his house the next morning, Grayson answers the door.

Without a shirt.

Wearing only gray sweatpants.

God bless gray sweatpants. And their inventor.

My eyes flick down to the bulge in those sweet, sweet sweats, and I can see the rather grand outline of his semi-hard dick.

Sigh.

I snag my bottom lip between my teeth as that familiar feeling of *need* darts right through me straight to my core.

I clear my throat. "Is my brother here?"

He raises a brow and slowly shakes his head. "They left for the museum an hour ago."

"You know I have work to do, don't you?" I say, a whole big dose of sassiness in my tone as I set my hand on my hip.

"Yep. And I have work to do, too." He yanks me into his house, and I giggle as I fall into him. He kicks the door shut behind me, and his mouth falls to mine. "I need you here with me," he says, his words punctuated with kisses. He tightens his arms around me. "Fuck, I missed you. More than I thought I would."

"I missed you, too," I admit. More than I thought I would, but I can't add that to my previous statement as he has intensified the kiss and now his tongue is thrashing wildly against mine and *God* do I want him.

So I'll be a few petit fours short of the extras I was planning to make.

This will be fully worth it.

We don't make it past the entryway. He shoves his hand down into my leggings. I didn't dress up to come here and bake, and he groans as he feels how wet I already am.

I mean…have you seen him? And those sweats? Of course I'm freaking wet. He's walking sex, and I'm absolutely powerless against his magic.

"Oh fuck," he snarls at me as I grapple for his cock. I rub him on the outside of his sweats, and then I dip my hand in and fist him. I stroke down his generous length before I stroke back up, and he shoves his hips toward me to show me he likes that.

"Fuck it," he mutters, and he pulls his hand out and yanks my leggings down. He pulls them all the way off, moving down so I'm no longer able to feel him, and when he straightens up again, he lifts me by my ass. I link my legs around his waist, and he yanks his sweats down, pulls himself out, and aligns with my pussy.

He thrusts his way in as he holds me. He shifts us until my back is against the front door, and then he really starts to move.

He drives into me as I grasp on around his neck, unable to really move or do much of anything except enjoy the ride.

And holy hell, am I enjoying this ride.

My body gives way before I even know what's happening, and I cry out as I start to come, my walls gripping onto him as pulse after pulse of pleasure racks through me.

"Fuck, yes, baby. Squeeze me with that perfect cunt," he murmurs as he wrings out every last ounce of my energy.

He keeps driving into me as my orgasm starts to wane, and he shoves up hard twice then lets out a low growl as he starts to come. I watch his face as it screws up with pleasure, and I'm not sure I've ever seen anything more gorgeous than Grayson Nash as he gives into the pleasure he's taking from my body.

"God, I love you," he murmurs as he carefully pulls out of me and sets me down. I feel his come as it oozes out of my pussy, and he reaches down to feel it, too.

His eyes absolutely light up as he feels the hot come he just pumped into me. He slides it around, focusing on my clit, and there's something so hot about feeling his semen as it combines with my own juices that the edges of pleasure start to pulse around me again.

I fly into a second orgasm, my body quaking as I grip onto his arm for support. If I don't grip onto him, I'll collapse onto the floor.

His mouth shifts down to mine, and he kisses me slowly, sensually, as he keeps fingering me through my orgasm. I drag in a heavy breath as the intensity fades, and he pulls his fingers out.

"Goddamn, that was hot," he mutters.

"Wanna help me bake now?" I ask brightly, and he laughs. "I'm teasing. I actually need to sit for a minute. And maybe a cup of coffee or a diet Coke or something."

"You got it, Cookie." He lifts me into his arms.

I smile at him as I wrap my arms around his neck. "You haven't called me that since…"

"Since I found out your real name? Yeah. But you once told me some people call you that, and I think it fits." He sets me down outside his first-floor bathroom and nips a kiss to my lips. "Be right back."

He returns a minute later with a washcloth and my pants, and then he gives me some privacy.

I take care of cleaning myself up and getting dressed again, and I collapse on his couch for a few minutes. He joins me with a cup of coffee.

"How do you like it?" he asks.

"Cream and sugar? Or…sugary creamer?"

"You got it," he says, and he brings me a bottle of vanilla creamer.

He settles in beside me as I sip my coffee, and we just take a few beats to *be* together. It's lovely. It's how I envision our future—quiet moments on the couch as we sip coffee and enjoy each other's company.

It feels like these moments are going to be fewer and further between as his season gets underway, so I will bask in every single one that I get.

Once my cup is empty, I force myself off the couch to get started on the day's tasks. Grayson helps me out, and he makes me lunch and forces me to eat when it's time. He forces dinner down me, too, and the way he takes care of me is really sweet.

He helps me where he can, and by the time we hear the doorbell telling me my brother and his family are back from the baseball game, my last batch of petit fours is done, and all I have left to do tomorrow is decorate the ones that haven't cooled yet.

I'm exhausted.

Between two orgasms this morning then being on my feet baking all day, I'm not sure I'll be much fun at tomorrow night's ball.

And it'll be weird pretending not to be in love with him for Beckett's benefit.

I rush to the door to greet my nieces since I haven't actually seen them yet, and they both yell, "Auntie Ava!" when they see me.

I squeeze them both, and we're regaled with tales of the fun day this party of four had. I can't wait to see what life's like for them when they're a party of five.

But first, we have to get through the charity ball tomorrow night.

Chapter 47: Grayson Nash

Do You Want to Bang It Out

"Holy shit," I murmur softly when she opens the door.

She's a vision in a silky golden gown. It's tight in the right places and falls down to the floor, and I can't believe I'm so lucky as to call her my date tonight.

She pulls me inside, and I press a soft kiss to her lips, careful not to smudge any of her makeup.

"You look incredible," I say.

Her eyes run up and down the length of my body as she sucks in a breath. "How am I going to keep my hands off of you tonight?"

I chuckle. "You don't need to. As far as your brother is concerned, we're faking it for the media. He'll be expecting to see us together. He just won't know there's nothing fake about us."

She raises a brow. "Nothing."

"I'll make damn sure of that."

She giggles. "You ready?"

"Is Kelly here?"

She shakes her head.

"Is she going with Austin?"

She shakes her head again. "I have no idea what's going on between them, but Kelly is out with her teacher friends tonight."

I glance back at the car and the driver waiting for us. "I know we have to go, but do you want to bang it out before we head out?"

She tilts her head as she contemplates it, but then she says, "I think we should bang it out after, okay? I can't mess up this hair, and besides, I want to get there and see my desserts. This way we can build the anticipation for our own dessert later tonight."

I chuckle. "Oh, I'm anticipating. But with you, I'm *always* anticipating."

"Right back atcha, big guy."

"Big guy...you're referring to the cock, aren't you?"

She giggles. "I love how you can take this nice little moment between us and make it about your cock."

"What can I say? I'm a man of many talents."

"You got that right," she mutters, and she grabs her purse and locks her door before we head toward the car waiting for us.

We arrive at a red carpet where photos are snapped and our names are called. The press knows who Ava is since she's been with me at almost every event I've attended in Vegas. We head inside to find a formal and fancy affair.

We take a sweep by the dessert table, and it's absolutely gorgeous with rows and rows of Ava's incredible pastries. I grab a truffle and pop it into my mouth, and my eyes roll to the back of my head as I try my hardest not to jizz in my pants at the fact that the woman I'm currently fucking made these.

They're incredible.

She is incredible.

This night is incredible.

And all I can think about is getting her out of that dress and pulling her on top of me so she can take a ride on the monster.

Fuck.

I have got to get it together.

I spot Beckett with Rachel across the room, and as soon as they see me, they head in our direction. It makes sense since they don't really know anybody else here aside from my brothers, but having to hang with my girlfriend's brother shouldn't feel like a drag the way it does.

I haven't seen him in ages.

I want to hang out with him.

He's my best friend.

But I don't want to hang out with him at the expense of having to act like I haven't fallen for his sister.

"You look gorgeous, as always," I say to Rachel, and she leans in for a hug.

"Oh, Victoria's here," Ava says, and she nods in her direction. "I'm going to go say hi."

I nod. "Excuse us," I say to Beckett, and I walk over with her to shoot the shit with my neighbors.

I slip my arm around Ava's waist, and she glances over at her brother. Instead of leaning into me the way she usually does, she leans a bit away from me. It's a little disconcerting given how close the two of us have gotten, but we're riding a bit of an odd line here where we want to make it believable to Beckett that this is still fake.

We mingle with my new teammates—in particular the ones who I've gotten close with during our workouts and practices—and I introduce Ava to the coaching staff. We chat with Lincoln and Jolene for a while, and we touch base with Asher, who showed up solo tonight with the hope of finding someone single to take home.

We run into my dad, and my mom made the trip out for the ball, too. Jolene's parents are here, and I catch up with them. Apparently at this same ball last year, Jolene's dad and my dad got into a public spat. I missed out on that one since I was in LA at the time, but so far this year, it seems like the two men are going to be civil. Or, at the very least, they'll ignore each other instead of interacting at all, which is probably preferable since one's son is the team's head coach and the other's daughter is married to the head coach.

We dance, and I hold her close as we sway to the music.

We're seated for dinner, and I'm at a table with other guys on defense, while Beckett and Rachel are at a table clear across the room.

It's after dinner when Beckett corners me at the bar.

"Is there something going on with you and Ava?" he asks me. "Because I have to be honest, Gray. I've never known you to be that good of an actor, but you've got everyone here fooled. And seeing you dancing with her...I can't help but wonder if there's something going on you're not telling me."

Dammit. I should've known his lawyer instincts would kick in.

He's always been good at reading people, but I've never really been the one he was reading before.

I'm not sure I like it.

And I'm even more sure from his tone that I can't admit the truth to him.

He's accusatory—maybe borderline angry. I can't tell him I'm banging his sister. I can't tell him I've fallen in love with her.

He knows better than anyone how I fuck up everything that's good in my life. He knows I hold immense power in my hands—the power to hurt her.

It's still my biggest fear. I still don't believe I won't.

But every day we spend together, I'm a little closer to believing we will figure out some way to make this work.

"What? Ava? Are you kidding me?" *Tone it down, Grayson. You're overacting.* I clear my throat. "She's still fifteen to me, bro. You know I'm just hanging with her to keep the media off my ass and keep my nose clean in Vegas."

"Is that so?" a voice beside me says.

I glance up to find Austin Graham standing behind me.

Oh fuck.

He's going to blow this for Ava and me. He's going to tell Beckett that Ava moved in with me, or he's going to tell Kelly what I said, or he's going to do *something* devious because that seems to be who he is.

He's going to...

Walk away?

He walks away, and I'm left confused.

And now I have to worry about whether his intentions are going to become clear some other time.

Chapter 48: Grayson Nash

A Fake What Now?

On Sunday morning, I wake up with the kind of hangover that reminds me I'm not as young as I used to be.

Beckett and his family decided to tour the Strip today, and I'm thankful they don't expect me to be their tour guide since I'm not exactly up for shooting the shit.

A shower and some ibuprofen help a little, and coffee helps a little more, but I'm still dragging. Part of me thinks it has more to do with Ava not being here than it has to do with how much I drank last night.

What the fuck is that shit? These feelings are unfamiliar as they pulse through me, and now I'm regretting that we didn't just tell Beckett the truth.

Especially when my phone starts to ring.

When I see who's calling, I have this gut instinct that I am going to need more coffee.

I answer on speaker as I make my way to the Keurig. "Good morning, Ellie."

"Hey, Grayson. I'm calling so we can put a plan together to mitigate damage." She sounds as tired and worn down as I feel. And…wait.

What?

Mitigate damage?

Maybe I drank more than I thought last night.

"Okay, first, let's back the truck up for just a second. What do you mean, mitigate damage?" I ask as the Keurig makes a loud whirring sound and starts to drip the coffee into my cup.

"Oh, you haven't seen the headlines," she murmurs. "There's a viral video of you at the ball last night telling an unidentified man that you're just hanging with Ava to keep the media off your ass."

"A viral video?" I repeat.

Austin Graham. That motherfucker.

"The comments are ripping you to shreds," she adds. "I'm so sorry to be the one to tell you, but you hired me to be the one who fixes this."

"How the fuck are we going to fix this?" My voice is a little frantic as the reality plows into me.

Why would he do this?

Because he fucking hates my family, and I'm the latest target since I'm the newest. Take out my brothers by taking me out.

Maybe I'm the most vulnerable since my reputation was already on shaky ground with the local media given the nepotism claims that have followed me here.

I feel like I've always heard the same thing from publicists. Don't listen to the noise. Ignore the rumors. Tune it out. Focus on the game.

That's all great advice, but this is different. This isn't just rumors about me and my latest hookup.

This is a personal attack *from a teammate*.

And it doesn't just hurt *me* this time. It also has the potential to hurt *her*.

Fuck, I can't let Ava see this, but it's not like I have any way of controlling it. And maybe she's already seen it anyway.

With Beckett here, it's not like I can overreact to it. Thankfully he'll be out for a few more hours at least, but when he gets home…then what?

Maybe it's time I just fucking fess up to him.

"A fake engagement," Ellie blurts.

A fake *what* now?

"What did you just say?" I ask, certain I didn't hear correctly even though I know what the fuck she just said.

"A fake engagement," she repeats a little more quietly. As if I didn't hear her the first time. As if her words don't tap into every fucking fear I have. "Listen, I know it's crazy, but you're already under fire for being here at all. We can't play it off like this conversation happened months ago since it's clear it's from the ball last night. Snubbing the media like this isn't going to do you any local favors, and an engagement is one way to show that you're serious about the girl. It's one way you won't even need to address this issue, and instead you show how much you're in love with her."

"That's crazy, Ellie," I mutter.

"Is it? Or is it just crazy enough to work?"

Her question is rhetorical, obviously, and I don't address it.

"Just promise me you'll think about it, okay? In the meantime, I'll work on other avenues of mitigation. What makes you a good guy? What can I capitalize on?" she asks.

What makes me a good guy?

Fuck. I don't know. Am I a good guy?

Maybe that's a better question for Ava…but if she's seen this video, she might be coming up empty right about now, too.

"I'm a good football player."

"Right. We're aware of that. But beyond that…what makes you *you*?"

What makes me *me*?

It's a great question.

I'm the life of the party, but lately I feel pretty damn lonely in a room filled with people unless Ava's there.

I can hold a conversation with anybody about anything.

I'm good at a lot of things, but I'm only great at one thing.

I'm tall. I have a big dick. I'm athletic. I'm in good shape. Some of my muscles have muscles.

Somehow, I don't think any of that is what she's looking for.

I'm thirty-two, and I'm terrified of commitment. My brothers are all at various stages in their lives where I feel like the odd one out. Lincoln is married with two kids, and he scored the head coaching position of his dreams. Spencer is engaged and loving life in Minnesota. Even Asher seems to be doing just fine coming off a yearlong suspension. He's thriving in Vegas, turning himself around to prove he belongs on the Aces despite his stupid wardrobe.

And then there's me. The guy who's new to town, who's trying to fit into a new team, who's spending more time with the girl than with the guys he's supposed to be building a brotherhood with.

And Ellie wants me to *propose* to her?

Fake or not, the entire idea gives me an ache in the pit of my stomach. It gives me anxiety like I've never known before.

I'm not ready for that step. Ava's not ready for that step. I'm not even sure I *ever* want to get married. I should know this shit. I'm thirty-fucking-two, and there's so much that's unknown.

Is this my last season?

What will I do next?

Do I want to get married someday? Have kids someday? Have a future with Ava—or someone else?

No.

If it's not Ava, it won't be anyone. I'm in love with her. Only her.

But that's not the point here.

The point is that Ellie's suggestion is making me think about things I've never thought about before. And it's not giving me the warm fuzzies.

Instead, it's scaring the fuck out of me.

I saw what marriage did to my parents. Sure, they had a lot of good years together. But ultimately, it ended—just like everything in life does. My dad has a penchant for fucking up everything good in his life. Guess who inherited that unfortunate gene?

"You still there, Grayson?" Ellie asks.

I clear my throat. "Uh, yeah. Sorry. I, um…I like to give back to the community. I'm passionate about football and fostering the next class of players. I'm more the kind of guy who prefers to give motivational locker room speeches than who runs kids camps, but I'm happy to donate and help with others' causes, too."

"Okay. I can work with all of that. Thanks, Gray. Think about my idea, and I'll be in touch."

We hang up, and I stare into space as our conversation punches me in the gut.

And then I get the sudden, ominous feeling like this is the beginning of the end.

Chapter 49: Ava Maxwell

Frozen Broccoli Will Do

I suggested dinner with my brother and Rachel on Sunday night while they were still here, but Grayson had some appearance he had to do.

He didn't invite me along.

I went to dinner with Beckett, Rachel, and the girls solo.

Maybe Grayson was tired of putting on the act with them or something. He was a little distant at the charity ball, and it seems like he's been ultra busy over the last two days.

Maybe it's my imagination.

Or maybe having Beck here made him feel just how real this has gotten for both of us.

We haven't talked about the viral video. He hasn't brought it up, and I haven't, either. But it's the elephant in the room.

Of course I saw it, but I also saw that he was talking to my brother. Of course he had to say that to him. I just can't imagine why he'd say it loud enough to be caught on camera, and worse, I can't imagine who would've posted it.

Someone who's trying to hurt Grayson, for sure, and maybe even someone who's trying to hurt *me*.

The only thing I can come up with is some jilted ex, but as far as I know, Grayson doesn't have any of those.

So I'm back to square one.

I've fielded three calls so far since the ball asking if I can cater private parties, and all the attention is exciting—but it's also going to keep me incredibly busy.

I don't want to turn anyone down.

I need a bigger kitchen. I need *help*.

Now that Beckett and his family are on their way to Hawaii, I'm thinking it's time to move back into Grayson's place.

But he hasn't invited me.

They just left this morning, and I thought we were beyond the point where I'd need an invitation.

Still, it feels awkward to show up without one. I decide to text him and fish for one.

Me: Hope you had a good Monday. Beck is on his way to Hawaii, and I miss you. And I have some exciting news.

His reply doesn't come until after dinner.

Grayson: Hey, sorry, I've been at workouts all day and I'm beat. Let's talk tomorrow, okay?

Grayson has a month and a half left of his offseason before training camp begins, and to him apparently that means it's time to start putting in the work.

But it feels like it means he's putting our relationship on the backburner, and I'm scared we're at the point where he's ready to run.

I don't know how to save things before he bolts.

I'm scared he's already bolted.

He always made me feel like I was worthy—like I was *loveable*. But in just two days, I'm back to feeling the same way I've felt my whole life: nothing more than *leave-able*.

I refuse to take this lying down.

Instead of responding with a text, I dial his number.

When he answers, it's loud in the background. "Hey."

"Where are you?" I ask, and I know my voice comes out more demanding than I mean for it to, but I can't help myself here.

"The Gridiron."

"Oh," I say flatly.

"I'm with the guys. It'll probably be a late night," he says.

"Okay. Well…bye." I hang up.

I can't be mad he's bonding with his teammates. That's where he should be since the season will get underway soon.

Still, it feels like there's more at play here, and I don't like the feeling pulling at me.

I'm in bed when I hear the doorbell.

At first, it scares the shit out of me.

I'm home alone, after all, and I'm not used to guests coming over at this late hour. I glance at the clock.

Okay, fine. It's nine thirty-seven. Still. It's dark outside, and I'm not expecting anyone.

I creep quietly toward the door when I hear the doorbell again, followed by banging on the door.

"Ava? Answer the door!"

I rush over when I hear his voice, and I toss the door open. "Grayson?"

It's dark, and I flick the outside lights on. He squints at the brightness, and that's when I see the blood trickling down from a cut just under his eye and what looks like the start of a black eye.

"Holy shit! What happened? Are you okay?" I'm throwing out the questions as I yank him inside. The car that dropped him here takes off as I slam the door.

"You should see the other guy," he jokes, but this is not a laughing matter.

And…is he slurring?

Is he *drunk*?

Did he get into a drunken bar fight with a *teammate*?

"Who's the other guy?" I ask, my blood turning cold as I usher him inside.

"That assclown Graham," he mutters.

Shit. I need to get him out of here. If Austin comes home with Kelly and finds Grayson here, it's going to get ugly…and it's not something I have any interest in being in the middle of.

I take him to the kitchen sink first, and he perches on the counter while I find some supplies to clean him up.

Once I gather my stuff, I move back toward him, and I move in between his legs. His hands find my hips, but I'm not exactly in the mood right now.

I use a washcloth to gently clean his wound. He winces as I dab at the cut. It's minor, but it's obvious Austin punched him. I can't help but wonder why.

Getting into a fight with a teammate is bad news. I can't help but wonder whether he'll be fined or suspended or *worse*.

"What happened?" I ask softly as I clean him up. His eyes fall tenderly to mine when I glance up into his, but I force myself to concentrate on what I'm doing.

He sighs. "It was him."

"What was him?"

"He posted that video of me talking to Beckett. Or, rather, he gave it to someone else to post."

My hand slips a little at his confession, and he winces when I scrape the washcloth against the cut. It's small, and it's not like it's gushing, but it's right under his eye, and it can't feel good. With his blood thinned from the alcohol, it's bleeding more than it probably should be.

"I confronted him at the bar, he didn't like what I had to say, and that was it. He got mouthy with me, so I gave him a right hook. And if I wasn't a few gins short of a bottle, I might've had the reflexes to duck his return." He shrugs and twists his lips wryly at the end.

I roll my eyes. "You punched him first? That was stupid, Grayson."

"What he did was pretty fucking stupid, too."

"He's your teammate, and you were out with players. You don't think this'll get back to the front office? You think you're untouchable because you're the coach's brother?" I ask, my tone demanding because, frankly…I'm angry.

"I've got a better shot at getting out of it than that asshole. And he had it coming."

"Be that as it may, you need to control yourself," I say. I finish cleaning the wound and toss the washcloth in the garbage can. I put some gauze and a bandage over the cut.

I head over to the freezer and fish around until I find a bag of frozen vegetables. I end up with broccoli. I think you're supposed to use peas on what's going to become a black eye, but I'm a pastry chef, not a nurse, and this is all I've got.

"Here," I say, and I shove the vegetables at him. I don't get close enough for him to set his hands on my hips again.

"I'm not hungry, and these are frozen."

I roll my eyes and set my hand on my hip. "Put it on your eye, asshole."

"Yes, ma'am," he says quietly—almost meekly. He does as he's told since I've never called him an asshole before.

But if the shoe fits…

"How do you know it was him who posted the video?" I ask.

"He was standing behind me when I said that shit to your brother. I didn't see him until it was too late. And you know I didn't mean it. I had to keep up the act for Beckett." He lowers the broccoli, and I push his hand back up.

"Keep it there," I say.

"It's cold," he whines.

"Too bad. Why would he post that video?"

"He's got it out for my family. I told you that from the beginning."

"But why would posting a video that had the potential to hurt your reputation help gain him a starting position?" I ask.

He shrugs. "No idea. Because he's delusional? But also…because he *can*. He knows he's not going to get in trouble since it would only look like Lincoln's playing favorites."

"Kelly needs to know what he's like."

"I think it's too late for Kelly, if I'm being honest. She doesn't see the side of him we do. He reserves that for us."

"If she knew he posted the video, she'd run far, far away." I purse my lips resolutely.

"Would she? Because I know you two are best friends, but if she's falling for him…" He trails off there. He doesn't need to finish that thought. I know where he's going, and it's not pretty. It's not something I want to think about.

"Yeah," I mutter. "Let's get you home."

He nods. "Don't put on more clothes on my account."

I glance down at my pajamas—a tight tank top and short shorts.

"I definitely need someone to stay with me tonight," he adds.

"Grayson, you completely ignored me for the last forty-eight hours, and you expect me to just forget all that and sleep over like everything's fine? It's not fine." I push a finger into his chest, and he holds up a hand.

"Okay, okay. I'm sorry. Let's talk on the way home, okay?"

I sigh but relent since his words make me think there must be more going on than I realize.

I pack a quick overnight bag even though I'm not entirely sure I want to spend the night, and I slip a sweatshirt over my tank top. We're in the car a few minutes later—thankfully before Kelly gets home with or without Austin.

"You said you wanted to talk on the way home," I say, pulling out of the driveway. "So talk. You've been distant for two days, and I want to know why."

"Ellie has a plan for me to mitigate damage. I've been thinking it over."

"Ellie has a plan?" I repeat. "What does that have to do with why you're pulling away from me?"

"I'm not pulling away from you," he argues as I cruise down the block toward the stop sign at the end. "I'm deciding if I want to take her advice or not."

"Then let's talk about it. What's this big plan?"

"A fake engagement," he blurts.

I slam on the brakes. "A fake *what*?" I screech as I come to a stop in the middle of the block. It's nighttime, and it's not a busy street. There aren't any other cars. I stare at him as I try to make sense of what he just said.

"I had a similar reaction, if I'm being honest, though yours is even better than mine was," he teases.

"And you're thinking about it?"

"Listen, it scared the shit out of me when she first told me, and I know we're not there yet. But an engagement, fake or otherwise, would throw the focus off that video, which would help me win over the media. They understandably lost all trust in me with those words I said when I thought I was having a private moment with your brother. I'm already on thin ice here since I'm playing on my brother's team with my other brother, so I need a win."

"*I need a win*," I repeat. "How fucking romantic, Grayson."

"This isn't my proposal."

"No, you'll do that in front of a huge crowd to ensure everyone sees it," I nearly spit at him.

But really…what am I so mad about?

Would it really be so bad to wear his ring on my finger?

No. Absolutely not. It would be freaking amazing. It's exactly what I want.

But I want it because he wants it. I don't want it because of some ploy to win over the media. That's just…ridiculous.

On the other hand, my stock is rising. People are interested in the woman with Grayson Nash, and they're interested in my pastries—something I haven't actually had the chance to tell him just yet.

And if my name is in the news again, that means this little side business I'm sort of starting up without even intending to will potentially also be in the news again, which means I'm another step or two or three closer to that dream bakery I've always wanted.

I blow out a breath as I creep toward the stop sign. "I'll do it."

He starts to choke, and I can't help but laugh once I glance over at him and see he's okay.

"You'll what?"

"I'll do it," I repeat. "Ask me publicly, and I'll say yes."

"What? Why? What? You seemed so…pissed off a second ago, and now you're okay with it?"

"I'm okay with it because of the thing I was excited to tell you that you still haven't inquired about," I say. I turn left.

"Oh, uh…right. I'm sorry. I've been preoccupied and busy getting into barfights. What was the news you wanted to tell me?" he asks.

"I've had three calls asking me to bake for various events since the ball," I announce rather proudly.

"Holy shit, Av. That's incredible. Congratulations."

I smile tightly. "Thanks. I was hoping I could use your kitchen. And, you know…you. For extra hands."

He nods. "Of course you can. I'm happy to help however I can, even if it's just to entertain you with sex in between batches."

I chuckle a little at that. "So, just to be clear…we're okay? We're back on the same page?"

"We were never not on the same page, baby. I just needed a minute after Ellie's big plan. Engagement isn't a small thing, fake or not. I still am not entirely convinced it's what I want out of my future after watching my parents go down in flames, you know?"

Disappointment lances through me. I don't say anything, and he keeps jabbering semi-drunkenly on, oblivious to the fact that I have real feelings pulsing through me.

Scary feelings.

Feelings that I *do* want that out of my future. I want marriage. I think I want kids—someday. I want it all, and I deserve it all.

But I want it with someone who is seven years older than me, and isn't sure it's what he wants.

And I have no idea how to be *on the same page* when I'm not even sure we're reading the same book.

Chapter 50: Ava Maxwell

A Lot Can Happen in Three Weeks

He hasn't gotten in trouble for the fight, though Lincoln called him in for a chat the morning after the fight happened. I guess Austin was there, too, and Lincoln made them work it out.

I'm not convinced they actually worked it out, but Grayson said they're good, so I'll take him at his word. Guy drama is different from girl drama, and maybe they really are fine. They sort of have to be ahead of the upcoming season.

I've been staying at Grayson's for the last few days, and I haven't been home to touch base with Kelly. I head that way after work on Thursday since I need some more clothes, and I cross my fingers that she's home alone so we can chat…even though I'm nervous for this particular chat.

I get my wish. She's on the couch watching a game show when I walk in, and she looks calm and relaxed since it's summer break. She still teaches summer school classes, but it's low-key and fewer hours than her usual workload.

"Hey Kel," I say, and she hops up and turns to face me.

"Avelina Marie! Where have you been?"

I offer a tight smile as I walk over and give her a hug. "Sorry. I've been either working or with Grayson. Can we talk?"

"What's wrong?"

We sit on the couch, and she relaxes back, setting her feet on the coffee table.

I sit up straight as I turn to look at her. "I'm sure you heard about the fight between Grayson and Austin, and I just wanted to talk to you about it."

Her brow crinkles. "The fight?"

"Have you been talking to Austin?"

She shakes her head. "He's been busy with workouts, and we had some fun together, but it pretty much just fizzled out."

"When did it fizzle?" I ask.

She purses her lips as she looks up to the ceiling. "A few weeks ago. Maybe a month or so. The last time I saw him was before their OTAs in May."

That was after I moved out.

Was he only seeing her to try to get to Grayson?

Once I moved out and Grayson stopped coming around here, he didn't have a need for that anymore.

But Kelly and Austin talked the first night I saw Grayson at the Gridiron. He wouldn't have known Grayson and I had a history at that point.

He also didn't go home with Kelly that night. As I recall, she wanted to go to the Gridiron again so she could see him again, and he'd seen Grayson and me together by then.

I don't say anything about any of that, though. I'd hate for Kelly to feel like he was just using her. If she puts that together, then fine—but I don't want to be the one to hurt her. Instead, I say, "He recorded Grayson talking to my brother at the charity ball and posted a video that went viral. Then Grayson confronted him at the Gridiron, and I guess it got physical."

"I saw the video," she says quietly. "Are you okay?"

I nod. "Yeah, I'm fine. We agreed to keep up the ruse with my brother a little longer, so he was just saying what he had to say, and Austin happened to be behind him, catching the whole exchange to share with the world."

"Ugh, I'm so sorry. What a dick," she says.

"I'm sorry he's a dick."

"Yeah," she murmurs. "It's okay. I never expected anything serious with him. It was more of a good time, and he was good at the sex."

"Are you heading back east this summer?" I ask. She heads to Louisiana every summer and spends a few weeks there with her parents before the next school year gets underway.

She nods. "The first session of summer school ends Friday, and I head out on the red eye for three weeks."

"I'm glad I came by to see you, then," I say. I give her a hug, and we settle on the couch for game shows and laughing.

Between work, organizing everything for the first of the three events I'm catering, and fitting in time with Grayson, I stay plenty busy in the next three weeks.

It's the second week of July when she gets back, and I head over to see her.

Training camp starts in two weeks, and Grayson and I have spent as much time together as we can. He hasn't proposed despite Ellie's suggestion, and we haven't spoken about it again. Instead, I appear with him at different community events, and we present a united front as we do our best to ignore the noise surrounding our true intentions with each other. It's nobody's business but ours.

I've learned over the last month that everybody has an opinion, but the only thing that matters is our truth.

"How was Louisiana?" I ask when I walk into the house.

When I spot her sitting on the couch, she's...crying?

I rush over and sit beside her. I sling my arm around her shoulders. "Oh my God, Kelly! What's wrong?"

I glance down between her hands and see the stick, and my heart leaps into my throat as I glance down at it.

Two pink lines.

"Oh..." I say. "You're—"

"Pregnant," she finishes.

"And it's—"

"Austin's."

"Oh, shit," I murmur.

Jeez, a lot can happen in three weeks.

And that's when I realize...

I haven't gotten my period this month.

"What am I going to do?" she wails. "We were just screwing around. Having some fun. And now...now I'm going to be tied to him for the rest of my life!"

"It'll be okay," I say quietly. Soothingly. But in truth...I have no idea what to say. On the one hand, I have my own racing thoughts running through my brain. I took the birth control shot, but we had unprotected sex during the first week I was on it. Lots of sex. So much sex.

What if I'm pregnant, too?

I know the odds are low.

But I also know...I'm new at this sex thing. I'm inexperienced, and I've never had a pregnancy scare before. I don't know if this is a scare or not, but I'm sure as hell scared right now.

I *want* to be tied to Grayson forever. I love him.

But I don't want it to be because a baby is pushing us together. I want it to be because he loves me—not because he feels obligated to stay with me.

And on the other hand...I need to push these thoughts from my brain. I need to be there for my friend. She actually *is* pregnant. The *scare* is over. This is the aftermath of the reality.

I rub Kelly's back as I try to push my own fears away.

"How far along do you think you are?" I ask.

She shrugs. "It's been...what, two months since I've even seen him? I couldn't bring myself to take a test at my parents' house even though I knew. I just knew. So as soon as I got home..."

"Oh, God, Kel. I don't even know what to say," I admit.

"I know. There's nothing *to* say."

"Are you going to tell him?" I ask.

"I feel like I have to, but I don't want him thinking I did this on purpose to trap him or something."

Would Grayson think that if it was me?

I have no idea.

She cradles her head in her hands. "I should've known better. We should've been more careful. I mean, we used condoms, but he might've slipped in once or twice, and it only takes once." She sucks in a breath. "I always wanted to be a mom. I mean, I love kids. I wouldn't teach kindergarteners if I didn't. But I never thought it would be like this. I never imagined it would be because I was messing around with a football player. God, I'm so stupid."

"You're not stupid, Kel. This could've happened to anyone."

"It didn't happen to *you*," she points out.

I clear my throat. I've never been good at hiding what I'm thinking.

"Oh, shit. Are you…" she asks.

I shake my head. "I don't know. I mean…probably not, but I didn't even realize I might've missed a period until I saw that stick in your hand, and—"

"There are extra tests in my box. Take one. I won't need them for nine months anyway, and by then they'll be expired."

I shake my head. "No. I'm not. I don't think I am, anyway. It's just the birth control shot or the stress…or something." I'm talking myself out of it being pregnancy.

It can't be.

She jumps up and leaves the room, and she returns a beat later with the box. "Take it. I don't need it anyway. Go take the test now. Maybe we can go through this together."

Shit.

I don't *want* to go through this together, though I'm not exactly in the right position to tell her that. "I'll take one later," I say, turning the box over in my hand as I stare down at it.

I get up and toss it on my bathroom counter, and then I sit with Kelly, and we talk about what this means.

She agrees she has to tell him, and we even discuss strategies for what she can say since she isn't sure she wants him around.

She's certain she wants to keep the baby, and she's also certain she'll figure out how to make this all work.

And then she throws out the thing that breaks my heart but might just be the right choice for her. "I don't even know how to say this to you, but...I think I'm going to move back to Louisiana to be closer to my parents as I navigate this."

I don't blame her, though tears pinch behind my eyes. "You should, Kel. But what am I going to do without you?"

"You'll never be without me. Instead of long talks on the couch, we'll have long talks on the phone." Her voice wavers a little at the end, and I start to cry, too. "It's just the right time, I think. If I'm going to move, I'd rather do it in the summer than once the new school year gets underway."

"I don't blame you. And it's absolutely the right choice. But I'm right here if you ever want to come back, okay?"

"I don't want to leave," she whimpers.

I reach over and squeeze her to me, and we both cry as we consider what a future might look like where we're no longer roommates and where we no longer even live in the same town.

We sit on the couch reminiscing about the day we met and all the adventures we've had together. It's dinnertime when my phone dings with a text.

Grayson: Will you be home for dinner?

I stand and stretch. "I should get home. Do you want to come over for dinner?"

She shakes her head. "No. I need to do some research about jobs by my parents and maybe make an appointment to make sure everything is okay in here." She pats her stomach, and the slightest twinge of something rushes through me. It's not quite jealousy, not quite fear, but some weird combination in the middle.

I should take that test.

I know it'll be negative. Of course it will be. But I also have this strange feeling like maybe ignorance is bliss, and I kind of want to live in ignorance a while longer.

I call Grayson on my way to his place.

"Hey," he answers.

"Hey. I'm on my way, and I haven't eaten."

"I haven't, either. Want to meet somewhere?" he asks.

"Sure."

He wants Mexican, so we pick a place not far from home, and I pull into the parking lot at the same time he does. On my way there, I decide I'm not going to tell him Kelly's news. It's not my news to share, anyway.

"You're quiet," he astutely observes after we order.

"Kel's going through some things. She's thinking about moving back to Louisiana to be closer to her mom and dad," I say.

"Oh, Av. I'm sorry. That must be hard for you. Is everything okay with her?" he asks.

I nod. "She'll be okay." It's just that her life is going to get completely flipped upside down, and I think I want that too.

I don't say any of that.

"I'm right here if you need me, okay?" he says softly.

I glance up at him, and I see the sincerity there.

"I know. Thank you."

I just hope Kelly has someone besides me in her corner, too.

I hope Austin does the right thing and steps up. But knowing him the way I do, I'm not entirely convinced he will.

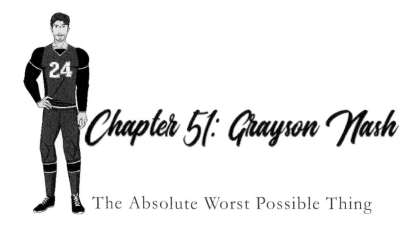

Chapter 51: Grayson Nash

The Absolute Worst Possible Thing

One week left until training camp, and I'm trying to soak in every possible second with Ava. I'm also pushing myself harder with our team trainers at the gym next to the Complex since we can't use our training facility until training camp officially begins.

I'm ready for this new season.

But first, I'm ready for some time with my girl.

Only…she's busy as fuck.

She's catering an event this weekend, which means she's been busy baking when she's not at Cravings, and she just found out Kelly is definitely moving back to be closer to her parents.

When I asked her why, though, she got all weird and dodgy on me.

Something happened, but she doesn't want to tell me what.

I don't press it. She's stressed as it is, and I don't want to add to it. I can't help but wonder if it has something to do with Austin, though.

Her event is this Friday, and she's losing her shit that she won't have enough time to get it all done. So I sit on the stool in my kitchen opposite where she's making her truffles as I ask what I can do to help.

"Sit there and look pretty," she says.

I laugh, but I do as I'm told.

"Actually, I do need your help with something. Kelly's moving out by the end of the week, and I'd love to get the rest of my stuff out of there and into here before you leave for camp. Would you mind just grabbing all the clothes in my closet and in my dresser tonight, and then I can go tomorrow and clean out the bathroom stuff and all that Radiance shit from my closet?"

I chuckle as I think about how I didn't even move my *own* shit when I came out here. I paid someone to do it. But for her...of course I will. "Yes. How much of the Radiance shit is there?"

"A closetful." She shrugs. "We had to keep buying products in order to hit the next bonus tier, and I'm just...not a salesperson. Now it's just sitting in my closet, and I don't know what to do with it."

I nod. "Okay. Oh, and I can help move your furniture, too. Want me to head over there now and assess what our needs are?"

"If you don't mind. I think Kelly's out. She said she had some people to, uh...to talk to before she leaves town."

"Some people? Like Austin?" I ask. "He won't be there, will he?"

"Honestly, Grayson, I have no idea." She's rolling her chocolate mixture into little balls, and she seems almost...angry.

"Is something going on with you?" I finally ask.

She sighs, and then she stops rolling her chocolate balls and looks up at me. "Kelly's moving. I'm sad." She clears her throat, and it feels like she's leaving something out. "I have an extra house key in my purse. I'll let Kelly know you're on your way over in case she's home."

I run upstairs and grab a couple of empty suitcases to fill with her clothes, and then I give her a quick kiss before I head over.

The house is dark when I arrive. I head straight for Ava's room, and I grab her bunny and nightlight first—though she hasn't had any nightmares at all since she's been staying with me. I pack the first suitcase full of clothes from her dresser drawers, and I head toward the closet next.

"Holy shit," I murmur when I see the sheer amount of Radiance shit in her closet.

It's…excessive.

Literally one entire wall is a shelving unit with Radiance Skincare boxes stacked from the floor to the ceiling. When she joked about having a closetful of this shit, I had no idea she actually meant an *entire closetful of this shit*. There must be thousands of dollars' worth of products in here.

I grab the clothes on hangers and take it all out to my car.

I fill up the other two suitcases until they're bursting, and before I take them out to the car, I stop to use her bathroom.

As soon as I flick on the light, I spot something sitting there on the bathroom counter.

It's a box of pregnancy tests.

Correction: A box of *open* pregnancy tests.

A pulse of fear races up my spine.

Is Ava pregnant?

Is she keeping yet another secret from me?

I thought I was past those secrets from the beginning when she lied about who she was. I thought I was okay with it. I thought we'd moved on.

But the thought that maybe she's keeping more from me is a terrifying realization. Will I *ever* be able to fully trust her?

I thought I could. I don't think I'm quite there.

It feels like the absolute worst possible thing that could have happened. It's all my fears combined into one manifesting itself in that open fucking box.

Kids ruin relationships. Secrets ruin relationships. Lies ruin relationships. And this has the potential to be all three.

It's not just another secret. It's not just another lie.

It's a *baby*.

I glance through the box mostly because I can't help myself, and I see that there's a test missing.

She took one. I'm not jumping to conclusions. The evidence is right fucking here in front of me. An open box of pregnancy tests on my girlfriend's bathroom counter.

I'm the only man she's slept with. At least I think I am. Maybe it's another secret. Another lie. The fact that she was a virgin came out of her stupid ex's mouth before it came out of hers.

She explained why she didn't tell me. I tried to understand.

But explaining away lies after the fact doesn't change anything.

Is this what she wants? Is she ready for kids and marriage and that whole life?

Maybe she is, but I'm not entirely sure I am.

It feels like a giant weight is pressing on me as I continue to hold the box in my hands.

I finally toss it down on the counter like it's on fucking fire, and then I bolt the fuck out of there. I grab the suitcases, toss them in my car, and decide to go to the Gridiron instead of back to my house.

I need a drink before I'm ready to face her and whatever this is. Make no mistake, though. I *will* face her. I will ask her about those tests and why they're on her counter.

Maybe I'm just jumping to conclusions. Maybe there's a perfectly solid explanation as to why she has an open fucking box of pregnancy tests on her fucking counter.

I suck in a few deep breaths as I'm at the point where I either have to turn left to go home or right to go to the bar.

I have her shit in my car. It's not like I can go drink and then drive home.

I turn left. I force myself to calm down.

It's not another secret or lie until she admits it is.

Then I can overreact.

I pull into the driveway and haul the first two suitcases inside. She's still making her truffles.

I head for the pantry, twist the cap on the Hendricks, and take a few swigs.

"What's wrong?" she asks.

She knows me so well.

I take another swig at the thought.

"Why is there a box of pregnancy tests on your bathroom counter?" I demand.

She freezes, and her face turns white.

That's all I need to know to confirm the fact that she's been keeping something from me.

She sets down the ball of chocolate she's forming, and she presses her palms onto the countertop. "Kelly's pregnant. She gave me the box after she used a test."

Kelly's pregnant? *Kelly?*

"Jesus. Is it Austin's?"

She nods slowly.

It's a simple enough explanation, I suppose.

But that box of tests wasn't in Kelly's bathroom. It was in Ava's.

Maybe every woman keeps a box of pregnancy tests on their bathroom counter.

Except...

I don't think they do.

And her face turned white. She froze as if she was caught.

There's more to this story, and I'm going to dig until I get to the bottom of it.

"But why would *you* need the box?" I ask, my voice a bit more menacing than I mean for it to be.

She clears her throat. "Are you accusing me of something?"

"Do you have something to confess?" I counter.

She sighs. "My period is late, okay?"

Of all the things I thought she might say, I don't think that was it.

Her words send ice through my veins. "Your...your period is what?"

"I started the shot, and we had sex the week I started it. Everything I read said it's fine, and I feel fine. I don't *really* think

343

I'm pregnant, but just in case, Kelly gave me the tests since she figured she wouldn't need them."

"And you just…decided to keep this from me? More secrets and lies?" I ask. I'm not really angry that she kept Kelly's pregnancy from me. It wasn't her news to tell.

But this? A scare?

This is something we could've faced together.

"It's not like that," she protests. "I'm scared, okay? What if I *am* pregnant? You're scared as hell of babies and commitment and all of this, and I'm not ready to lose you because of something we didn't get the chance to plan."

I take another swig of my gin. "You've got it all figured out." I shake my head as I mimic a woman's voice. "Grayson is too emotionally immature to handle a baby, so I'll just deal with it on my own." I cut the voice. "Well, what if you are? What then? Were you just going to lie to me and hide it until you could train me to accept it?"

"Are you kidding me right now? I've been fucking terrified to take that test because I was scared of what your reaction would be if I was, and so I haven't. I know I'm not, but I still had that five seconds of fear. What if I was? What then? How would you handle it?"

"Fuck, Ava!" I roar. "It's yet another complication we'll never know the answer to because you don't trust me enough to tell me the truth!"

She looks small and scared standing there behind her chocolate, but I'm finding it hard to muster up any sort of sympathy.

"I'm sorry," she whispers.

"So am I," I hiss. "I'm sorry you can't be honest with me. I'm sorry that this," I say, waving between the two of us, "just isn't working for me."

I leave those as my final words as I storm out of the room.

Chapter 52: Ava Maxwell

The Absolute Worst Possible Thing

He's angry, and I get it.

He has every right to be. The absolute worst possible thing in his eyes is more secrets and lies. It took a long time to get past that first one, and I finally felt like we were in a place where he trusted me—where we'd make it through anything because our feelings would be enough.

I should've put the box under the sink, but I haven't been back to the house in weeks. I did a little research and learned a good chunk of women don't get their period at all with the birth control shot. I'm guessing I fall into that percentage given that I don't *feel* like I'm pregnant.

I should take the test just to rule it out.

But does it matter now?

He made his feelings clear. I suppose it's not the fact that I might be pregnant or the commitment factor. It's the fact that as he sees it, I'm keeping something else from him.

I get that he's sensitive about the whole thing, and maybe I should've just told him about the test and my fear and all of it. He's probably right about that. How are we going to have a future together if we can't talk about these sorts of things?

Emotions are high tonight, and he overreacted. By morning, he'll cool down. We'll talk it through, and we'll get back on the same page again.

We have to. I gave him my full honesty when I told him I wasn't ready to lose him. I know his instinct is to run. I know his instinct is to fuck things up. This is him putting up a shield, and it's up to me to help him work through that so we can come out on the other side stronger than ever.

Only…that's not what happens.

I give him time to cool down before I head up to bed, but he's not actually in bed. I'm not sure where he is at all. I'm not even sure if he's still at home.

The bedroom—*our* bedroom—is dark and quiet, and I lay there wondering if having a pregnancy test on my bathroom counter that isn't even mine is really going to be the thing that breaks us.

As ridiculous as it sounds…it is.

I get up way too early after a restless night's sleep.

Or, not completely restless, I suppose.

I fell asleep crying, and I woke with a nightmare at some point. I never fell back asleep after that.

When I open the bedroom door before my shower with the hope of running into him, I find suitcases with all my hanger clothes stacked on top of them just outside the door.

Does this mean he still wants me to move in with him? Or was he simply emptying out his car?

I head down to the kitchen and find him there.

He's grabbing something from the fridge and wearing his workout gear, and I can't help as my eyes dart to his calves.

Damn, he's in good shape.

I force that thought to the back of my mind. "Morning," I say quietly.

He spins around at the sound of my voice. "Hey," he grunts.

"Can we talk?" I ask.

"I need to get to the gym."

"Thanks for all my stuff."

"You're welcome." His words are stilted and cold.

I press my lips together. "Are you okay?" It's not what I want to ask. Are *we* okay seems like the more appropriate question.

"No."

"Because of the box of tests that aren't even mine?"

He shakes his head, and he moves to walk past me. "I said I need to get to the gym."

"You're just going to walk away? After everything we've been through? Grayson, I love you. That has to count for something." I'm begging, and my voice is desperate, but I guess when you're pushed up against a wall, you'll do whatever it takes to hold onto the one you love.

He slams his Gatorade on the counter. "It's not the fucking box, Ava. It's what that box means. When was the last time you were at that house?"

I lift a shoulder. "I don't know. A couple weeks?"

"Exactly. So you've been thinking about this…this…this *thing* for a couple weeks all by yourself when you could've talked to me about it. It's a *thing* that affects me, too, deeply, but you chose not to say anything. And that's…that's just bullshit." He shakes his head. "Secrets tore my parents' marriage apart, and that's why I had a hard time at first with the ones you kept from me. Okay? And seeing that box there…yeah. I jumped to conclusions. My first thought was that you were lying to me. That you were keeping something from me. You know what that tells me?"

He stares at me for just a beat that isn't long enough for me to respond.

"It tells me that I don't fully trust you." He sighs. "And you know what? I don't know if I fully trust *anybody*. Maybe this is a me problem. I need to work it out. But I have a season coming up with a new team, and I have to prepare for it. I can't have all these distractions when I need to focus. I have shit to do, and worrying about what secrets and lies you're keeping from me next isn't on that list."

He grabs his Gatorade and storms out of the room as I stand staring after him, and I hear the door slam to signify that he just left.

If the worst possible thing for him was more secrets even though I still don't feel like I was actually keeping one, the worst thing for me is that feeling of abandonment.

Of course he left.

He was always meant to.

He admitted he fucks up everything good, and I'm so leave-able that he decided to run at the first sign of trouble when it wasn't even actual trouble.

I fall to the floor in a heap as I start to cry.

Eventually, I pick myself up because I have to. I have a full schedule today, but also…I will find a way to fix this. I have to. He's worth it. *We* are worth it. He's just angry right now, and he's trying to focus on the season, and the only version of him I've ever known in season was back in high school. The stakes weren't very high back then, and I was too young to care about the game.

I force myself into the shower. It's one task at a time. Shampoo my hair. Wash my body. Get ready for my day.

I'm putting in a half day at the bakery so I can get back here to tackle the pastries ahead of this Friday's event, and even at work, I'm just going through the motions.

I head back to the house I've lived in with Kelly for the last three years, and I find her in the kitchen as she empties the shelves, stacking everything on the counter for the two of us to sort through.

She can have it all. I don't need it since Grayson's place has all this stuff, but am I still welcome there?

We didn't get to that part of the conversation.

He wouldn't just kick me out on my ass, would he?

If he did…then I guess I *would* need this stuff.

"You should take it all," I say, and she jumps when she hears my voice.

"Oh!" she gasps as she turns to face me.

"I'm sorry. You okay?"

She nods, and I move in to help her empty another cabinet.

"How'd it go with Austin?"

She clears her throat. "It was…okay. Better than I expected, I guess. I'm still moving to Louisiana, so it's not like he made some big play to get me to stay so we could raise the baby together and have our own happily ever after."

"What did he say?"

"He said he wants to be part of the baby's life, and he will do what he can to help me financially." She shrugs. "He didn't say he wants to be part of *my* life, though."

"Do you want him to be?"

She snags her lip between her teeth. "I'm not sure. He didn't say he *didn't* want that, but I don't know."

"That's not a no," I point out.

She shakes her head. "No, it isn't. I don't like what he did to Grayson. I think he has some growing up to do, and maybe once he does that, there might be a chance for us."

I reach around her and squeeze her in a side hug. "You're really the best. Do you know that? You are going to be the best mom ever."

"Thank you," she murmurs. She shakes her head a little. "What about you? How's everything?"

I sigh as I set down a stack of bowls and back up until I'm leaning on the island. I shake my head a little. "Not great."

"Why not?" She pushes some dishes out of the way then lifts herself up to perch on the counter opposite me.

"He saw the box of pregnancy tests on the bathroom counter, and I think we're breaking up." My voice cracks at the end.

She gasps. "Because of the pregnancy tests?"

I lift a shoulder as I swipe away an errant tear. "He says no, that it's because I kept another secret from him."

"What secret did you keep?" she asks, her brows drawing together.

"The fact that I was worried I might be pregnant when you said you were."

"Oh, God. I feel like this is my fault."

I hop down off the counter and squeeze her arm. "It's not. At all. It's his issues. I think the idea of commitment and babies and love—everything, all of it…it's freaking him out, so he's running scared. He's saying he's got a season to focus on and doesn't need these distractions, and now I'm halfway moved out of here, and all my stuff is at his place. I have no idea if I'm even still welcome there, but then he set my stuff outside the bedroom door last night. It's so confusing and conflicting." I shrug at the end.

"Did you ever take the test?" she asks softly.

I press my lips together and shake my head.

"You got your period?"

I shake my head again.

"Do you want to?"

"In my heart, I know it's negative. But, yeah, I guess I should." I glance toward the bathroom, and it feels like the clock of doom is ticking.

"I'm right here, okay?"

I nod. "Okay."

I head to the bathroom, read through the directions, and take the test, and then I call her in.

"Is it done already?" she asks.

I shake my head. "No, but I need moral support while I wait."

"I set a timer and walked away," she admits.

"Well, I'm planning to stare at it until I have an answer."

She giggles, and that's always been the difference between us. She has patience. I do not.

I don't want to wait for Grayson to figure out that we belong together.

But maybe I need to take a page from Kelly's book and give him the time and space he needs to work through this.

I watch the control line as it turns a pale pink.

I wait to see if another line appears. It doesn't.

"Yours was really obvious, right?" I ask.

She nods. "I mean…I waited the full three minutes, but yeah. Two pink lines."

"How long has it been?"

"You didn't look at the clock?" she asks.

"No! I was too busy peeing on a stick!"

She giggles even though it's not very funny. "No idea. Thirty seconds, maybe? A minute?"

I blow out a breath. "Fine. Can you set a timer for two more minutes?"

"Of course I can." She pulls her phone out of her pocket, and we watch the two minutes tick down. The pale pink of the control line deepens a little darker, but no second line appears.

The timer ticks down to zero, and her phone quacks.

"Seriously? A duck?" I ask.

"I use the timer a lot in my classroom, and the kids respond to the quack."

"You're a quack," I say, and we both giggle.

"And you're not pregnant. Will this ease Grayson's worries?"

"Not likely." I snap a photo of the negative test. "But at least I have evidence to show him he has nothing to freak out about."

I'm not really all that sure it matters at this point. He's beyond the point of being rational, and even though I want to fight for him anyway—for us and for the future where we stand together watching this same kind of test but hoping for a different outcome—I'm not sure it's a fight I have any chance of winning.

Chapter 53: Grayson Nash

Does Anybody Actually Know You

I glance up from where I'm focused on my leg curls when I see something out of the corner of my eye, and I spot Patrick waving his hands at me.

"Nash!"

I yank out an AirPod after I lower the weight. "What?"

"Are you okay?"

I blow out a frustrated breath. "Fine. Why?"

"I've just never seen you go this hard."

"Yeah, well, we haven't known each other that long."

"I've also never seen you this grouchy," he points out.

"I'm not grouchy," I say. It's a lie. I'm definitely grouchy.

"What's going on, man?" he asks.

I sigh. "Nothing I want to talk about."

"Okay. Well, I'm here, you know," he says.

"Yeah. Thanks."

"And I'll be right here all season," he adds. "It's not like you can get rid of me. So you might as well get it off your chest so we can move forward."

"I'm just going through some personal shit. It's nothing to worry about."

"Got it." He presses his lips together and nods, and then he studies me thoughtfully for a beat. "You know, you're one of those guys who seems like he's everybody's best friend, but does anybody actually know *you*? The real you, I mean."

It's a fair question, and the answer is complicated.

If anyone does, it's Ava.

Beckett comes close, but given that I've been lying to him for the last four months about what's really going on with his sister, I'm not sure I can still claim him on the people who know me well list.

He walks away, clearly asking a rhetorical question, but it's the kind of question that kicks me clean in the stomach when I'm already down.

It's the kind of question I'll take some time to ponder.

Yeah, I can talk to anybody. I can entertain a room. I can make everyone feel like they're my best friend.

But the vulnerable side of me locks a lot of myself away. Maybe it's some small part in the back of my mind that thinks people only like me because I play football, or because I have money, or because I have connections.

It's the part of me I refuse to acknowledge most of the time, but I've never heard that pushing away your real feelings is a solid way of dealing with things.

Except...it's how I've dealt with things my entire life.

Until Ava.

I showed her the real me. Didn't I?

Patrick's words play on my mind the rest of the day. I'm not in any hurry to get home. I'm not interested in talking things out. I just want to bypass all the relationship shit and get to the season already, and it's clear that she's affecting me. If Patrick could see it, then anybody could, and I can't let this take me down.

I also can't go to camp in this frame of mind.

I need to fight for my starting position. I'm new here, and I need to use camp to prove that I belong here—whether it's for one year or for ten.

Fuck, maybe I'll keep playing past this year. Maybe I'll love the Aces so goddamn much that nothing else will matter.

It's what I tell myself, anyway. I need that internal motivation to get to camp and leave it all out on the field, and I can't do that if half of my heart is still here struggling through the bullshit.

That's what leads me to my decision.

It's late by the time I get home. Admittedly, I stay at the gym far longer than I need to. I'm exhausted, and I treated myself to dinner solo after a shower at the gym.

But she's still awake. She's working on decorating those little mini cake things, and she's beautiful. She's smart. She's talented. She's everything.

But she can't be mine.

I knew we were doomed from the start, and not just because of the lies. I knew we'd end up right in this moment—or maybe I manifested it because I so strongly believed in it. Regardless, here we are, and I'm about to fuck this up like I fuck up everything.

"Hi," she says quietly.

"Hi." I move across the room and wind up on the opposite side of the island from her, and it's like we're facing off.

She sets down her piping bag and sets her palms on the counter. "I took the test today. It was negative."

I should feel relief at her words, but strangely...I don't. I feel indifferent. "Oh. What took you so long to take it?"

She lifts a shoulder. "One part fear, one part knowing what the result would be. It was a literal flash through my mind when Kelly said she was. I never actually believed I might be. It was more of a scare since I'm new to this whole, you know...sex thing."

"Right." I press my lips together. "Well, I guess that's good then."

I feel her eyes on me, but I keep mine averted to the counter.

"Listen, I leave for camp in less than a week now, and I'm not focused. And when you're not focused, you're risking injury." It's a quote from a former college coach. "I can't risk that when I'm new here."

"What are you saying?"

"I'm saying I need to end whatever this is between us." I rush the words, as if I have to say them quickly to get them out. "I was supposed to protect you. I failed. But at least now we don't have to lie to Beckett anymore."

I glance up at her, and she's clenching her jaw at my words.

"You can stay here for now, or whatever. Your rent is still paid up at the other house through the end of next month." I shrug. I'm not sure how to say I would like for her to move out when I'm not sure in my heart of hearts that feels like the right thing.

"Why are you doing this?" she whispers.

I hear a sniffle, and I can't look at her. I can't glance up and see tears tracking down her cheeks. I can't handle hurting her.

I thought this would be easier—that I could just walk away the same way I've walked away from every other relationship I've ever attempted.

But that's the thing. She's not every other woman I've ever walked away from.

It's just because she's my best friend's sister. It's just because there's more at stake here.

I can justify it however I want. The fact remains that this is harder than I thought it would be.

"I'm doing it because we never belonged together, Ava. It's only going to hurt more in the end if we prolong it."

"We never belonged together?" she hisses. "Are you kidding me?"

I finally glance up at her and watch as she brushes away a tear. I blow out a breath. "You once said I wouldn't have given you the time of day if I would've known who you were. I think maybe you're right. I certainly wouldn't have slept with you, and we never would've ended up where we are right now. We were always doomed to fail."

"We're only failing because you're allowing us to. You're running because you're scared. I know you, Grayson. Maybe better than you know yourself. You love me, and I love you, and I refuse to believe that our love isn't enough."

I clear my throat. "Well, it's not. For me, anyway."

She nods and draws in a deep breath. "Okay. I'm not going to beg, and I've got a lot of work to do." She picks up her piping bag and gets back to her desserts. "If it's okay, I may stay while you're gone for camp so I can use this kitchen since all my shit is here anyway. I'll figure out a plan once you're coming back."

"Okay." I watch her for a beat before I turn and walk out of the room.

Maybe it's just her focus on her task since she has a big event she's working on, but she seems okay with it. All of it.

But as I walk away toward the guest room I slept in last night, I'm not sure *I* am okay with it.

Any of it.

Chapter 54: Grayson Nash

Football is the Distraction

"Just stay away from him. Okay?" Lincoln demands, and I nod.

"Yes, Coach." I use the term more as one of endearment than as one of respect, but it works either way.

"I mean it. Don't get cute on me."

"Full disclosure…you know what happened, right?" I ask.

He sighs. "Yeah. The viral video, the fight at the Gridiron…I know all of it."

"I know you know that since you yelled at the two of us and told us to work it out like grown men. But did you also know that he was fucking around with Ava's roommate and got her pregnant, and now the roommate is moving to Louisiana to get far, far away from Graham?"

Lincoln narrows his eyes at me as he crosses his arms over his chest. "No. That I did not know."

"Well, now you do," I say.

"I guess I do. And I'm still telling you the same thing. Stay away from him. I don't need you causing issues your first year here when my other brother was suspended his first year here. Got it?"

I blow out a breath, but I mutter my agreement. "Got it."

He confronted me the second we arrived in California, where we're going to be for the next two weeks. The Aces always travel for the first two weeks of camp as a way to completely immerse ourselves back into the game.

And I have to say, it's nice to be back at it.

Nice isn't the right word. It's incredible. It's the exact distraction I need.

But I've never thought of football as the distraction. Everything else was always the distraction. Football has always come first. Everything else is secondary to that.

It's how I was raised, and it's how I've always lived my life up to this point.

It's that exact mindset that drove me to do what I did before I left for camp.

But now…something feels off.

Something feels *wrong*.

Despite having the *distraction* of football—my job, my life's work, my livelihood—there's still something that's just plain missing right now.

I refuse to let myself think it, but what it is that's missing is obvious.

Over the last few months, something else seems to have edged its way past football on my list of priorities, and being back at camp, building a brotherhood where we all share a common goal…it's a reminder that *this* is what matters.

At least…that's what I keep telling myself. Whether or not it's true is another matter entirely.

We're working on footwork skills today—my least favorite of all the drills we do. I love the mirror drills where I mirror the movements of a receiver and stay in tight coverage. I love coverage drills through a route. I especially love ball drills where we focus on deflections and interceptions.

But today we have hip flips, and fuck if I'm not going to be feeling that tomorrow. It's my least favorite partner drill where we have to change direction—from shuffling to planting, or from backpedaling to sprinting as we cover the receiver running routes.

I put my all into it, proving I still have speed and agility despite my advanced age.

After skills, we head into a scrimmage, and all of that is before lunch. After lunch, defense hits the weight room, and we move into meetings with our position coaches before dinner.

We have some walkthroughs of our newly installed plays after dinner, and then we get free time before curfew, though free time is mostly rehab and rest ahead of going hard again tomorrow.

Lather, rinse, repeat. It's two weeks of the same routine, but it's a routine I've come to rely on. And seeing Lincoln at the helm of all of it is something else entirely.

He's my big brother. I always idolized him, and then somehow we became actual friends. But now…he's at ease in this position. It's as if it was made for him. His deep knowledge of formations and plays is impressive, and his motivation to create a cohesive team experience is some of the best coaching I've ever worked with in my decade in the league.

And that's my brother.

On other teams, I've seen divisiveness. It's the offense against the defense. Here, we're all one unit, and what's even more impressive is how Lincoln fosters bonds between players of the same position when each of us is out here fighting for our own playing time and spot on the roster.

The only weak link I can seem to find is Austin Graham…but it helps to watch Asher kick his ass in camp.

I haven't spoken to Asher about what happened between Austin and me, and I haven't admitted to Austin that I know about his baby with Kelly.

I've stayed as far away from the guy as I can at the request of our head coach, and I've largely ignored my phone because the constant reminders of Ava are overwhelming.

I fucked up.

I know I fucked up.

And I don't know how to fix it.

It's the end of day eight at camp when I get back to my room. I've been sharing with Patrick, who has become a good friend—though I've been careful not to talk about Ava.

No distractions.

Football is the distraction.

I'm so goddamn confused.

I check my phone after my shower and see I have a new voicemail from my mother.

"Grayson Michael Nash, it's your mother."

Oh, shit. I got middle named. That's never good.

"What's going on with you and Ava? I just spoke to Sandra, who didn't even know you were dating, and then she checked in with Beckett, who said you two were just faking it, but it didn't seem awfully fake to me, and then I saw this video online that seems to confirm that it was fake…so what is it? I know you're at camp, but you better make time to talk to your mother no matter where you are. Okay, love you honey, bye!"

I chuckle at the end of her message, though the message itself really wasn't all that amusing.

I don't really want to call her back, but I also don't really think I have a choice. She did middle name me, after all. Patrick is still in the shower, so I don't bother leaving our room to make the phone call. I realize it's late in New York, but I am also fully aware that she's going to be waiting for this call. The longer I make her wait, the more trouble I'll be in when I finally call.

I click the call button, and she answers almost immediately. "Grayson Michael Nash, what is going on?"

"Sorry, Mom. It's complicated."

"What's complicated? Either you're with her or you're not."

Theoretically, she's right…but in practice, it really is a little more complicated than that.

I launch into the story from the beginning. "When we first got together, I didn't realize who she was. I guess she had some unrequited childhood crush and didn't know how to come clean with who she really was. We had a great connection, and then I found out a week later that she had kept the truth about who she was from me. Around the same time, I had to come up with some explanation since Beckett saw some photos of us kissing after he specifically asked me to watch out for his little sister. She suggested we tell him that it was a fake relationship. The lie seemed better than having him feel like I betrayed him even though I didn't do it knowingly. Eventually, I got around to forgiving her for keeping that secret, and I started to fall for her. I'm pretty sure she fell for me too, and things were going well until I uncovered another secret. But this time…it just triggered that flight response in me. I saw what these secrets did to your marriage. I can't be in the kind of relationship that was doomed to fail from the start because of secrets. Not after I watched you and Dad fall apart."

"Oh, honey. Baby." She sighs. "I'll admit, I was hurt by some of the things your father was keeping from me, but just because the end was rough doesn't mean I would trade in the first forty years we spent together. Well, maybe except for the last couple." She chuckles a little at the end, and that little laugh there tells me that she's okay. She's fine. She lived through it, and she emerged on the other side. Laughing.

"You really wouldn't trade it in? You wouldn't do it over if you could?" I ask, and I hear the begging sound in my own voice.

"No. And I was never quite as sure about that as I was when we were together as a family in Jolene's hospital room and I held my first grandbaby. I sat there, and this realization plowed into me that as hard as it was in the end, this is what we created. We created this beautiful family of four boys, this new generation. Things weren't always perfect, and maybe we messed you guys up. But if I traded those hard years with your dad to make it all easy, then I wouldn't have the four of you. I wouldn't have my first grandbaby. There were thirty-eight mostly good years before the last two, but honey…that's life. Sometimes it's hard.

Sometimes it's messy. Sometimes it's sad. But sometimes it's beautiful and lovely and *happy*."

She pauses for a beat as I process her words, and before I get the chance to say anything, she adds, "I really want you to think long and hard about whether whatever secrets are between you two are so bad that you'd give up even one more minute of the delirious happiness I saw when you were with her. Maybe you told Beck you were faking it, but you can't fake those genuine smiles I saw on both of you."

I blow out a breath. "Okay. I'll think about it."

"Promise me. Because I have to tell you, honey, the pain was worth it for the happiness I had for a long time. And she's worth it, too."

I clear my throat of the sudden clog of emotion that seems to gather there. "Fine. I promise."

"Okay. I love you, baby. Forever."

"I love you forever too, Mom," I mutter just as Patrick walks back into the room.

We say our goodbyes, and Patrick glances over at me. "That was your mom?"

I nod.

"Heard she's single."

"Shut the fuck up," I warn.

"Yeah...probably not a smart plan to hook up with Coach's mom, anyway." He smirks at me.

"You know I can kick your ass, right?"

"Pfft. In your dreams, maybe." He shrugs, and while the exchange is meant in good fun, I'm not feeling very *fun*.

Not after my mom issued so many points for me to ponder.

Is she right? Were we really that happy together?

Am I giving up things I never even knew I wanted because I'm scared?

Yes. Only, I'm not *scared*. I'm fucking terrified, and I don't know if I'm strong enough to battle against those fears to find my way back home to her.

Chapter 55: Ava Maxwell

Eventually They Come Crawling Back

He's coming home today. It's the moment I've been simultaneously dreading and anticipating for two long weeks.

We haven't spoken since he essentially ended things between us before he left. I've thrown myself into work over the last two weeks.

Because when I'm not working, I'm crying or dwelling on what I've lost.

Kelly left me the same time Grayson did, and it only worsened my chronic leave-ability condition. It showed me *yet again* that everyone in my life eventually leaves.

Even my friends.

To be fair, Kelly has called or texted me every day since she moved back to Louisiana. I know I'm not alone, but it does feel very much like Grayson left me at one of my lowest points. He knew my biggest fear was abandonment, and he chose to press on that fear when he left for training camp at the exact time my best friend skipped town.

And the fact that he hasn't attempted to make any sort of contact with me since leaving only confirms how very over this is.

I'm even thinking about changing the recipe for my cookies.

I know I can't. I know they're the bakery's best seller, and taking out my special top-secret ingredient will change the entire composition of the cookies.

But that's of little concern to me when that secret ingredient reminds me so much of the man who broke my heart.

"Do you wanna come?" Cora asks. "Ava? Ava!"

"Huh?"

"To the Gridiron tonight," she says. "Do you want to come with Dom and me?"

"Oh…no. No thanks."

"Are you sure? Rumor has it the team gets back today from training camp, and I'm sure the hot single ones are all going to need a drink when they get back in town." She wiggles her eyebrows and says the words as if that will be the thing that convinces me.

In reality, I'd like to stay as far away from the Gridiron as I possibly can.

"Oh, uh…I have some things I'm working on. A couple of side projects…" I keep it vague, just as I have since I got the first call for desserts after the charity ball. I haven't admitted to Cora, Dom, Poppy, or anyone else at the bakery that I've been taking business on the side.

As long as I'm using my own recipes and supplies and not the bakery's, there's nothing stopping me. I haven't made my famous cookies for any of my side projects, but not because I can't.

Thanks to work and those side projects, it hasn't been all sadness and tears. With each day bringing us closer to this one, with every moment that my phone remained silent, anger started to take root.

It burrowed its way in and held on tight as the pain and sadness shifted into frustration.

Each passing day seemed to get a little easier despite the many setbacks I had. But now that it's been two weeks and I haven't heard a damn word from him, you better believe I'm angry as fuck.

I realize he has been at training camp, and I know he has to focus on the game. He made that clear.

But Kelly heard from Austin.

It was just to check in and see how she was feeling, as far as I know. He didn't get in touch with her more than two or three texts over the last two weeks.

But it's two or three more times than I got from the guy who told me he loved me.

It's hard to buy that he really loved me, because if he did, he wouldn't be so easily able to cut himself out of my life. That's what I keep going back to. Maybe it was just fun and games for him.

It was more than that for me.

But since he won't bother getting in touch, I can't ask.

I could call him—and I did.

Once.

I didn't leave a message, and he didn't call me back.

So now I'm at a point where I'm not even sure I would give him another chance if he did come crawling back.

It's not worth smashing the little progress I've made to regress back into something with him when he is so unbelievably sure that we were always doomed to fail. I can't be with someone who doesn't believe we can make it with the same conviction I have.

I was so sure that we were right for each other. Now I see how blinded I was by some stupid childhood crush on a guy who never even gave me the chance to get to know who he really was.

I thought I knew him. I thought maybe I was the *only* one who really knew him.

But the guy I fell in love with never would've been able to walk away so easily.

Two of my three events are done now, and word of mouth is picking up. I did the ball for free minus my expenses, but these other events have been quite profitable.

I just need to keep saving my money and keep my focus. I'll get to that goal…eventually. I'm more than halfway to what I think I'd need since I have a trust my dad set up for me in his will. I haven't touched that money, but I know it's what Beckett used for law school, it's what Alexander used for med school, and it's what Oliver used for his master's degree.

As for me…it'll be part of what I use to open my own bakery before I turn thirty.

I can do it. I have five years to save up to hit that goal, and I'm more determined than ever.

If I could just sell that damn Radiance shit, I'd be even closer.

I push those thoughts out of my head while I finish up the cake I'm decorating, and it's just as I'm getting ready to leave for the day that my phone starts to ring.

I yank my phone out of my pocket to see who's calling, my heart lifting with hope that maybe it's him.

I'm not sure *why* I allow myself to fall into that trap. It *hasn't* been him once in the last two weeks, so why the hell would it start now?

But it's not him.

Instead, it's someone I'm even *more* surprised to hear from, if that's possible.

It's my mother.

I finish the cake, say my goodbyes quickly, and rush out to my car to call her back.

"Ava, hi darling," she answers. She sounds…more coherent than the last time we spoke. I think it was…six months ago? Before Grayson and I reconnected, for sure.

"Hi, Mom," I say. "You called?"

"I did. I spoke with Missy Nash. She said she saw you a couple months ago and you're dating her son now?"

"Yeah…we were," I say softly. "Sort of. It's over now."

"Oh," she says. "I'm so sorry to hear that. He always seemed like a good boy. Are you doing okay?"

"I will be." I think. I'm not really sure, but I can't keep going home to his house when I know it's over. "What about you, Mom? How are you doing?"

She clears her throat. "I'm doing well. I actually joined a local group and made some friends who have been through a loss similar to mine, and through that, I met someone. We've been seeing each other, oh, a few months now."

"You're seeing someone?" I repeat. My dad died seventeen years ago. It still sounds weird to hear that she's seeing someone.

But…good for her. Nobody should have to face this world alone.

The thought is depressing. I'm more alone than I've ever been. I jumped from Colin to Grayson literally overnight, and now I'm on my own.

And maybe I want to *stay* on my own a little while longer. Maybe this isn't such a bad place to be.

I'm talking to my *mother*. And she sounds *okay*. Normal, even.

Maybe I'm not as alone as I thought. When one door closes and all that.

"Yes. Is that weird for you?" she asks. "It's okay if it is."

"No. It's not. I'm happy for you."

"Are you sure you're okay? I'd love to come out to Vegas and spend some time with you. Tell you more about Thomas. Maybe even bring him out."

"I'm totally okay, and I actually have a spare bedroom if you'd like to stay with me. My roommate just moved back home to Louisiana, so it's just me." Sort of. Once I move back into my place.

The house is going to feel so empty without Kelly, and just like I wasn't sure if she could afford it without me, I don't know if I can afford it without her.

But I'll figure something out. Maybe I'll get my Radiance group on Facebook going again.

Ugh.

Just the thought of hitting up my friends and family to buy all that shit has my skin crawling. Maybe I can look into other independent consultants and see if they'd like to buy some of my stock.

"Okay. I'll be in touch. Maybe Oliver or Alexander will meet me there. It would be nice to see my kids a little more. Even *hear* from them a little more," she hints. She backpedals quickly. "I know I haven't been a very good mother to you four. I know Beckett stepped up more than he should have. And I've also learned that it's not too late to fix your mistakes…if you can find it in you to allow me to try."

I'm wary of the promises. I don't know who this Thomas guy is, but so far it sounds like he's good for her. I never expected a call like this one.

It doesn't necessarily make me feel any less alone, but it does do one important thing.

It makes me see that even if it's easy for people to leave me, they don't forget me. Eventually, they come crawling back.

Chapter 56: Grayson Nash

What is with Today

I'm not sure what to expect as I turn onto the street my house is on, and my chest tightens when I see the little red Versa in the driveway.

My mother's words to me have not left my mind since she said them.

I promised her I'd think about it, and I have.

It's *all* I've thought about.

My mother wanted me to weigh whether being angry over the secrets was worth losing her, and it struck me that she was right.

Both my mother *and* Ava.

Ava said she knew me better than I knew myself. She said I was running scared.

She was abso-fucking-lutely right about that.

I did run scared. I told her it was over to save myself the pain of it all coming to an end later anyway.

But my mom was right, too, and she made me see that I was giving up the good times because I'm scared of the bad.

I can't live life scared.

Ava really didn't keep a secret from me. It's not like she was knocked up, but seeing those tests on her counter pulsed a fear in me I didn't quite understand at the time.

I'm not ready to be a father, and I still don't know if I even want that in my future.

I thought we were protected. I thought we were safe. And that's the root of my issue. As it turns out, my issue wasn't with her or even that box at all—it was my own fears that I was going to fuck this all up, and I made it into a self-fulfilling prophecy.

I did fuck it up.

I realized it two days ago, but by that point, I figured I should just wait to see her in person to admit the truth.

And now here we are. I'm moments away from walking through the door and making my big confession so I can pave the way to winning her back.

Only…that's not exactly what happens.

When I walk into the house from the garage, I hear some grunting. When I turn the corner, I find her.

She's as gorgeous as ever, and my heart palpitates wildly in my chest at the sight of her.

God, I love her.

How did I think I could walk away? What the fuck is wrong with me?

She's struggling with one of her suitcases as she yanks it down the stairs, and I walk up to take the suitcase from her.

"Oh!" she gasps when she sees me. Her hand flies to her chest. "You scared me."

"Sorry," I murmur, and even from here I can smell that fresh-baked cookie scent that somehow now only serves to make me horny as fuck.

I keep it in my pants.

For now.

We have to talk first.

I have to tell her how sorry I am for what I did.

I get her suitcase down the stairs, and I pause with the handle still in my hand. She seems to be waiting for me to keep moving it along, maybe even out to her car, but I don't want to do that. I want her to stay right here.

"I'm sorry. I had planned to be out by the time you got home. You're earlier than I thought you'd be."

I rushed home so I could see you.

I let the words die on my tongue. "You don't have to leave."

She purses her lips. "Well, it doesn't make much sense for me to stay when you made it clear that things are over."

"What if they aren't?" I ask.

"Wha...um. What?"

"What if things between us aren't over?" I ask.

She sighs. "Can you, like...be clearer?"

"Sorry," I say. "I don't want things to be over. I fucked up, Ava, just like we both knew I would, and I'm sorry. I want to try this with you. I want to be with you. I love you."

She's quiet as she touches a hand to her forehead for a beat.

I wait with bated breath for her to leap into my arms.

"God...what is with today?" she wonders quietly, and I can't help but wonder what she means by that.

I don't get a chance to ask because she plows forward. "I love you, too, Grayson, and once upon a time, I thought that was enough. You told me it wasn't. So...I'm sorry, but no."

She twists her lips as her words pack a punch to my gut.

"I never thought I'd be the one to say it," she continues, "but I've realized over the last two weeks that I need to be with someone who believes in us—who believes in *me*. I need to be with someone who won't run at the first sign of trouble. I deserve that. I deserve someone who might go away for two weeks but who can't possibly not call me every single one of those days. I deserve someone who doesn't leave me like everyone else leaves me, especially not when you knew that was my biggest fear and you bailed on me anyway. You showed me exactly who you are, and I wish who you are could line up with what I want, what I deserve, but it just...doesn't." She presses her lips together, and then she reaches out and squeezes my arm.

She squeezes my fucking arm when I'm expecting her to fall into them at my confession.

I thought this would be so easy.

Clearly...I was wrong.

She's not the girl who's going to forgive me with one apology.

She needs to see that I'm all the things she deserves—that I believe in her. I believe in us. I believe in our future together, and I won't ever leave her again.

I need her to see that this was just my fear that I needed to deal with, but it was knowing she'd be there on the other side of it that eventually showed me how to get the fuck over it. She needs to know I can't and won't go a single goddamn day without hearing her voice.

And maybe most of all, I need to show her that one simple question from my mother turned me into someone else.

I'm not the same guy who left two weeks ago for camp.

That guy would have heard her rejection and walked away. That guy would have believed it wasn't worth fighting for.

I'm better than him. I'm the guy who's going to fight to win her back…whatever it takes.

And I know just where to start.

She leaves, and I put my plan together. I make a few calls and get some things lined up.

I bide my time and wait for the next morning when I'm sure she'll be at the bakery.

It's my one day off before the local leg of training camp begins, and instead of taking the day to rest and relax as was recommended by our coaches, I'm on a mission.

I still have the spare key for her house, so I grab a few empty boxes and toss them in the bed of my truck before I jump in and head over. The house is quiet. She's the only one who lives here now, anyway, and she's at work.

I grab a couple of the boxes out of my trunk and head toward her closet. I have absolutely no idea what this shit might be worth, but I looked up a local consultant who was happy to take a look at the inventory and let me know what it's worth in exchange for a pair of tickets to an upcoming game.

Am I using my connections to try to get what I want? Fuck yeah, I am. What's the point of having connections if you don't use them?

I start emptying the shelves of the Radiance skincare products. There are hundreds of white boxes with black writing on them: cleansers, toners, serums, scrubs, soaps, moisturizers, haircare, suncare, retinol, makeup. At the beginning, I look at every single label. By the end, I'm tossing shit into the boxes, hoping that I brought enough empties with me to get all this shit out of here.

I navigate over toward the coffee shop where I agreed to meet this consultant. It's obvious which one is her since she has a giant sticker in the back window of her car that lets the world know she is a Radiance Independent Consultant—along with her social media handle to make it easy to find her.

She must really be into this shit. Ava clearly is not.

I get out of the truck. She must recognize me because she gets out of her car at the same time.

"Melanie? I ask.

"So nice to meet you," she says. "Let's take a look at what you have."

I open the boxes for her and show her all the stuff Ava has stored in her closet for who knows how long.

"Wow," Melanie breathes. "This is…well, it's a jackpot. It's a tier five VIP box."

It's a little incredible she can look through a few boxes and know exactly what she's looking at. "What does that mean?"

"All the consultants start out at fifteen percent commission, but each tier gets you a better rate. By the time you're at the tier five box, consultants keep thirty percent commission."

"What are you?" I ask.

"Tier five. It's the max."

"So…do you want all this shit?"

She narrows her eyes at me like calling it *shit* is an insult.

"How did you find all this? Is it…" She glances around. "Is it an underground, back-alley kind of thing?"

375

I can't help but laugh at that. Do people really do that? "No," I say as I hand her an envelope with two tickets in it to our home opener. "It's my girlfriend's. I'm just trying to help her offload it."

She nods and twists her lips as she eyes the boxes. She's right there. I can tell. It might just take a little, tiny nudge.

"Do you want it?" I ask.

She sighs. "It's a lot of money. I'm not sure…"

"What did my girlfriend pay for it?" I ask. I'm hoping she tells me the truth, but it's easy enough to look it up now that I know what it is.

"Ten thousand."

Whoa.

She paid *ten thousand dollars* for this shit? What the fuck was she thinking?

I sigh. "You can have it all for five thousand." I'll pay the difference. I just want her to have her money back.

"Oh, wow. I…I don't know what to say."

"Say you'll get this shit out of my truck."

She laughs. "Okay." She nods as she says the word. "Yes. Let's do it."

I suck in a deep breath. Mission fucking accomplished.

I just hope it's enough for her to see that I'm making the types of sacrifices that she deserves.

Chapter 57: Ava Maxwell

Bring it On

I stay at the bakery until it closes, and then I stay a little longer.

If I head home now, I'm just going home to the empty house I used to share with Kelly. And it's not just that.

I'm not okay.

I know telling him no was the right thing to do. I know walking away is what's best for my heart. These are the things my brain keeps telling me.

My heart, however, is on a different page entirely. My heart thinks it's all wrong, and today I'm sitting in that weird place of conflicting thoughts and feelings.

I hate it. I hate all of this, and I wish I'd never met him.

Sure, if I'd never met him, I would've missed out on the good stuff, but it was so short-lived that it feels like a blip in time that I'll never get back again. Dwelling on it isn't helping, so I throw myself into baking.

Only…it's not helping the way it traditionally has.

I'm not just sad. I'm heartbroken. But I had to walk away. I had to do it on my own terms. I had to let him know that I won't go back to how things were. I will wait to get everything I deserve, just like I told him I would.

When I get home, the kitchen light is on.

I didn't leave the kitchen light on when I left this morning. In fact, I made sure I turned it off when I left, and since it was dark outside at the time, I nearly tripped over a chair on my way to the garage, and I had to turn on the flashlight on my phone to see where I was going.

Someone was in here, and when I spot a rather large sum of cash on the counter along with a note…well, I know who it was.

I read the note.

Ava-

I used the key you once gave me. Hope that's okay. I want to be what you deserve, and you deserve not to be stressed out by mistakes of the past any longer.

-G

Stressed out by the mistakes of my past? What the hell is he even talking about?

I count the hundred-dollar bills on the counter.

There are one hundred of them.

That's ten thousand dollars in cash just sitting out on my kitchen counter.

What mistake from my past is worth ten grand?

As soon as the thought registers in my brain, I run to my closet.

"Holy shit," I whisper as I take in the now-empty shelves. I run my hand along the middle shelf. It's all gone, and in its place is the cash I wish I would've held onto in the first place.

I never used the products. I didn't like the way they smelled, and having to sell them made me realize how very much I am not cut out for direct sales.

Yet I was dumb enough to purchase ten grand worth of products with the promise of bonuses and vacations and even a car.

I didn't get any of them. Not a single one. They made it seem so easy when I sold out of my welcome pack right away, but once people realized how cheap the products actually were, I had little chance at success.

I have no idea how he offloaded all that stuff, but I feel very grateful.

I think about sending a text of gratitude, but a phone call feels more personal and genuine.

"Hey, Cookie," he answers. His voice is warm and rich in my ear.

"Thank you for what you did," I say softly.

"You're welcome."

"How'd you do it?" I can't help but ask the question.

"I looked up local independent consultants, picked one who seemed like she had a lot of interaction on her Instagram page, and sold it to her."

My brows rise.

That's actually…a lot of work. Plus, he hauled it all out of here, and there were nearly seven hundred products in there.

Today was his one day off. He spent it making sure I knew that he was trying to prove he had changed.

And he did.

"That was really sweet, Grayson. I don't know how I'll ever be able to thank you."

"You don't need to do anything. But I wouldn't be opposed to, you know, having you come over so we can make up and put all this to rest."

I blow out a breath. "As tempting as that is…I told you. I can't run back and risk being hurt again. This time was hard enough, and I can't put myself through that again. Not when you so strongly believe we're doomed from the start, and not when my feelings for you run so deep."

He clears his throat, and I'm ready for the protest.

I don't get it.

"Okay. I understand."

"You do?" I ask, clear awe in my tone.

He chuckles. "Yes. If you're not ready to take me back, then that means I still have work to do."

"So, what…you're just going to badger me until I relent?" My own tone sounds frustrated.

"No, babe. I'm going to keep showing you how sorry I am that I ran out on you. I'm going to show you that I don't believe we're going to fail. I believe in you, and us, and even myself. And I'm going to figure out how to prove that to you."

I'm quiet a beat as I try to process that. This is him fighting for me, but I've already made up my mind.

I can't do this. I can't tiptoe through life as I wait for him to decide he's done.

I'm not sure what would be enough to prove that he won't run scared again.

But if he wants to keep trying…well, then bring it on.

And he does bring it on. When I get home from the bakery the next evening, there's a box on the kitchen counter in the same spot where the cash—which I deposited into my account today—was sitting yesterday.

Inside is an envelope sitting on top of a Vegas Aces jersey.

I pull it out of the box and turn it around. Nash 24.

I open the envelope and find two tickets to the preseason game this weekend, along with another note.

Ava-

Looking for plans this Sunday? Come hang at the stadium and cheer on your local pro football team. Seeing you in the stands wearing my number would mean everything to me.

-G

Oh, I'll go to the game, all right. But wearing his jersey?

I don't think so.

I'm tempted to wear Austin's just to grate on Grayson's nerves and see what he does.

I'd never actually do that.

Instead, I invite Cora to attend the game with me, and I wear a black Vegas Aces T-shirt paired with jeans.

I didn't bother looking at where our seats were located until I got to the stadium.

As it turns out, section one-thirty-five is immediately behind the Aces' bench, and row one is, well, the first row.

The team is out on the field doing warm-ups when we arrive, and Grayson spots us and jogs over as we take our seats.

"You showed up," he says.

"Free tickets to a game," I say a little flippantly.

He grins. "I knew you wouldn't wear the jersey." He runs over to the bench and grabs something before he runs back to me. "It's why I have this spare one waiting on the bench—just in case you forgot it."

I roll my eyes despite a small giggle, and he winks at me before he races off to finish his warm-ups.

I slip the jersey on, and it's a perfect fit. He finds me from where he is on the field, and he glances down at my shirt. He nods approvingly, and I just smile and shake my head.

"What's going on with you two?" Cora asks me. "And can I get in on some of that...but maybe from a different player since Nash twenty-four is obviously into you?"

I have to admit, there *is* something special about being here. And Grayson really is trying. He called me every day this week when he got home from practice, and he's really putting in the effort.

Seeing him on that field...well. It does things to me.

He's a man in uniform, though not in the traditional sense, and those tight white pants are really something else.

He looks so...tough. I've never really paid much attention to the game before, but I find that when he's on the field, I can't take my eyes off him. And when he's on the sidelines...well, I can't take my eyes off him.

Except when we get nachos. Then I can't take my eyes off my nachos.

I miss a play when I'm digging in for more cheese, and when I look up, Grayson seems angry as he stalks toward the bench.

"What happened?" I ask, my mouth full of chip.

"Nash missed a block," the guy to my left tells me.

Oh. Sounds bad—whatever that means.

I have a beer, which isn't my favorite drink but seems to go down well here at the game. The atmosphere is positively electric. The Aces are winning by the end of the first quarter, and most of the starters are benched when the second quarter begins. I need to remember to ask him why that is.

He runs right by me before the players run into the locker room at halftime, and he stops. "Are you having a good time?"

He's so sweet, so sincere, as he wants to make sure I'm enjoying myself.

I give him the honest truth. "I'm having a blast." And watching him do his thing is nothing short of absolutely incredible.

He grins before he follows his teammates to the locker room, and Cora and I head up to grab another beer.

I like Cora—she's fun to work with, and she was game to come here with me today—but I miss Kelly. Cora is definitely not a Kelly replacement, and I'm sad that I'm not here at this game with my best friend as we cheer on our men.

I mean…as I cheer for Grayson and she cheers for Austin.

Neither of which is either of our men.

Still, the mistake was made in my own brain, and I'm starting to wonder what I'm missing out on by pushing him away.

It's been just under a week, but so far, he hasn't shown any signs of slowing down. At what point is taking the front-row tickets and the cash overstepping some imaginary line?

I can't quite be sure…but I'm tossed into a weird state of confusion as I fight against my feelings.

Has he changed?

And if he has…am I willing to take him back?

I've told him no.

But I'm not really quite so sure anymore because when things were good, things were *good*.

And I'm starting to think I want to get back to that place again.

Chapter 58: Grayson Nash

The Only Path Forward

I'm running out of ideas. The last one I have is also the biggest, and it's a combination of several things that I think will be enough to win her over.

I'm getting closer. I can tell. I'm not giving up, but I saw the way she looked at me during the game. I saw the way she smiled when I had a big play.

I saw the way my jersey fit her like a fucking glove. I don't want her to just wear my name.

I want it to be *her* name, too. And *that* is a realization that would have been terrifying to me a few weeks ago.

Now, though, the only thing scary about it is the fact that she could say no.

A rejection after I lay it all out on the line would kill me, but if it's what she wants and what she truly believes is going to make her happy, then I won't stand in her way.

I continue to call her every day, even if it's just to leave a voicemail because she doesn't pick up. Sometimes we talk, but more often than not, I tell her I just wanted to hear her voice.

Training camp is still kicking my ass, but getting to go home every night helps. And hearing her voice at the end of each day is the balm I need to soothe my aching muscles.

It's the motivation I need to go harder tomorrow.

I tell her that, too.

She's flattered.

"I love you," I say to her one night.

"I know you do. And you know how I feel."

Do I, though?

I don't question her, though I'm starting to feel a sense of desperation.

As we wait for our defense meeting to start, I overhear Dave Redmayne talking about how his daughter's birthday is coming up and they have no idea where to go to get a cake.

"I know someone," I tell him.

I give him her number.

I look for ways to promote her talents.

And it's as I make a final decision about her talents that I finally realize…I need to call her brother.

I need to be honest with him.

It's the only path forward for us.

I'll never have her dad's approval, but having Beckett's is just as important.

I've never been nervous to call him before, but I've also never called him with the sort of confession I'm about to make.

I'm not just worried about his reaction. I'm worried I'm putting our friendship on the line for something that isn't guaranteed. If anything, it's something she has made clear she doesn't want. But I finally know what to do to get her to believe that I trust in her, us, and our future.

And it's the absolute guarantee that there *is* a future for us. The only way to do that is to invest in something we can create a future from.

I draw a deep breath, my chest tightening as I get ready to make this call.

"Grayson Nash," my best friend answers. "To what do I owe the pleasure this time?"

"Just checking in on you, old buddy."

"I figured it had something to do with that viral video of you that I was in, too."

"Eh, that's old news at this point." It really is, though. The charity ball was nearly two months ago, and has it really been that long since I spoke with Beckett?

"I'm glad it blew over. I figured it would. These things always do."

"How's Rachel?" I ask.

"She's incredible. Glowing and feeling great. How's Vegas? How's my sister? Still faking things?"

"About that," I begin.

"Uh oh…"

I know he's trying to be funny and play it off like it's some big joke, but it's not a joke, and it's not funny to me. It's my life, and this is me trying my damnedest to straighten it the fuck out.

"I have a confession to make, and I'm not real sure how you're going to take it."

"Well, now you're kind of scaring me," he admits.

Just do it. Get it over with. Rip off the bandage.

"When I first moved to town, I saw a girl at a bar and felt this instant chemistry. I took her back to my hotel, took her out to dinner, questioned whether it was right to spend the night with her since we had a connection beyond the physical, and then did it anyway."

"Oh, shit. You're about to tell me you're fake breaking up with Ava for this chick, aren't you?" he asks.

"Uh…not exactly. Fast forward a week, and I went to the address you gave me to check on your little sister. Imagine my surprise when I saw the girl I'd hooked up with at the same bakery." I clear my throat. Here it comes. Confession time.

I must freeze longer than I realize.

"Grayson?" Beckett asks.

I blow out a breath. "I had no idea she was the same girl who used to lift weights in your family room in some attempt to impress me all those years ago. She looked completely different than she did back then. She happened to know who I was, so when I hit on her at the bar and she accepted my invitation, she gave me a nickname, and when I took her back to my hotel room, I had no idea she was little Ava Maxwell."

Silence greets me on the other end of the line, so I plow forward.

"When I found out who she really was, I ended things with her immediately. I felt like she made me betray my best friend, and I wasn't okay with that. I told her I couldn't continue seeing her, but then her ex showed up, and I pretended like we were a thing to protect her. He took a picture and sold it to the media. My plan to stay away from her was fucked when she told him we were together, and then you called and questioned me about the pictures, and it sort of *was* fake for his benefit, so that's what I told you. But then we were forced to spend time together to keep up the act, and both of us developed feelings."

"What kind of feelings?" His words come out stilted and forced—like he's speaking through a clenched jaw.

"You know what kind of feelings," I say quietly. And then, just to clarify, I add, "I'm in love with her, Beck."

He's quiet on the other end.

"And, naturally, because I'm Grayson Nash, I managed to fuck it up."

"I swear to God, if you hurt her, I will come out there and kill you myself. With my bare hands." He's seething.

"There's no need for any of that. I'm working my ass off to show her that I've changed, that she's the only one for me, only...she won't take me back."

"What the fuck did you do?" he asks.

I decide to go for full honesty. It's the only way I'll win him over. "Before I left for camp, I saw a box of pregnancy tests on her counter. She's not pregnant, but it stopped me short as I had to sit and think about whether it was what I wanted out of my future."

"And?" he presses.

"And I still don't know the answer, but I told her I needed to focus on the upcoming season, and I couldn't do that if I was distracted by what was happening between us. I told her it was over, she called me out on my bullshit, and I ran anyway."

"Then you deserve it. If she won't take you back, it's because she's protecting herself from having to deal with your ass again, and to be honest, Gray, I don't blame her." He's blunt, and he sounds angry...as any good brother should be.

"I don't blame her, either. Which is why I'm trying so goddamn hard to show her I've changed, and the first step to that was confessing all of this to you."

"She doesn't know you're telling me all this?" he asks.

"No. And I'm sorry if you're mad. I know you told me to protect her, and honest to God, I tried. It's how this whole thing began—I saw her fighting with her ex, and I acted like I was the new guy in her life to get him to back off, and here we are five months later, and I've never felt like this before. I love her, man. I want to marry her. I want to spend my life giving her everything she deserves."

"This is going to sound harsh, but I've seen you go through women like fucking Tootsie Rolls. I think this is a terrible idea." There he goes, being all blunt again, and it's an epic shot right to my heart.

"I know. She deserves better. But I'm hopeful she'll end up with me anyway."

He sighs. "With that said, I also know that you're a good man to your core. I don't think I could've maintained a friendship with someone for this many years if I didn't believe that. I know if you're calling me to tell me all this, it's real. It's serious. And to be honest, I more than suspected it when we were in town. She loves you, too. It's obvious, and so I can't be the one to stand in your way. You better not fuck this up, though. You hear me?"

"I won't. At least, I won't *again*."

He chuckles wryly.

"So do I have your blessing to ask for her hand in marriage?" I ask quietly. Nervously.

"If it's what she wants, then there's nothing I'd like more than to call you my actual brother."

My chest swells at the thought of it. It seems so simple now, but it's been a conversation I absolutely feared for months.

Now that it's all out in the open, I feel…free.

Chapter 59: Ava Maxwell

Thoughtful Fleeting Things

A giant bag of Tootsie Rolls appeared on my kitchen counter yesterday. Last week, I got a phone call from someone who plays defense for the Vegas Aces asking me to bake a cake for his daughter's birthday party. This week, I've had more phone calls asking for a variety of different types of desserts for different events.

I know this is all Grayson's doing. I know he believes in me and my abilities when it comes to baking.

And I think it's starting to slowly get through to me that he believes in me as a person—as a *partner*—for him.

I'm teetering on the edge of wanting to slowly dip my toe back into trying things with him. The season is well underway now, but it hasn't stopped him from calling me every day to check in. Sometimes it's late into the night. Other times it's first thing in the morning. But regardless, he hasn't let a day go by where I haven't heard his voice and he hasn't heard mine.

And this is his season. He's busy. But he's making time—time for Tootsie Rolls and jerseys and Aces shirts. Time for tickets where he sees me in the stands. Time to come over and say hi and make sure everyone in the stadium knows he's taken. By me.

Even if he really isn't.

The media hasn't picked up on us being apart, and I think it's because people assume he's busy. He is in season and not attending the same number of events he did in the offseason, and he's still greeting me at games.

Or maybe he's choosing to stay home because he doesn't have a date since I'm still holding back.

At least that's what he indicated when we were talking the other night. I told him I didn't want to hold him back from doing the things he wanted to do, and he said he wouldn't find any joy in them if he didn't have my hand to hold.

The more time that passes where I'm not at his house, not in his bed, not by his side, the more I wonder whether I'm just being stubborn. I'm not sure what it'll take to push me over the edge to run back into his arms.

I told him I need him to prove he believes in us, and I guess I need him to prove to me that I am the future he wants. Giving me tickets and jerseys, or selling my skincare line, or stopping by with Tootsie Rolls—these are all wonderful and kind and thoughtful actions.

But these things are fleeting. These aren't the things that tell me I'm a permanent fixture in his life.

Football season is in full swing as the scorching heat of summer fades into the milder fall weather. Halloween is right around the corner, and while he has continued giving me all sorts of attention, he hasn't pressured me into taking him back. Despite that, he's still there, calling, texting, and letting me know he's thinking about me every single day.

I'm starting to get the hint.

He wants me to take him back when I'm ready. And I think I'm getting closer to being ready. I think I want to jump in and try to trust him again.

And then one day my phone starts to ring, and I see it's Beckett calling.

"Hey," I answer.

"Hey. Mom said she wants to come see you in Vegas, and I have a free weekend coming up, too. Can I join her?"

"Just you? Or the whole fam?"

"Just me," he says. "Rachel is sicker than a dog at six months pregnant but says she can handle the girls by herself for one weekend."

"I'd love to see you. You're welcome to stay with me."

He clears his throat. "I know, but I'm guessing Mom will take you up on that, so I asked Grayson if I can stay with him."

"You're staying with Grayson?" I ask.

"Yeah. And, uh…just for the record, he told me everything."

"Everything?" I repeat. "What everything?"

"Everything everything. From that first night at the Gridiron when he didn't know who you really were up through the box of tests on your bathroom counter."

"Oh," I say softly. "So when you say everything, what you really mean is *everything*."

"Yeah," he murmurs.

He told my brother everything? When? How? Why?

A million questions plague my brain.

He's the one who was scared to tell my brother, and my brother just confessed that he knows everything, and he's so casual, so *cool* about it, and I'm pretty much confused as hell as I try to piece out why Grayson would tell him *now*—after it's been over for months.

Because it's not over for him, a little voice in the back of my head tells me. Maybe this is his way of trying to clean the slate so we can start over.

My chest warms at the thought.

"Are you okay with it?" I finally ask.

"I mean…yes and no. But you're not together now anyway, so does it matter if I'm okay with it?" he points out.

"I guess not."

"Why aren't you with him, again?" he asks. "I'm a little fuzzy on that part."

I chuckle. "It's not always very clear to me, either. But more or less he left me when I felt like I needed him most."

"He left for camp. He didn't have a choice."

"You're hearing his side," I point out. "He broke up with me. He left *me*."

"And according to his side, he's been working overtime to make that up to you." He makes a damn strong point.

I wander around my kitchen as I make a confession to my brother. "I miss him, but I also can appreciate the friendship we've formed. I've been on my own now for almost three months, and that's the longest stretch of independence I've had since I was a teenager. Isn't that all sorts of screwed up?"

"Not really. I haven't had much independence since I met Rachel, and I wouldn't trade a second," he says.

"But you two are perfect together." I roll my eyes as I think of how sickeningly perfect they really are.

"Don't you think you and Grayson could be, too?"

"Sometimes I do because for a moment in time, we *were*. But I'm so scared, Beck. What if he leaves me again? I can't go through that twice in one lifetime." I sigh heavily as my brother extracts the fear that has pulsed beneath the surface for months.

"What if he doesn't?" he counters. "Isn't it worth the risk?"

I'm not sure how to answer that.

"Anyway, I have to go. I just wanted to check in with you and see if you're taking visitors. We're looking at the second weekend in November. The Aces have a home game, and I'm planning to stay through Wednesday so I can hang with you and Grayson."

"I'll get the dates on the calendar at the bakery," I say.

"I'm sure I'll talk to you before the trip, but I'll see you then."

We hang up, and even though it's still a few weeks away, I'm excited to see my family...even if my brother is staying with my ex.

Chapter 60: Ava Maxwell

A Girl's Gotta Eat

The two weeks pass by quickly. Despite having cut my hours, I'm spending more time at the bakery, and my personal calendar has filled with the projects Grayson's teammates keep sending my way.

I'm burning the candle at both ends.

I've started taking Sundays off so I can watch Grayson play, whether I'm in person at the stadium because they're playing in Vegas and he sent me yet another jersey to wear, or I'm at home watching from the comfort of my couch with my slippers on.

And when I watch, I feel this strange sense of ownership over him. *That's my guy.*

He is. Except…he's not.

When Friday rolls around, Beck texts me that their plane landed. My mom brought her boyfriend, and they're both going to be staying with me, and it all just feels so *weird.*

But if she's happy, if she's out of the fog that's lasted since my dad died, then I'm happy for her.

Beck rented a car, and my doorbell rings about an hour after I received his text.

My brother stands in front of the group, looking clean-cut as always, and I glance beyond him while I hug him first.

My mom looks…different. Cleaned up or something. She's wearing a dress, and her hair is dark when it was always platinum.

She's wearing makeup, and the deep bags that were under her eyes for so long seem to have lifted. She looks like she has joy inside her again, and this woman reminds me of the woman I knew when I was six or seven. She looks like the kind of mom I would have loved to have had when I was a teenager and needed my mom.

My eyes flick to the man she brought with her. He's tall and handsome, and he's wearing a suit. They look like a power couple in town on business, and somehow...it suits her.

"Mom," I say, and she squeezes me tightly. She holds on a few extra beats, and she smells exactly like I remember her smelling. "It's so good to see you. You look great."

"I can't believe this is the first time I've been out to Vegas to visit you since you moved here," she says softly.

"Eight years now," I say. "Better late than never, right?" It's something my dad used to say to us all the time.

I still remember it in his voice when I think hard enough.

She presses her lips together and tilts her head, a secret acknowledgment of his words, and then she looks at the man standing beside her. "This is Thomas," she says. "Thomas, my beautiful and talented daughter, Ava."

"Pleasure," Thomas says as he shakes my hand.

Weirdly, he doesn't remind me of my dad in any way, but I still like that he's here. I like that he's perhaps the vehicle that helped my mom feel like she could enjoy life again.

"Come on in," I tell them. I show them to the guest room—which happens to be Kelly's old room—and leave to let them get settled in while I meet Beck in the kitchen.

"You okay with dinner tonight?" he asks.

"A girl's gotta eat," I say, and he shakes his head.

"Are you okay with Grayson being there, I mean."

"Oh, uh...yeah. Of course." Of course I can handle a meal with Grayson. I love him.

And that's the whole problem. I've been so skittish to jump back in that I've been content with seeing him on Sundays at his home games, talking to him during the week, and staying far, far away so I don't fall into that body-betraying syndrome where I'm so attracted to him that I can't help but get naked and jump on top of him.

Not that I haven't thought about it. Especially late at night when I'm home all alone with just my vibrator.

"Great. We have reservations tonight at Prime Cellar. Eight o'clock. Can you get Mom and Thomas there?"

I nod. "I sure can," I say, and my tone is a little *too* bright.

It's fine. I can eat a meal with my ex, whom I still love, and his best friend, who is also my brother, plus my mom and her new boyfriend. No problem. It won't be awkward at all.

And since I'm the driver, I won't even get to drink.

Cue all the self-pity.

As it turns out, Thomas says he'll spring for a car so we can all partake in a glass of wine. Instead of wine, however, I plan to partake in some vodka.

Stat.

Grayson isn't there yet when we arrive, and lucky me…Beck leaves the seat between us open, which means the very second the man walks close enough, I can smell his familiar woodsy scent.

Just like the first time, it still does things to me.

"Mrs. Maxwell," he says, greeting my mother. "It's been far too many years. How have you been?"

"Much better than I once was," she says with a smile as she hugs Grayson.

Ugh. Why does it have to feel like he's already part of the family?

Why do I feel like I want him to reach over and slide his hand along my thigh?

Why do I wish I never gave him up?

He hurt me, yes. But we all make mistakes. Even me.

And I think it's a mistake that we haven't fixed this yet.

I haven't shared a meal with him in months. It's been easy to pretend it's nothing when I'm at work and he's at work, and we haven't been in this close proximity except when he runs over to greet me on game day. Somehow he's sent me two tickets every single week for the same front row seats, and he always has a backup jersey to pass over to me just in case I don't show up in the one he leaves on my counter.

It's these little things that mean so much, but it's the big things that really matter.

Dinner turns out to be less awkward than I had anticipated. Thomas seems to be a really great guy, and between having him and Grayson at the same table, it's like some sort of intense battle of charisma for who can carry the conversation the most.

I think maybe Grayson is winning, but then Thomas starts in with another story that has us all laughing. Thomas is long retired, but he worked in education his whole career. He's a former high school principal and has eight grandchildren of his own—all of which my mom, who just has two, has met.

His whole family resides in New York, and his kids attended the rival high school to my own. I vaguely recall playing volleyball against a girl who I think might be his daughter. As I recall, she was aggressive and mean as a teenager...but I'm sure she's nice now.

Once that revelation came out, I couldn't help but think what a small world it is. Who would've ever guessed that my mom would end up with a guy like this when she seemed so vehemently against any sort of relationship after we lost my dad?

It's kind of a lovely thing to see, and it's also kind of pulsing this different feeling in me. It's a reminder that life is short and unexpected things can happen. Do we really want to waste time when we're not guaranteed tomorrow? I think I finally have my answer to that, and I want to talk to Grayson alone.

I want to tell him how I'm feeling. I want him to know that I never stopped loving him.

I don't get a chance to, though.

"Sorry to cut out early, but we have early practice in the morning. I need to get home and get my solid eight."

Beck stands to give him one of those bro backslaps. "What a great dinner, man."

"It really was," Grayson says, and he glances over at me. He seems to say something with his eyes, but I'm not entirely sure what he's trying to say. He presses his lips together into a sort of apologetic smile. "Good seeing you, Ava."

I stand, and he gives me a hug. The way his arms wrap around me is more than just a friendly hug goodbye.

His lips find my jawline—not quite my cheek, not quite my neck—and he gives me a short, quick kiss before he backs away. It's too short. Too quick. I want more. I want it all. With him.

But it's not in the cards tonight. I've waited this long. I can wait a little longer.

"We'll be at your game Sunday, and are we still on for lunch Monday?" Beck asks.

Grayson nods, and his eyes find mine again. "I'd love for you all to come. There's this great little place on the Strip that's brand new. Come check it out with me."

"I'll be there," I murmur, transfixed by the way his eyes are silently begging me to come.

I'll duck out of work for lunch…or I'll quit or something. Anything to be there Monday, to have the chance to sit beside Grayson, maybe to have the chance to pull him aside and tell him the things that have been playing on my mind all through dinner—all through the last few weeks.

I have a text from him when I wake up in the morning, and it tells me he got up even earlier than I did.

Grayson: Dinner last night felt like old times, didn't it?

I'm not quite sure how to reply. On the one hand, I want to let him know how I'm feeling, but on the other, I don't want to distract him ahead of tomorrow's game. And I don't really want to say anything over text.

Me: It really did. I had a lot of fun sitting next to you.

His reply doesn't come for about twelve hours, but when it does, it's in the form of a phone call.

"Hey," I answer.

"Hi. How was your day?"

"It was good. I made a ton of cookies and worked on two cakes. How was practice?"

"Good. We're ready for the Jaguars tomorrow."

"Are you at a hotel tonight?" I ask. He once mentioned that the entire team stays at a hotel the night before a game, even if it's a home game, so coaches can make sure players aren't distracted.

"Yes I am. Got a room all to myself this time."

"Nice."

A beat of quiet passes between us, and then we both start to say something at the same time.

"Grayson…"

"Ava…"

I clear my throat. "I feel like I have a lot I want to say to you, but I want to do it in person."

"I want to do it in person, too," he says lewdly, and I chuckle at his joke. "In all seriousness, we can talk tomorrow night after the game. Does that work?"

It does, but I have an idea.

I have no idea how much trouble he'll get into, but it's worth a shot anyway. We need to have this conversation in person.

"Yes," I say instead of any of that. "So tell me about your hotel."

He launches into a story I'm half-listening to while I pack a quick bag, and then I wish him luck at his game tomorrow before I tell my mom I'm heading out for the night.

And then I drive.

Chapter 61: Ava Maxwell

You Have a Guest

Nerves tackle my spine as I get closer and closer, and once I'm there, I pull into a spot at the back of the lot.

I look up at the large buildings sprawling out in front of me, and I pull up a map to try to figure out where I'm going.

He told me his room number when I asked about the hotel. He has no idea I'm showing up tonight.

I count buildings, and then I count windows, and rather than go inside where I might get caught, I toss a little pebble at the second-story window when I think I'm in the right place.

The curtains slide to the side a moment later, and *oh shit,* it's Patrick Harris.

I duck behind a bush as he glances around, and then he pulls the curtains shut again. I look at the map on my phone and back up at the windows, and I pick up more pebbles to try the one next to Patrick's.

"What are you doing?" a voice behind me says, and I whip around.

"Lincoln!" I gasp.

"Are you trying to sneak in to see my brother?"

Heat rushes to my cheeks. "No!"

"Really?" he asks. "Because if you are, I can get you in. If you aren't, you'll probably be arrested."

My eyes widen. "Fine. Yes. He doesn't know I'm here, and I don't want him to get into any trouble. But I need to see him. I need to tell him I love him."

Lincoln blows out a breath. "Finally."

"What?"

"You heard me. Finally. I can't deal with his lack of focus another second, so get in there and do what you have to do to get him on track for tomorrow."

"He's not focused?" I say. He's seemed fine to me during his games.

"He's in love, and the woman he's in love with has been holding back. Trust me when I say I know what that's like. Now do you want to see him, or do you want to stand out here talking to me?"

"Him," I say immediately. He looks a little offended, and I laugh. "As lovely as it is chatting out here with you."

"Of course," he scoffs, and then I follow him through the complex and toward Grayson's room...which, by the way, is in another building entirely.

"Gray, it's me," Lincoln says as he bangs on a door.

The door swings open. "What the fuck do you wa—" Grayson's jaw drops, and his eyes widen as they land on me. He draws in a sharp breath.

Lincoln steps aside and urges me in. "You have a guest. Don't stay up too late."

Grayson's eyes don't leave mine as he murmurs, "Thanks." I step into his room, and the door closes behind him. "What are you doing here?"

"It felt like we left some things unsaid, so I figured I'd swing by so we could talk."

"Some things unsaid?" he repeats, and we walk into the room. He perches on the edge of his bed, and I sit on the couch right across from him.

I nod. "You go first."

"I miss you," he says quietly. "I loved being with you last night. It felt so good and right, and I'm trying so hard to give you space and time, but I just…I miss you."

Heat pinches behind my eyes as I have the urge to rush into his arms. I don't—yet. I stay where I am because we need to clear the air before anything else happens. "I miss you, too," I admit. "Last night was good. Really good. Having you right next to me felt so comfortable. You just fit. And being with my mom and Thomas, it all sort of came crashing down on me—the reality that life is short and unexpected and scary and beautiful."

His eyes move to mine. "I love you. You were the one who was fighting for me to see that we belong together, and now somehow those roles have reversed. We belong together. I'm fighting for you. I *love* you. Can't you see that?" His tone is riddled with frustration that we *aren't* together even though we should be, and I'm finally feeling it, too.

We've been apart long enough.

"Of course I see it, Grayson. And I love you, too. I never stopped, and I never will."

He's silent for a beat, and then he finally asks, "Then why are we apart?"

"Because I'm scared."

He stands, and he closes the short distance spanning between us. He reaches out, and I set my hands in his as he pulls me up off the couch.

"I don't know what else to do to prove to you that you don't have to be scared. I'm not going anywhere. It's been months since we were together, and I haven't stopped thinking about you. I haven't so much as looked at another woman. My chest aches all the time when I think about you and us and how good we were together before I fucked it all up. I'm so sorry, and I will never run scared again. You are it for me—any way I can have you, even if it's just as a friend like it has been for the last few months. You're my future. No one else. Before, the thought of kids and marriage scared the hell out of me. But it's nothing compared to the thought of not having you in my life. I promise you, Ava. I won't run again. I won't leave you. I won't hurt you. Because doing any of those things would kill me."

The heat pinching behind my eyes forms into a tear that drops onto my cheek. I brush it away. "I…I don't know what to say," I admit. "I want to be with you, too."

"That's exactly what I've been waiting to hear for three and a half long months," he says, and his mouth crashes down to mine.

He kisses me like he's trying to make up for lost time, his fingertips diving into my hair as the urgency of his mouth on mine intensifies and deepens. We're both crazed with need and lust, but overpowering all of that is this deep *love* spanning between us. He pulls my body against his, and I wrap my arms around him as I give in to the feel of having him in my arms again.

It's where we belong.

But before we can seal this with more intimate promises, I pull back.

"I do have a couple conditions," I warn.

"I would expect nothing less," he says, his eyes hooded when they meet mine.

"For starters, you don't run. If you get scared, you come talk to me like an adult, and we work it out."

"Deal. Done. What else you got?" he asks.

"No more secrets. No more lies. On either side of this."

"Deal," he agrees. "I have a condition, too."

"Oh, you do, do you?" I ask, my tone full of sass. "What is it?"

"That I hear your voice every single day."

"Agreed," I say softly.

"Anything else?" he asks.

"Just that you take me to bed and rock my world."

He grins. "Now *that* I can do."

And he does.

He lifts me into his arms as if I weigh nothing at all, and he tosses me down onto the bed. I giggle as he climbs up over me, and his eyes find mine. His are dark with desire, and I feel it too.

This time apart has shown me that I never want to be apart from him again.

His fingertips trace my jawline then dip down, tracing a line down my torso to my belly. He moves his hand to my hip as his lips fall to mine, and this kiss still has the same urgent undertones, but it's slower—as if we have all the time in the world.

We don't. He has to get up early, and he needs his rest ahead of tomorrow's game.

But tonight…he's all mine.

He reaches under my shirt, and he yanks down my bra to expose one nipple. His thumb brushes over it, and my hips jerk toward his.

It's been a minute since I've had a man's touch, and this feels so…different.

Sure, we were in love the last time we were together like this, but there wasn't the undertone that it was meant to last forever.

Now there is.

We've been to hell and back. We've been broken. But now we're piecing it all back together, and the intimacy of this moment is heightened by the emotional connection that's stronger than ever before.

He breaks the kiss to trail his lips down my neck, and then he pulls back to pull my shirt off. I yank on the hem of his, too, and he pulls it over his head. I run my fingertips along the abs that are even more cut than they were the last time we were together. His body is different. It's all muscle and hard planes. This is *in season* Grayson as opposed to the *offseason* Grayson I was with before.

He sucks a nipple into his mouth, and I moan my approval as I feel his tongue flick against the tight bud. I grab onto the back of his head, urging him to keep doing exactly what he's doing, and he drops a hand down. He pushes past my jeans and dips into my panties, and then his finger slips right inside me.

He grunts as my hips jerk again, but it doesn't stop him from the work he's putting into my nipple. He only stops to start trailing kisses down my body. He pulls his hand out and works my jeans down my legs, tossing them on the floor. He pulls my panties down next, and he gets naked, too.

Then he dives headfirst into my pussy.

He shoves two fingers in while he sucks on my clit, and I love it. I love every second of it. It's hot and intimate, but I've been waiting too damn long for him. I need him inside me like I need to take my next breath. I can't take not having him there another second longer.

I grip his shoulders as I murmur, "Grayson?"

"Yeah?" he whispers against my hot, wet pussy. His breath is warm, and it nearly pushes me into an orgasm.

"I need you inside me."

His eyes are so dark with lust they're nearly black in the dimly lit room. He shifts up the bed until he's hovering over me, and his eyes fall to mine as he reaches between us and pushes himself inside.

"You can take it, baby," he murmurs as he pushes all the way in, and I clutch him to me as my body stretches again after too long apart.

But it's like our bodies were made for this. I adjust to his size as my body squeezes him inside me, and he stays still for a few beats as we both relish the feel of each other.

I wrap my legs around his waist as I urge him to start moving, and he groans as he starts to fill me with his heavenly, deep strokes.

"Oh God," I gasp as he starts to pick up speed.

He grunts as he rocks into me, pushing my body to its limits as I fight the urge to give in and come. I'm not ready for it to be over. It feels like it just started, and I want to lie beneath him forever as he continues to drive those deep strokes into me.

Trying to stop my body from giving into the pleasure is like trying to stop a freight train with my bare hands. "Oh yes, yes, yes," I cry out.

"You like that?" he asks as he starts to move even faster.

I arch into him as I claw at his back, my orgasm within reach as he pushes me to some new, sublime state I've never experienced before.

It's that land of love, where I'm skipping through the forest with his hand in mine, and at the same time, the land of pleasure where I'm teetering on the edge of my entire body exploding.

It's the heady combination of the two that pushes me over, and the tidal wave plows into me.

"Fuck, baby, fuck, I'm coming, fuck," he grunts as he crashes into his own release.

Our bodies move in perfect synchronization as we rocket through the pleasure together, pushing the boundaries of our emotions and our love and our intimacy.

It's sexy and sweet, and a little forbidden since I'm not supposed to be here, but we're finally free and clear of the lies and the secrets, and nothing stands between us any longer.

"God, I love you," he says, his voice emotional when our bodies start to come down from the high. His lips drop to mine, and he doesn't pull out of me right away. I feel his cock twitching inside me, and my pussy seems to squeeze him inside, trying to hold him there forever.

He kisses me slowly, luxuriously, as if we have forever.

And maybe we do.

It's not something I ever believed before…but I sure as hell believe it now.

Chapter 62: Grayson Nash

Nash's Nibbles

One more game.

One more day.

One more night.

And then, finally…I can reveal the secret I've been working on for months.

It's what kept me away, though I'd never admit it to her. But in order for everything to be in place, I had to be here as much—if not more—than I was at the Complex for practice.

My days have been long as I went from one place to another every single day, and I still managed to fit in time to let her know she was my top priority.

I wouldn't have done all this if she wasn't.

I hope she can see she made the right decision in taking me back, and it pulses something else in me.

Another idea to prove to her that *she* is my future—as if the secret project wasn't enough to prove that.

I see her grab her seat with Beckett beside her. She gave the other two tickets I scored to Sandra and Thomas, and all four of them are wearing Nash twenty-four jerseys.

My heart is beating wildly as I run over to see my girl before the game.

"Nice jersey," I say.

She leans over the guardrail, grabs my face between her palms, and plants a kiss on my mouth.

I grab her and pull her down onto the field, and she squeals as I press my lips to hers again. "I love you," I say as I lean my forehead to hers.

"I love you, too. Now go win this game, and we'll celebrate later."

I grin at her and help her back up to her seat, and I fist bump her brother, who's grinning at me. Holy shit. I just kissed Ava in front of Beckett…and it didn't feel weird.

What a fucking day.

We roll through the first half of the game against the Jags with two tuddies—or *touchdowns*—and we hold the Jags to only a field goal. I'm having one of the best games of my professional career with one interception and one forced fumble among other achievements. I'm blocking the hell out of wide receiver James Christian, and I don't know if I've ever felt more freedom playing this game before.

Asher grabs a tuddy late in the fourth, so it's all about the Nash brothers this game. The quarterback decides he can't get it to Christian with me in the game, so he starts throwing to the other side of the field.

All in all, it's a perfect day that started with my woman in my arms and a kiss before the game and ends with a kiss after the game and my woman in my arms again.

She gets up early for work on Monday morning, and I have the day off since we won yesterday.

Lincoln was giving me the day off regardless, but it feels even better to have earned it.

Beck comes with me to the Strip to check on things, and everything is in place.

It's perfect.

All our hard work has really paid off, and I'm so excited for her to get here.

I finger the box in my pocket a little nervously.

I'm ready to go, and it's even sweeter that we got back together two nights ago. I didn't want *this* to be the driving factor in what helped her decide she wanted to be with me, but the whole idea behind doing it was to show her how much I believe in her, in us, in our future together.

I still don't know what the future holds. I don't know if I want to play another year, or move onto coaching, or something else. But I do know that I want to spend nights here watching her do her thing, and I can see little kids—*our* kids—in a gated corner where they can safely play. I see long hours and probably frustrations as we work together, but I also see all the things I feel most when I'm with her—laughter and brightness and happiness.

Everyone is here. I can't believe we actually made this work.

"It's time," Beck says to me.

That means she's on her way.

She thinks she's coming here for lunch. She has no idea what's really about to go down.

I head out front so I can intercept her as soon as she arrives, and I spot her walking down the sidewalk.

I should be nervous. I have no idea how she's going to react to this. But I don't feel nervous, and maybe it's because I finally got something right. Maybe I don't fuck everything up. Maybe it just took the power of finding my other half to do things right for a change.

My heart swells as I take in every detail. Her blonde hair swings gently around her shoulders, and she's wearing sunglasses and a dress with flowers on it today. It's early November in Vegas, and the weather is perfect—sunshine and seventy with a light breeze.

A perfect day for my perfect girl.

She smiles when she sees me, and she picks up the pace, walking quickly through a throng of people to get to me. When she does, she practically crashes into my arms. I grunt at the force but smile as my eyes move down to her face. I drop my lips to hers.

"What is this place?" she asks when she sees where we're standing.

"It's new. It's not quite open to the public yet, but I got us in to give it a try. You ready?"

She nods, and I go in first, holding the door open for her.

"Surprise!" the huge group of people gathered yell, and her eyes are drawn to the bright pink neon sign perched behind the counter that will eventually be the cashier stand: *Cookie's Cookies.*

Her jaw drops as she spins around to face me, but I'm already down on the floor. She gasps as she sees me kneeling.

"Ava Cookie Maxwell, I love you. I love your cookies and your cakes. I love your talent. I love your drive and your ambition. I love your kind heart and your sweet soul. I want to spend forever with you right here, whether we call it Sinful or Cookie's Cookies or Ava's Haven or Nash's Nibbles. This place is yours now, but it's *our* future, the place where I envision long days and late nights filled with laughter and recipes and experiments and fun."

My big, planned speech that I rehearsed hundreds of times seems to have flown out the window at the pressure of having her entire family looking at me.

"But it's not just this new bakery I want you to have today. I'm also handing over my heart. You've owned it since the day we reconnected at the Gridiron. I want to spend the rest of my life with you, whether it's here at this bakery or kissing you from the sidelines. This place can be our first baby, and if and when the time is right for us, we'll have more. All I know is I want to be with you, and I want to give you everything you deserve."

The room falls silent. Deafeningly silent.

I pull the box out of my pocket, and she gasps as I flip open the lid.

The diamond glints in the light, and her hands fly to her mouth.

"Ava Louise Maxwell, will you marry me?"

"Oh my God! Yes! Yes, I will marry you!"

I laugh as I yank the ring out of the box, shove it onto her finger, and rise to a stand so I can pull her into my arms and kiss her properly.

It takes a solid beat before I realize people are clapping and cheering. I think it's Beckett's loud whistle that brings me back from the cloud where I'm floating back down to solid ground.

I pull apart from her lips. There will be plenty of time for that sort of celebration later, but I have a lot of details to share with her about this place, and her entire family is here ready to celebrate with her.

The first person who comes rushing over for a hug once we pull apart is Kelly.

"Oh my God!" Ava squeals. "I can't believe you're really here!"

"I can't believe you're really engaged!" she squeals back. "Congratulations!"

Ava reaches down and rubs Kelly's growing stomach. "You look so good!"

Sandra moves in for the next hug while Beckett claps me on the back.

"Holy shit, man. You actually did it. Congrats."

I chuckle as I give my future brother-in-law a hug. "Thanks, man. For everything. For being here. For not getting mad that I'm banging your little sister."

"Dude. Our friendship doesn't have to change, but if you ever say that again, it will."

I laugh. Oliver and Alexander are here, too, and it's been a full decade since I've seen either of them. Beckett actually did bring lunch, so after the excitement starts to die down, we sit at the tables that were left behind from the last restaurant that moved out a little over a month ago.

I'm sitting beside Ava, and as she digs into a sandwich, she asks, "So how soon until we can have this place up and running?"

I laugh. "I have a business contact who can help us with a lot of the lifting, and I thought long and hard about whether I should finalize the details or not, and ultimately I knew you'd want it to have your own touch. It's your dream, so I just had the place painted white and cleaned out so you could build *your* dream from scratch. But I also want you to know that you're not doing this alone. I'll be right here every step of the way, and together we'll make your vision a reality."

She leans over and presses a kiss to my lips, and when she pulls back, she bumps my shoulder with hers. "The neon sign is a perfect touch. I think I might have to go with that name after all."

"I'm kind of partial to Nash's Nibbles," I admit.

She laughs, and it's that sweet, musical sound that I can't wait to hear for the rest of my life.

Chapter 63: Grayson Nash

Marrying the Defensive Back

I look around at the transformation this place has made over the last two months. It's unrecognizable from how it was when I first found it, but a lot about my life is unrecognizable from how it was as little as a year ago.

Coach Nash led the Vegas Aces into the playoffs for a second year in a row, and that means we're preparing for another game in a couple weeks. Because of our record during the season, we get a bye while the wild card games are played this weekend. It also means we get a week off from practice, and I have to admit, as excited as I am to make the playoffs, I'm incredibly excited for a week off.

Soon I'll have to announce my decision regarding next season. I know what I want to do now, and I've discussed it at length with Ava.

"I can't believe the first batch in *my bakery* is almost ready," she says, and the excitement in her voice is pretty much everything I dreamed of when I paid for the lease on this place.

These cookies aren't for the bakery, though. They're for a party she's catering tomorrow. We finally got the kitchen in working order, and she's been itching to test out the equipment ahead of our opening.

We're not having our official grand opening until the first of March. It gives us almost two months to make sure we're ready to roll. We still have employees to hire and a few more decisions to make about equipment and seating, but we're close to ready. She wanted to wait until I was out of season so we could have a good couple weeks to focus on something aside from football.

I know where my heart is, though, and it's no longer on the field. It's planted firmly in Ava's hands.

"Can you cut more of my super-secret ingredient?" she asks.

"Only if I can eat some." I pop a Tootsie Roll into my mouth, and she giggles.

"Stop, or I'm going to have to make more." She decided to make homemade Tootsie Rolls rather than using the store-bought ones like she always had in her kitchen sink cookies at Cravings, and I have to be honest…her homemade ones are even better than the original.

Maybe because she made them with love.

I set the rope onto the cutting board and make the slices just like she told me. We're not calling them *Kitchen Sink Cookies* here. Instead, the special title she gave them was *Nash's Nibbles* since she loved the name but didn't want to use it for the bakery. And also since she already knows it'll be our number one seller, and she wanted my name—her future name—attached to it.

For the bakery, she went with Cookie's Cookies and Cakes.

This is our future, and I see her in every detail as I look around. She went with a polka-dot wallpaper made up of pastels, and the result is cheerful and happy—two adjectives I'd definitely use to describe my Cookie. Instrumental dance music plays softly in the background, and occasionally she dances around the kitchen with pure abandon and glee. I feel like she'll do that thousands of times in the future.

What a road it has been. Sometimes I can't believe it as I glance around, but this is it. This is our future.

I had no idea that when I looked beyond the game, I'd be the owner of a bakery with my future wife.

And it's not just the bakery that's different. It's also the fact that our wedding is a little over two and a half months away.

She'd always dreamed of a May wedding, so the first weekend in May—two months after we open our bakery—we'll be saying *I do* right here in Vegas.

And I can't wait for the bachelor party the week before. We're having a weeklong celebration, and Spencer and Beckett are both flying out for the whole week with their fiancée and wife, respectively.

Nobody ever would've guessed that I'd be next after Lincoln, but here we are. And as nervous as I was about marriage before Ava and I got together, now I see that just because my parents made mistakes doesn't mean that we have to repeat them.

And we won't. I lost her once. I'm not stupid enough to ever do it again.

"Where are we at on those Tootsie Rolls?" she asks.

I chuckle. "Coming right up, ma'am."

"Thank you, sir."

I glance up, and my eyes connect with hers at her use of *sir*.

"Say that again," I dare her.

She giggles. "No!"

"If you think I'm not about to fuck you right here on this counter..."

"Grayson Michael Nash, that is *so* unsanitary," she scolds.

I roll my eyes. "You're no fun."

"Excuse me? I was debating between bending over the counter or just going to my office, but if I'm not fun, then I guess both options are off the table."

My jaw drops as I glare at her.

She laughs. "I'm teasing. I'm totally down for bending over. You know, once we get the next batch in."

I wiggle my eyebrows and get to cutting a little faster.

I'm just about to make my way over to ravish my sweet little baker when my phone starts to ring. "Dammit," I mutter under my breath. I see it's Spencer calling, so I pick it up.

"Sup?" I answer cheerfully.

"Wedding's off and I don't even know if I'm staying in Minnesota," he blurts.

"Wait...what?" I ask, completely confused by his announcement.

"You heard me. I've got more calls to make." He hangs up.

My brows dip together.

"Who was that?" Ava asks.

"Spencer. He said the wedding's off and he's not sure if he's staying in Minnesota."

"What?"

"That's what I said. He said he had more calls to make and hung up on me."

"What the hell is going on?" she asks. She walks around the counter over toward me, and she slips her arms around my waist.

"No idea," I murmur, pressing my lips to her temple. "But I'm sure we'll find out more soon."

"Hopefully it's just a misunderstanding," she says.

I nod as a bit of worry fills me for my brother. He's the most logical out of all four of us. He's strategic. He's smart. He's cautious and unimpulsive. Calling me out of the blue to let me know his wedding is off seems...out of character for him.

But I guess opening a bakery with my best friend's little sister might've seemed out of character a year ago for me, too.

Yet here I am with all these new dreams coming true—dreams I didn't even dare to dream as little as a year ago.

"Hey, I have a surprise for you," I say as I try to push Spencer out of my mind for now.

"What is it?"

"Instead of bending you over this counter, which, please believe is going to happen multiple times over the next forty or fifty years, what if I take you to the place where it all started?"

Her brows crinkle together. "The Gridiron?"

I shake my head. "I was thinking dinner at that little café at the Palms before I bring you up to that same corner suite and fuck

416

you right up against the windows. And I have it booked for tomorrow night, too."

Her jaw slackens. "Are you serious?"

I raise a brow.

"Because that café has *the best* nachos."

I laugh as I pull her into me, and I drop a kiss to her lips. "Oh, it's not the nachos you'll be thinking about all day tomorrow."

"You're right. It's the cheese pretzels." She giggles, but then I stick my tongue in her mouth, and she's not giggling so much anymore.

She pulls back. "Whew. I am one lucky girl. I went from fake dating the defensive back to owning a bakery with the defensive back to getting banged against a window by the defensive back."

"And pretty soon you'll be *marrying* the defensive back."

Her lips tip up in a smile. "And I can't wait to get started on our happily ever after."

Epilogue: Ava Maxwell

My New Stepsister Spiked My Face

"**O**h my God, yes, yes, yes!" I scream as I claw at the window.

He slams into me harder from behind, and then he reaches around to brush against my clit.

That's when I fall apart completely.

I'm wearing a dress, but knowing anyone could look up to the top floor and see me getting banged against the window is somehow…hot.

I never thought of myself as an exhibitionist, yet here we are.

In the back of my mind, I think I know nobody could really see us. Well, maybe someone with binoculars. But the risk is still sexy.

"I'm going to come so hard in this tight cunt," he growls, his voice low and raspy close to my ear.

"Do it, Grayson. Give me all your come." Whoa. Was that me?

"Oh fuck," he says, and he rubs my clit a little faster as he starts to come. Hearing his sexy groans and growls only pushes me faster into my own orgasm, and I fall apart the same time he does, both of us writhing in total and complete ecstasy against the window, our moans a beautiful chorus of our pleasure.

"Fuck, baby," he groans once our bodies are depleted, and he pulls out slowly, careful to reach down as his come drips out of me. He slides it all around my already wet pussy, and I freaking love it when he does that. It's illicit and hot, like he's marking me as his.

I am his. Only his—now and forever.

It's not the only time he's banged me up against that window. Every few months, he books this suite—usually for special occasions, but not always.

The house we share has become a bit of a revolving door. Everyone wants to come visit—whether it's his mom, or one of my brothers, or my mom and Thomas, so having our little suite to escape to is especially nice.

He's already booked it for the night of our bakery opening since both my mom and his mom will be staying with us. We can still have sex at home when we have guests, and we do, but we can have the special sort of loud, headboard-banging sex without worrying anyone will overhear us here.

"So fucking wet. Always," he murmurs.

"Only for you," I admit. I never got this wet with Colin, who any sort of below-deck experience was limited to before Grayson, and it was never very good, and it was never sex.

"I love that." His eyes are already heated on me again, but I shake my head.

"Oh, no, big boy. We have a wedding to get to."

"Fuck," he moans.

It's actually why we're here tonight. We're attending a wedding at a little chapel just south of here, and we figured it was closer to get to from our favorite hotel than from home.

And, you know, the window sex. It's always good motivation to book this room.

"I know. And we need to be there in twenty minutes, so get dressed." I run to the bathroom to wash up first, and then I slip my panties back on, and I'm ready to go.

The window sex happened when I came out of the bedroom already dressed for the wedding, and he couldn't help himself.

I wasn't complaining. And I know him well enough that I emerged fully clothed and ready to go a full forty minutes early to give us time for what we just did.

No regrets.

He puts on the suit I packed for him, and hell if I'm not ready to rip him right out of it.

He's just so…hot.

I saw it when I was just a teenager with a massive crush. And now? Now I'm engaged to this man who I still have a massive crush on all these years later.

Only he's better than the teenage me ever could have imagined.

He's given me everything I could ever ask for in the way he loves me. He proved to me that I was his future. He asked me to marry him, and he didn't want to wait. He's the one who wanted this year when I said I'd always dreamed of a May wedding. I figured we'd wait a year. But it'll be just under six months from the day he proposed to the day we actually get married.

We're keeping it simple. Because of his status as a celebrity, we're just going to do it at home. Beckett will be his best man. Kelly, who I just saw two weeks ago when I flew to Louisiana for the weekend when she had her sweet, precious baby, will be my maid of honor. Lincoln will preside. Family and close friends will be present, and it'll be perfect for us.

Just like this wedding today will be perfect for my mom and Thomas.

They didn't want any fanfare over it, but they were ready to tie the knot. They chose Vegas since it's the land of wedding chapels and quickie weddings, and Thomas flew out his entire family along with ours.

I'll finally get to see that volleyball bitch…I mean my new stepsister.

I promised Grayson I'd behave, and of course I will. But I still like to call her that when I'm talking to him—it keeps him on his toes, and it makes me laugh when he thinks he might really have to hold me back from slamming a volleyball into her face the way she did when she spiked a ball at me ten years ago.

I'm over it now.

But it hurt like hell, and I thought my nose was broken. It wasn't.

And wouldn't you know it? When we arrive, she's the first person I see. I definitely recognize her, and she still looks like a volleyball player—all lean and tall and long, and I feel short next to her as she approaches me with a smile.

"Hold me back," I mutter to Grayson, and he laughs.

"You must be Ava," the woman says. She holds out a hand, and I shake it.

"I am. You must be Erica."

"That's me."

"You once spiked a volleyball at my face."

"Oh my God, I am so, so sorry. I was an angsty teenager, but I promise I don't spike anything anymore." She holds up a water bottle. "Except my drink."

I link my arm through hers. "I always wanted a sister," I say, and Grayson laughs as I walk off with her toward the bar.

He finds Beckett, and I glance at him across the room. His eyes are on me, and I eat up every second of it.

We hold hands as we watch my mom marry the love of her life.

We dance at the reception.

We have more sex against the window.

Yep…I think I can get on board with this new life of mine. And soon, I'll be married to the man of my literal dreams.

That's when life will truly begin.

Bonus Epilogue: Ava Maxwell

Football-Themed Cookies

It's never what you want to see.

I was thinking I'd be down on that field celebrating the victory as the confetti flew all around us, but instead, it's the 49ers celebrating as they'll be the ones advancing to the big game in two weeks.

My heart drops for Grayson. I know how hyped he was for this game, and it's sad that this is how the entire season is coming to a close. But they had a great run this year, and that's something to be proud of. It's only Lincoln's second year as head coach, and both years he led the team to the playoffs. It's no easy feat considering the season before he came, the Aces won the Super Bowl and half the team retired with that victory. It takes time to rebuild, and they're doing it well.

But those words won't make any of the players feel better when they were so ready for a victory today—especially on their home field.

I glance up at the Jumbotron and see close-ups of some of the players as they look at the field as if they can't believe they just lost.

The 49ers scored a field goal right at the last second when the teams were tied going into the last two minutes of the game.

I used to think, *oh, the team who won must've wanted it more.* I don't think that way anymore. Nobody wanted it more than the Aces, yet they lost.

Grayson takes a lap around the field. He doesn't watch the celebration for the other team, but he does take a few deep breaths as he closes his eyes.

He walks over toward me and waits for me to bend down.

"You played your ass off, Grayson," I say to him as I get closer to him.

He presses his lips to mine. "I love you."

"I love you, too," I say, and he takes a few minutes to himself, staring up at the Jumbotron before he finally heads toward the locker room to be with his team.

Rather than run down to the field like the wives and girlfriends of the opposing team are now doing, I head down toward the tunnel where I can greet Grayson once he leaves the locker room.

I expect him to be down when I see him, but…he's not.

He's smiling.

He looks…*happy.*

"What a great run, am I right?" he asks when he spots me. He pulls me into his arms.

"An amazing run," I agree.

"Let's go home," he says as he laces his arm around my shoulder.

I grab his hand as it dangles over my shoulder, and I glance up at him. He's looking down at me, and a soft smile graces his lips.

"I told Lincoln," he says. He leans down to kiss me again.

"Are you sure it's what you want?" I ask when I pull back.

"I've never been so sure of anything in my life. And I texted my agent. I'm holding a press conference tomorrow when I come in for our end-of-season exit interviews."

"I'll be front and center," I say.

He shakes his head. "You'll be on the stage with me. And you better wear that new shirt I had made for you."

I gasp a little, and heat pinches behind my eyes as I nod. "Okay, I will."

We head home, and we drink to a great season before he takes me upstairs and makes love to me slowly, sensually, as if we have the rest of our lives together. Because we do.

When morning dawns, I shower and make breakfast before we head together toward the Complex.

I hang out in the press room with Jolene as I wait for him to finish his exit interview, and the room starts to fill with members of the media while we wait.

It's a little before noon when the team owner, Jack Dalton, takes the stage. "Thank you for being here," he says. He nods at me. "Come on up."

I make my way to one of the chairs on the stage.

"We have a special announcement today from one of our players. I'd like to introduce Mr. Grayson Nash and his fiancée, Ms. Ava Maxwell."

The media claps as Grayson walks out and joins me on stage. He gives me a quick kiss, and my cheeks flush as he turns toward the crowd.

"Good afternoon, and thank you for coming today. After eleven seasons playing the greatest game known to man, I have decided to retire."

A few surprised gasps come from the crowd, but really, they had to have known what this was about.

"My future wife and I will be opening a bakery on the Vegas Strip on March first, and I'm hanging it up to help her run this new venture. So be sure to come to Cookie's Cookies to get your pastries made by none other than Ava Maxwell, maybe with a little help from Grayson Nash himself."

That garners a chuckle from the crowd. We take some questions, and Grayson does everything he can to hype up the bakery along with our catering department.

It gives me a thought, and I blurt it out before I have a chance to talk it over with him. "We'll be making special football-themed cookies every Sunday during the season and offering catering, too, so come on by to grab yours!"

I glance over at Grayson, who's looking at me, and I swear I can physically see the love he feels when our eyes connect.

That's the image that graces the headlines a few hours later. *NFL Star Retiring to Help Run Bakery.*

Our phone has been ringing off the hook with new catering orders, and we're busy before our grand opening even occurs. We hire more local pastry chefs to help fill the orders, and Grayson hires the best business manager around since he knows that as much as I want to run every aspect of this place, my heart is in baking and decorating—not on the business end of things.

The morning of March first, I'm antsy. I didn't sleep at all the night before, and Grayson tried to help me relax with multiple orgasms even though we were both exhausted as we prepped for today.

It helped, obviously, but I'm nervous and excited and anxious as we pull up to the bakery before the sun is even up.

And there's already a line.

A longer line than Cravings used to have on Saturday mornings…and we don't even open for another three hours.

I'm beyond thrilled with the turnout, but just because we're here now doesn't mean we're taking business from Cravings. Their loyal customers will continue to support their favorite bakery. And anytime we *can't* take an order because we're overbooked, the first place I recommend is Poppy's store. She's been amazing in helping me prepare for my own grand opening, and she's become somewhat of a mentor for me.

Cora and Dom have been great about everything, too, and the last time I spoke with Cora, it sounded like she had just started seeing the kicker for the Aces, Nick Dawson.

As I walk by the line to open the front door, I spot the first person waiting. "Kelly!" I squeal.

She hugs me tightly. "Congratulations, Avelina! I had to be your first customer!"

"I can't believe you're here! What time did you get in line?"

"A little after midnight," she admits.

"Come on in," I say, and she follows me in while Grayson signs some autographs.

I flip on the lights, and she looks around in awe.

"Wow, Ava. It looks so different than the last time I was here!"

"And so do you," I say, nodding at her belly. "Where's Mia?"

"With her daddy."

"And how are things with her daddy?" I ask.

She shrugs. "I'm not sure. I told him I can't forgive him for what he did to Grayson, but he's trying. He feels really bad, and he invited us to stay with him. I guess right now I'm not ruling anything out, but he has to earn my trust back first."

"Please, please, please tell me this means you're moving back here," I beg as she follows me back to the kitchen. I turn on the ovens, and when I glance back at her after she doesn't say anything, I see a wide smile on her face.

She shrugs. "Never say never."

I gasp. "Are you?"

"No. I mean, I don't have a job or anything, but I think Austin would like us closer, and I'd like Mia to grow up knowing her father, so…maybe."

"You're hired!" I squeal as I throw my arms around her.

"What?" she asks.

"Come work for me! We need more help!" I'm still squealing, but the possibility of my best friend moving back to town with her sweet baby girl *on my opening day* is overwhelming.

"I don't know how to bake! You know I'm a mess in the kitchen!" She's squealing, too.

"Then you can run the cash register, or do office stuff, or marketing—whatever. Oh! You can be my moral support with Doritos and vodka any time I need it. We'll find a spot for you and sweet Mia. And I'll teach you how to bake!" I'm crying by the time I'm done trying to convince her.

"Okay, then! Yes! I'll be your Dorito and vodka girl!" She's crying, too, and we're hugging, and then we hear a voice.

"What kind of freaky shit did I just walk in on?"

We both laugh as we pull apart and face Grayson.

"Kelly just agreed to move back to Vegas and come work here."

"Did I?" Kelly says.

"You did," I confirm, and we're both wiping our eyes.

Grayson walks over and hugs Kelly. "We couldn't be more thrilled to offer you a place here."

"Gosh, Ava. He really is dreamy," she says.

I giggle, but she's not wrong.

He brings over a glass of champagne once Kelly heads back toward the line to be our first customer, and he clinks his glass to mine.

"To the right place at the right time," he says, and I smile as I think back to the first time he toasted me with that line at the café our first night together at the Palms.

It's early for champagne, but it's perfect.

We get moving on all the things we need to do to get ready for our first day. When seven o'clock rolls around and our doors open for the very first time, Grayson sells her the first Nash's Nibble.

I watch my former defensive back as he hands a cookie over the counter to my best friend.

I'm not quite sure how I ended up here, but this is definitely the road to my happy ending.

THE END

Acknowledgments

My first thanks as always is to my husband. Thanks for inventing hours for me to write, for supporting me, and for being the best dad to our sweet babies. I love having you as part of my team, and I love the family we've created together.

Thank you Valentine PR for your work on the launch of this new series.

Thank you to Diane Holtry, Christine Yates, Billie DeSchalit, Serena Cracchiolo, and Autumn Gantz for beta and proofreading. I value your insight and comments so much.

Thank you to Renee McCleary for all you do.

Thank you to my ARC Team for loving this sports world that is so real to us. Thank you to the members of the Vegas Aces Spoiler Room and Team LS, and all the influencers and bloggers for reading, reviewing, posting, and sharing.

And finally, thank YOU! Thanks for being part of this Vegas Aces world. I am SO EXCITED to bring more football and more Nash family! I can't wait for what's coming next!

Cheers until next season!

xoxo,
Lisa Suzanne

About the Author

Lisa Suzanne is an Amazon Top Ten Bestselling author of swoon-worthy superstar heroes, emotional roller coasters, and all the angst. She resides in Arizona with her husband and two kids. When she's not chasing her kids, she can be found working on her latest romance book or watching reruns of *Friends*.

Also by Lisa Suzanne

VEGAS ACES

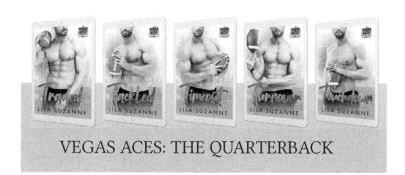

VEGAS ACES: THE QUARTERBACK

FIND MORE AT AUTHORLISASUZANNE.COM/BOOKS

Printed in Great Britain
by Amazon

43527101R00243